Claire McKenna is a speculative fiction writer from Melbourne, Australia. Claire grew up in Auckland, New Zealand and came to Australia when she was young. Her stories decided to come with her.

A longtime writer of short fiction with a background in environmental sciences, *Monstrous Heart*, the first book in the Deepwater Trilogy, was Claire's debut novel.

You can follow her on:
Twitter @mckenna_claire
www.clairelmckenna.weebly.com

Also by Claire McKenna

Monstrous Heart

DEEPWATER KING

BOOK TWO OF THE DEEPWATER TRILOGY

CLAIRE McKENNA

HARPER Voyager

Harper*Voyager*
An imprint of HarperCollins*Publishers* Ltd
1 London Bridge Street
London SE1 9GF

www.harpercollins.co.uk

HarperCollins*Publishers*
1st Floor, Watermarque Building, Ringsend Road
Dublin 4, Ireland

First published by HarperCollins*Publishers* Ltd 2021

This paperback edition 2022
1

A catalogue record for this book is available from the British Library

ISBN: 978-0-00-833721-6

Set in Sabon LT Std by Palimpsest Book Production Ltd,
Falkirk, Stirlingshire

Printed and Bound in the UK using 100% Renewable Electricity
at CPI Group (UK) Ltd

MIX
Paper from
responsible sources
FSC™ C007454

This book is produced from independently certified FSC™ paper
For more information visit: www.harpercollins.co.uk/green

For Paul H

The Saint of the Islands

The history goes like this. Two centuries ago a child came into the world with a vast and terrible ability. At the moment of her birth, the delivery-forceps at her crown recoiled into a tight rose of metal and crushed the unwashed fingers of a drunken surgeon just-returned from the dissection of a cadaver. At her cry the lenses in the midwife's spectacles cracked in their frames.

In her fifth summer she touched a spoon with a licked finger, and it stood up on its end, danced a jig before knotting into a silver ball.

That day she destroyed most of the cutlery before her servant-girl mother found her on the kitchen floor, giggling among the ruins of their employer's silverware.

At eight she tripped on the road and struck her chin upon a tram rail. Sixteen lengths of iron spun curlicues about her like a cocoon.

At twelve, she killed a man because he'd hissed a cat-call from an alley, tried to pull her into the damp shadows. A hot, unfamiliar spike of anger shot through her, and when she'd heaved a huge mouthful of spit into his face, he'd let her go, run headlong into the spinning leather belt of a steam-mill.

It was then that she realized she could move men as well as metal.

In ways both violent and uncanny she had made him lose his mind. Ostensibly this girl was *sanguinem*, a bloodworker, but far away from typical. The common sanguis of Lyonne were small cogs in the great machine of Lyonne's economy, and their abilities were limited to small, individual things, brief moments, tiny movements. Theirs was not an inexhaustible talent. They would see sacrifice in blood loss, and would remain prudent in what they did.

However it was one thing to light a lamp, or move a weight. The girl could move metal and men with just a taste of her own blood.

Such a thing was dangerous. To a person. To her family. Every night she would pray before the icon of her father's adopted church, *take this burden from me, God, for I cannot bear it.*

The Redeemer of Lyonne, forever bound upon His rock, merely gazed down at her in silent disapproval, too busy with His own stone sufferings. His marble eyes stayed blank milky cataracts. The stone mouth said no word, and even with her voice that could command metal she could not command it of Him.

Although the girl was born to parents from rural, backwater Fiction, she was a citizen of Clay City, the teeming northern capital of Lyonne. When it soon became publicly apparent what powers she obligated, the city masters were quick to act. The girl was taken into their care, and under watch of a platoon of musket-men they mapped out the margins of her power. Over the course of a week three men died, another five fell into madness, and she built a small steam-engine by whispering a song to copper leaves.

In the end the testers made their diagnosis: *Sanguis Orientis – Direction of Mind* – and *Sanguis Mandatum – Instruction of Matter.*

The *orientis* was useful enough. One could always find value in manipulating men. But it was the *mandatum* that complicated matters entirely. She could talk to metals and chemicals related to metals, sing them into assuming a joint, a connection, make them twist into a form. Prior to her, even the best sanguis bloodworkers of the age could barely compel a steel bar into a right angle.

The *Lyonne Investigatory Order and Nomenclatures*, that secret society whose business it was to manage such powers, burned many lamps dry on the long nights they discussed the girl. The Lyonne Order could see her future keenly in the entrails of their dead men. She had the means to kill them all. A girl who could pull iron foundations out of concrete with a breath could with a lone tantrum reduce the city to rubble.

But then the Order also knew all too well the economic value of someone who could spin metals and command both objects and men. The sanguis bloodlines were weakened from over-breeding. Even in the south country of Fiction, where the blood still ran wild in the old families, the talents were frail and undecided. For all that she was dangerous, there was still a use for her.

We shall send her away, they decided. *And if her companions in isolation survive our girl's adolescence then . . . then we will see.*

So it was in her thirteenth year that the Order found a place where the girl could grow up safe and isolated from civilization, in a distant archipelago in the cold south waters of Fiction. She was remanded to a religious order of anchoritic nuns upon the flat, broad island of Equus, the ancient country of her forefathers.

Apart from the nuns, the island was at that time mostly uninhabited.

In the winter it was visited by the nomadic leviathan-hunters of the old Deepwater religion. In the mild summer months the petralactose prospectors came from Lyonne and drilled for the rockblood layered in the limestone shale, which they stored in barrels on their rusty iron ships before transporting the crude rockblood to Clay.

'We'll come back for you,' the Order promised the girl, even though they had no real hopes that she would survive her adolescence intact. 'Once you learn to control that temper of yours. You must learn to be less a devil and more a saint.'

For a long time after, communications were few and far between. There would be brief letters to her family, her gifts of dried flowers pressed between torn book-leaves, a sea-serpent scale, a perfect shell, a limestone pebble with a hole worn in the centre.

She would write of the nuns, their lessons, and their daily prayers to the Redeemer. She wrote of the shy folk who visited the northern shores, the deepwater people that hunted the sea-serpents and kraken of the Darkling Sea. The Anchorage Mother provided positive reports, unremarkable in their brevity. Their charge was hard-working and kind, and there was little else they had to say.

The months became years, and old political orders moved aside for new ones. The Masters of Clay shifted oversight of the girl with her powers of *mandatum* and *orientis* to another department. The old Lions of the Order retired, clutching their redacted memoirs. A fire in an archive room destroyed the records of that miraculous week in the Tower. The young cubs that came after were more concerned with the government of present sanguinem than of the one exiled far away.

After the span of a decade, she was forgotten.

But industry is industry, and its expansion occurs in strange places. It came to the notice of the new guard of Order that the petralactose production out of Fiction, once so seasonal, had become reliably constant. Those businesses that needed such an elixir to power their iron smelters and illuminate their streets began to seek out the now plentiful southern petralactose rather than rely on local Shinlock shale. Venture capitalists sent ships of pig-iron and copper southwards, asking, and in return came inconceivable amounts of the precious liquor. New-minted thousandaires walked the streets in krakenskin coats, spoke of fortunes to be made in the southern Sainted Isles.

Twenty years had passed by the time Order investigators returned to Equus. They found, to their astonishment, a great row of derricks on the western shore, pumping petralactose out of deep wells. The roughnecks who worked the derricks called the liquor *rockblood*, preferring the old name. Their forgotten girl had taken the teachings of the anchorite nuns to heart: in holy service she had given her talents to help the prospectors, spun derricks for them out of scrap iron, commanded the pipes to drill deep into the ground, made reservoirs and barrels, and combustion chambers to fraction the petralactose into fuel.

This information was brought back to the Order offices. Puzzled and delighted, the Lyonne Order instructed that the investigators should wait without contact, and keep eyes upon her.

Over those remaining years they watched her build an industry among the rockblood prospectors. Just as she had done in the testing-yard she sung life into the copper cables, made tanker-ships that needed no captain. Sensing an opportunity for wealth, people had come from all parts of the world to prospect for rockblood from Equus. A city sprang up in Burden Town, a river mouth settlement that had not more than ten years earlier been a ruin of stone against which prospectors would pitch their tents.

The anchorites had given the girl a purpose. Driven both by the song in her blood and the nuns' humble lessons, she served both Man and God, and found her life's joy in both.

There are very few missives left from that time, and they are museum letters kept under glass. Reports from the Order investigators, by then already under her *orientis* spell.

The last letter ever sent tells how the prospectors worship the girl now, who seems ageless despite being a woman in her middle years. The local folk have built for her temples out of seashells and ichthyosaur bones. They call her the *Saint of the Islands*. She rules them like a benevolent god. As for the anchorite nuns, nobody remembers what happened to them.

Perhaps they took residence elsewhere. Perhaps they grew weary with age and went into the potter's ground. More likely though, they forgot who they once gave duty and prayers to, and turned their songs towards their blessed girl.

And then one day she is gone.

Fresh agents are sent to investigate an island without its saint, for in the interregnum between watchers the girl has slipped away. The pumps still bob, and the rockblood still flows and the ghost ships still move back and forth between island and Fiction coast, but they do so without her instruction. Nobody could say why the Saint of the Islands fled. She was in her fortieth year and not so old. She had no enemies, and had no reason to fear the Order attention. All anyone knew was that after twenty-five years of service the saint had abandoned her islands and left behind her pumping derricks and her ghost-captained ships and congregation of worshippers.

After a fruitless search the agents reported that she had gone for good. Whichever star had been her orient, whichever horizon had called her away, the journey was one without a return. She would not come back.

Those few who were in charge mourned openly in the dim corridors of power, but in secret, the Order was relieved. The Saint of the Islands had always been a case on the verge of calamity. She had been miraculous, yes, but dangerous, and like any avoidable occurence they thought it best they never chance another one like her again.

Before – The Deepwater Funeral

Stefan Beacon saw them first. The hunters returning in the afternoon on the tide-rise, six small black figures striding through the grey slosh of the sheltering bay. They dragged behind them a small, shallow shoreboat.

He'd been suspended halfway up the long column of his father's lighthouse with a rag and bucket of soapy water to wash the salt-grimed windows when the seabirds started their aggrieved squawking. Down in the harbour one of the men fell to his knees once they cleared the breakers, rolled on his back. Another knelt beside him in the rocky sand, slid off his hat. More followed along the pier.

From his high position Stefan Beacon counted three ships in the small bay, all blowing the dark smoke of a death on the waters. Something had gone wrong with the hunt, for it was unusual that all three boats returned at once. Normally two monster-boats might stay out on the open ocean, while the third returned to process their cryptid catch.

Stefan put down the cleaning rag and released the counter-weighting gears of the bosun's chair. The little platform brought him to ground level where he struggled free of the retaining ropes. It had been easier to haul a chair up and down the lighthouse as a child, but on approaching his seventeenth year, his body seemed to have grown an extra foot overnight. He would need to find more stones for the counterweight, he thought, but first his father would need to know what he had seen.

At his son's call, Jorgen Beacon came stooped from the outhouse, braces hanging down below his hips. He squinted through the drowsy mist at the scooped land below the cliff. It was navigationer's sight he used – that sharp vision all Beacon men were born with, sharp enough to make out a face from a mile away.

'Missing a man,' he said gruffly, and if any emotion moved him, Jorgen hid it under the shade of his dark brow. He rubbed his hands, and the fingerless gloves of his fire-sympathetic profession.

'How do you know?'

'Takes seven to run *Sehnsucht*,' Jorgen said, indicating the largest monster-boat, a massive paddle wheeler as white as fog. 'Someone's gone to the King. They'll be mourning him tonight.'

Stefan caught himself frowning. It was a Hewsday, and nowhere close to the Sabbath. The Clay Church had strong laws for when one might show grief, and Stefan knew that better than most, for in a few days he would head to Clay City and start his collegiate years in a seminary, and train for the priesthood.

His look of judgment earned a chastising glare from his father.

'I didn't say anything,' Stefan protested.

'Could see it. Those folks might visit a Clay Church on a Sunday morning Mass and give their prayers to the Redeemer of Lyonne, lad, but the nights belong to their abyssal gods. Don't let them see any northern attitude from you, son.'

Stefan did not argue with his father. Something in Jorgen's face had changed.

He sent Stefan back up the lighthouse tower to finish cleaning the windows. Stefan stayed up there until the sky became sullen with the encroaching evening. He only came down when the mist soaked through both his shirt and jacket and made him shiver.

The lighthouse had a base broad and stout, enough for a bed and a bathroom. He hesitated in the doorway at the solemn sight of his farther grooming his whiskers over a soapy basin.

'You don't think it could be Zachariah, Da? He usually takes out *Sehnsucht*.'

Jorgen tilted his lathered chin up. 'If it were Zach, someone would have already come to bring the news. So clean up, boy. We have a funeral to attend.'

After hurrying his son in front of the wash basin to clean up, Jorgen loaned Stefan a dress uniform of navy broadcloth and red pipe. A Seamaster's Guild uniform, unworn since Jorgen had left the hot wharves of Clay Portside to tend the last lighthouse on the Lyonnian navigation chain. The trousers ended above Stefan's ankles. Once dressed they made the short walk into the Cleave-Riven compound with the sunset in their eyes.

Stefan fell behind his father's sombre step. The leviathan-processing factories run by the Riven family and their dependants were a fifteen-minute stroll from the lighthouse, and the path to reach them traced along a narrow ridge of land that made up the promontory. To the left was Vigil Bay, where the Vigil township crabbed against the shore like barnacles to the pier, and to the right the broad shallow curve of Dead Man's Bay. The mist had cleared off that side, and Stefan could see the rockblood refineries in the distance.

The compound was large enough to be called a fisherman's town in its own right. Fifty people lived within its sprawling perimeter, and perhaps another ten further along the rutted, single-track path that led to the mainland. In the factory-sheds they would strip down their monstrous catches to oil, bone and leather. From there the sea-harvest was sold onwards for the trade disciplines of medicine, food and clothing. Eight families, all descended from those first deepwater fisher clans the Baron of Vigil had, a hundred years ago, brought from the Sainted Isles. They had not needed much incentive to leave their island home, for the waters around Equus had become sterile and barren from rockblood poisoning. If they hadn't left for the mainland, they'd have all died.

But they were shorefolk now, mainlanders, hunting close to the Vigil coast and never venturing more than a few days eastwards and never close to the deepwater abysses of their forefathers. Out beyond the Sainted Isles the land slipped away into the true abysses, but there were no souls left alive who dared chance running a fishing line into those depths.

Jorgen took Stefan's elbow before they came too close.

'We come out of respect tonight, son. But remember, it's not our place to participate in their funeral.'

'But you're their friend.'

'It's *their* ceremony. Their lost fellow must return to his god.'

Near the beached pontoon a mourner went into the water, chasing eddies of cold blue bioluminescence. A woman, perhaps the missing man's widow. To Stefan's shock and surprise she began to slice ribbons from her shoulders with a knife until her pale arms and chest appeared black in the dying light.

Others joined her, and these folk more vocal, wailing a cacophony of curses and song. The wind kicked up harsh and cold.

With all that blood they might attract something hungry into the shallows, Stefan thought with a horrified thrill. Even though he was baptized into the Redeemer's church, Stefan knew a little about their beliefs just from living close by. They were mostly converted to the Clay Church now, but the shorefolk kept provisions in their religion for the Deepwater King's offence. If the dead man was not accepted into the court of the King, he would become a lost spirit of a sort, a bitter source of bad luck and spoiled hunts. If he had been especially wicked, the King might also see fit to finish off the mourners at the benighted fellow's own funeral.

Much to Stefan's relief, no monster came to the small beach that evening, not even a jenny-ray, and by full nightfall the deepwater folk-rite was complete. The mourners moved out of the water to the safety of land, bound up their wounds, embraced each other and shared bottles of liquor between them.

A large man in a coat of tooled ichthyosaur leather came out of the shadows and enveloped Jorgen with his embrace so fully it was as if he had eight arms instead of two.

'Beacon,' he mumbled through his embrace.

Stefan's father leaned back slightly to look his friend in the eye. 'Ah, Zach, my condolences. Who was he?'

'Ishmael,' hissed the brute through his teeth. 'Ishmael Cleave.' The shark-tooth tattoos on Zachariah Riven's pale cheeks twitched. By daylight he would not be permitted the speaking of the dead man's name, so he would say it through the long Deepwater Night. 'Barb to the chest, dead before his head went under.'

'Ishmael Cleave? Oh no, was he not married to your sister?'

'For a year. My sister has no luck with the men of her affections. The King also loves them too much.'

Zachariah Riven held Jorgen by his shoulders, looked him up and down. Took note of the uniform, the respect of it.

'It honours him, you coming.'

'How's Thalie holding up, really? I saw her give the old rites for him down by the water. Her love must have been great, to take such a risk.'

Zachariah nodded, clearly agreeing. 'She is not at her best. I think she hoped that . . .' He trailed off. 'Well. Who knows what my sister hoped. Now my nephew will have no father to teach him a man's ways.'

'He'll have you, Zachariah Riven. You're his uncle, his blood.'

'I have my own son to worry about.'

Stefan saw Jonah Riven, Zachariah's nephew and the one the men spoke of, standing awkwardly nearby. He was a slight, raw-boned boy who Stefan had known most of his life, but in that distant way when separated by a three-year age difference. Stefan raised his hand hesitantly, unfamiliar with funeral etiquette.

Jonah shook his head at Stefan's greeting and faded into the darkness.

Stefan shivered as the closing songs were sung on the beach. He had heard whispers about what the Deepwater rites were supposed to do. Something sinful. Something unholy.

Jorgen Beacon took Stefan's shoulder and directed him back towards the ridge. 'Let's leave our friends to their grieving, my son,' he said. 'We have been granted a rare sight, but the rest of the night is not for us.'

Stefan glanced back at the water line, wondering if he had missed a slumping shadow past the breakers. Maybe there was something out there, something called by the mourners. But the sea was dark, and offered up no secrets.

'I heard someone was invited to a ritual last night,' Bellis Harrow said archly from her high position on the tide-wall. She slid a brassy lock of yellow hair behind one small ear. 'A funeral for Ishmael Cleave.'

Stefan hid his surprise with a shrug. 'Don't believe all the gossip, Bellis. The townsfolk talk too much.'

'Was not the normal gossips.'

The Postmaster's daughter tilted her blonde head towards Vigil's crooked little boat-harbour and its jumble of marina berths. 'Mx Modhi – the Harbourmistress – she grouched at me all morning about Jorgen Beacon's shirking. He got completely drunk at Mr Cleave's wake. Missed the morning helioscope signal, and now she has unexpected visitors.' Bellis pointed to a boat at the far end of the marina, a big ghostwood hunting ship with a high bow and side wheels for churning through weed-fouled waters. 'Harbourmistress Modhi takes a dim view of your father's friendship with the Islanders.'

A defensive loyalty towards his father made him respond in a temper. 'Would she rather the Vigil lighthouse keeper be *fighting* with them? Because he'd miss a few more if he got beaten up by even one of those fellows. They're *huge*.'

She smirked, and nodded, for shorefolk tended to grow as tall and broad as the cryptid creatures they hunted. Bellis Harrow herself was tiny, an elfin little thing. Her Lyonnian ancestors might have done duty as chimney sweeps and mine-workers due to their small size. It was generally agreed that she was beautiful, except for an uneven cast in her face. It was as if the vital clay in the hands of her Creator had been dropped, then patched together again in a hurry, leaving her unsymmetrical.

'She also suspects your da doesn't *fight* with the Riven leader as much as he does the *other thing*,' Bellis said with a wicked smirk, and gave Stefan a playful shove with her toe when he pretended to be aggrieved. Of course Stefan knew about the relationship between the two men. There was not much else to do on long nights on the promontory, and the Beacon family history was full of hot-blooded and ill-advised love affairs.

'You are an awful tease, Bellis.'

'I could be more than a tease, handsome Stefan,' she wheedled, winking. 'You have yet to take your priestly vows.'

It was Stefan's turn to shove her, but under his playfulness was an air of caution. An uncanny kind of feeling always accompanied Bellis' presence. She was by turns completely magnetic and utterly awful – becoming more mercurial as they had grown up together in their little fishing village. The boys in town had lately begun to fight over who would squire her to the monthly dances. Let them fight. Stefan hated such confrontations. How awful, if he were to be dragged into the same madness that enchanted them.

'I suspect Mx Modhi loves hearing about promontory drama,' Bellis went on. 'It gives her more entertainment than watching boats come in and out all day.' She leaned in conspiratorially. 'So is it true? What happened out there during the Deepwater Rite? Did someone lose a hand or a foot?'

'I cannot say. It was private.'

'Then I must bribe you. Is bribery a sin for a priest? Tell me it is not so!'

'I'm not a priest yet, so show me your bribe, Bel.'

Bellis winked, then took out a small packet of tobacco from her coat pocket. Some strands of brown leaf had already been rolled into cigarettes with scraps of cotton paper. She offered Stefan the least bent of her treasure trove.

'Where did you get this?'

'My secret!'

He looked about uneasily before accepting a lit strike-match and coughing through tobacco smoke. Bellis had a way of wheedling contraband from the sailors that was not exactly innocent. She used a certain charisma upon the men. They gave her everything she asked, even objects that were not theirs to give.

'These better not be stolen cigarettes,' he grumped. 'Last time we got chased into the Black Rosette because of that whiskey incident.'

'Ha, I remember it well! If the night-ladies hadn't hidden us in their pleasure-huts, we'd have been flogged by the watchman.' Bellis then gestured otherwise. 'No, these were a gift to my father, from the new Mrs Sage.'

Even speaking of her powerful father caused Bellis to pull a disagreeable face. The Postmaster was overprotective and authoritarian. There was no love between father and daughter.

Bellis re-lit the strike-match to ignite her own twist of tobacco paper. She blew smoke rings, pulled a knee to her chest, inspected a hole in her stocking. 'So, did the funeral call the dead man out of the water, huh? Would have been a sight to see.'

'Don't make fun, Bel! It was a very solemn rite.'

'Of course it was.'

'Could have been a tragedy if there was any leviathan close enough to shore to pick up the blood-scent.'

She shook her head. 'I would not make light of it if it were that dangerous. Maybe if there really were monster-callers of the old blood among them, they might have called something up. But they're just simple shorefolk now. Everyone knows the deepwater folk went extinct when the Baron Justinian brought them here.'

Bellis looked wistfully towards a scrap of shoreline revealed by the low tide. Jonah Riven stood in the rock pools, picking idly through the stones. He was as small as Bellis was, though at fourteen years old it was hard to tell if he would take on the towering shorefolk height or more likely resemble whatever townsman his mother Thalie had tumbled with instead. His features were more delicate than those of the rest of his shorefolk family, and there was an air of feyness about him, as if he were not completely hewn from this brutal coast.

They suited each other, Stefan thought. Two people not quite tied to this harsh world. Had Jonah not been younger than Bellis, he might have joined the town boys in squabbling over her strange affections. As it was, he was more interested in the goings on at the tideline, like a child. His stained shirt rode up his thin back each time he bent over. Black gouges inflamed his pale skin, fresh deepwater tattoos. By his twentieth summer he would wear the squid-ink tattoos all over, even in the unmentionable places of a man's body.

Bellis sighed and tucked her chin into her palm. 'His people once believed they could bring the dead back, if they asked the Deepwater King in a way that pleased him.'

Stefan felt the same shiver that had afflicted him on the funeral beach. The sun had gone behind a cloud, or at least it *felt* like it had. A looming chill.

'Some kind of *aequor profundum*, they used to call it,' Bellis continued. 'Profound water, a resurrection rite. Isn't it a strange pagan idea? So barbaric.'

'If they could do that,' Stefan said, 'they'd not have had to evacuate their island, would they? Wouldn't have had to come here and be baptized in our ways.'

'I guess not.' She turned her head. '*Jonah*,' she called in a chiming voice. 'Come and sit with us.'

The boy did so, and gave Stefan a shy, brief smile before perching next to Bellis on the tide-wall.

Wherever Bellis went, Jonah was not far behind. Last winter, when Thalie Riven had been courted by Ishmael Cleave, that was when Bellis had unofficially taken the lonely and ignored Riven boy under her wing. Their odd relationship might have been fine back then, but with the mounting attention from the town boys, it seemed altogether risky. Stefan could see in his mind's eye an aggrieved suitor suffering an attack of the jealousies before the summer was out.

Jonah accepted the last lit cigarette like a wild thing snatching a treat. The sweet tobacco smoke surrounded him like a wreath. Then a brief joyous moment occurred, as a belly of sun showed out from behind a cloud, and the small quartz chips in the grey granite stones sparkled as if they were diamonds. But enchantments can sometimes obscure dangers.

Stefan no longer wanted to taste the bitter smoke, and discarded the tobacco butt inside the mortar of the tide-wall.

'I'd best get back home,' he started to say.

He stepped back, and to his surprise collided with two huge figures in bronze krakenskin coats and grey knitted sweaters.

Stefan startled at the sudden, silent appearance of these men. He may as well have run into a wall of solid meat for all the movement the massive figures made.

Both men had black chevrons carved into their hands and trinkets piercing their cheeks. A brace of scabbarded flensing blades swayed at their leather-clad thighs.

One of them, elder and taller, was Zachariah Riven, unmistakable in both height and the tattoos below his grey eyes.

Zachariah grunted, 'Watch it, lad, my knives are sharp.'

'Sorry,' Stefan mumbled. But Zachariah's attention was elsewhere. 'Jonah,' said Zachariah brusquely, his words like mill-rocks grinding. 'Tide's up soon. Come away.'

The boy clung mutinously to the wall. 'But there's another hour to go.'

'Come.'

Jonah's uncle did not wait to see if the boy followed. He only swayed, knife-clinking, back to the harbour, where his massive ghostwood paddleboat *Sehnsucht* knocked against the pontoons. A wet drizzle drifted sideways out of the fog bank. The sun had stolen away and taken the sparkling moment with it.

The other Riven man, Jonah's cousin, looked exactly as Stefan imagined Zachariah would have done if he were younger, minus the broken nose and the deep furrows on his salt-corroded brow. Zachariah's son spoke harsh words in the old Fictish language to Jonah. Red-faced, Jonah discarded the cigarette and climbed off the wall.

Bellis jumped in between them, like a bird might jump before a bull.

'You leave him be, Jeremiah Riven!'

Iron in her voice again. Stronger than the tone she used to wheedle tobacco and cigarettes from besotted sailors. Stefan stood up, sensing something in the air. A weight in the atmosphere, like a coming storm.

Jeremiah Riven scrutinized Bellis, his eyes squinting. 'Say what, Harrow?'

'You. Leave. Jonah. *Be*,' she said again, fierce with command. 'He'll stay with us this afternoon. There's an hour before the tide turns.'

Jeremiah's terrifying face became blank for a second, before he winked and snatched the pouch of tobacco out of Bellis' bosom. 'Looks like this'll have to come with me as well.'

'Hey, give that back!'

Jeremiah shoved the pouch in his pocket and loomed over Bellis. Wetted his lips with his tongue and let his gaze fall on her in a way that made even Bellis Harrow shudder. 'Why not come to the sheds and we can work something out.'

She hissed at him. 'Brute. My father would have you put in the stocks.'

Jeremiah snorted, already bored. The exchange had been mocking anyway. He had never shown any interest in Bellis, not even when she had developed a woman's body and drew attention from everyone from the night-soil collectors to the Baron's son. 'Your father knows where I live. Tell him to swing by.'

Bellis glared at him, but to no avail. Jeremiah shouldered Bellis aside and pushed his young cousin along ahead of him. 'Move it, Jo.'

'Bye, Bellis,' Jonah said belatedly, earning himself a clip over the ear.

'Don't talk to her,' Jeremiah grunted.

The two Rivens followed their patriarch down to the harbour where their white boat *Sehnsucht* was moored and waiting for the rising tide to take her out of the harbour mud.

Bellis, frowning, went back to her perch on the sea wall. 'He is a fiend! If I ever told Father half the things that beggar says to me, he'd be over to the promontory with ten men and a dozen firearms!'

'Ah, come on, Bel, don't sulk. You can't expect to charm everyone,' Stefan said at last. 'Especially not a Riven.'

'I was not attempting to charm him! He treats Jonah abominably, is all. Jonah's so alone.' Then she gave a great sigh.

'What's wrong?'

'I keep being reminded what day it is. Four more days until Saturn's Day, you will be leaving me and I will be alone as well!'

'Alone with all your admirers.' He gestured towards the fog-shrouded Manse Justinian, set high on an uplift of land watching over Vigil town. 'And perhaps your eventual husband. They will keep you busy until I come back.'

Bellis shook her head and smiled unconvincingly. 'You won't come back. Once the church has trained up their handsome young priest, they'll send him across the Summerland Sea to some gaudy Vinland cathedral. We may never see each other again from this day. Oh, you tell me of my admirers, but they love a shell and not what lies beneath.'

'They'll come to know you.'

'Will they? Have you ever cracked open an oyster, and seen the little monster inside? They will not love that.'

'Are you not forgetting the pearl?' Stefan reminded her gently.

'That started out as an irritation.'

'Bel, cheer up. It's only a few years, not long at all. Who else but me would keep you out of trouble?'

Without warning she lunged over and hugged him tight. She

laid her head on his sternum. 'Promise you'll come back, promise with all your chest else *die* from it!'

'I promise. Bel, what's got in to you?'

He could smell her skin pressed against his own, a hot smell like burnt rock, or raw petralactose. He shifted away with discomfort. His body wasn't reacting with desire to her. Something else. A complication to her, a veil covering her true intentions. Although she was his friend, there had never been anything *attractive* about Bellis Harrow to him, and she knew it. It was clear that frustrated her but perhaps that was why their friendship had lasted.

'I am always safe with you, Stefan Beacon. You are not like Vernon Justinian, who looks at me with lust in his heart, and I don't have to watch after you in worry the way I do Jonah. You are my shelter and my anchor, and I am afraid of what will happen when those things are gone.'

Suddenly her need . . . whatever it was . . . became cavernous and he was falling into it, a voice in his head like a bell chiming, *I will stay, I will stay* . . .

With a gasp Stefan pulled out of Bellis' small hands. He could hardly bear to look at her. It was *her* voice he'd heard in his head. Bellis' voice, commanding, making him forget himself.

She looked at him guilelessly. 'What's wrong?'

'The Rivens are still waiting for the tide,' he said, uncertain and confused about what had just happened. 'I think I'll see if they'll take me as a passenger.'

'Will I see you again before you go?'

'I'll try. I might not see you before the Lyonne ship comes, though. My father wants me to do all the chores before Saturn's day.'

Bellis gave a wry smile. 'Go then, my friend, and serve God well.'

He nodded, and left, and told himself his haste was only to reach *Sehnsucht* before the tide pulled her away from the pier, and not because for a second Bellis' commands had risen up as if to choke him, like a fist at the back of his throat.

* * *

Stefan presented himself to the Rivens upon the docks, and though he received a glower from Zachariah's son, the patriarch guffawed benevolently at his neighbour's flustered request for passage home. He let Stefan on board.

Not long after the waters rose and *Sehnsucht* floated free of the harbour mud. Stefan stood at the bow and hung on to the guy ropes. The ghostwood hunting-boat thundered through the leaden water towards the promontory at the other side of Vigil Bay. Each time a rogue wave bucked the bow up higher, the guy rope knocked him in the back like a disapproving arm. The local boats ran on both propeller screw and side wheels, a quirk of the weed-fouled waters, but heavy water could catch the paddles and make the boat kick.

They'd barely made it out of the harbour before he was wet through with sea-spray, and miserable from the chill.

'I couldn't speak to you at the funeral. It was forbidden.'

He startled out of his preoccupations. From both the wildness of voice and accent he could not be sure if it was Jonah or Jeremiah Riven that had come up behind him.

Stefan turned about as best he could without releasing his grip on the guy ropes. It was little Jonah. The boy had pulled a threadbare wool sweater over his thin shoulders. The scoop of unravelling stitches at his neck exposed a delicate filigree of squid-ink tattoos. Shorefolk grieving marks, probably put on by a drunken hand through a haze of tears. Jonah's expression was wary, like a pale crow that at any moment might take fright.

'Well, it was really my da was invited, I just came along.' Realizing that he might sound abrupt Stefan added. 'I'm sorry about Ishmael. He sounded like a good man.'

Jonah perched up on the bow, and drew up his bare feet while his expression remained inscrutable. His hands brushed over that fresh tattoo scab at his collar, and he nodded absently. 'Yes, he was, and I am too. Sorry. That he died.'

'Your ma's still young, right? She can get married again?'

Jonah gave Stefan a look that was both affronted and withering. 'No, she can't,' Jonah said with the aggrieved patience of a teacher talking to a particularly obtuse student. 'She made the promise to the Deepwater King and she stays married until she dies. No man can touch her now.'

Stefan nodded, and remembered his father's warning not to show judgment upon his face. 'Oh, yes. I forgot. My apologies.'

The ship hit a swell and a sheet of grey water splashed up from the bow. They were re-entering the shallows. The side wheels took over with a strained creaking. Jonah climbed off his perch as the boat sidled up to the long, thin pier. The other hunting ships, golden *Sonder* and dark *Saudade*, were tied off, not having moved since they'd arrived the afternoon before. A pair of shorefolk put the finishing touches to a decorative row of circles painted across each hull. The circles reminded Stefan of sucker-scars from a kraken attack. Superstitious wards of some kind. Both paint and cans looked awfully similar to the lighthouse whitewash, and Stefan suspected they'd helped themselves to the official paint.

Jonah Riven slid overboard and onto the pier with his hands full of rope, preparing to secure the ship onto the hawser cleats. Zachariah called to Stefan from the wheelhouse.

'Don't go yet. Walk with me, lad.'

Even though he'd known his father's neighbours for as long as he could remember, Stefan still found Mr Zachariah Riven thoroughly intimidating, with his cryptid-skin coat and the scars of his hunting profession so evident on his skin. Some marks were flat and shiny, others were a deep keloid purple. In summer the shorefolk swam at a hot-water beach on the other side of the promontory, and Stefan knew there was hardly a place on him that was not similarly scrimshawed.

'Jorgen tells me the Clay priesthood is about to gain a new novice.'

'Yes, three years at the seminary, then three in service of the church. By God's grace, I may then apply to be His priest.'

'And you were not . . . how do they say it . . . sanguis?'

He pointed at Stefan's hands. Stefan shook his head.

'My father tested me at home, but I showed no talents.' He put his hands in his pockets, for compared to Zachariah Riven's they must have seemed so soft and sun-touched, not scarred and bleached by water. 'Not even metal, or storm-calling.'

The man nodded. 'Sometimes that is best. Now go fetch your father. Tell him I wish to see him.'

Stefan

Stefan Beacon woke up with a start.

Not just to silence. A low tolling in his head, the ringing aftermath of a cry in his dream, as if someone had called out to him at the moment he woke, and he could not be sure to which state he belonged.

Stefan lay in the semi-dark of the light-tower's upper alcove, felt the baffles of the coldflame turn high above him. The grinding harmonic of the motor spinning the light seemed to have lost its comfortable familiarity. Something discordant in the sound, as if the world had moved just a little bit sideways and off-key. He sat up and looked around his room. It was a garret barely wide enough to stretch his full length, with the only light coming from a thin slice of opaline glass that had gone grey with dawn.

A feeling moved in him. Stormteller trouble, almost. Blood heavy in the air, and thick on his skin. He had been correct when he'd told Zachariah about his failed tests for sanguis talents, but just because he couldn't enact sanguis bloodwork did not mean he could not sense its presence.

Stefan slid into his strides, padded downstairs. His boots stood by the door, but not his father's. The bed was rumpled and cold and the pot-bellied stove had exhausted its fuel. A shy light filtered through the windows.

And a call on the wind. His father's voice. Not shouting. *Screaming.*

Stefan shoved his feet into his boots and had barely opened the door to the cold day . . .

. . . when his father pushed him aside as if he weren't there. In a flurry of rain and wind Jorgen ran for the telephone set on the equipment desk, wound the handle furiously, shrieked incoherent words into the handset.

Blood on his face and clothes. Bloody handprints over the desk, and the door.

'Murder . . . massacre . . . all dead . . . dear God, Gertie, send help . . .'

An icy finger of apprehension touched him. Stefan stumbled into the day, and the air about him pressed as still as a cathedral's void. Beyond the promontory, a blanket of smoke clung to the cliff edge. A man's body lay on the slender path. By the trail of viscera Jorgen had dragged the corpse all the way from the promontory factories to the lighthouse.

With his heart in his mouth Stefan approached the corpse. The full damage turned out worse than he had imagined. The great barrelled chest hollowed out so that the spine showed through like a row of white flags. No legs beneath the knees. Kraken-sucker scars ribboning a shoulder.

Zachariah Riven, dead.

Stefan's breath stuttered. How could a monster-caller suffer monster injuries?

In a fugue of bewilderment he followed the trail of gore. More bodies, and these ones of people who'd tried to escape whatever had gone on here. Disturbed dirt, slithering gouges from legless, boneless things.

Out of all the people working in this compound how had not a one of them sounded an alarm?

The largest of the factory houses had been reduced to blackened ribs, still smouldering. They'd tried to use fire against the invasion. A slimy, suckered squid-arm lay hacked off and wetly on the ground in a death-grip around what was clearly a human limb. A woman's hand marked with Riven chevrons, the upper arm scored with knife-cuts through the meat.

Someone had tried to use heavy sanguis blood to stop the beast, Stefan reasoned wildly. Tried and failed. What in God's name had happened here? The scouring, heavy tracks had come up from over the beach-bluffs, tearing out the stone foundations from the old missionary ruins before heading towards the factories.

He stood in the centre of the compound, aware of Jorgen calling him, but he wasn't ready to leave, not yet.

A sound made him startle.

He turned about, and Jonah Riven slumped shirtless near the tanning vats. At first glance Stefan thought Jonah was dead as well, before the thin ribcage flared with a breath.

'Jonah?'

He reached out to touch a clammy, bony shoulder. Oddly there was no sign of sucker-marks on the boy, but the tops of his forearms were crusted with stripes of dried blood. He'd clearly tried to make the cuts shallow and vertical and at some point lost control of the knife.

Jonah had been crouched there a while. The blood had soaked into the crushed quartzite stones of the Riven compound. The boy rocked, eyes wide as he met Stefan's own.

'It wasn't supposed to be this way.'

Stefan backed off. 'Jonah, what happened here?'

The attention fixed on Stefan. A terrible, almost luminous blue beheld him, eyes that had no feeling behind them. For the briefest moment, something else lurked behind Jonah's eyes, then it was gone.

'I went into the water. I called Ishmael back.'

'Jonah . . . Jonah, *what*?'

Defiance replaced the horror on Jonah's face. 'I called him *back*. I stood on the shore and demanded the Deepwater King give me back my *father*!' Jonah heaved a breath. 'And he came!'

Stefan swallowed. His words came out creaky.

'You called the monsters out of the water?'

'Not monsters! Ishmael! My sea-father in the name of the King!' Jonah implored, his eyes begging him to understand. 'It was Ishmael . . . at first.'

At first. Through the confusion came the glimmers of an awful understanding. The Deepwater Rite was a funeral rite, but the old sanguinities of monster-calling still ran in the shorefolk veins. Jonah had believed in a folk tale of bringing the dead back from the sea, resurrecting a man. Jonah had gone to the water and made the offerings.

Whatever he'd raised out of the ocean had not been Ishmael alone. The ocean had fathomless depths where the monsters of the permanent night lurked. Drawn to shore by the invitation, they'd massacred every living thing that had stepped in their way.

Someone had to have encouraged Jonah to such a foolhardy act. Someone he trusted completely. But nobody in his family, certainly not his mother, would have—

Bellis.

'You evil—!'

As silent as a shadow, Jorgen had come up behind Stefan and with one great yank tore Jonah to his feet. Struck the child down with a fist.

Picked him up and struck him down again. Stunned, the boy didn't even attempt to fight back.

'Rotting little bastard!' Jorgen shouted. 'Filthy slut-born devil! You called the monstrosities out of the fucking deeps and killed your family! Your rotting carcass will rot in hell!'

Kicks to the ribs, and Jonah only reflexively rolled into a ball and let Jorgen punish him.

'Da, stop!' Stefan cried. He grabbed the older man and pulled him away. '*Stop!*'

'I'll kill it! I'll kill the beast and hang its hide for the devils to find!'

'If we kill him, it will only make it worse for us, Da, please! We'll wait for the . . .'

He searched for the word, and the only one that came was *Lions*. The Lyonne Order would definitely come, the shadowy folk of the Lyonne government whose business was to control bloodworkers. The Lions would investigate Jonah, and Bellis. The Lions and their poisons and their accidents.

'We will wait for the Magistrate,' Stefan finished. He shook Jorgen's collar to agitate some sense into this weeping madman. 'When they come, they can investigate properly, all right? We don't really know what's happened here. Monsters come to shore all the time. The sea is always hungry.'

It was a lie under God, but necessary now. Jorgen fought Stefan for his freedom, fought him savagely. Only by Stefan's height and youth could he hold his father back. Wailed words. *Killed him, killed him. Oh, Zach.*

'I know, Da, I know,' Stefan soothed as Jorgen collapsed in his arms. 'I know this feeling.'

He did not know, not really. *Eros* existed as a foreign emotion, and Stefan was well joyful to be immune from the trouble desire wrought. He did not know romantic love. Yet still, he knew pain.

And Jonah, more corpse than boy, lying in the dirt, left with the enormity of what he'd done.

All of a sudden Stefan had been crowned the lone, sane adult in this theatre of suffering. Stefan ordered his devastated father down to the pier, to await the arrival of the Vigil constabulary. Harbourmistress Gertrude Modhi would have already called them after receiving such an alarming communication on the rarely used short-wave.

Despite everything, Stefan found room to experience a twinge of pity for Jonah Riven. This disaster was not entirely the boy's fault. If Bellis was behind the suggestion to work a rite of resurrection, then she had only suggested Jonah do the rite out of curiosity, maybe. Out of her misplaced sense of concern. How could she have known it would lead to this?

'Best get up and into the house, Jonah. Bind up those wounds,' Stefan said. 'We can't have another episode of devilfish coming ashore.'

Slowly, it dawned on Jonah that there would be more to face than just grieving. He had committed a terrible crime. He stared at Stefan. 'What'll happen to me?'

Stefan exhaled. He couldn't get the stink of the day out of his lungs.

'The Magistrate will have questions. If you're lucky, maybe he'll see it as a rogue monster attack, nothing more. He'll see you've suffered enough, and let you go.'

Book One: Equus

PRESENT DAY

1

Talk about fortunate

'Talk about fortunate they didn't immediately hang him in the town square. That's what Mother always said,' David Modhi concluded with a sigh. 'The townsfolk were righteously angry, and scared.'

'Would they have hanged someone so young?'

'Fourteen is old enough in Fiction.'

Yes, people grew old before their time in the cold south waters. Arden Beacon, Lyonnian and niece of Jorgen Beacon of Vigil, peered at her shipmate. The half-light of the boat's below decks made David Modhi of Vigil seem aged beyond his eighteen years. The mention of Jonah softened his expression. Arden could see his mother in the young man's face, the Vigil Harbourmistress who had been a spy for the Lyonne Order.

Mx Gertrude Modhi had spent twenty years writing missives of the comings and goings of the townsfolk, the shorefolk, and the lighthouse keeper.

Twenty years of letters via the Postmaster of Vigil, Alasdair Harrow, whose cunning, curious daughter had made copies of them all.

Inside the hull, the black mangrove wood of the hunting

ship *Saudade* swallowed up anything brighter than a candle flame, so the dark loomed in close and intimate. A time for secrets.

'Mother said if Mr Riven's tragedy happened a few months later, he would have received an adult's trial, and an adult's punishment. And murder in Fiction is punished by execution.'

'But a *child*,' Arden repeated, even though her heart broke a little from the speaking of such a thing. She smoothed out the waxy paper. Postmaster Harrow had owned a spirit duplicator, and his clever daughter had put it to good use, painstakingly taking her own copies of all the classified mail that went through his office.

At some point Bellis – a loving Bellis not yet drowned in malevolence – had gifted the more pertinent letters to Jonah, back in those first days after his return from the Harbinger Bay penitentiary. An offering of knowledge to a man who'd lost half his life. Tied them with a ribbon and wax seal, left them in *Saudade*'s map desk for him to find.

To Jonah, from Bellis.

But he had never found them. Or if he had, he'd declined to break the seal. They'd remained bound until Arden had found them this night.

'According to this other official letter from Postmaster Harrow, what happened on the promontory was a random . . .' she waved her hands in the air, trying to grasp the full meaning of the tragedy, '. . . devilfish attack. It makes no sense. Why would the Magistrate sentence a boy to the worst prison in Lyonne for a bloodworker accident?'

'Because accident or not, he still called to monsters and killed his family,' David replied.

'But that's just not how a bloodwork accident would normally be dealt with. Life imprisonment in another country? It all sounds far too convenient for the Lyonne Order's business, having Jonah be removed from Bellis so utterly.'

David Modhi nervously rubbed his hands, seemingly uncomfortable at Arden's observations. Though he was *sanguis ignis*, and bloodworked fire, David Modhi would never be a servant of Lyonne. Because of their flight into the free waters of the Darkling Sea, he would never be bound up in oaths to the Lyonne Order and the Eugenics Society. Arden Beacon, an invested Lyonnian bloodworker, had once dreamt of that kind of freedom with a man she had begun to love. For a little while, Jonah Riven had made her believe it possible, and then it was taken away.

But if Jonah had never managed to be truly free of the Lions, how could Arden have done the same? She had foolishly chased freedom, and now she was a fugitive and he was dead.

'I think,' David said carefully, 'they sent him away because Jonah was Bellis' friend.'

Arden nodded. 'Yes. I think so too. The Order wanted her isolated. So they could watch her grow without interference. To have as much influence over her as possible.'

They fell quiet and the boat creaked around them.

'Do you think he survived Bellis?' David asked. 'I mean, after you escaped from *Sehnsucht*?'

She shook her head wearily. In her mind's eye she relived the last time she saw Jonah's face, receding from view while aboard the petroleum Queen's ghost-white ship.

A Lion spy had been on board Bellis' ship, and he had helped them escape. The spy, Mr Absalom, had given Arden's companion Chalice Quarry a secret locket full of gathered information. Commanded her to bring those items back to Clay City, and the Order.

But the spy's help had not extended to Jonah Riven. While the women fled, he had remained on board. Chalice might have survived the water with Arden, but she had been under Lion instruction and had been ordered home not long after their eventual rescue.

Arden sighed, still missing Chalice utterly, another layer of regret added to Jonah's loss. Chalice could never have stayed. She was completely beholden to her Order masters.

'No, he would not have survived Bellis. I have thought many days and nights about what Bellis Harrow would do to Mr

Riven in punishment for disobeying her prohibitions, but at the end, letting him live long was not one of them.'

With more force than she intended Arden dropped the copied letter file and its contents into the map drawer, closed it with her knee and winced as her hand hurt while turning the lock. The bloodletting grommet snagged and pulled under her fingerless gloves. Bellis Harrow – the Queen of the Sainted Islands – had been the trauma of Arden's summer. It was nearly midwinter now, and though they'd been sailing for almost a week, she was still hurting.

Three seasons ago Arden had come to a springtime Vigil to run her uncle's old lighthouse. She had thought she was primarily *sanguis ignis* back then, and had been able to trammel a little portion of fire to provide light and do her duty.

What she hadn't known, and it galled her like a wasp's nest in wood, was that the Seamaster's Guild had not employed Arden due to her meagre talent with flame. She was a Lion's tool. They had used her as bait to goad her neighbour Jonah Riven into remembering the hungers of man.

Not a proper seduction though. He was too remote and wary for that. Arden's presence, they expected, would jog his memory. Even though she and Bellis looked nothing alike, Arden would remind him of his powerful wife in hiding somewhere in the Sainted Isles. They suspected Arden's vulnerability would arouse in Jonah an equally protective need to find Bellis again.

Arden had been disposable to the Lyonne Order in light of the greater prize: it was the matter of Bellis' restraint that the Order sweated over. It was Bellis they devoted their energy towards. Bellis had the old *orientis* ability to influence people, but fearsome Jonah Riven, new-returned to Vigil after serving his sentence for a massacre, Jonah been the only person who could influence Bellis in return. Two monsters, two of a kind.

The Lyonne Order required him to tighten Queen Bellis' leash.

But the Lions had not expected Arden and Jonah to fall in love. Hadn't expected that Arden would be with Jonah on *Saudade* when he was reunited with his long-lost love. Instead of a marital reunion between man and wife, the meeting had turned into a three-way, jealousy-fuelled disaster.

Arden's last image of Jonah remained a scar on her mind. Him shackled and bleeding off the bone-white bow of *Sehnsucht*. The last second's rebellion before he was beaten to death on Bellis' command.

At least it would have been quick. Arden could not have borne the thought of him suffering.

Before she could speak to David further, a strange shiver trembled through the hull of their becalmed boat.

Arden sat up straighter. 'What was that?'

An unearthly voice echoed in the waters beyond the sanctuary of *Saudade*'s hull. Not whales or plesiosaur. It sounded too human.

'It's fin-folk,' David answered breathlessly, his eyes wide with excitement and fear. He tilted his head and frowned. 'A pod of them. Close perhaps. Those are hunting songs!'

'Fin-folk?'

'They call them *merrows*, sometimes?'

'I know what merrows are. Oh, that's not good news at all.'

'They'll not harm us. They don't dare go near black mangrove wood.' He rapped on the desk, the same dark wood as *Saudade*'s hull. 'It reminds them of kraken haunts.'

Arden nodded. 'My father kept a book describing the southern species of merrows,' she said. 'And I know that mangrove wood or not, they've been known for boarding ships at anchor.'

David snatched up his boots and began to pull them on.

'I need tell Sean to keep watch. Hillsiders don't have much of a sea-sense.' Then the boy yawned, and stumbled over his feet as he stood up.

'Hold on,' Arden scolded, leaving the map desk. 'I'll go tell Sean. You get some rest.'

'I don't feel that tired—'

'Tired enough to tip over the edge of the boat in a rogue wave, David Modhi. Look at you, weary-drunk as a dock-bound sailor.'

'I'm not weary either!'

'If I count the days we took from Vigil to Garfish Point, this is your third night awake. Now sit. I'll go warn him. Get some sleep.'

Despite her uniform dress being warm enough for the strongest gale, Arden slid into her dark bronze krakenskin coat before slipping outside. The coat lay heavy on her shoulders. It was true deepwater clothing, a hunter's garment, but cut for a woman. Arden had once thought the coat belonged to Bellis, but it had really been the garment of Thalie Riven, a *cunning-woman* among the shorefolk of Vigil's promontory.

Thalie Cleave-Riven, Jonah's mother. Dead in the same massacre that had taken his family.

Arden climbed out onto the deck, where the empty sky – all but the brightest stars washed out by the waxing moon – might have well been cut from funereal black glass. Once there she gulped down the breaths she had not permitted herself in *Saudade*'s below decks. Jonah's face there every time she closed her eyes, blood-drenched and defiant to his dying. Each time she thought her grief had dulled, an image of him would catch like a burr, taking her breath away.

Despite the kraken-boat's supposedly unsinkable design, it was not safe to run the engines on a night like this, not while there were *monstrum mare* about. They were powered down for the dark-time hours. Ballast anchors kept *Saudade* from drifting too far off course. The fin-folk singing receded faintly into the distance. The waves sloshed gently against the black mangrove hull. *Saudade*'s bow dipped and rose. She had much of a tugboat informing her design, as her forecastle was long and wide, the abaft even longer, and the wheelhouse the only high point. Most of the vessel's mass was below the water, making her harder to capsize when a creature as large as herself was trying to drag her down to the deeps.

The waters below *Saudade* flashed electric pink as a fever of giant rays schooled beneath them, disturbed by the presence of the merrows.

Jonah's mother had been briefly married, Mx Modhi reported in her letters, to a man who'd died at the barb of a giant ray. Ishmael Cleave had been his name. His people had given him the Deepwater funeral on the night before they died.

Deepwater rites, Arden repeated to herself. A prayer on Deepwater Night. Jonah had implored it of her the last time she had seen him alive.

Arden bent over and pressed her cheek to the dark wood of the gunwale, imagined by its natural warmth she could still sense Mr Riven's palms having rested there. It would be hard to let *Saudade* go when the vessel reminded Arden of Jonah, every beam and plank. As she rubbed the wood she felt the coins catch inside the leather, and grimaced.

'Do they hurt?'

The darkness had not been entirely unpopulated. Sean Ironcup stood further down the deck in a woollen jacket, indigo-cotton leggings and rubber fishing boots.

Arden startled. 'Sean! I hadn't realized I wasn't alone.'

His slender body leaned heavy on his staff. The palsy dwelt in the left side of his body more than the right. One arm was perpetually folded like a bird's wing, so that Arden could not help but be reminded of those myths of men turned by witches' spells into swans by morning.

'I'm sorry if I interrupted. I thought you knew I was here.'

'Don't be. I was inattentive when we cannot afford to be, out here.' She remembered his question, then, and held out her palms with their fingerless gloves and a small stitch work of flames in the centre. 'My hands don't really hurt. It's my coins that are a little tender though. It has been a year, and I'm due replacements.'

A sudden wave of inhibition came over her and Arden tucked her hands into her dress pockets. Even though they were both Lyonnians, Sean's family had been Hillsiders, people from the high, cold tablelands that bordered the sprawling capital of Clay. They were perennially suspicious of the sanguis-endowed, forever sensing an interference with the ways of nature.

'What happens if they aren't replaced?'

She gestured indifferently with her chin, pretending the issue was of so little concern she had not thought of it. 'Then I would get very sick.'

Sean had no more questions about her condition. They stood slightly apart on deck and viewed each other with the chary caution of fighters sizing one another up. A smudge of blue kraken-grease still dappled Sean's blond-stubbled cheek. Seeing that it was David who worked the engines, it could only have come from an impromptu encounter between them.

Theirs was a forbidden relationship too. David Modhi, a runaway sanguis whose genetics were too precious for him to make his own decisions, and Sean Ironcup, a man involved in Arden's attempted murder and therefore a felon. Arden could see in Sean's eyes an equal suspicion of her. She was far too highborn and deep in her privileges to be making decisions that would affect all of them, in his opinion. Even after two nights and a day in flight she knew she still looked like genteel old money, a sanguis with a complexion like a bright copper burner, dark eyes better to be reading in a library than looking out to sea, and her mahogany hair still coiled elegantly upon her head.

Although he was not long past his twentieth year, Sean Ironcup had already developed the rough, uncultured face of the poor farmers from the Clay highlands. He had thinning yellow hair the texture of corn leavings, a hairline still somewhat too close to his brow. David had given up a lot for this raw young man. Too much, maybe.

He leaned casually upon the gunwale, but his expression was still suspicious. 'David said you were taking us to Libro Island.'

'Yes. I hope if the weather stays fair we will arrive by tomorrow. The map shows a sheltered port on the south side, and a town with welcome-marks.'

He gave a sceptical grimace. 'The map on this very boat said Maris Island was uninhabited, and then we found out that Bellis Harrow had put an army there.'

'In all fairness, it is a very old map.'

'So nobody knows the islands very well, right? I mean, not even Leyland knew, and he considered himself an expert.'

The mention of Sean's wicked relative made Arden bristle, and her reply a touch too forced. 'Mr Ironcup, I am more than certain Libro Island is our destination. Bellis took a Libran girl as a prisoner, and we have suffered equally under her tyranny.' She tried to give a comforting smile. 'They are farmers like yourself. You'll find a home among them, I'll make sure of it.'

Even in her impatience, Arden still tempered her feelings, tried to be kind. Sean Ironcup knew she disapproved of him, of what he'd done to her when under the wing of his family – and of his relationship with David Modhi. He had taken a great many choices away from David's future. As a *sanguis ignis* David would have been welcomed in Clay City. He did not have to throw in his lot with a Hillsider criminal.

Sean's hand trembled, a tell for his anxiety. 'I wonder . . . Would there be a chance while we are there . . .'

'A chance of what, Mr Ironcup?'

'Of finding my sister Helena. If we made a small detour to Equus, we might be able to track her down.'

Arden sucked her teeth and gave Sean a pained smile. 'Like I explained before, Equus Island is far too much a dangerous place for any of us. Even if we don't have someone from Bellis' crew recognize us, we cannot put this boat or any of us at risk among such desperate people as Equus prospectors and pirates. I am also still quite vexed about the whole attempted murder thing.'

Undeterred, Sean pressed on. 'I only want to confirm Helena's safety, Mx Beacon. Maybe send a message? I know she would never leave Gregor, but her children need to know their mother is all right. I could not care less about the other two. They can become kraken-food for all I care.'

A sea-spray kicked up as the boat dipped into a wave-crest. Arden brushed aside a damp lock of hair from where it tickled her eye. 'All right. When we get to Libris, I'll see if we can arrange someone to make inquiries.'

Sean opened his mouth to speak more and then uttered no sound. His head tilted.

'Wait,' he said. 'Is there something out on the water?'

She frowned, and suddenly remembered her reason for coming out. 'Merrows?'

'No, a ship is out there. A big one!'

Arden listened, to little effect. Sight was her talent – she had ears no better than anyone else. Strangely, her navigationer's sight seemed reduced in this darkness, as if a black veil had been draped about them.

Sean didn't bother to explain, instead thump-limped on his staff towards the lantern house. 'Our engines are stilled. We need to get a musket-flare up,' he said urgently. 'We need to hail them, so they can avoid us.'

Gradually the sound came across the dark water. No splash and whip of a craft at sail. Not the shallow beat of a wheelboat either. This one had a deep rhythm of long pistons through a big engine block. The stars winked out just above the horizon.

Over by the rope-chests, a small musket-flare clicked in Sean's best hand. He clumsily loaded a phosphor cartridge into the breach while using his armpit for leverage. His tongue poked out in concentration.

'Can you see it?' he grunted mid-load. 'Are they close?'

'I can't see anything. I should be able to, but I can't . . .'

The air stilled. A feeling of something coming close, yes, but nothing in the silvery night apart from the disappearing stars as if—

Arden gasped, lunged at Sean and snatched the musket out of his hands.

'What in God's . . .?' Sean protested.

'Shush! Quiet!'

'We need to warn them that we are here . . .!'

'*Quiet!*'

With a cry of alarm Arden threw her arms about both Sean and a nearby post, else they would have been toppled by the great grey bow wave. There was no time to fire up the boilers again and away. The death-grey ship passed right by them with barely inches to spare. *Saudade* rocked wildly.

A lungful of the ship's paying load hit her and Arden reeled. That volatile stink of petralactose and rusting iron. Rockblood filled the ship like a wound might fill with infection. In the darkness the hull had no colour, only a flat moon-shadow grey.

Through the mist and the lantern glow Arden stared wordlessly up at the rusting flanks of the old iron craft as it slipped by. Sean dropped the flare-rifle and hugged the post until the rocking faded.

'Is it gone?'

'It's gone now.'

'What was it?'

A door clanged open as David fell out. By the way he held his head the near-collision had thrown him off the couch. 'Did something hit us?'

'We were nearly capsized!' Sean shook his fist at the dark water in protest. 'The boat pilot tried to run us down!'

Arden ran to *Saudade*'s stern and squinted into the night. The lightless boat had disappeared into the gloom, the engine a distant receding thrum. No craft followed behind them. She turned back to where David comforted the Hillsider lad as best he could, but Sean was having none of it.

'Was that ship trying to run us down on purpose? Are we being hunted?'

'No pilot crewed that ship, Mr Ironcup,' she said tartly, and shook the water off her coat.

'It makes no sense!' Sean still trembled from the near miss. 'How can it not have a sea-pilot?' He turned to David Modhi for confirmation.

'She's right, Sean. If that was a ghost ship out of Equus, there would have been nobody on board. Not a living soul. They are like clockwork, wound up once and then keep going until the metal turns to dust and sinks into the waters.'

Arden nodded in agreement. There had been days in old history, where a thousand captainless ships out of Equus had operated in a chain, one behind the other. Automated iron tombs filled with rockblood. The undead instructions might last forever, but metal was certain to fail eventually. Ships would sink, or get carried north by storms. There were perhaps less than a hundred rockblood ships out there now.

'But how is that possible?' Sean asked.

Arden picked up the rifle from where Sean had dropped it, took the flare cartridge from the breech and checked the paper was still intact. Then she looked at Sean.

'It's an obscure bit of Clay City folklore, but have you heard the story of the Saint of the Islands?'

Sean shook his head. 'I thought when they said the Sainted Isles they meant the Redeemer . . .' he said, referring to the messianic figure who'd drowned and resurrected from a lonely pirate rock.

'According to my father, the Lyonne Order centuries ago exiled a very powerful bloodworker onto Equus,' she explained. 'Someone who made all the rockblood pumps and refineries, the clockwork ships. Set them going forever. Many sanguinem can have more than one endowment, a greater talent and a shadow talent.' She tapped her chest, then shrugged at the thought. 'Every once in a while some individuals can have two very powerful ones.'

'*Sanguis orientis* and *sanguis mandatum*,' David interjected, wanting to prove himself knowledgeable, for he'd have no doubt heard the tale from the Black Rosette traders back in Vigil. 'Direction and Instruction, but combining to form something new, something that can keep machines going forever and men compelled to work them!'

Arden nodded. 'That's the talk around dinner tables, when the sherry makes an appearance and the adults think the children are in bed.'

Sean frowned. 'I've never heard of *mandatum* . . . or *orientis* for that matter.'

'Nobody has, not really,' Arden said. 'They are drunkard's myths more than anything. Had I not learned about archival sanguinities in my academy history classes, or seen Bellis-damn-Harrow work *orientis* on twenty men—' She snapped the flare-rifle shut. 'I'd not have bothered to remember them.'

Arden locked the rifle away, and put the paper cylinder back with its two other remaining cartridges in a box that had once held closer to thirty.

'Because of this saint's talents, an automatic ship can still work after all this time?'

'Yes, if the metal still holds. Because of the *two* instructions. We are on a path far from Equus, thank goodness, but we may still cross more than just a lone corpse-boat and must keep watch.'

A new terror dawned upon Sean. 'It is a sin.' He grabbed David's elbow, to impress upon him the gravity of his words. 'It's a sin, David, to give life to something *inanimate*, to play God!'

'It is the economy of rockblood and the petroleum islands,' Arden corrected him, as she locked the gun box tight. 'These are sightless lands, Sean. Especially for me. Something is getting in the way of my vision. Let me decide who we signal or not from this point, all right?'

Sean pouted, but succumbed to David's hugs and pleas for understanding.

'I am right. Now be gone, little devils. I'll take this shift. We may have a long night ahead of us, if we are on an *orientine* sea-road.'

After the two young men begrudgingly took their leave, Arden climbed into the wheelhouse. The moon showed as a hard little dot high above the horizon. A collection of spindly shapes moved through the water beside the boat in silver reflections that could only be a plesiosaur pod, coming to the surface to feed upon the shoals of fish that followed behind the lich-ship's wash. The kraken would soon follow as the great apex predator of the Sainted Seas. She knew she should by rights have let one of the pair take the morning shift as she too had hardly slept. However, the sudden appearance of the ghost ship had filled her with an undertow of concern. Something worrisome in the way they'd crossed the perimeter between mapped land and the unknown so quietly in the night.

Arden reached into the pockets of her skirt and took out one of the few possessions she had taken with her on her flight from the mainland. The iron ring from the promontory beach, the one cast in the shape of a giant sea-serpent, ridden by the small figure David had identified as the Deepwater King. An almost unbearable weight was on her. Grief and duty. She pressed the iron to her lips.

'I'm on my way, Jonah,' she said quietly. 'I'll give you the prayer soon.'

David's footfall caused the ladder's creaks as he made an unannounced entrance into the wheelhouse. Arden, still holding on to the old relic, slipped it back into her pocket.

'Two brandies and an opium tincture in quick succession,' David said. 'Sean'll be right come morning.'

'I rather thought I ordered *everyone* go to sleep,' Arden said, rearranging the olive fabric of her oiled skirt as she sat up. The cold weather tended to make the fabric stiff, and the kraken-oil heater at her feet was set to Riven levels of warmth – which was to say, barely above freezing. Even if she'd managed to get one of the *ignis* lights going, *ignis* flame burned cold. With a pang of regret, Arden wished Chalice were here. Even as a spy pretending to be a keeper's assistant, Chalice Quarry would never have let a heater burn down. Arden imagined Chalice in her stormbride dress, spluttering with indignation, red hair awry, hauling a stove into the wheelhouse.

'Can't sleep any more, Mx Beacon. Too many things going around in my head.'

'Likewise, Mr Modhi. At least our sufferings won't be for much longer. Once we start up the engines at first light, we could be in Libro by suppertime tomorrow.'

He shot her a tight expression before kneeling to warm his hands on the heater. 'If you say so.'

'They *will* give us shelter, David. When I was a brief guest of Bellis Harrow on *Sehnsucht*, I saw a servant girl who called herself Persephone Libro. She will have a family, and a real name. A family who will want to know she is still alive. We will bring them glad news of their daughter.'

'Mx Beacon, if Bellis has already taken Libran prisoners, they may no longer have safe harbour to provide us.'

'Still a safer harbour for us than a desperate place like Equus, with ten thousand men all scrapping over the same patch of dirt. Taking one prisoner does not mean she's taken them all.'

'I'm just trying to keep an open mind.'

'David, if a man must stay up and whisper doubts in my ear, he can also fetch me some tea in the meantime.'

The young man smiled tentatively and stood at the doorway but lingered, not quite finished.

Arden exhaled impatiently. 'Speak, Mr Modhi.'

'Mx Beacon,' David started with hesitation in his words. 'You told me Mr Riven asked for a prayer in his memory?'

'Yes, for the Deepwater Rite, or as close as I can come to it. At the time I didn't understand what he meant by a *prayer*. So specific. But I had a lot of hours to study the old Island mysteries while I was recovering at Mrs Sage's apartments. Her husband was translating medicinal journals from Fictish to Lyonnian. He had several old books. I suspect Mr Riven didn't mean just a prayer, but a *ritual*.'

'I have heard of it.'

'Yes. Your mother more than once spoke of the shorefolk rituals in her intelligence-gathering letters. Ishmael Cleave had the Rite performed in his memory, the night before the massacre.'

'I just don't think it's safe,' David said, shaking his head. 'It's a hard service. Back home we'd get fisherfolk coming into the harbour with hands and limbs missing because they'd called up something *huge* during their funerals.'

'Monsters?'

David nodded.

Arden rolled her eyes. 'With due respect, I'm not going to

secure the help of a rum-addled sailor who can't keep his hands inside a boat while performing the rite, David. We are going to islands where the old religion still holds. Equus might have been poisoned against the deepwater ways by the rockblood industry, but even I've heard Libro never suffered like they did. It's a peaceful and spiritual island. I can find a priest on Libro who remembers the old ways. I'll exchange the last of my Lyonne gold for them to complete the ritual on Mr Riven's behalf. Will that be a problem? If it is, tell me.'

Taken aback, David swallowed. His apple jumped in his throat.

'I would do anything for Mr Riven. But I can't understand. Why even come all the way out here for a prayer? Why not go home to Lyonne, and pay a priest there? Sean tells me that the God of Clay and the Deepwater King aren't that different.'

'Maybe the gods are not different in a Hillsider's opinion. But *I'd* know the difference.'

He pointed at her hands. 'Those coins are hurting more every day. I saw what happened to your uncle, Lightkeeper Jorgen, when he decided he wasn't going to do what the Lions told him any more. He lost feeling in his hands, they turned black with sepsis and he died. You don't have much time left either.'

Not wishing to meet his eyes, Arden plucked a pilled thread from where the fabric wore down at the knee-line of her skirt. She noticed at once how her fine finger skills took much more effort. No, she did not have time. Eventually she would lose the use of her hands and become a liability to her own survival, but she had yet to think much beyond that.

Refused, even. Not until she'd given Jonah his due.

Morning had yet to find the boat. A greenish light on the southern horizon spread higher than the permanent storm. An aurora's mantle, she thought. Of all the bad-luck omens.

She lifted her head. 'It is true, I can't live out here. But when I pay Jonah his last respects here it will be *me* doing it. Of my own volition. Once I go back to Lyonne I am a sanguis, a cog in the Lyonne Order's great machine. I will be no different than that pilotless ship, carrying out instructions laid down a century ago.'

She pressed her hands together. They hurt, but it was a more welcome pain than the fog of grieving, and the regret that would follow her always, were she *not* to do this.

'Why is fitting in so bad, Mx Beacon? It would be nice, to belong somewhere, be part of something.'

'If I were you, it would be wonderful. And it would be, if ever you were to change your mind and go. But I fear when I go back to Lyonne, I'll forget what it's like to be *me*. I'll forget *him*. Then Jonah will truly be lost, and he will never find his way back to the cathedral of the King. I'm already responsible for the death of his body. I'll not allow the loss of his immortal soul.'

David looked at his feet, then nodded. 'Doing it for him, then.'

'Yes. So go on, Mr Modhi. Fetch me some tea and join me for the sunrise, for Libro is waiting for us.'

2

The sea gods were malicious

The sea gods were malicious, for on sunrise when *Saudade* came to pull anchor and fire up the kraken-oil engine, the boilers refused to catch alight. Arden pumped the priming handle for all it was worth, and received not more than a spark for her efforts. The four great pinions that steered both side wheels and screw groaned piteously in their valve seats.

'What's the matter?' David asked when he pushed his dark tousled head into the wheelhouse. 'Daylight's here. Shouldn't we be on the move?'

Arden made an impatient gesture at the priming handle. 'We have been stymied by physics, Mr Modhi. I cannot get the engine started.'

David pondered the handle. 'It may be the oil seats down in the engine block. It shouldn't take long. I'll go and tighten them, and we'll be on our way before breakfast.'

David's confident appraisal of their problem didn't shake her doubts. For all that *Saudade* had been repaired by Mr Fulsome in the Vigil docks several weeks before, there were a myriad little things that could go wrong with a boat left abandoned on a storm-tossed sea for over a month. *Saudade* had spent a long time alone, knocking about with the whales and sea-rays before a fishing boat had towed her in.

The devils of misfortune and the salt water had, in that time, found their way in through the vessel's nooks and crannies. It was not an ailment particular to these waters. The same happened to the Clay Portside wharves that were rarely used and fell into ruin. Desertion made them haunted.

David's best experience in engine repair had been with the small single-stroke generators at Mr Riven's promontory lodge, not with twelve massive valve chambers as mysterious as a thief's maze in a Pharaoh's tomb. At full sun-up they had yet to find a solution for their stilled engine, and Arden admitted that *Saudade* was now adrift.

The boys didn't give up trying to fix her, so, jangled with anxiousness, Arden had nothing else to do except pace the deck, and shuffle through all the scenarios of rescue she could think of. Though they were in neutral waters, she still half-expected to see the big Lyonnian clipper from two days before. It had pursued them a short time after they'd left the mainland, only turning away upon the sunset when *Saudade* had crossed into the Darkling Sea.

'Devilment,' she said to the empty air. 'Don't let me get to a point where I start wishing for Lions.'

No other craft disturbed the flat expanse of the north-passage sea-road. The wind remained a fair easterly one and the weather stayed kind. The fauna of the ocean did not bother with this black mangrove wreck upon their watery kingdom. In the afternoon sun Arden saw a large shadow pass under the ship – she feared a great shark or sea-dragon until recognizing it as a giant armoured isopod, tumbling lazily below *Saudade* before moving on upon a cold, hidden current.

David and Sean took the kraken-oil engine completely apart, fashioning a block and tackle upon the forecastle deck, disinterring brass levers and glass oil-cups the size of a man's ribcage, ceramic rings wrapped in copper wire, valve seats of a tough black rubber, worked around pistons as large as rum barrels at the end of tree trunks.

By the late afternoon, the combined wisdom of the ambassadors of Clay Hillside and Vigil were stumped by the engine's complexity. David threw Arden an apologetic glance and shook his head.

'We might wait for someone to come along,' he said at last.

'That could very likely be the Lions,' she said. 'Or pirates. If you can't fix the engine, at least get the parts back together again in the engine bay. We can't afford to lose a piece over the side.'

The drowsy day with its hint of chill at last got the better of her, and she left the wreckage of the decks for the relative quiet of *Saudade*'s dark below. She did not mean to nap, but the sound of the waves heaving against the hull, the faint camphor of the rare wood and the low lights behind the yellow sconce-glass made her drowsy as if she'd taken opium. She lay upon the ray-leather chaise longue without removing her boots, and the ship rocked her to sleep . . .

. . . until a whooping cry from David snapped her awake.

Disoriented, Arden sat up. *Boats*, he was yelling. *There's boats!*

Boats? Her competing desires jostled for attention. Had the Order found them?

Upon making her way outside, she found *Saudade* was no longer alone on an empty sea. During Arden's unplanned afternoon nap a small flotilla of sloops and yachts had come upon them. One sizable paddleboat bore a yellow flag. Clay City, but it was not an Order flag, or a nautical flag. These were civilians, which meant they could be anyone.

'Hoy,' David shouted. 'Hoy!' He lit a saltpetre cartridge, sending lurid red smoke careening over the decks and off with the wind. 'Over here!' The cold pink eye of a phosphor flare hung in the mist above.

Devilment! He was not a Beacon *ignis* with her family's brilliant eyesight, so David couldn't have even *seen* who he'd signalled. He'd lain out the best tableware! In a hurry Arden righted her waxen skirts and fastened her boots before leaving the wheelhouse, preparing to scold him.

David's expression was luminous as he turned towards her. 'I think they saw us,' he said joyfully. 'We're saved!'

Almost speechless with disagreement, Arden pointed at the signal smoke as it drifted over the water in a red tail.

'Saved by who? Now they know we're vulnerable, and look at them – they are all from Lyonne! Have you boys no sense, David Modhi, Sean Ironcup? You tell *me* to be careful!'

David pouted. 'We *are* vulnerable. We need their help.'

'We don't even *know* these people.'

Arden looked down at her hands, and all the cautions of a lifetime came over her. She yanked off her flame-embroidered fingerless gloves, and dived into her dress pockets for a roll of crêpe bandage.

'Quick, help me tie the bandage on. Over my coins. We need to hide them, fool!'

David, having expected gratitude, gave her a baffled frown, did what she asked. Once bound she grabbed his hand and turned his arm over. Most of the small cuts could be passed off as common engineering injuries, but in one instance she could see he'd deliberately inserted a phlebotomist's needle into a vein, bruising his skin in such a shockingly obvious blood draw even a commoner could see it.

'Roll those sleeves down,' she said urgently. 'I'll do the same. My hand wounds are rope burns from hauling up the engine. You cut yourself on glass, by accident. Other than that, let *me* do the talking. Understand? Not a word to them. Tell Sean.'

'Won't we get preferential treatment if we say we're sanguinem?'

'We won't get *anything*. Have you been listening to what Sean has said of what Hillsiders think of rich bloodworkers? David, in my home city, sometimes people can't find work because one of us has replaced a hundred of them! We may be the entire reason the people over there have been forced to make this fool journey out to this excremental place!'

By David's face she could tell they'd not had such a discussion. Arden shook her head. 'Just go get Sean and tell him to keep his mouth shut. Disguise those cuts and let me handle this.'

Chastened, he ran for the cabins, to prepare Sean for their visitors, and inform him of his required silence.

She slid her gloves into one of the roomy pockets of her dress, before checking the honey-wax seals on her hands. If she didn't do anything strenuous, she would not bleed through the coins and give away her disguise.

It took a while for the scouts of the meagre little flotilla to approach *Saudade*. Three tough-looking men and one woman wearing waxed garments so cracked and ill-fitting they could only have been obtained from a jumble-sale stall. Each tunic bore a clumsily embroidered rosy cruciform decoration on the chest, of which the constant damp of harsh sea travel had unpicked most of the stitches. She recognized the symbol as being the Redeemer's Rock, so these folk could belong to any one of numerous Clay City Church offshoots servicing the more disaffected and contrarian of the flock.

'Hoy there,' Arden said, slipping into a common Clay Capital accent. 'I'm glad we found such welcome assistance. I wasn't relishing another night with the Old Leviathan below us and the merrows so hungry.'

'How long has your boat been drifting?' one man called to Arden from his position on the tender-boat's bow. Not unfriendly, but he was not offering to help, not yet.

'A day and a night. We left Garfish Point on Maunday, late noon.'

The folk exchanged glances and nodded. 'Must have just missed the embargo then,' said one of the men.

'Embargo?'

'We came out of Morningvale on Hewsday morning, tried to spend a night in the Point,' the woman said. 'The whole town is under guard by the Lyonne–Fiction militia. Some criminality afoot. How blessed we were, to have the supplies to keep going this long way around. Others were not so blessed and were confined to the port.'

'Thank goodness then, for not being tardy in leaving,' Arden said. Her hands tingled as her coins responded to her ever-tightening fists. She wanted to scratch them. Could they not beg a ride soon and be on their way?

'No, it is God we must thank,' the woman said. 'And the Redeemer Who Walks the Way.'

All four kissed their knuckles and crossed themselves.

So she had been correct in identifying these fellows. 'Do I welcome Clay Church pilgrims?' Arden asked hopefully, looking at their chest patches and their familiar shape. The most sacred island around here was most certainly Libro: according to Clay Church tradition, the unnamed holy teacher had placed the soles of His feet upon Libro when He first walked the world, in the days of His brief ministry. It was certainly the last place He'd walked, as He had died at the hands of angry unconverted pagans, tied upon a rock until the tide rose and drowned Him.

Even though the Sainted Isles were shrouded in mystery, Libro remained a virtuous place in Clay lore, with well-kept records from the missionaries who had first ministered upon the green, fertile shores. Arden recalled Sean thinking that the Sainted Isles had been named after the church's most holy person, and a shy hope bloomed in her heart.

'Thank the One Who Walks the Way,' Arden said.

'Yes,' the woman replied. 'We are pilgrims, all of us bound to the Sainted Islands to do our duty by God. One of our congregation – my late husband – he had a *vision*.'

'Well, that's incredibly convenient!' Arden exclaimed.

They stared at her rather stonily.

Arden coughed. 'By that, I mean, this vision has become a benefit to all of us, God helping many with the one act of charity. See, I am . . . I was . . . on a pilgrimage of my own.'

'In such a massive craft?' The woman's attention went up and down *Saudade* as if she were inspecting an inappropriately dressed debutante. 'And built out of such a heretical wood?' She tutted at the black mangrove, which would have seemed to the woman's Clay eyes as malign a material as ever was carved into an unholy deepwater idol.

'I was gifted passage on this ship. I cannot speak for the craft's amorality, I am afraid.' By now Sean and David had worn out their patience below decks and had sidled back out through the cabin door to peer down nervously at the pilgrims.

Arden continued, 'The owner is this young man here, Mr David Modhi of Vigil, and I have paid passage to Libro to recover the body of my dead husband. He . . . he was taken to the Islands and never returned.'

Something in the way she garbled the last words and gulped a breath afterwards clearly softened the woman's thorny heart. Madam Pilgrim nodded to one of the men, gestured that he throw a rope to Arden so she might tie on.

Arden lowered the boarding ladder to allow them up onto *Saudade*'s side. This took time, for by the ill look in some purge-hollowed faces, they were not all of them used to water voyages.

Aboard, the Clay pilgrims inspected the boat with narrow, prying interest. There appeared no malice in their curiosity, only homespun common sense. David showed the menfolk the remains of his engine repair. The woman took off her wide-brimmed hat and offered Arden her hand.

'I am Mrs Phillip Cordwain, and these fine fellows are Messrs Tega, Gallo and Le Shen respectively.'

Arden gave a nod and shook the cold fleshy hand in return. 'I am . . . I am Mrs Richard Castile.' She kept her grip light, willing herself not to leak blood through the bottom of her dress-sleeves. 'My given name is Arden.'

'Ah, but Mrs Richard Castile is just a fine enough name for a widow to use,' Mrs Cordwain chided gently. 'I too lost a husband. Was yours young?'

'Far too young,' Arden said by rote, before she turned back. 'I have introduced Mr Modhi already. This is Mr Sean Ironcup, who is searching for his sister who became lost to the Islands, and left behind three children.'

Nods all round at such a worthy reason. The flotilla had drifted closer, sensing that the greetings had moved up a notch.

'I have very little available coin to pay for a tow,' Arden continued. 'I do have kraken oil in the hold however. If the motor vessels require it, I can give more than enough.'

The man identified as Mr Le Shen nodded and turned to his companion. 'We could use the fuel, Mrs Cordwain. We were meant to take on provisions in Garfish Point. If we are cursed with anything other than what little rearward winds we've been blessed with so far, there will not be enough fuel to get us all to Equus.'

At the very mention of the rockblood island, even the wind seemed to stop blowing.

'Excuse me,' Arden asked. 'Is this flotilla not bound for Libro?'

'No, it was *Equus* that my beloved husband – may his soul rest in peace – saw in his vision, Equus the Horse Island, the Burden Town Island, where hard work is rewarded, where the Redeemer once said, *God helps only those who help themselves*. T'was an epiphany he had, as awe-inspiring as a saint receiving a blessing of the Spirit.'

'But I . . . I thought you might want to go to Libro, being that the Redeemer . . . well, being that He . . .' In the storm of panic Arden tried to find the words. 'Being that He walked the world upon Libro first.'

Mrs Cordwain blinked at her, in the slow manner of a cold-blooded thing who has found its likely supper sleeping.

'The Redeemer would not think us worthy if we did not do the *work* first. To Equus we go, to work in God's service, work the milk from the stone, and draw up the petralactose from the devil's bosom! Then when we have suckled the devil dry, then we may be invited to join the Redeemer upon the holy isle.'

Now the flotilla surrounded *Saudade*, and the souls aboard thought it quite the place for a holy hymn. To Arden's ears it might as well have been a dirge.

'At least we have such a similar path,' Arden said uneasily.

'The Libro island group is only a short ways beyond Equus. If we could impose upon your graciousness with a double payment of . . .'

Mrs Cordwain's face turned grey, and hard. 'Would be a sin to take penitents there, when they have not earned their invitation. Would be a sin for a widow not to see the true work that awaits her in heaven before she returns to her earthly duties.'

A cold sweat stung Arden's brow with ice. While she tried to think of another tack that would enable her to avoid the chaos of Equus Island altogether, Mrs Cordwain continued, 'Though one is very much welcome to stay here and wait for a more appropriate vessel to tow this craft, I fear Great Lyonne has stilled all the boats in the Garfish Point harbour for an unspecified number of days. One may be waiting quite a long time.'

'Devilment, how bad *is* this?' Arden fretted.

'I'm sure it's not that bad,' David said. 'The prospectors go there to make their fortunes, right? Even those pilgrims are taking a detour. We are sitting on a fortune's worth of kraken oil in this ship. We will arrive rich, in Equus. We have money for the Old Guy.'

She shook her head at his invocation of the payment-collecting spirit of the Sainted Isles. '*Oil* is definitely something the people of Equus are not lacking for, David.'

'We could be in and gone within a few days.'

'I don't want you boys near that cursed place,' she said. 'I won't have it. There's no getting out once the island has a man's mind in its grip. Have you not heard any warning I've given you? People go there in enslavement to the rockblood industry, they give their labour and die!'

'It can't all be rockblood mining,' Sean added churlishly. 'Maybe the pilgrims aren't being so absurd by wanting to go to Equus first.'

'Really now?'

'Listen, Leyland used to say Libro was an island in decline.

Farming and fishing, and not much of either. But think, we could have real financial opportunities in Equus. I've had enough of being a farmer.'

'*Leyland* used to say? Sean, that mendacious man was only thinking about the wealth in his pocket, and was willing to sell his grandchildren for it!' She shook her head in exasperation at Sean's optimistic ignorance. 'He was willing to kill me for his fortune, and he certainly as hell was responsible for Jonah Riven sailing after him to his death!'

The galumphing of feet interrupted them, for the pilgrims on the flotilla had decided it would be a fine opportunity to stretch their legs all about the decks, to pull out the sheet anchors and unspool the rope coils from where they had been neatly placed and put the most impossible knots in them. Earlier on Arden had counted at least thirty travellers, with some spare children to round out the misery. Having them climb all over *Saudade* was like having Mr Riven's body desecrated all over again.

'You're terrified of going there, Mx Beacon,' Sean said. He was not willing to concede. 'Is it because the Equus folk won't do any sort of stupid ritual for Mr Riven? Because from what I hear they would more likely celebrate his death and spit upon the krakenskin coat rather than give him a proper funeral!'

Arden opened her mouth in speechless affront, then glared at David.

'You *told* him about that, Mr Modhi?'

'I didn't mean it that way, I was only discussing history.' He turned to Sean. 'Come on, Cup, we agreed we wouldn't say anything!'

'I never agreed to this! Look where we are, D! Stuck in the middle of the ocean with nowhere to go but into the water because we're chasing a dead man's ghost!' He sat up as tall as his palsy would allow him. 'A dead man hated by everyone! All Mx Beacon's effort is about Mr Riven. We are an afterthought! A burden so she can enact a sinful worship to a demon!'

As David vacillated between defence of Mr Riven and

supporting his friend, Arden waved them down. 'Mr Ironcup, I agree with you.'

He glared at her suspiciously. 'What?'

'I should have let you both slip into hiding on Fiction and not dragged two innocents along with me on this cursed expedition. Jonah would never forgive me a Deepwater Rite on his behalf if I put you both in danger on Equus. Imagine if Bellis' people recognized us.'

Sean Ironcup, having puffed himself up for a fight, deflated somewhat. Sullen as a silenced child, he held David's hand and watched Arden pace the map room.

Then Sean gave up his crumb. 'Bellis Harrow won't ever go back to Equus,' he grumped. 'It's impossible for her.'

'This is the deduction you've come up with on your own? Sean, when she got kicked out last time she was a silly girl, and now she is a woman with an army. Argument with the locals won't keep her away.'

'Not even her army can make her welcome! When my family were on the *Fine Breeze*,' he paused, because the little boat had belonged to Arden and its theft was still raw, 'the sailors came across us in their white boat. *Sehn . . . Sehn . . .*'

'*Sehnsucht*,' David said.

'Go on,' Arden said warily.

'I stayed hidden as they boarded. I overheard the sailors talking. About the people of Equus who had cast Bellis out, and of a man who lived there.'

Something about the way David said '*man*' gave Arden pause.

'Someone who put the fear of God into Bellis Harrow,' David finished. 'A rival on Equus Island. She had no power over him and it vexed and scared her. Even now. Maybe this is someone who could keep us safe better than the Libro Islanders ever could.'

Arden tried not to let the disappointment at being left out of this confidence show. 'Should I not have been informed of this theory earlier?'

The two young men hunched down in defiant shame.

Clearly the mutinous pair had already been discussing potential scenarios that hadn't involved Arden. Maybe they'd even been planning for a time when they could not rely on her at all.

David shrugged, deeply apologetic at having been caught out. 'We should have shared it. I'm sorry.'

Arden sighed again. 'And who was this rival?'

Sean spoke. 'They said a name. 'Miah . . . Miah *Anguis*. Like the sea-serpent.'

David nodded emphatically. '*Miah Anguis*, Mx Beacon. An Equus man called Miah who made Bellis afraid. Her army wouldn't cross him. Sean heard her go quite spare and maybe – maybe Mr Anguis might be the one to shelter us.'

Arden rubbed her temples with her sharp-twanging hands. She wanted desperately to agree with them about this safe harbour Bellis could not breach, but they were grasping at straws. Without proof, their saviour story was a figment of desperation and hope. Many violent denizens of the Lyonnian underworld had dealings in Equus, drawn by the potential criminal profits of the unregulated prospectors' island. Even if someone was formidable enough to resist an *orientis*-empowered Bellis Harrow, trying to win the help of such a one would be next to impossible.

'Even if this person exists, I cannot for the life of me see how we could buy an influential man's assistance without anything to exchange.' She frowned at them both. 'And don't mention kraken oil again. Like I said, it has no value on a petralactose island.'

'No, we could trade something else entirely. See, that bastard Leyland . . .'

'Helena Tallwater's father-in-law, David. And she is Sean's sister. His family still.'

Sean's complexion had permanently settled into a shade of mauve. 'Leyland thought he'd sell your blood to some Islanders to gain entry. He told me it was because crude rockblood won't burn, not unless something sets it alight. A *catalyst* he said . . .'

David jumped in, and finished off. '*Sanguis ignis* blood has value! I could sell them my blood in return for our safety.'

Arden could barely talk from the disbelief at what she was hearing. 'No, you are not going to bleed yourself! Devilment, David Modhi what are you—'

Another voice said: '*One could always just go home.*'

Arden stopped, and turned about to face the direction of the sudden voice. It had been so familiar . . .

'Good day, Miss!' David said to the visitor, standing up and giving a little bow. So caught up had she been in her miserable conversation, Arden had failed to notice the entry of another person into the map room.

Chalice Quarry, in a floppy hat and pilgrim's tunic, leaned on the map desk casually and spun a brass protractor on one end. 'I said *darling*, you could just go *home*.'

'*Chalice?*'

'Hello, darling,' said her erstwhile stormbride. 'It's been a while.'

3

Arden knew

Arden knew she could not truly forgive all that had happened between her and Chalice Quarry. The lighthouse assistant's friendship with Arden had merely been a rat's-coat disguise, for Chalice had turned out to be a Lyonne Order agent, a woman vowed to keep *eyes upon*. And what about Jonah's death, that Chalice had both aided and witnessed? Arden should rightly throw her out on her ear.

But all she could do was stagger into the arms of the one other familiar face on this empty sea. Close to tears, she clutched the sturdy shoulders close. 'I am so angry, and I haven't forgiven you one bit.'

'And justly so. It's all gotten rather away from us, this situation.'

As Arden suspected, Chalice wore the same style of dress as the other pilgrims, from her trousered skirt to the hastily embroidered rocky crucifix upon her tunic. She released herself from Arden's embrace and made a stern face at the two young men.

'Boys, a private moment, please.'

Muttering apologies, David half-dragged a protesting Sean upstairs, leaving the women alone in the map room. Even though she was shorter than Arden, and as stout as a tugboat, she'd somehow passed for any one of the menfolk clambering all over *Saudade*'s broad decks.

'How could I have overlooked the smallest fellow in the group with the biggest bosom? A right *imp*, Chalice Quarry, to have not revealed yourself to me straight away! Oh, these people should have seen the horns on your head and your cloven hoof.'

'Even the devil can be charismatic sometimes, as we are all too well aware.' Chalice pushed her hands on either side of Arden's cheeks. '*Someone* looks only a little better than when I saw them last. My dear, you are half-drowned and going dusty with *ichor meritis* poisoning. And who did that hair? Certainly not me. Why, you're fraying like a night-lady's corset.'

It was all Arden could do not to hug her and sniffle a teary spot into Chalice's scarf. Chalice who she loved and hated in equal measure. Chalice, enemy and friend.

She choked, unsure if she was laughing or crying. 'Oh, devils! You mendacious *vixen*. You utter *fiend*, why chase me all the way out here? Don't tell me of a secret sanguinity for finding lost people, or I will be utterly affronted.'

Chalice released her to find the polished silver mirror on one wall, and tried to pat her riotous red hair in place so it might fit back under the Sou'wester hat she'd been using as the bulk of her disguise.

'Let's just say my heels had cooled somewhat in Morningvale when I first caught word of *Saudade*'s flight. Took me all the powers of persuasion to get on the last boats allowed out of the harbour before the coast shut down.'

Then she left her image alone, and turned about.

'And you know why I'm here.'

Arden had known the Order's command would reach her, one way or another. Wasn't it Chalice's first statement when stepping in this room?

'Ah, Chalice, of all people I thought you would understand why I had to leave.'

'I'm sorry, darling, but that is what it is. The Order would not allow me out of the country without my at least trying to bring you back.'

'Then what about Sean and David? Sean's a wanted criminal in Lyonne, and David won't go anywhere without him. If they end up on Equus . . . Chalice, you know what that place is like. They won't last six months and I'll never forgive myself if I lose two more lives. Destroying one was enough.'

She couldn't stop the twist of pain showing on her face, and turned about so Chalice could not see her. Behind her Chalice let out a small *hmm* of consideration.

'Where did you intend to take them before you were waylaid?'

'Libro,' Arden said. 'It's the only place they could be safe.'

Chalice shook her head. 'No.'

'Yes, Chalice! It's the perfect place.'

'No! Remember the locket Mr Absalom gave me, before we left *Sehnsucht*?'

'The one with his secrets—?'

'There was a thread code embedded in the silk. A catalogue of all the nonsense our Queen Bellis has been up to since she started her *orientine* gallivant about the Sainted Isles. The girl in the yellow dress on board Bellis' ship, she was the lone Libro prisoner.'

'Persephone.'

'Wren, her real name is. Wren Halcyon Libro, maybe she'll be the last of her people.'

'I don't understand, Chalice. The last?'

'The last, darling. There are none of her kind left. Three years ago Bellis Harrow killed every Libros adult her army could find, then dropped the children into the sea. Libro is no more.'

Even if the ground had fallen out from beneath her feet, Arden would not have felt so weightless as she did then.

'But nobody else knows the old ways except the people on that island. David and Sean were going to live with them, and I was going to ask about . . .' She trailed off.

Chalice gently guided Arden to the daybed and took her hand. Arden did not fight her. Her hope had drained away as utterly as if a knife had nicked every vein.

'Why don't the Lions stop Bellis?' Arden asked hollowly. 'If the Order is so aware of her brutality?'

'I suspect the Lyonne Order is happier having our Queen monstering a few fishermen and assorted farmers rather than turning her sights towards Clay City. They prefer her out here and away from anywhere of importance.'

Without warning Chalice grabbed Arden's wrist. She pushed the bandage off the wax-stoppered coins and pressed hard on one silver disc with her thumb.

Arden pulled her hand free. 'Ow! That hurt.'

'They shouldn't hurt.'

'They won't hurt if they're not poked!'

'Darling, a sanguinem can't stay out here forever roaming the islands like a wailing, lovelorn spirit. Those coins need replacing each year, else your body will begin to corrode about them.'

Annoyed, Arden yanked the bandage back into place. 'I've already had this conversation with David Modhi, Chalice. Why do you think I'm being driven like I've got demons with pitchforks chasing me? Time is not on my side.'

'Which is why I want to *help*.' At Arden's frown Chalice continued. 'I also heard what Jonah said before we jumped off the back of *Sehnsucht*. You're not out here just to find the boys a home, are you, darling? If your lost man needs a deepwater prayer to rest his errant ghost, then let me put my significant skills to effecting those words.'

Arden was confused by this helpful Chalice. 'So this is not a Lion with a switch telling me to turn the boat around right now?'

'As if my wilful friend would listen? Goodness, I'm not a monster.' Chalice smiled and caressed Arden's cheek. 'If the Order investigations are correct, there is also an heretical Clay City priest on Equus who converted to the old island religion. After he performs a funeral ceremony, we can leave Equus and find a place in South Lyonne for the two boys to slip away. Much of the land south of Harbinger Bay is lousy with rebels and swampland secessionists. The Order gets there as much as they do the Isles. See? Everything in its place, and your homecoming to boot.'

After being buffeted by so many conflicting emotions in such a short time, Arden could barely say a coherent word. The only recognizable feeling in the tumult that flooded through her was relief.

'I suppose it sounds achievable,' she croaked breathlessly.

'It is achievable. Cheer up. I'll help you make those confessions and acts of contrition to whatever church of love exists upon Equus. And then, once we have done what you need to appease that guilt, let me take you home.'

4

They called it day

They called it *day*, but was it daylight that they saw when they came into the harbour of Burden Town, the main township of Equus Island? A roil of smoke from a hundred fires coated the sky in bruised blacks and furious crimsons. A thousand boats in this curl of bay, and a stench beyond anything Arden had suffered before, even greater than the stink from the ghost ship. A sour-sweet miasma of salt and organic rot from poison waters mixed with effluent and bituminous rockblood.

Beyond the harbour squatted an edifice that looked as if a dozen great slum dwellings had been built one on top of the other. A small city of a thousand rooms, each balanced precariously on the roof of one below, all enclosed by a low ragged wall of limestone like a great square tomb constructed piecemeal. Countless constellations of tiny electric lights scattered over the apartment-city's surface, making the dark plains beyond the wall all the more grim.

A place for work and working, not lives and living.

The Equus morning showed blood-red on a horizon ragged with pumping-derricks. The pump-heads bobbed laboriously along the coast. Beyond the walled city, Arden could make out a landscape of uninhabited plains where not even trees grew. The wasteland was as open and featureless as if it had been graded flat. Anxious, she adjusted her gloves so that the stitches in the leather secured against her skin, and tried to still her quick, fretful mind.

'You can feel it, yes?' Chalice stood alongside her, having slipped back into her pilgrim disguise. She had previously promised Mrs Cordwain that she would keep watch on *Saudade*, for the pilgrim leader had quickly realized a hunting boat filled with kraken oil would be worth the price of docking in Burden Town. 'The *orientis* and *mandatum*. It's everywhere.'

Arden nodded. She felt it sliding through her lungs with each breath. More than felt it. The old talents were suffocating in their strength here.

Chalice took her hand and gave Arden a concerned look. 'Your *evalescendi*'s playing up?'

Arden stilled her urge to pull her hand away. Chalice had every right to worry. With her shadow talent of *evalescendi* Arden could take someone's very small portion of talent and make them stronger, make them the opposite of small, make them exponential, make them uncontrollable. Chalice had experienced the runaway amplification of *evalescendi* well enough.

But Arden shook her head and gestured to the oily water below them. 'Those sanguinities feel strong, but they're remote, somehow. Aged. Like the rope connecting to them has been cut.' She gave Chalice a wan smile. 'I'll be all right.'

Chalice stood up straighter and released Arden's hand with a consoling pat. 'Talking about cutting a rope, we need to take care of a much more present one. The harbour pilot is here.'

Chalice sidled down the gunwale before leaning over the starboard deck. The pilot boat that had pulled up alongside *Saudade* was in possession of, thankfully, a live man inside the wheelhouse. His grimy coat gleamed a bilious yellow in the cold light of a chemical lantern. Chalice Quarry spoke with him, and offered coins from her purse.

I will have to be careful with Chalice, Arden thought. *Even if she does say she is helping me. I don't know what the Order's plans really are.*

The pilot was pleased with Chalice's payment and recovered the tow-lines from Mrs Cordwain's boat, much to the vexation of the widow who'd expected to secure several hundred Djennes from *Saudade*'s sale. Her indignant curses faded into the distance as the black mangrove ship was hauled away.

Now with her fate fastened to the pilot craft, the harbour man towed *Saudade* a distance from the chaotic main wharf to a quieter section north of the dredged river mouth. A long, thin mole of rock and metal girders protruded into a less populous harbour. The docking fees must have been exorbitant, given the better class of boat also secured at the pier. Though Chalice might have been acting outside of Lion auspices, they had certainly given her the funds to dispose of as she saw fit.

Arden unscrewed *Saudade*'s priming pump handle from the ignition block, and took it below decks.

'I need someone to stay and look after *Saudade*,' she said to Sean Ironcup privately, once she had sent David off on the errand of keeping an eye on Chalice. 'I can't leave the boat alone while we look for Chalice's supposed fraternity.'

She tucked the handle into Sean's palm then, after much deliberation, took out the Lyonne gold she'd meant to pay the Librans for the Rite. It was unlikely she would ever pay for their services now. She folded the coin pouch into the twists of his fingers, and pressed them tight against his chest.

'What am I supposed to do with this money?'

'Effect repairs on this boat. Hire some shipwrights. Fix her. Keep her safe while she's docked here.'

'How do I do that alone? We don't have weapons apart from a flare-gun.'

'Pay a local to stand guard. I saw some mercenaries patrolling the other ships. Offer half the money now and the rest later. It will ensure their loyalty.'

'*You* pay them, Mx Beacon. I could help in Burden Town. I could come along. I might not be able to cover much ground with my walking staff, but I know about the Hillsiders who come here. I know these people.' A sweat of alarm sprang out on his high forehead.

Arden squeezed Sean's shoulder. He clearly didn't want to be alone. 'David doesn't realize it yet. He needs more than just a lover. He is sanguis, valuable in a land where he's never had value before. If he decides on foolishness and wants to make his own way here, I cannot stop him from leaving us.'

'He would never.'

'Because his connections to Mr Sean Ironcup will keep his good sense about him?'

Sean sucked on his cheeks. His palsied hand drew up tighter, and she knew his tells well enough to know him deeply worried.

'Is Burden Town that dangerous of a city?'

Arden met his eyes. 'There's no future in this place. There's death all over. If you survive the year, the rockblood fumes will rot your brains, send you spare and shorten your years by half at least. This is no place to make a life.'

'Then don't take him too far, Lightmistress.'

'I promise I'll bring him back, Mr Ironcup.'

Sean waited on the deck while the others loaded themselves with only their most essential luggage.

David was talking animatedly to Chalice as Arden approached. '. . . saw a lich-ship pass us on the way here. *Mandatum* and *orientis*! Or at least, that's what Mx Beacon says.'

One of the pilgrims stood with them, a stout man with a neat moustache and a waistcoat of a marbled brocade that reminded Arden of the endpapers in a book. She recognized Mr Le Shen, one of the figures from the pilgrim ship who had boarded first.

'Mx Beacon is correct,' replied the man to David. 'There was once a person who had both talents and they were exiled here for a convenient forgetting. They were much too powerful to keep in Lyonne—'

Chalice cleared her throat upon seeing Arden. 'Lady on deck.'

Arden stepped forward. 'Don't stop on my account.'

'Oh, Mr Modhi was regaling us with the encounter with one

of the rockblood ghost ships,' Chalice said. 'Arden, this is Mr Rex Le Shen, from the Clay Capital library. He'll be coming with us.'

'Yes, we met earlier. You are a librarian, sir?'

Mr Le Shen was average in height and solid, with a figure more suited to a street-brawler than a librarian. His face was smooth and broad with puffy bags under his eyes from long nights reading books in dark galleries. His hair silvered his temples with wings. He shook her hand and gave a quick, cautious nod, as if he were used to dealing with nobility but not ready yet to be obsequious to it. A golden key dangled from a leather cord about his neck, the gold bright and soft, like a ceremonial necklace. Something about him rang at her memory.

The man bowed gently. 'Lightmistress.'

Arden inclined her head. 'I find your face familiar, sir. Not just from yesterday. Have we met before?'

'We may have crossed paths. The Clay City library was a favourite haunt of Portmaster Lucian Beacon and his children.' He gestured politely to her.

It stung her, that sudden upwell of homesickness. She managed a smile. 'Oh, of course. My father took a membership wherever he could keep his ear close to the city.'

'How goes Lucian?'

'I've not seen him since springtime. But he was well when he last wrote.'

'And his brother Jorgen? He was also my friend in our springtime days. We lost touch, to my eternal regret.'

'He passed away last year,' she said. 'Blood poisoning.'

Mr Le Shen smiled with genuine tenderness. 'My condolences, Mx Beacon. I tried very much to maintain the friendship with Jorgen but Fiction was so very far away, and after his son – Stefan – died, he stopped corresponding altogether.'

'His son's death weighed hard on him.'

'Stefan would have been your cousin, I presume? It puzzled me, how a healthy young man could have been lost. I was told it was a crime of passion.'

'I'm not sure either. We were never close. I only met Stefan once or twice, as a child.'

Arden decided not to tell Mr Rex Le Shen the full extent of her uncle's tragedy, the loss of Stefan three years ago into the maw that was Bellis Harrow, Jorgen's descent into despair. He did not need a day coloured by sadness, and she was not fully sure of this man.

'So, what brings a librarian to Equus, Mr Le Shen?' Arden asked, changing the subject. If he was a companion of Chalice, there had to be Order business afoot. 'I'd expect the cultural artefacts of Clay City would be the first things discarded once anyone got here.'

'Exactly, correct! I am chasing *discards*, a far different mission than that of Mrs Cordwain and her followers,' he said with a nod towards the main harbour, and the path Mrs Cordwain had gone down. 'When prospectors come here they'll trade away priceless family relics. A penny for the Old Guy, as the saying goes. Books, the likes that have never been seen in Clay. Rare volumes, hundreds and thousands of them, all sinking into the private collection of a man I would like to meet.'

'Also,' Chalice interrupted, 'this same fellow who has the private collection also has some Order debts he hasn't quite paid off. So he owes us some favours, and today we are going to call them in.'

Arden took Chalice aside. 'We don't have the time to socialize, Chalice. Aren't we going to see this priest of yours?'

'We have to secure safe haven first.' She pulled a wad of damp folded papers out of her coat pockets and waved them at Arden. 'But if we wander around here without a chaperone and the stink of powerful protection, we are sitting ducks on this polluted lake of rockblood thirst.'

With that Chalice took the lead, as if she knew exactly where she was going.

A line of shabby traders in rockblood-vinyl coats accosted them at the end of the pier, having seen the newcomers come in and be granted a most expensive berth. The smell of fish and sweat mingled with the esters of rockblood, and Arden found herself close to repulsed utterly by it all. Unlike Vigil's marketplace, which had been rather staid and antiquarian, there was a riotous air in this dockside mall, as if the traders were snatching up minutes that did not belong to them.

Not so far away a squad of men in patchworked fish-leathers and flat caps shoved a protesting fellow about his trestle table. The other traders began to pack up hurriedly. Chalice plucked at Arden's elbow. 'The militias are enthusiastic, I see. This way, let's get out of this chaos.'

Arden grabbed David's hands and dragged him through the press of bony, starved bodies, afraid she would lose sight of Chalice. But Chalice was not about to go too far. She led them around to the side of a building ruin to a wall set behind the busy main street. Arden puffed some fresh air back into her lungs, only to find that without the reek of fish and half-dried seaweed, a more insidious smell of rockblood had replaced it.

Chalice opened the paper wad carefully along its folds. 'Now, let's see where we are.'

Arden caught a glance of hastily drawn lines, small icons, a compass rose. Chalice's papers were a street map. Even with Chalice's spidery hand, Arden's memory twanged all at once. Mr Absalom had secretly given Chalice that silk map in a metal locket on Bellis' *Sehnsucht*, before they had jumped overboard to save their hides. Of course Chalice hadn't given it over to her Lion masters without making a personal copy first. She was much too cunning for that.

'This way,' Chalice said, orienting the map against the pier and pointing at one street. 'This is where our book collector lives.'

Then they were back into the crowd, their route wending through the tangle of tents and tables, up a flight of worn steps laid in by a civilization so ancient even the stone had forgotten the carvings it had once held, to a road away from the mole dock, and into the walled city of Burden Town.

5

Inside the town boundaries

Inside the town boundaries, the air changed, became heavy and stale. The constant stink of raw petrolactum brought with it an uneasy vertigo. A fine mist veiled the close-walled, foetid streets. The buildings were tall in this crowded, dense city; at least twenty chaotic levels high apiece. A foul-smelling rain dripped down through the tangled wires that connected one edifice to another.

Twisted, gaunt faces loomed out of the darkness as if they were reflections through smeared glass. Doorways were illuminated in flickering sodium reds. Shadows lolled there, watching them pass. Everyone they passed appeared lean with starvation, their expressions hollowed.

Arden tripped over her own feet like a drunkard. Chalice ran to help her up.

'Darling?'

Arden waved Chalice away and got up. 'Just a little dizziness,' she said, brushing her tender knees. 'It's quite airless here, isn't it?'

Her excuse to Chalice earned her narrowed eyes, a glance at Arden's hands, and a low disbelieving murmur.

'I'm sure it *is* dizziness. We'd better get going. There are already eyes upon us. There's people here who'll take advantage of any innocent within these walls.'

Despite it being midwinter, the Islands benefitted from the hot-water currents from the south and the climate was mild, if dreary, with an ever-threatening shower. Waves of rockblood fumes buffeted them in between sharp, rain-scented air. The road from the harbour soon crossed a stone-lined drain that might have once been a river or an aqueduct before finding final purpose as an open sewer.

Chalice's map led into a quarter of Burden Town that was mostly suspended above the water upon stilts. Ragged men in their iron coracles paddled through muck and murk. One fisherman dragged up a net writhing with eyeless horrors, a species of white fleshy blob-fish with sharp crystal teeth.

One of the stilt houses was larger than the other huts. It was a literal hut-mansion, three storeys high with a wide veranda all around, and broad eaves to protect it from the constant rain. At its roof was a bush of gaudy plastic scales that fluttered in the hot petroleum-laden wind. Above the large doorway lintel, carved into the wood, a single word: *Abaddon*.

Chalice knocked upon the iron-banded door until a peephole opened to a pair of gaunt male faces looking out.

'What is it?' gruffed one of them. His head was missing a tooth. Like other Equus locals, they were both thin and underfed, and they wore the same kind of flat caps and poorly cured leather coats as the men who had prowled the docks. There were similar men in the worst parts of Clay City, private armies and mercenaries who could be hired out for a few copper coins, and who would murder anyone for a pair of rag-paper bank notes.

Chalice raised her chin. 'I have come to see Lord Abaddon. Ask him if he cannot help a Widow's Son.'

'The what?'

'Just go get him and repeat my words, sir,' she huffed.

The militiamen at the door were not altogether happy. Two women, a scholarly man and a youth were clearly not Lord

Abaddon's regular callers. They discussed this at length, before letting them in.

Chalice clasped Arden's hand, as if ready for any kind of malfeasance. Inside, the house opened to a small, dim and greasy foyer decorated with a jumble of decadent Clay carvings and utilitarian Fiction furniture. One corner was entirely given over to candlesticks, cutlery, plates and empty gilt picture frames, piled with thieves' bounty. Upon any surfaces angled flat, a dark patina of oil beaded and smeared.

'I hope you still have a blood-letting knife, dear,' Chalice whispered out of the side of her mouth. 'The lord of this house belongs to us but I don't know about the hired *assistants*.'

Arden put her free hand at her bodice where the plesiosaur ivory handle poked out unassumingly.

'Did you say this collector is a lord?'

Chalice rolled her eyes. 'An entirely self-styled one. With enough money and power he could call himself King Abaddon if he wanted to.'

'Have our visitors arrived, Harmal?' a voice demanded from the camphorous recesses of the next room. Moments later a man walked into the foyer, resplendent in knee-high stockings and an untied gown of a shiny thread. He wore a wig of white judiciary curls, tattying as they fell below his shoulders. The gaping robe showed an affronting nakedness from neck to knee. He did not bother to conceal himself, only smiled broadly.

Arden tried not to look but he was so contrary to the skinny citizens of Burden Town that she had to stare. The man's body was pale and well-fed as a hog for slaughter, a physique purposefully meant to display his wealth and prestige – everything soft and rolled as bread dough, blond pubic hair and his manhood somewhat lost amid its gold mass. A blur of rouge upon his face. By its smear she guessed he had only acquired it second-hand.

The strange lord-by-self-decree stopped speaking upon seeing his guests and his eyes folded into aggrieved slits. 'These are not who I expected.'

The moment was fraught. Chalice stepped forward.

'I am Chalice Quarry.' Chalice gave a hand signal that meant little to Arden. The Lord Abaddon knew that sign however, and he huffed with a barely disguised rage.

'You are a Lion.'

'My employers advised you that one of us would come eventually. Surely this agreement is well remembered when you accidentally procured the family of a very vexatious Parliamentarian? Oh, and these are my companions. Rex Le Shen from the Great Library. Lightmistress Arden Beacon of Clay Portside and David Modhi from Vigil.'

The lord gave Arden a look of caustic disgust. She stood taller and returned the look to him, cool.

With a yank he closed his robe shut and tied the ends together. 'I didn't believe a Lion would make it out here so soon, if at all.'

'We have journeyed with pilgrims. Better us than the Parliamentarian's own militia, who I hear *always* get their man.'

'Huh.'

Chalice eyed the man up and down. 'I don't think I need to remind Lord Abaddon of the oath he gave, when the Order saved his life.'

'I have not forgotten my oath,' Lord Abaddon sniffed, before stalking off through the dark oily corridor.

'The Lions certainly pick these allies carefully,' Arden said once out of earshot of the lord. She inspected the equally dark, greasy foyer. The mansion house occupied the footprint of a large Clay City apartment. With all the piecemeal and clearly ill-obtained bits of furniture, it was as cluttered as a bazaar.

'I had little choice,' Chalice replied *sotto voce*. 'There aren't infinite squares on this game board of ours, so we have to use him.'

Arden noticed the mark of a Clay traders' guild carved in one lintel under a garishly designed family crest of twin derricks, mid-bob. 'How does he get so wealthy trading rockblood when everyone else is starving?'

'Oh, it's not rockblood he trades, it's *people*. He has agents in Clay who will smuggle them here for every penny in their pockets and the food out of their children's mouths. He makes quite a profit out of it.'

Arden mouthed *people*, as the true horror of the lord's profession became evident. Of course, that was how he came to the Order's attention. He was a people-smuggler, a trader in human bodies. Such fiends started as pimps and touts from the lowliest Clay City gutter, but Equus had a way of uplifting the most undeserving.

Chalice elbowed David, who had the baffled face of someone caught swimming well out of his depth. 'Chin up, Mr Modhi, don't look so guilty. You'll make our host think we're here to commit a crime.'

Lord Abaddon, for all that his evil profits had turned him into a man of great standing, had very little in the way of domestic staff apart from his manservant militia. He showed them to the guest rooms himself, flinging open the plastic-panelled doors to a ludicrously stocked library-turned-bedecked-boudoir. The floor was a riot of plush cushions and pink satins, velvets, muslins and sheer fabrics, all draped over the bookshelves. By the fug the room was not often aired out after its energetic use.

He addressed the body gruffly within. 'My sweet, we have company.'

There was much in today that had Arden staring, so one more novelty should not have had her descend to such rudeness, but what she saw made her swallow and stare. A young man was sprawled across the central pillowy chaise, in much the same state of undress as the lord. Utterly naked, he had suffered a most grievous injury to the parts that made him male.

Or at least he had a long time ago, for the puckering of pigmented skin between his legs suggested that when he had been emasculated – so terribly and completely – the wound had healed a long time ago.

The most pressing concern, however, lay in his rolled-back eyes and his blue lips.

'Devils!' Arden dropped her bag. 'The boy is dying!'

'Ah, the runted whelp,' Abaddon cursed. 'Johannes! Harmal! Come quick!'

Chalice, the closest, darted forward and grabbed one limp arm and pulled him over sideways. Vomit spilled from the boy's lips.

Arden, still stumbling over the discarded pillows, saw at once the cause of his collapse. She picked up an empty slump-glass bottle that had rolled an arm-length away, and sniffed it. The rush of fumes that followed made her cough.

'Devilment, he's been drinking distilled rockblood spirit.'

'Awful,' Chalice said. 'Come on, lad, cough it up, there's years left in you yet.' She turned to Lord Abaddon. 'He's made a bit of a mess. Hot water too, if it can be spared, or if this damned island even has it.'

'Of course we have it,' Lord Abaddon said from the doorway. 'We have water on Equus. Good clean water with just a hint of healthful radon. Comes out hot and boiling! Not this river-muck. I will bring it personally.'

Arden kicked the soiled rags that were either clothes or furnishings into the corner of the love-room. She raised one warped, etched window from the sill, but the hot waves of rockblood coming in from outside were just as bad as the smell within. Reluctantly, she pulled the frame down.

She turned to David, still gawking uselessly at the scene.

'Find a robe for the lad, Mr Modhi. Give him some decency.'

'His . . . his . . .' David pointed at his own crotch.

Mr Le Shen answered.

'It's called a hunter's scar. The result of the complete and desperate removal of genital organs to be cast in the water to draw up some foul devilfish from his abyssal lair.' Mr Le Shen fished in his pocket and drew out a behemoth-leather notebook.

Arden and David exchanged a meaningful glance. Only the night before they'd spoken of the rites that called things from the sea and the sailors with their missing hands.

When Mr Le Shen frowned quizzically at their unspoken communication, Arden explained quickly before David could speak too much. 'A woman I stayed with in Vigil – Mrs Sage – told me of exactly the same thing once.' She frowned at the recollection, for it had occurred directly after the first time she had seen Jonah Riven. 'I didn't quite believe her then. It seemed so outrageous an idea.'

'The tales of the *terrible rites* used to be somewhat true in days of antiquity. That self-mutilation, it's borrowed straight from the old sea-monster worship. They did love pain, the old deepwater folk. Thought it made them stronger. And it attracted the beasts they hunted. I can guarantee there are similarities in the way sanguinem use blood to access their sympathies. Blood or body part, it's all the same.'

David couldn't help himself. He blurted, 'Does it mean he follows the Deepwater religion, sir?'

'Appropriates the religion, most likely. He will be part of an homage, a watered-down local tribute movement or cult. Such fraternities grow like wildflowers here. The genuine belief died out a century ago when the saint brought the automata and rockblood drills to this island.'

'It can't be appropriation. This injury is too extreme for just homage.'

'This is an extreme place. I studied these islands extensively for my Librarian Master's Degree. Deepwater religion may have begun here, but now it is just a farcical folk tradition. Street theatre. An excuse for a carnival and an orgy at the end, to take the rockblood workers' minds off the work that has them dying.'

Chalice flicked her attention at Arden, her thoughts loud on her face. *You still want to do this ritual for Mr Riven, then?*

Arden folded her arms.

'All right, all right,' Chalice said when met with Arden's stone-faced stubbornness. 'Let's not stand here discussing our new friend's choice of body modifications. David dear, don't pay it all too much mind. People do what they can in Equus to take their mind off other sufferings. There's a bathrobe on the stand. Pass it over, please.'

David pulled down a gaudy wormsilk robe from the nearby hat stand and tossed it in Arden's direction.

As Arden prepared to throw the robe over the skinny back, the jags on the boy's skin caught her eye. She had previously noticed that the youth was tattooed when they had first turned him over and not paid it much mind; such an expanse of skin was a common sailor's canvas. Now, in this quiet time after the worst of the peril had passed, she took a proper look.

Chevron scales, like the sea-dragon *maris anguis*.

Arden quickly covered the young man up before anyone else might look further and come to the same conclusion. He had not quite so many tattoos as Mr Riven had had, merely a flare across his lower pelvis and some creeping up the spine, but they had the same keloid raise as the shell-and-squid ink of the traditionalists.

Of the Rivens. Of the true deepwater people. This is more than a deepwater homage.

Lord Abaddon came back then, a sulky manservant trailing behind with a bucket of steaming water and some rags. Under the lord's watch, Arden bundled the soiled blankets into a sheet and bound it up, before helping the groggy boy wipe his face with a fresh cloth.

'There is something of a nursemaid about you, as well as a sanguinem,' Lord Abaddon grumped to Arden. 'I thank you. I am no monster; I don't wish my lover injured, much as they spend their *life* trying to cause me grievance. I trust you to take care of this precious thing that I own,' the lord said.

'Sir.' Mr Le Shen stood up with the pencil still in his hand. 'While my companions are caring for your friend, may I speak to you about the books in your keep? I hear you have collected many fine volumes. I too am a collector.'

Lord Abaddon smiled broadly. 'Of course, fellow collector. Come and see how many rare editions are gifted to me by many guests . . .'

His voice faded out down the corridor as they left for another part of the house, leaving Chalice and Arden to their privacy with the wretched boy.

'*Own*,' Chalice scoffed. '*This precious thing that I own*. Like a dog. Like a pet.' She paused. 'Like a *slave*,' she added.

The owned creature only moaned and vomited wetly into the bucket, and Chalice patted the heaving back. 'There, there, dear, better out than in.'

The boyish face, framed by fallen copper hair, looked up at Arden with rheumy eyes. He had sensed her watching him with more than just a healer's attention. From being almost half-dead, he had crawled back to some semblance of life.

'Hello.'

'Hello back,' Arden said, even as a hundred questions prepared to follow, and none of them safe to ask while Chalice was around.

'I am Malachi Abaddon.' He held out his bile-sopping hand as if he were a queen expecting a curtsey and kiss, realized that he was not and would get neither, before returning to the circumspection of his bucket.

Who are you really, Arden wanted to say, and caution made common sense press an invisible finger to her lips. 'Um,' Arden said gently. 'By what address are you known?'

'Mister,' he replied in exhausted languor.

Chalice nodded towards his waist. 'So what brings your misadventure?'

He tilted his chin up with defiant pride. 'My injury shows the sacrifices I have given to *maris anguis*.'

'Huh,' Chalice said. 'Well now, it seems the women of Vigil's marketplace aren't entirely talking out of their rears, when they gossip about the *greater castration* of the men of the Darkling Sea.' She hung her coat up on the hat stand. 'You sea-worshipping fundamentalists can do all the lopping and cutting you want; you'll be wishing for your brain removed come next morning. This gut rot will bring on a dreadful headache. Whatever were you thinking drinking an entire bottle of spirit?'

'Escape,' he said with a sigh and a regretful hug of his bucket-idol. 'My lord's appetites can be fearsome, and . . . *unusual*.' He grinned wickedly then, a handsome flirtatious boy even deep in suffering.

He turned to David and flashed an angelic smile. David blinked and returned the smile, for despite Malachi's wretched state, he still had an aura of enchantment about him.

When Chalice went to slop out Malachi's bucket, Arden dragged David aside and behind the curtain of the dressing room that winged off the ridiculous boudoir.

'Don't go having ideas, Mr Modhi,' Arden scolded once they were alone, and batted aside an oily chiffon scarf hanging from a crossbar. 'No feeling tenderly towards another broken boy, when the last one we fished from death's maw is still sitting on a boat waiting for our return.'

'I know he is,' David said, blushing.

'Then stop staring at Malachi like a fool. We don't even know this person.'

'I wasn't staring! I mean, I thought Mr Malachi was unusual, that's all. He reminded me of Mr Riven, with his tattoos and scars.'

Arden felt her righteous strength leave her. He had made the same connection. Shakily she sat down upon a dressing-seat. 'Yes. Yes they do remind me of him too.'

He joined her on the seat. 'Then why would Mr Le Shen say that they aren't real? A *homage*, he said. Was he lying to us?'

Arden shook her head. 'Most of the time tattoos like that *are* false. Not all of Mr Riven's ink was genuine either.' She flicked her eyes towards the gap in the curtain. 'But his are real.'

'How can you tell?'

'Jonah got a lot of his adult work finished off in the Harbinger Bay prison hulks. Oyster blue dye, not kraken-ink. I could feel it under my hands when . . .' She trailed off before she could say, *when I made love to him*. 'I could feel the difference between the Riven marks made by shell and those scored by a needle by a Harbinger Bay tattooist. The shell leaves deeper scars, not like a prison tattoo, which feels flatter. I felt the difference just now on that boy. His marks are genuine. He's the real thing. The *real* thing.'

She rubbed her cramping palms. The thought of young Mr Riven in a Harbinger Bay hulk, paying a prison tattooist to complete his dead family's marks, made her want to cry for the child he'd been, and what he'd lost.

From the boudoir came the creak of a phonograph cranking up, and the whir of a cylinder before scratchy operatic music played loudly and forlornly through the adjoining rooms.

Through a gap in the curtain Arden watched Chalice return and look about for them. Nearby, Malachi was draped over the chaise longue like an intoxicated forest sylph that had been unceremoniously dragged out of a gutter.

Arden leaned in close to David's ear. 'Say nothing to Chalice about the ink on Malachi. I don't want her curious about it. It's too much of a complication right now.'

'But wouldn't she want to know—?'

'The Lions know *everything*. We cannot spend any more than a day here. Once my business is finished, my priority is you and Sean, Mr Modhi. I need you off this island as soon as possible, all right?'

David nodded, his lips pressed together with promise. 'I'll keep quiet.'

'Oh, there you are,' Chalice said when they emerged from the dressing room. 'Looks like we have our passports to walk safely through the streets of Burden Town.' She held up two white ribbons on the end of dress-pins. 'Our marks of protection. But first we need to join our host for dinner.'

6

After a supper of slimy kelp

After a supper of slimy kelp and dried meats that Arden declined to touch – mostly because both Malachi and Chalice had both shaken their heads at her when she gave a forkful a cautious sniff – came a dessert of stale dried fruits and crystallized honey. The menservants stood watch at the doorway and glared at the three guests and their appetites – politely minimal as they were – with hungry, baleful expressions.

Lord Abaddon's attention was fixed upon Chalice and her bosom. His previous ill-feeling towards Chalice's arrival had clearly been forgotten. Malachi and his tatty, thin feminine aesthetics were ignored. Arden could clearly see the boy was not at all jealous of being spared the attention.

The only time Malachi seemed less than in a half-dead doldrums of a rockblood-spirit hangover was when David asked Lord Abaddon timidly if he had heard of a Miah Anguis, who was rumoured to live upon Equus and was a man of some standing.

Malachi looked up from his boiled seaweed briefly and frowned at David, before returning to his hunched-over position.

'Never heard of him,' Lord Abaddon harrumphed. 'Go into

Burden Town if you must, and ask around. There are a great many ruffians and touts who will call themselves men of standing. Why do you ask?'

'Oh, all right. I just thought you might know Mr Anguis. We were thinking he could help us with a problem.'

'Any problems are best solved by going through the proper way,' Lord Abaddon said. He indicated himself with a thumb. 'By going through me. I don't take kindly to competition on this island, which is why I have none.'

Chalice maintained a friendly professionalism, even though the slightest bump would have sent Lord Abaddon's face tumbling into her generous cleavage. 'That's exactly what I said to Mr Modhi,' she said, and glared at David. 'When he first brought the matter up.'

When their meal was finished Chalice at last announced that as much she enjoyed the lord's company they needed to go into town for important Order business.

'Make sure you wear my ribbons,' Lord Abaddon said. 'They'll be a warning to anyone who wishes to do you an unkindness.'

'Thanks to you, Laurent,' Chalice cooed, tickling the lord under his rotund chin, much to his delight, before snatching Arden's hand and dragging her out into the oily corridor.

'*Laurent?* I never took you for much of a seductress either,' Arden said as they retreated to the washroom.

'One does what one has to do,' Chalice said with a shrug. 'I needed to pay him off for the *protection* somehow. Let's get some of the stink of travel off us before we go and visit our holy man.'

The outhouse was suspended perilously above the water with no more than a hole cut in the floor, and it took Arden a grim few minutes of indecision to lift her skirts and relieve herself, it being initially unconscionable that she pollute the water supply beneath her further still.

Chalice raised her head over the waist-high modesty divider that separated them and said, 'Darling, as our host said, they use deep-well artesian water for drinking. This dreadful cloaca is a plain old open sewer, so don't fuss about doing some business in it.'

Water splashed into the dim recesses of the crude sanitary as Chalice sluiced herself clean from a bucket nearby. The water had a peculiar smell to it, like rotten eggs. Limestone. The drinking and bathing water indeed came out hot from the pipes, clearly from deep bores.

The city of Burden Town might have been a despicable crust on the land, but Arden could sense old infrastructure here. Civilization even older than the Saint's constant presence. Even the corroding stone walls spoke of a primeval city beneath the hurried settlement of rockblood prospectors.

As if Chalice knew what Arden was thinking she said, 'The ancient Islanders did know their way around plumbing before they degraded into sea-shore savages ripe for conversion to the Clay Church.'

Arden finished cleaning herself and went to wash her hands in the carved jadeite bowls set out for the purpose. The soap slimed about her fingers from lard that had not been aged long enough. Something meaty was in the smell, and the uncured lye stung her hands.

'It's unpleasant here, is all. The lord is unpleasant. What he demands of Malachi is awful.' She realized she had spoken the deepwater boy's name and willed herself silent, else Chalice would turn her interest towards him.

'Maybe he is awful, Arden. I'm certain there's worse horrors found in the township proper. We aren't going to stay long enough to get used to Burden Town or Lord Abaddon. Have you got your gloves on? It smells very flammable here.'

'I'm not going to ignite anything,' Arden replied defensively. 'Besides, rockblood doesn't burn naturally otherwise those foolish boys of ours wouldn't have been planning a fire-sale with David's bodily fluids.'

'Hopefully they can plan a nice holiday in South Lyonne by the end of the week. Come on, put your big-girl clothes on and let's get this funereal task over and done with.'

They left the House of Abaddon and walked along the fire-lit riverside, gasping petrolactum-scented breaths through their charcoal masks. The masks made the walk easier, and Arden's head did not spin so much from the rockblood fumes. But the background ache of *orientis* and *mandatum* instructions still hummed all around her. If anyone stayed here in Burden Town long enough, the sanguis whispers would work their way into a person's mind, create an awful obsession about the rockblood. The victims would constantly dream about fetching up the milky liquor from the ground, about joining the pumps and the derricks like living machines. They would forget friends and family, and forget eating, and sleeping. Eventually they would subsume themselves into the churned dirt of Equus, and make room for more doomed prospectors.

'Now,' Chalice said, breaking Arden's disquiet, 'our holy fellow did not travel far. Mr Absalom's map clearly showed the position of a church in the centre of town.'

Arden despaired at the chaos of camps and ramshackle apartments that lined the decayed boulevard. 'Will we stand any chance of finding him in all that mess? I saw a bigger church down on the main docks when we were coming in.'

'Which is exactly where a Clay priest thrown out on his ear would *not* go. He'd have a hidden church for sure, not that cattle-house on the dock for any pious Lyonnian newcomers to find.'

Chalice stepped around a large pothole and avoided a dribble of water from a high, dark pipe with the all the grace of an Equus native. 'Ah, here it is – we are getting close.'

'Are we?' To Arden one alley in this town looked much the same as another. As befitted someone born to a lighthouse-keeping family, she was best with wide open spaces. Close spaces made her disoriented.

'It's what the map says.' Chalice patted her pocket where her copied map was stored. 'It's been accurate so far.'

They had reached the walls of Burden Town, pressed through narrow streets and gaps between buildings impossible to navigate without tilting shoulders, through jungles of pipe and over cesspits brimming with their awful contents. Woozy with anxiety, Arden searched the close, foetid streets for anything that could remotely pass for a church. There were architectural hints in each gloomy passage of shop fronts and barber surgeons and portals to any imaginable sin, but no evidence of a sacred space.

A man lingered too long at one end of a blind, narrow boulevard looking at them, and Chalice pulled Arden down an even narrower alley, where they could not have easily stood two abreast.

Arden found herself pressed up against a crudely painted snake on one wet-slimed wall.

A snake in a circle. Frowning, Arden dug her hand into her coat pocket and pulled out the iron ring, the serpent-idol she had found on the Vigil beach near her lighthouse. She held it up to the mural.

A voice barked: '*Where did you get that?*'

Arden gasped, and jolted away from the wall, nearly knocking Chalice over in the process.

A gaunt face beheld her from a high gantry. Great, sorrowful lines bisected his cheeks, and small blue eyes squinted in the red sodium light of a nearby lintel. She could smell kraken-musk in the darkness, a heady spice.

'I said,' repeated the man through his thin lips, 'where did you get that?'

He was pointing at her relic-find. Arden rubbed the rough iron nervously, before holding the snake ring up.

'The Deepwater Rite,' she said breathlessly. 'I need someone who can say the prayer.'

'The prayer,' Chalice echoed, in a decidedly less enthusiastic tone. Her hand clasped Arden's grimly.

The man sidled off his gantry-post and slid down an iron ladder. He wore familiar Clay Church robes of black and crimson underneath a grey fish-leather coat. 'How is it a Lyonnian speaks of the Deepwater Rite?'

'My friend,' Chalice said before Arden could reply, 'has to undertake a funeral promise made on a man's death.'

Without a word the priest snatched the sea-serpent icon from Arden's hand and examined it.

Arden had to add, 'I picked this up from the beach at Dead Man's Bay, near Vigil of Fiction. There are ruins there.'

'I know those ruins.' He squinted into Arden's face, a hundred questions in his watery eyes. 'Vigil? You came from there?'

'Not more than five days ago.'

'Follow me.'

It wasn't quite what Arden would consider worshipful, this hot, low breezeway that smelled decidedly of sweat and urine and far too many bodies in close quarters. The strange holy man drew them through a mouldy door on the side of the alley into a small remnant hall, a church of plastic and iron. A half-dozen pews filled the floor in the Lyonnian style, tatty upholstery of various scavenged fabrics with scratches and a thousand fingernails dug agitatedly into soft wood.

One or two greasy-backed figures bent in prayer, as oblivious to the newcomers as if they were smoke-wisps from the votive candles.

The church could have been in any illicit meeting hall, if not for the spread-eagled figure wrought in scrap metal upon the far wall. Worn seashells dangled from the idol's chin. Some ex-voto objects hung from the cable-tendons of the Redeemer-figure's flesh, tiny boats, tools, and little person-figurines made of twisted wire. A candle-float burned upon a bowl of murky liquor at the icon's feet. From this liquor came the smell of kraken-musk.

The priest placed the iron ring on the altar with the other icons, then turned to them.

'You have both come a long way. A long way and bearing stories that do not belong to you.'

Arden released Chalice's hand, to her stormbride's dismay, nodded towards the door. 'Wait for me outside, Chalice, I need to speak to him in private.'

'Arden . . .' Chalice protested.

'Give me this, please.'

Grumbling, Chalice Quarry went to take up position in the rear pew, while the priest ushered Arden into the confessional box that stood at the far end of the room, beneath the figure on the wall.

She sat in the confined space with its walls of black mangrove, the rare wood that had once grown only upon the island of Equus. *Saudade*'s wood. An achingly familiar smell surrounded her, of kraken-musk, camphor and agarwood.

A small arabesque screen separated her from the priest. Hers was not a confession, so he slid the panel open so they might speak face to face, albeit privately. Arden told the priest her name, her purpose. He listened in silence until she had finished her brief introductions. She hesitated on disclosing the full extent of her relationship with Mr Riven. Called him a neighbour and friend. Told him how they had been tricked into following some Hillsiders out into neutral waters, and had come across pirates. She had escaped, Arden hedged, but Jonah Riven had not.

'He has no next of kin,' she finished. 'So I suppose the burden of a funeral is on me.'

The priest stared at her a long time before speaking.

'The Deepwater Rite is a sacrament. A plea to send a soul into the court of the King. It is not for outsiders to appropriate for their . . .' He made a face. 'Posturing. I won't disrespect the old ways just to make a Lyonnian feel better about themselves so they might go back unburdened and ready to forget.'

Something ferocious and painful nestled in the hollow beneath her heart. Jonah had echoed the same doubts about her affection for him. He'd thought she might tire of him, and discard him. 'The Rite is not for me. I'm doing this for a deepwater man,' she replied forcefully.

The priest paused. A stray facet of light gleamed in his eye as he looked at her, and she began to suspect that he fully understood their relationship now.

'There have not been true deepwater people on Equus for a hundred years,' he said flippantly, as if she had spoken nonsense. 'They sailed away to Fiction and became Vigil shorefolk. They lost their old ways within a generation, converted to worship the Redeemer on His rock.'

'Then why would he ask it of me with his dying breath, Your Reverence? I have read letters, official documents. They were still doing Deepwater Rites in Vigil for their dead not more than fifteen years ago.'

He waved her words aside dismissively. 'Shorefolk were doing it. Symbolic, that is all. It pains me to say that you have come to the wrong place, Lightmistress Beacon. Seek out his shorefolk family in Vigil and ask them to say a prayer, for it is out of my remit.'

Arden dropped her hands out of his sight so he would not see her wring them together. 'Your Reverence, like I said, my friend has *no family left*. They're all gone. I need to do the funeral rite for him, even if it is just symbolic.'

'You should have asked me for a simple Clay prayer, Mx Beacon. For all my knowledge, I have not the physical faculty for such a ritual.'

'But I was told you knew the deepwater ways,' Arden protested, feeling a flush of anger towards Chalice. 'Unless your reputation is completely predicated on a lie.'

'God gave me a longing for the ocean. The call of the King compelled me all the way to Equus, the furthest place the land could go. But as for talent? As for an ability to summon the old deepwater spirit from the sea? Not enough for your needs, Claywoman. I have some, but hardly more than a shadow of it.'

'A shadow?' She leaned towards him, unable to stop herself from grasping his bony forearm in urgency. 'I have a talent that could increase that shadow of yours.'

'I'm not sure—'

'*Sanguis evalescendi*. I make stronger whatever was weak.'

The priest gave a short exhale as he digested her words. 'Ah. One of the forgotten talents.'

'If I could strengthen your *physical facility* enough to perform a Deepwater Rite, would it be possible then?'

He extricated his arm and straightened the sleeve of his

fraying robe. 'As much as my curiosity is piqued, my common sense says: no. Mx Beacon, there is something in you that makes me afraid. We are only meant to have what God gives us. *Evalescendi* could uncover a part of me I've long tried to keep hidden. I do not wish to walk that path.'

Had she been held up with hot air and not bones, a great rent in her side would not have deflated Arden faster. She fell back upon the hard chair in a half-daze.

'Don't say you won't help. I've come so far. Please. Every time I find someone who could give my friend the Deepwater prayer, they are taken from me.'

'I'm sorry,' he said. The darkness had carved more hollows into his face, his eyes were set so far back she'd have imagined no eyes at all, just smudges like an extinguished candle wick.

He took the hand which still rested upon his arm, then raised her hand palm up. She allowed him to press his wizened finger where it fell soft upon the button in the heel of her hand.

His touch hurt her, but in a different sort of way, as if he were touching a deeply private place inside her. 'I can see you are suffering. Once someone blessed you with *aequor profundum*, the holy waters.'

In her mind Jonah dragged her onto the stony beach when she had been half-dead from blood loss, irretrievably gone, or so she had thought before he called something to shore. The intimacy and violation tasted like salt in her mouth, the memory so raw she wanted to gasp at it. They had done something there, baser than lovemaking, an act so desperate and violent for a moment she'd thought him transformed into one of the very monsters he had called up.

'But there's so much more to the deepwater ways than a few muttered words. The King exacts terrible payments. To do the ritual properly would take days. You would need to give yourself over utterly, surrender yourself, know despair and sacrifice and sorrow and . . .'

'I'll do anything,' she said, and in her mind she thought of the Harbourmistress' letter to the Lions, a detail of the funeral of Ishmael Cleave, Thalie Riven cutting herself open to summon the King.

He trailed off, his cadaverous face absent with memory. When he spoke his breath whistled through a crooked tooth. 'Love makes you speak rashly.'

She jerked her hand away.

'I never told you that I loved him.'

'It is written all over your face. To guide your lover to the halls of the King would require a sacrifice.'

He observed Arden with the coolness of one of his icons, and mysteriously a flicker of light appeared in the cavern of his eye pits.

'What sacrifice? Blood? I can give blood.'

'Not blood. It's meaningless to Him, He gets enough. *Love*. Yes. He will take that from you, if He has not already done so.'

He reached out again and caressed Arden's hand, and what had before been damp and dry was now cold, and wet. The voice that issued from the priest seemed changed. Husky, deeper and low with seduction. 'Would you lie with an intermediary of the King, surrender your body to Him to pay the sacrifice? Would you part your legs and soul and take the King into your body? Will you forget your lover and let Him take you?'

Taken aback by the sly rasp in his voice, Arden snatched back her hand and stood up. 'I think not!'

The smell rose up again, kraken-musk and the cadaverine stink of dying, as if a third body had squeezed into the darkness and watched their proceedings.

'Too late . . . it is already done. You lost your love for the man the moment you set foot upon Equus. The King has already seen your face. He will have you in the darkest ways, Arden Beacon, whether you want Him or not.'

Gulping air which had become as thick as seawater, Arden slammed her way out of the confessional. Had the priest reached over and touched her in her most intimate place, she would not have felt so molested as she did right then.

Chalice stood up as Arden approached.

'What happened?' Chalice asked, her fists clenched as if ready to fight. 'Did he hurt you?'

'This was idiotic,' Arden snapped at her, struggling to hold back angry tears. 'I was thoughtless in believing you actually knew a proper deepwater priest here and not a common Clay ghoul making a clumsy sexual pass! There's nothing here, Chalice! I've wasted time, and put everyone in danger, for nothing, nothing at all!'

Chalice kissed her teeth as she followed Arden into the breezeway and onto the stinking streets.

'Darling, we were always chasing believers in a god whose people either died out or scattered to the four winds. At the back of your mind, you must have known this.' She ran to catch up.

Arden stopped and whirled on Chalice, a fight upon her tongue. The religion *was* alive, it was alive and terrible beneath the cassock of an excommunicated Clay City priest and drawn on the skin of Malachi Abaddon.

But if it existed, its entry was an emotional labyrinth Arden could not enter. All it took was a priest speaking of profane intimacies, and she was lost, stymied and afraid to go further, to enmesh herself into a world that might not exist.

The priest's words had not been lecherous. They had been exactly what was required by a religion washed in oceanic violence, and she had fled at the speaking of them.

'I'm sorry,' Arden said, defeated. 'I'm being overemotional and irrational. I know you tried your best, Chalice. It's not your fault I couldn't do what was required.'

'I understand,' Chalice replied, rubbing Arden's arms. 'It's been a dreadful few days and you're completely worn out by all *this*.' Chalice waved her hands about.

'He knew too much. About me and Jonah. That's all. Asked too much of a price. I panicked. Jonah's memory is the only thing keeping me together at the moment. I fear if I lose it, then I'll lose myself.'

Chalice hugged her, forgiveness on her face. Arden returned

the hug, but could not get the priest's words out of her head. *Love. He will take that from you.*

'Come back to Lord Abaddon's and get a night's rest,' Chalice murmured. 'Sean should have hired men to repair the boat. By tomorrow we will be on our way to Lyonne, and the sweet air of home will take the sorrow away.'

Arden stepped back and shook her head.

'I can't go back home without having done something for Jonah. You know that. That was our deal, remember. If I go now, he'll haunt me forever.'

She'd never seen such a look on Chalice's face as she did then, wrenched with hesitation and resolve. Chalice took Arden aside from the curious onlookers smoking cigarettes from high balconies, into an alley.

Overhead, hot incandescent wires buzzed inside a glass globe the shape of a persimmon.

'What is it?' Arden asked, concerned by the way Chalice had slipped into such a severe mood and what it meant for what came next.

'Before I worked in Vigil with you, I was a stormbride in Harbinger Bay, with Lightkeeper Pharos. We would often watch the shorefolk of South Lyonne enact their own ceremonies to the deepwater gods, along the beaches south of the estuary.'

'Your stories are of no help to me right now,' Arden wearily complained.

Chalice's fingers dug into Arden's forearm. 'They would *burn* the boat of a dead man. Something he owned, often with him on it. Put it on the water and set it alight. We saw the shorefolk funerals from the lighthouse. A gift to their own Deepwater King. They worshipped Him differently, but they still gave Him devotion as best they could.'

Arden stilled. Chalice's hands slipped down into hers.

'No,' Arden said. 'His boat comes back with me.'

'And what does a dock girl do with a boat too heavy to get past the canals of Clay Portside? Let *Saudade* flounder on a wharf until the borers eat her into paper? Would she sell *Saudade* like chattel so other hands might turn her into a messenger boat?' Chalice gave a sad smile. 'They'd strip that old girl to pieces for the black mangrove wood, sell her treasures bit by bit. If Jonah's soul is in that boat, think of him torn apart, disrespected, hmm? Think how he would prefer to dispose of his earthly remains if he had the choice.'

Arden leaned back against the brickwork. She *had* thought about it, every moment Mrs Cordwain's pilgrims were walking all over the deck, every time she had touched the wood, or smelled the *oud* of the black mangrove when in the cabins.

Above her, rust-scented rain threatened to break through the constantly shifting canopy of clouds. A few coppery drops fell on her cheek. The boat was the only thing Jonah loved before Arden—

Her thoughts stopped. They'd never known each other long enough to speak truly of such things as love. Jonah had feared Arden would abandon him once she'd worn out her curiosity. Maybe he even died doubting her commitment to him.

What kind of thief would she be, discarding *Saudade*, or selling *Saudade*, or leaving Jonah's boat to rot in some inland harbour?

Chalice let Arden's hands go.

'Perhaps it's too much, darling,' Chalice murmured apologetically. 'Forget I spoke.'

'Wait,' Arden said quietly. 'Perhaps, it's not too much. Everything that is left of Jonah is in the wood and beams of that boat, and everything you've said is true. I need to think about what to do with her, in a way that honours him.'

'It was only a suggestion.'

'It's a good one, Chalice. I think . . . I think it might be how I deliver him back to his King.'

'Then let us get to the safety of Lyonne, all of us. Make your decision once we are on familiar shores.' Chalice nodded in determination. 'In the morning we will leave this place.'

7

Arden woke later in the true

Arden woke later in the true night – she supposed it was that, for the light through the lower windows had changed from the dull yellow to a dark, chemical scarlet.

She sat up from the too-soft mound of cushions, disoriented momentarily. The night was animated with scents and sounds, the murk and shudder of the river below them, the distant roaring of the pumps and derricks piercing the brittle limestone earth, the pestilent hum of Burden Town. A hot breath of air puffed in through a slightly open window, not quite so tear-jerkingly rancid with fumes. The wind had turned about, bringing in a sea breeze heated by warm currents.

Was it time to go?

Deeper in the house a clock chimed twelve times, followed by its stolen brothers. Arden sighed from disappointment. Too many hours. It was midnight still, and dawn was at least six hours away. The old talents of the nameless saint pressed all around her, making every muscle tense with anxiety. Arden could sleep no more. She had dreamt of *Saudade* burning, and she was certain it was no trick of her mind, it was her future, clear as day.

Chalice snored with an epiglottal burr beside Arden, a book

tumbled off her lap. Arden slipped a thumb under her fingerless glove and absently rubbed her aching hand, considered waking Chalice up. Her own thoughts seemed too much to bear right now, that place where Jonah's image faded as if through darkened glass. Could she really destroy *Saudade* on behalf of a dead man?

As she lingered over Chalice, Arden heard someone moving about one of the adjoining rooms of ill-gotten gains. Mr Le Shen, still awake.

She recalled how he had studied the religions of the coast dwellers. He would have more to say about her intentions, even advice. How to approach them. What to ask.

Arden pulled her boots on and quietly stepped out into the corridor. In the dim light she collided with a side table and sent a mismatched pile of Lyonnian lead crystal vases clinking. Stolen treasures that Lord Abaddon had collected from his desperate arrivals. Their facets flashed silver, as from a high clerestory window the full moon was shining through the parted clouds.

Once the table had stopped trembling Arden let it go. She stepped through louvre doors and into the high room that served as the library. The space was taller than it was long, with a small mezzanine level made accessible by a corkscrew staircase. Like the front foyer it contained yet another thieved trove of payments and taxes. Fur coats and embroidered dresses hung on an ornate clothes dresser, polished shoes, jewellery, clocks and pocket-watches, precious mechanical devices. Most of all, books.

Mr Le Shen slumped, snoring, at a desk at the back of the room. He had fallen asleep upon his forearms, one water-damaged tome still open from a pile. She turned down the lamp at his face and let him be.

Before she turned away, a *thunk* from above caught her attention. A huge moth was up there, caught in the clerestory, and it batted its furry, mouse-sized body against the high glass windows with a constant, aggrieved stutter. She stepped quietly up a curled staircase of iron to a low mezzanine, reached up on tip-toes and pushed the window-lever open so it might escape.

After securing the window closed, Arden found more books stacked haphazardly alongside things more suited to children. Delicate porcelain dolls still bearing the marks of having been dumped in greasy water and recovered, string-toys, cutlery to feed babies. She swallowed an ache of concern, for there was no place on Equus for children yet desperate, rockblood-enchanted parents had still brought them here.

She had seen no children on the streets of Burden Town.

He will take the love from you.

She covered her face and crouched in the moonlight, waiting for the wave of loss to wash over her and pass. *Jonah*, she thought. *I shouldn't have come here.*

When she raised her head to wipe her eyes Malachi Abaddon sat in a corner of the mezzanine that had been empty before.

'Hello,' he said in an oddly clipped accent. 'Don't mind me.'

Arden forcefully heeled the last of the dampness from her cheeks. 'A gentleman would have made his presence known!'

'Your business did not look like something I could readily interrupt.'

'Well, we all appreciate good manners.' She stood up. Since the deepwater priest had rattled her so much, Arden did not want to speak to a boy wearing chevron tattoos.

But Malachi swung into her path, his blue eyes going silver in the window-gleam.

'As for manners, Lord Abaddon was aggrieved that the expensive meat Harmal served at your greeting meal stayed on the plate.'

'I recall someone signalling me not to eat it.'

'The *person* the meal *once was* thanks you, for all that he was a criminal and not worth the sauce he was cooked in.'

He grinned at Arden's expression as it dawned on her what he'd meant. 'Is it really that bad? This town has fallen to cannibalism?'

'Used to get all our food from Libro Island,' Malachi said. 'Not now.'

Of course not. Because if what Chalice had said was correct, Bellis had come across the island of farmers and decimated them. Equus might have survived for a time buying their supplies from Lyonne or Fiction, but the threat of piracy would have made merchants think twice about risking their crews.

Malachi flicked his eyes towards the high windows. 'What business did two Lyonnians have in town?'

'Business that was private, and it is done. We are leaving in the morning.' She stepped onto the iron stair, only to have Malachi slip in front of her again.

'Oh, my lord will be upset at such a quick departure. He has developed a fascination for the Lion who came on . . .' He paused, and grinned. 'Zachariah Riven's boat.'

The name took Arden aback. 'Excuse me, it's not *his* boat. Anyway, how would you know of Zachariah Riven? He was a Fiction man, and eighteen years dead.' She peered at him anew. 'Which almost certainly pre-dates you.'

'Don't think me so young. I could count nine winters when he died.'

Arden examined the catamite's face. She had thought Malachi young, but that was the emasculation softening his features. Perhaps he really could be a man in his late twenties.

'I knew Zachariah Riven,' Malachi continued. 'A shorefolk patriarch from Vigil. His ancestors were brought to the mainland from Equus a hundred years ago. We are somewhat related.'

Arden peered at him, and knew he was telling the truth. Malachi's hair was the same shade as Jonah's beard after a few days without shaving.

'Zachariah divided his time between here and Vigil,' Malachi continued. 'He was not afraid of hunting in deep water. Owned three boats, a gold waxwood named *Sonder* for plesiosaur-running and one white pirate ghostwood called *Sehnsucht*. Then lastly a boat made when he had secured his fortune. This one hewn in black mangrove, and magnificent.'

Malachi counted them off on his fingers and he threw Arden a challenging look when he finished.

'That last boat was *Saudade*. The boat that came this morning into the harbour and from which you disembarked.'

Arden stepped back from the stair, startled by his words. She noticed how Malachi was dressed in waxed cloth and leather, for a journey. So it was he Arden had heard moving about the library earlier. The satchel slung over his shoulder bulged, and a silver soup ladle stuck out from under one unbuckled flap.

'Where are you going?'

Malachi brushed back his snarls of copper hair. 'I am not just a whore to Lord Abaddon. He knows I have fed myself in pieces to the ocean and that sometimes I must return to give fealty.' He gave a short, sardonic bow. 'Otherwise the sea might again rise from the insult and take all of us.'

'Tonight?'

'It's full moon. Spring tide. We need to summon the Deepwater King to feed His people.'

Her heart thudded against her chest and her breath came loud. Now it was she who manoeuvred in front of him, to stop Malachi leaving with questions unanswered. 'Deepwater King? You're doing a deepwater ceremony? A real one?'

'Is there any other?' Malachi went to sidle past. 'I will tell Miah Anguis your greetings, and that Zachariah Riven's boat has been kept in reasonable condition.'

'Miah Anguis?' Arden repeated, suddenly aware that she was being lured, and unable to refuse the bait. Below the floor, the chatter of a rockblood engine sounded as a small boat moved through the filthy river beneath them.

Miah Anguis.

The man Bellis fears, who drove her from this island so utterly and trounced her so completely she could never return, not even with an army.

'Didn't your companion ask about Mr Anguis at the table?' Malachi asked with a sly wheedle. 'Miah Anguis has been an object of discussion, has he not?'

'I never thought he was a *deepwater* man,' Arden said with a shake of her head. 'He came across as being someone like . . . like Lord Abaddon. Someone legitimately with power, and in Equus that only belongs to a certain kind of person.'

She shook her head at her misunderstanding. She had imagined a warlord with an army equal to Bellis Harrow's, a Lyonnian criminal with weaponry and even a fleet of ships, yet all that Burden Town could produce had been this tatty smuggler and his hired help.

'You believe a deepwater man could not be powerful, Mx Beacon?'

'To be honest, I was told all the true deepwater people had been taken from Equus a century ago. When the rockblood poisoned most of the waters.'

'Some of us get by. We live on the northern shore, keep the old ways. Or find work in Burden Town.' He gestured about himself.

A burning curiosity came over her, greater than the desire to wait until morning and escape this place. She wanted to see the man who could make Bellis Harrow scared. She needed to know what boundaries the murderous Queen could not cross, what frightened her the most, how a man could have prevailed over her when Jonah couldn't.

'Then I will come with you,' she said vehemently. 'To this Deepwater King summoning, and speak to Miah Anguis myself.'

'But aren't you intending to leave in the morning? Whatever will your Madame Lion say when she finds you missing?'

'She can wait for me. Allow me to get my coat.'

The long, narrow punt bobbed in the sewer, and going by the extended groan from a distant horn, the time had just clocked two hours past midnight. The woman steering the boat knew Malachi and had been waiting for him, but she glared at Arden's krakenskin as if Arden were a thief who did not deserve such finery. The coat's crusted kraken-rings glowed blue in the dark. Arden realized, passing under a small gas lamp, that her bronze coat was, in the moonlight, the same colour as Malachi's hair.

'What is your name, kind sailorwoman?'

The boatwoman merely pursed her lips, and continued to stare with eyes milky with both age and superstition. 'Lys,' she said at last through a rasped throat, then dipped the hood of her rockblood-fibre jacket down to signal that she was not interested in talking.

Malachi nodded sympathetically at Arden's flustered dismissal. 'Best way to get by in Burden Town is by keeping people at arm's distance. It's not customary to ask a name.'

'I didn't realize. I should have. I'm sorry.'

'A person's worth is only in what they can pay. Have a penny ready for the boatwoman, Mx Beacon, and Lys will think kindly of you.'

Lys didn't seem to have any opinion on the matter, and wordlessly steered the chattering boat through the ancient canal, past glacial crusts of refuse, floating mortuaries picked over by men in stilts and carrion-feeder's helmets. Even in the deep night people worked with desperate haste.

At least the air had cleared and Arden could finally breathe properly, for a fresh night breeze came from the western ocean, away from the pumps and refineries. A signaller's lantern on the bow of Lys' boat outlined small islands of congealed muck that would occasionally bump alarmingly against the hull as the craft passed.

'Don't fall in,' Malachi cautioned with a wink, as Arden peered over the side. 'There's beasts in these waters that will devour flesh, dead or alive.'

She withdrew, fastened her coat tighter about her, and suffered Malachi's laughter.

In time Burden Town and the city's scab of human habitation sloughed away, and the punt slid into a slimed watercourse that ran through the open rockblood fields. The moonlight confirmed what Arden had seen from the boat. The land had been scoured flat, and not even a blade of grass grew from the muck. Trundling steam and petralactose machines worked in their constant pierce and overturn of the soil, having forever cleared and smoothed the ground for two centuries. Just as with the ghost ships that brought the rockblood to the mainland, there were no human operators inside.

'The iron folk,' Malachi said with a grin. 'When I was a child the elders would talk about a great machine inland, a great copper devil who might come past the mangroves and steal us from our beds if we were not careful to keep Him away.'

Her hands stopped itching and started burning. She tucked them under her armpits. Her body longed to join and strengthen the forces at work. If her *evalescendi* was reacting so strongly now, after centuries, imagine what it must have been like when the instructions were freshly cast?

The river turned into a canal again, and belonged to another river system, for they cleared an uplift in the land through a suspended aqueduct and a creaking, leaky water lock, before they came upon a harbour utterly different from the one they'd left in Burden Town.

There were no stilt houses here, no fishermen and wailing horns or milling people along the riverside. No town or evidence of a chaotic, desperate life. Only the bleak grey ships of the rockblood refineries moved through the locks, twin ships to the one that had passed *Saudade* in the previous night.

A pair of grey boats waited against a corroding skirt of rubber to receive rockblood into their tanks through a tangle of pipes, as if a child had arranged the ships like toys in a row. Another pipe was broken at the valve and disgorged rockblood into the water, oblivious to there being no boat to receive the liquor.

Lys had brought them to their journey's end. She slowed her boat down at a small pier on the other side of the harbour. The pier had been lashed together with hand-sawn pressure-pipes and metal, and was the first structure since Burden Town that had not been bloodworked into shape.

'This way,' Malachi said, scrambling over a ridge of sandy ground past the pier's base. He waved an unlit lantern. 'Light?'

'No, I'm all right,' Arden said. 'I'm from a *sanguis ignis* family, I see well in the dark.' She glanced back at Lys, to find the boatwoman had already put her feet up on a seat-board and slid her hat down over her face, settling in for a long nap. 'Or at least I did. It's a little different here.'

As she returned to follow Malachi, Arden felt the sand beneath her boots become interrupted by a knitted carpet of vegetation, the first greenery she'd come across since arriving in Equus.

When she reached the top of the ridge, a flat scrubby coastal plain spread out before her. This was wilderness, sere and salt-scored. This was the other side of Equus, a place where the machines had not touched. Several miles away a natural barrier of swampland and black mangrove wood had most likely stopped the earth-moving machines from encroaching onto this side of the land.

With inexplicable timing the clouds parted, and the sullen moon gave off a hard, clear light. Equus' true land's end was a long, straight black-sand coast with a border of white phosphorescence.

With an instinct well suited to observe the maritime environment, Arden noted the perfect lines of waves rolling in to shore, the white spume glowing with almost unnatural brightness in the midwinter moonlight. The borderland was lit by a row of bonfires along the beach, barrels of half-distilled petralactose. Unrefined rockblood wasn't rich enough in vapours to explode, but volatile enough to keep a steady, smoky fire.

Figures moved from barrel to barrel, setting more alight. Fifty at least that she could see, milling about in restless motion. Pre-laid rope coils made silver shadow-gashes in the deep black sand. They were preparing for something, to bind something up, drag something ashore. The wind came in strong gusts fresh from the endless ocean, stinking of ozone and electrical energy.

'The bait is already out,' Malachi said. 'Let's hurry down, before it comes.'

'*It*?' Arden asked, trying hard to navigate the slope without falling. 'The Deepwater King is out there?'

Malachi laughed good-naturedly, before reaching up and taking her hand, and helping her onto more level ground.

'More than that. We're bringing Him ashore. He who has tasted my flesh, and has meat aplenty to return to us.'

It has to be a monster, she thought. Arden knew little about hunting *monstrum mare* apart from the Vigil krakens that had made up the bulk of the Riven industries, and even then Mr Riven had taken pains to tell her the creatures would be halfway dead before coming aboard *Saudade*.

But this air, ringing with electric tension, this sea so black and white, was nothing less than alive. The heightened feeling about her was elemental, fecund and terrible, and she could almost taste it, the vertiginous lurch towards slaughter, for no creature would ground itself voluntarily. Had this been what Jonah had felt as a boy, when he summoned the creatures that would go on to kill his family?

'What kind of large sea-monster could breach land, though? I've seen pictures in my father's books. Nearly every species is huge, and they can't be dragged past the shallows.'

'Hopefully it'll beach itself,' Malachi said with a wink. 'With the right bait.'

A knot of men and women waited at the base of the dune, with hard, weather-scored faces and eyes like grey iron in the closest boat-burning firelight. They wore coats cut the same way as Arden's own, and she realized with a thrill of recognition that some of the men had chevrons at their collars and the women bore serpentine whorls behind their ears, black as the night ocean.

One said to Malachi, ''Tis 'bout time you showed up, lad. What kept yeh?'

'Offerings,' said Malachi, patting his satchel of stolen goods. 'And guests.' Malachi stepped aside, and showed them Arden. A painful silence greeted her. One man took his pipe to his mouth and sucked smoke from the end. The salt wind blustered about them, skittish and mocking. They looked mostly at her coat, a garment she did not properly own.

'Malachi,' a man gruffed, shaking his head. 'What is this? Bringing a stranger on fucking Deepwater Night of all days.'

'There's no time for reprimands, Gareb,' replied a woman's voice from further back. She sounded older and husky from either smoke, drink or giving commands. 'Malachi – just get the visitor to the watchtower. Anguis and the others have already gone out into the dark. If he comes back empty-handed, there will be questions put forth to answer.'

Malachi waved off the criticism. 'He'll not come back without a catch, Mrs Seaworthy. He'll put blood into the ocean, you can be sure of it.'

After he handed over the satchel to the woman, Arden was obliged to stumble after Malachi Abaddon into the sand when he left without proper introductions. She did not feel comfortable standing with these people she didn't know. As she walked her own shadow appeared on the sand, and Arden took anxious note of the sky. She had known instinctively it was winter, and the moon full, but was too used to following a Lyonnian mathematical calendar rather than a Fiction lunar one. Jonah Riven had asked for a prayer on Deepwater Night, but Arden been so intent on finding a priest to say the words that she'd neglected the date that Mr Riven had implored of her. The prayer of that last full moon before the days grew long again. It was tonight.

'. . . don't mind them,' Malachi was saying. 'It will be Miah Anguis who you will want to meet.'

She welcomed any subject that diverted her attention from her despair. 'So this Miah Anguis – he is your clan leader, or whatever it's called?'

'No. He's got blood talent for monster-calling and has made enough applications, but there's more to being our leader than a few lucky catches. A man needs to be born here, and Miah is an outsider, unwedded in the eyes of the King. No, the person who chiefly administrates our group and affairs is Mr Cleave up yonder.'

Mr Cleave. It sounded a familiar family name, as familiar as *Riven*. Was he a relation of Ishmael Cleave, Jonah's stepfather?

She wanted to ask more about why a man powerful enough to turn away Bellis Riven was not leader of the deepwater people, but the wind rose up and lashed them ferociously and quite took her voice away. They waded through the loose, stinging sand until they reached the watchtower, a small raised platform of iron pipe welded together inside a puddle of firelight. Human welding she could see from the rough seams, not bloodwork.

A high red lantern gave off a small, intense light through air thick with smoke from the burning petroleum in the barrels. A lone, bearded man on the watch-platform nodded at Malachi and tossed down a straight-razor which Malachi caught and opened. The blade had been sharpened so many times the almost paper-thin edge was ragged from the whetstone.

'You here? Get into the water, lad. Help bring Him home.'

Malachi Abaddon hesitated, his attention swinging between Arden and the man on the platform. He nodded then, took a handful of his hair, opened the razor and sliced a handful away. 'We'll eat tonight, Amos!'

'We'd better. You're the last one to go in.'

Malachi turned and loped for the water line. Arden had to stop herself from calling out, and begging him to stay with her. Instead she found herself left alone with this man haloed in blood-red light, this stranger she did not know. He wore krakenskin too, from a minor part of the beast. A flank or arm, she thought, torn between anxiety and excitement. A monster-hunter's garment. She couldn't get much of a clear view of his face, only that he was not young. Not very old either, perhaps sixty years on him. His head was shorn down to the scalp and his full beard – once dark blond or auburn – streaked with grey.

He did not look at Arden when he said, 'Don't stay down there if you don't intend to help.'

She clambered up to join him. As she reached the top platform a chant started up from the dunes behind the beach. An old

Fictish chorus in rising and falling harmony, the sound of empty petroleum barrels struck in strange syncopation. Fin-folk sounds. A man cried out in the darkness. The metal of the platform hummed under her hands. Her breath caught and released.

Mr Cleave glanced at her, and nodded as if he knew exactly what she was experiencing.

'Has the weight of the hunt fallen upon your brow?' he asked. He did not take his hooded eyes off the unseen horizon. 'The dark places of this world are full of the habitations of violence. The beast comes, drawn by sacrifice and burning rockblood. They are out there, summoning the King to shore.'

Arden nodded mutely. There was a weight upon her, the same potential as when she drew blood, the *orientis* and *mandatum*, but fresh and potent. 'Ishmael Cleave,' she asked breathlessly. 'The one who lived on the Vigil promontory twenty years ago, did you know him . . .?'

'Yes, he is a distant relation. Amos Cleave is my name. My family were Islander-born since before the cataclysm of the rockblood machines. This nation was whole back in those days, and no bloodwork infected the metal.' An odd accent to him, a lilt she'd heard in Jonah sometimes, when he was tired and dropped his flat Fictish vowels.

'And this hunt, it's also a ritual? One of the Deepwater rituals?'

'A ritual that brings food to us folk surviving the wilderness? Yes, certainly. Call it a ritual.' He took an unlit pipe from his pocket and jammed it between his teeth, flashed a grin at her. 'My people tell me you were the one to sail Zachariah Riven's boat into the harbour yesterday morning.'

'I did come in on *Saudade*. But sir, I must make a correction. *Saudade* is his nephew's boat, not Zachariah's.'

Mr Cleave moved his pipe about. 'How is it a Lyonnian woman came to know Jonah Riv . . .?' Mr Cleave started, then stopped. A cold, hard gust of wind interrupted him. Though Arden could not see it, a downdraught had been exhaled from the massive clouds out to sea. The distant southern tempest and the hot northern currents whipped the climate into chaos. All the great mountains and valleys of air were at war.

Then, as if a great hand had shaded it, the moon disappeared. They were plunged into darkness. The barrel-islands of petra-lactose fires began to extinguish one by one along the length of the beach.

Mr Cleave leaned over the watchtower rails. 'What's going on?' he shouted at an unseen figure below.

'The fires are going out!' a woman cried back. 'How will they find their way ashore?'

Mr Cleave grabbed the red lantern from its hook and signalled wildly. 'Gather the wood fuel!' he shouted into the dark. 'As much as you can! Keep the fires, go, go!'

With an odd, remote sense of alarm Arden counted a dozen figures scrambling through the darkness, all trying to build up a single blaze against the rising wind. But the wind was too strong and the fuel did not catch.

'Where the watery hells is Mr Stone?' Mr Cleave bellowed. 'Where's my stormcaller?'

In answer, three people stumbled out of the dark with a third, a bare youth slung between their arms, bleeding out from great gashes across his thighs.

'What happened to him?' Mr Cleave reproached.

'He got carried away, Amos,' the woman of the pair said, her voice between scold and sympathy. 'His wounds are bleeding too heavily. Mr Banks, come quick!'

A thin, bare-faced man came out from the murk with a satchel, unloaded it to bind up the young man's wounds. Mr Stone had cut himself the way Mr Riven did, clumsy and deep, knowing only blood, and not subtleties of bloodwork. Mr Cleave looked on, shaking with frustration.

'Devil's abyss, how bad is he? I need some damned ball lightning or a St Elmo's fire or *something* out of the wretch! We have no light.'

'Is there no other way to get light? Arden said out of turn, needing to ask despite her being the stranger here. 'This child shouldn't have had a knife go near him, no matter what power he has!'

Mr Cleave turned about, his face expressionless except for the rivulets of reflected gasoline-fire across his cheek and forehead. After an uncomfortable moment of silence he spoke. 'We need him. Crude rockblood won't ignite on its own.' He looked down at her hands and her little flame-embroidered gloves. A hope danced in his eyes. 'You trammel fire?'

She dug her hands into her pockets and shook her head. 'Coldfire,' she said.

'But still light?'

'It could be.'

The *evalescendi* in her blood yearned towards the bleeding boy. They had propped him up against one of the platform pylons beneath them. Through the slats of the watch-platform she could see a medic approach and fuss. The yearning feeling was akin to disgust. She'd gotten very sick the last time she'd used *evalescendi*.

But she had been weak from a day adrift on the ocean then, and things were different now.

She spoke before thinking it through, but a thought was forming in her mind, an idea that repelled her and excited her at once. 'What can the boy do, Mr Cleave?'

'He can make the rockblood burn, for one thing. Don't know how. He only calls storms, and yet . . .'

Of course, Arden thought with a lurching insight. She recalled her studies in the Clay Academy, her Portside education of the manifestations of climate, and weather. The boy called up storms, which meant *pressure*. The great mountains of air concentrated upon one small spot. And pressure could make the weak fumes from crude petralactose concentrated enough to be flammable.

As could *ignis*, made stronger by the catalyst of *evalescendi*.

Could those talents work together even if they weren't all in the same body, or if their portions were separated by time? Arden slid the coin-knife from her bodice stays, felt it scrape against the soft ribs of fabric as if she were sliding it out from under her own skin.

Was there already pressure enough in this air, and all the fire needed was a little kick?

Arden stepped towards the ladder.

Mr Cleave was not ignorant. He knew what a hidden knife in the hands of a woman wearing fingerless gloves meant. He stood in front of her.

'And where do you think you're going?'

'Let me help,' she said in a small voice.

'If Mr Stone gives any more blood, he'll die,' the deepwater man growled in warning.

'He doesn't need to give any more. I can do it now.'

The moment stretched on, as Mr Cleave wrestled with his caution, then nodded. 'Go.'

Compelled by a desperate self-belief she climbed down the ladder and onto the dark, damp sand.

A hundred paces away the pitiful remains of one extinguished barrel of rockblood in a shallow trench gave off the last scraps of heat. She could sense the boy's blood-tithing, the work he'd attempted by the way she struggled to breathe as she came closer, by the weight in her head and her throat.

Arden closed her eyes and pulled off one glove. The small coin in the side of her hand was numb; she barely felt her knife pierce the skin. Again she felt herself falling into the memory of the last time she'd called on *evalescendi*, when she and Chalice were in the salt water of the Darkling Sea, choosing either this . . . or death . . .

Lost in her little oblivion Arden almost missed the blue eye of flame forming in the centre of the barrel, a circle radiating outwards.

With an exclamation of warning she fell back and scrambled to her feet.

'Tell them all to get away,' she wailed at Mr Cleave, who had in his curiosity climbed down after her. 'As far away from the trench as possible.'

His attention fell upon her bare, bloodied hands and her silver coins. The delay lasted only a second, and then Mr Cleave was shouting to the others, *get away, get away, we're going to have light . . .*

No telling how far she got when even the world seemed to take a deep breath, and a brilliant white pillar of vapour-driven coldflame shot into the sky.

8

The shock hit her

The shock hit her with the power of a fist, knocked Arden face first into the sand. White flame behind her, crackling upwards, like a whirlwind inside a storm.

From the size and strength, it was a man who hauled Arden into an upright position.

She clung to him, heaving breaths. She met Mr Cleave's startled, rain-dripping face. He still puffed from exertion, but was, in the whiffling white firelight, overjoyed.

'A nice trick,' he shouted, smacking her shoulders enthusiastically. 'A nice trick indeed.'

'Is there enough light?'

'Should be adequate,' Mr Cleave said with a wry grin. 'That eruption – why, they'd have seen it all the way to Libro! Quick, girl, back to the watchtower, we can't abandon our posts.'

He supported her over the black sand. Arden's shadow cast long and dark before her, a giant's silhouette.

'You wear the gloves of a *sanguis ignis*.' Mr Cleave helped her up onto the platform and followed close behind. 'Though I've never seen a lone *ignis* shepherd such a blaze.'

'It's really Mr Stone's talents. I just made them stronger,'

Arden said, trying to talk and climb at the same time. 'Maybe a little of my *ignis* was in there, all mixed together.'

'That can be done?' Mr Cleave asked once they had returned to the safety of the watch-platform. 'Two separate people making one talent?'

'Yes, I've managed it before.' She petered off as the dark-breaking foam of the ocean began to congeal and writhe, taking on a shape that was not the action of wave on shore.

Encouraged by the new light, the drumming of the oil barrels along the beach became a furore that echoed into the night. A bullroarer wailed out, and its high-pitched sibling replied from behind the dunes. Some of the singers stopped their chant, and ran across the sandy expanse, hooks in hands and flares billowing orange phosphorus smoke behind them.

'Light and sound!' Mr Cleave sucked in a great breath. 'Light to guide them, sound by which we shall bring them home. Watch now!'

Arden cried out a warning. A sinuous black shape that end to end could match a locomotive and ten carriages whipped from the water less than a quarter-mile from her perch on the observation platform. It scoured a great half-moon across the beach, leaving ploughed sand and a cresting wave as high as a house. At least five runners tumbled head over heels to avoid being crushed. The platform quivered as if in a strong gale.

'*Breach! Breach! Control the tail!*' Mr Cleave roared.

Small longboats were coming in behind the shape in the water. From her elevated position Arden found herself gripping the rail in dread and anticipation.

'*Maris anguis*,' someone screamed.

'The King comes!' Mr Cleave nodded at Arden, whooping with triumph. 'Comes to face His death!'

'How . . . how will they kill it?'

'No man nor woman alive can kill such a bedevilled creature.' He slapped Arden on the shoulder with a great, broad paw. 'Eyes up and bear witness!'

The great barbed tail lashed sideways again, impaling a nearby man through the middle so absolutely that when the tail rose, he rose aloft with it, thrown skyward and screaming, his flare-marker rising at least twenty feet high.

And then Arden beheld the terrible body of *maris anguis* rising up out of the water, the image of their god, the Deepwater King.

Outlined in *ignis* flame and phosphorus flare, a thousand serrated ridges glistening wickedly in the night, each one like the tooth of a giant saw-blade nailed to a small mountain. Its head was a reptilian wedge dishing flat at the porcine snout, curved tusks erupting from a jutting lower jaw.

The beast might have been impervious to death, but it was certainly injured into fury, for it rolled towards the sand until the very earth shook and the platform swayed in its foundation.

Arden would have tumbled off if Mr Cleave had not caught her, held her firm. Now less than fifty yards away, in the glow of Arden's blood-light the grim chevron scales of *monstrum mare* shone bright as polished opal; it lashed a head the size of a motor car and raised a frill of thorns. Several hunters fell beneath the scaled bulk, the others swerved sideways, pulling their ropes after them, executing a dance of smoke and distraction.

One runner stabbed his hooks onto the edge of the beast's innumerable scales, scrambled up a moving mountain of bloodied armour. Another followed.

'Secure it, quick!' Mr Cleave shouted. 'The head! The head!'

Enraged, the beast gave a great, whipping movement, enough to dislodge all annoyances save the one who had climbed first, a lone figure clinging to the rough crown. The second figure flopped on the end of a short length of rope. The platform swayed again at the thundering shock of the monster scraping a giant furrow through the sand in an effort to free itself of hunters. Arden held tight to the railing this time, made herself secure while she fought her own instincts to flee.

The man at the head had dragged a contraption up with him, a weapon that belched smoke. In a flailing, desperate moment

Arden saw him alone and tied down, brass harpoon gun in his arms, driving a steam-powered spike through the serpent's skull.

With a loud felling crack the head collapsed hard into the shallows, but the rear half continued to flail. Mr Cleave grabbed Arden's wrist, made her watch the brutality, what cruelty survival required of them.

'It comes! The end comes!'

The tail-spike, still bedecked with the flare-burning corpse, doubled back on itself, striking and striking, lashing and flailing, until the entire sinuous horror of a monster-body had writhed halfway up the beach. She had not misjudged her senses when she had calculated the thing to be as long as a Lyonne express train, for it had to be longer, three times as long. Enough to roll and crush them all, were it to forget the man stuck to the largest of its head-spikes.

Literally half-dead, the giant beast raised its spiked tail and stabbed down, straight through the man and into its own stilled and sightless eye. The *whump* of its giant head hitting the sand sent a shudder through the watch-platform. The platform swayed alarmingly. For a moment there was no sound save for the metal singing through the guy-wires.

Arden let go of the copper platform rails and her hands hurt from how hard she had gripped the corroded pipes.

Mr Cleave said quietly, 'It's over now.'

With a final tremble, a miserable O of death, the entire creature slumped into the shoreline. Now it had turned from life to death, a monument of a thing, a great shadow from the water. The silence extended to encompass all that the hunt had cost them, before a throaty roar of victory came up from one bedraggled knot of hunters.

Then quite suddenly the witnesses of the Deepwater hunt erupted from their sheltering dunes and the beach was overrun by bodies, a hundred, maybe even two hundred people in the dark morning, converging and cheering as they rushed to the body of the beast.

'Tonight we feast!' Mr Amos Cleave screamed at the crowd

from the platform. 'Tonight we do not go hungry, your elders eat, your children eat, you wear the clothes of the leviathan's hide!'

Still trembling from her exertions Arden remained with her bird's-eye view and watched the wild victory celebrations spill out across the sand. It stunned her, the open outpouring of weeping and shouts of gratitude, as all the emotions of the hunt had risen not to the kill, but in this overwhelming crescendo. It was almost religious.

Or whatever this was. Arden's thoughts found no purchase, for how could Clay Church with its old books and statues and morose dogmas have ever competed with this kind of celebration? The missionary churches on the Vigil promontory had long gone to stone ruin while the deepwater folk still dragged their gigantic gods from the sea.

Several of the faces were Lyonnian, so clearly they'd had no problem in attracting converts.

A rowdy song sprang up from one quarter, and quickly spread to the rest of the gathered celebrants. Among the group were children, and a dozen of them were passed overhead to the dead *maris anguis*, their small hands reaching out fearlessly to touch the scales of the sea-dragon. Even when lifted by the tallest man they could not stretch halfway up the creature's flank.

Slightly apart from the others was Malachi, nose streaming blood, clutching at his wrist. He limped out of the crowd. With a belated exclamation Arden scrambled off the platform and ran clumsily for him over the sand.

'Malachi! You're all right!'

'Did you see that?' he asked, still too caught up in the collective hysteria to notice how truly hurt he was. 'Rolled right over the top of me!' He coughed, wincing and smiling at the same time. 'I broke ribs! I gave pain to the water!'

'I certainly did see, Malachi Abaddon,' Arden said kindly, not wanting to begrudge the young man his victory. She felt quite out of breath and dazed herself, with a lingering ache from using *evalescendi*, but nothing so bad as the broken bones he may surely have suffered. 'But you'd best go see your medical man about that arm of yours. I still need a guide back to Lord Abaddon's house this morning.'

She found herself trailing off.

Before what, she thought. Leaving? That had been a decision made yesterday, before knowing about this place and these people. She had thought Equus a dead end, a place of forgotten memories, and all of a sudden it had exploded about her with possibility . . .

'Riven,' someone shouted, 'Riven, Riven!'

Arden whirled about at the speaking of the name. Had she been on the platform she could have seen where the voice was coming from, but on the ground with the milling strangers in the cold darkness it seemed as though the name came from everywhere at once, as one person picked up the cry and repeated it. *Riven, Riven!*

'Mr Riven?' she said, half to herself. 'Jonah?' The old poison in her veins lurched. *Could it be? Did he get away? Did he come home?*

The blood in her ears roared as if from a long, endless tunnel. Arden left Malachi and fell into the dense press of the crowd nearer to the serpent's head as she tried to follow the name. Her body was shoved and ground in between wet leathers and hot breaths.

Arden's frantic attention moved to where everyone else's was: the ichor-dripping wound in between the beast's horns.

Two corpses there, one on the rope, one still holding grimly on to the brass steam-spike. The flares fizzled and went out.

Except the corpse at the steam-spike twitched and moved with purpose, began to yank himself free. His upper half was bulky and bare, with plesiosaur-leather breeches that ended at the knee. In the flare-light he stood, tall and grave, marked with monster-scale tattoos upon his flanks and belly, daubed in dark blood.

Her legs would have given way if not for the press of people about her. She keened out Jonah's name and the man's head turned to her in the darkness. The victor was oblivious to the crowd's wild worship. He shook himself free of them, waded into the crush to seize up Arden in both his hands.

Frozen by memory, she let him lift her until her feet dangled.

'What are you?' he yelled over the exultant noise.

This man's entire hide was a riot of tattoos across skin as pale as a nightmare. He was larger still than Jonah across the shoulders but not as tall. His nose was broader, an old split crooked one lip under a ragged beard woven with metal charms, like the ex-voto offerings pinned to the icon of a saint.

And yet there were similarities, in the shape of their eyes, their face.

In her blood-drunken confusion she had not – for a moment too long for comfort – been able to tell the difference between her lost lover and this bloodied creature.

He let her go with an inhale of almost disgusted confusion. 'You stink of *aequor profundum*. It's everywhere.'

What had come over her? The man was not like Mr Riven at all, for he was much older, with the years making a face cragged and raw, chest winged with dark hair. Jonah's hair had been lighter and not quite so bestial.

And yet, the familiar abyss in this one's deep-set eyes . . .

Mr Cleave lurched out of his own knot of people to get in between Arden and the man. The crowd had begun to pay more attention to the prone sea-serpent now, for having established their victor was alive, they were more concerned with the spoil of the hunt, and Arden was now alone with Mr Cleave and this achingly familiar stranger.

'Miah, this is Malachi's friend from the city.' Then remembering his manners he said belatedly, 'Arden Beacon, this is Miah Anguis.'

'Miah Anguis?' she repeated.

'Beacon?' he said at the same time. 'Like Jorgen Beacon, from Vigil?'

He glared at her fiercely and all she could think was, *why do they call you Riven? Why is there a ghost in your face?*

Mr Cleave continued, 'She is *sanguis ignis*, she brought the light to us. And she brought Zachariah's ship back to us as well.'

'Wait a minute,' Arden protested, 'I didn't bring her back . . .'

Miah Anguis spat blood out of his mouth before accepting a bucket of water thrust at him, drank deep. The blood on his face and neck made dark verticals down his broad throat as water dripped down.

He then stared in dismay at the breeches torn on the inside of his right thigh and grimaced. 'Dirty horn got me right in the god-damn *leg*.'

'Better there than in the other place, Miah,' Mr Cleave said with a laugh.

Arden could stay silent no longer. 'They called you Riven. Why did they call you by that name, sir?'

'You heard wrong. I'm Miah Anguis,' he said dismissively as he turned to leave. 'And strangers aren't supposed to be here. Mr Banks – come with me. I have need of a steady hand and some thread.'

'If you are a Riven, then it was one of your family who brought me here,' she called out to Anguis' back. 'Jonah Riven, who saved my life when people tried to kill me. He called up a sea-devil itself himself to bring me back. It was him that put *profundum* in me.'

Miah stopped, but did not face her. A muscle jumped in his heavy shoulder, the way a horse might shiver off a fly. The moment stilled. He said something to Amos Cleave, and then limped on, as if he had not listened to a single word.

'Where are you taking me?' Arden found herself corralled down a foot-track through the black dunes behind the beachfront. 'I know I shouldn't have come here. I made a rash and foolish decision. I would quite like to go.'

'Sorry,' Mr Cleave said. 'We're not done yet.'

'But my friend is waiting for me in Burden Town.' Arden tried to stop and turn, only to have the group of Islanders firmly, if apologetically, block her path. She returned to Mr Cleave.

'Sir, this is a kidnapping.'

'Then burn us alive if this is such an imposition,' Mr Cleave said. He took a pocket-watch out of his leather waistcoat and wound it casually as he walked. 'I know you can do it. Otherwise it is an hour until full daybreak. If you have intruded upon one half of our night, then please exercise some respect and join us for the other. We are returning to camp, and will speak further out of this weather.'

She grumbled, and fastened her krakenskin coat to her neck in the sleety rain. The water pounded off the hood in crackles. The wet did not bother her for it was a lighthouse keeper's climate after all, but the night had exhausted her, and made her hungry, and she was out of sorts for having had to attend to her bathroom needs earlier with little more than some spiky grass for privacy.

Added to that, in an hour Chalice would be wondering where Arden had gone, if she wasn't already. Her departure from Lord Abaddon's had been so sudden she had not thought to leave a note. In her rush of curiosity about Bellis' enemy and the hidden deepwater folk, Arden had quite abandoned her good senses.

As the sky turned pale grey, the folk who remained upon the killing shore quickly set about their task of butchering the serpent. Their work-songs floated eerily through the sea-mist. The burnt smell of wet flares still lingered about the sodden beach to mix with the musky cryptidness of the serpent.

Past the dunes, the island's limestone protruded in slabs and shales, and a rude encampment of flax-canvas tents and flat-bed wagons chaotically occupied a large sandy clearing in the land. The tents were somewhat sheltered by the mangroves from the worst of the coastal weather. Some tough-looking ponies grazed on the scrub nearby, their long wet tails flicking streaks of mud along their shaggy flanks. The smell of ash and petroleum lay strong over the salt.

Arden looked over a small uplift of land and almost cried

out. Anchored a little way out from a corroding pier floated a familiar black mangrove boat.

It took her all her effort to hold her ferocious tongue. They'd taken *Saudade* from the dock and either sailed or dragged her to the other side of the island. Is this what the priest had meant, when he said the Deepwater King would steal the love from her?

Oblivious to her silent outrage, Mr Cleave and his entourage escorted Arden past an ad hoc tangle of copper plumbing set apart from the encampment that provided the most rudimentary of washing facilities. A pressure container rested over a bed of wood coals, and hot water bubbled from a whistle-cock.

Nearby, a motley assortment of naked, bloodied people waited to stand under the flow, rinse the sticky serpent ichor from their faces and scissor-shorn hair, launder the muck from their clothes at the same time.

Arden noticed Miah Anguis-Riven in the wash line with the other deepwater hunters, coarse and muscular, slab-like pectorals glistening where the wiry hairs of his chest curled, his waist thick with hard work. His terrible head pressed against one of the pipes and he'd fallen half-asleep under the streaming, lime-milky water. The bleeding cut in his thigh painted one leg scarlet. And she found herself observing that his male parts were intact, and he had not sacrificed himself to the ocean the way Malachi had done.

Something in Arden's concentration on him woke the man, and the Riven cousin beheld her with his cruel-sea eyes as she passed, and she suffered it again, that kick of synchronicity.

You're sanguis, she thought bitterly. *But more than that . . . something else that I cannot speak of with a human tongue.*

It could be the only reason that she was feeling from him a thrill of recognition above and beyond his likeness to Jonah. It couldn't be that the lines of his body were deeply familiar to her, or that she'd mistaken him for a Jonah Riven allowed to grow older and wild. This was the man Bellis found unbearable and frightening. Indeed, Arden decided, Bellis was not far wrong.

Gently, Mr Cleave took her distracted elbow and guided her into the camp circle, where he approached the wax-stiff opening of the nearest tent.

'In here,' he said.

'Mr Cleave,' she started, then stopped, and blinked into the dim cavern.

She was not solely among strangers. Another figure was in this tent with her.

Sean Ironcup gave a bashful, panicked smile.

'Hello, Mx Beacon.'

9

Oh devilment

'Oh devilment, Sean. So much for looking after our boat, then.'

He was clearly ashamed to have Arden see him like this. They'd never had the best of relationships in the first place, and he was proving all her doubts to be very true.

'They outnumbered me,' he explained churlishly. 'One even had a musket. And how was I supposed to know she was a stolen boat?'

'*Saudade*'s not stolen, Sean. She's legally David's boat, not theirs.'

'They said she was theirs!'

Such was the confidence of Mr Cleave that he'd let them speak alone briefly, but Arden knew there would be ears outside, listening. A stray wind heaved against the damp tent canvas.

'All right. Let's start with how this matter happened, then we can work out how to get out of it.'

Sean apologetically launched into the tale of a boarding by several men not more than an hour after their arrival, followed by a difficult and extended confession about *Saudade*'s provenance and ownership, and of being rudely tossed below decks while she was towed to the northern beaches. Along the way the deepwater folk had questioned the Hillsider lad thoroughly, from his missing family, to David Modhi, to Arden and yes, Jonah Riven.

It became quite obvious Sean Ironcup was the source of Mr Cleave's expedited information about Arden and all her trials to get to Equus.

In between his begrudging apologies Sean described someone who could only be Miah Anguis, the hunter interrogating Sean about Jonah's life, his death, and mostly about the relationship with Bellis Harrow.

Terrified, Sean had kept no secrets. Whatever he knew about Arden and Chalice and Jonah and Bellis, they knew now.

'I'm sorry,' he finished. 'I'm sorry!'

Despite her exasperation, Arden deferred to her better self and gently patted the Hillsider's scraggly corn-coloured sideburns and chin.

'Nothing we are doing is with malice, Sean. *Saudade* does not belong to them. The rules of inheritance are clear. Mr Riven owned her and he passed her on to David before he died. She's David's boat to administer, not these people's.'

'I tried to tell them that. They didn't really want to listen. The big Mr Riven-looking one became furious when I brought it up, so . . .' He shrugged. 'I kept my mouth shut about ownership afterwards.'

So, he *had* noticed Miah Anguis' familial appearance too. Malachi was not the only distant relation here.

'We may have many more conversations about who owns what before this day is out,' Arden said, not wanting to show Sean how worried she really was over *Saudade*'s contested ownership. 'But my concern is getting both you and the boat back. Perhaps this Mr Cleave fellow can be open to discussion.'

Sean looked aside then, and she wondered why he seemed so evasive. Did he not believe her?

'How? Could we trade the kraken oil? We don't have anything else.'

Arden could still smell the dead serpent's scent upon her skin, and gave him yet another of her tight smiles, despite her jaws aching from having clenched them for so long. 'I suspect they don't want much for anything cryptid. Let me see what I can find out.'

Vexed by her new problem, Arden could do nothing else except take off her coat and found an inconspicuous corner to shake out the rain. The tent had a touch of a constant traveller's dwelling about it, with hippocampi-hair rugs across the floor and wax-flax weavings insulating the walls. Not completely a prison. The iron stove in the centre of the tent, repurposed from a section of welded pipe, held a small flame in its belly. Arden held her hands before the glass window and put some feeling back into her chilled fingers. Too long indoors had taken her body's natural capacity for warmth from her.

To add to her misery, she was developing the thunderous ache behind her eyes that would grow into a full-blown bloodworker headache.

Sean joined her. 'And David? Is he all right?'

Arden sighed at Sean's priorities. 'Much safer than us. He is with Chalice and Mr Le Shen in the library house of Lord Abaddon. He is the official here who is giving us shelter for now.' She paused, as she gave the issue more thought. 'Though how safe that shelter will remain depends on me getting back soon with Malachi Abaddon, who it appears is somewhat of a favoured pet.'

Sean must have seen Malachi at some time this morning, as he gave a nod at his name.

'The one with the craze-cut hair who brought me food before? He is handsome,' Sean said, gruffly, having known at once where his jealous heart oriented. 'I suppose David finds him handsome.'

'It doesn't matter what our fool companion thinks, we have to get *Saudade* back. I cannot allow her to be snatched from us. She's ours, not theirs!'

The canvas tent door flapped open, letting in a gust of chilly salt wind. Mr Cleave stepped in, willing Arden to finish her conversation.

'So. Seems our small privacy has expired,' she said. 'Good morning, Amos.'

'Are you satisfied we have treated this sickly lad of yours well?'

Sean butted in to reproach Mr Cleave for calling him sickly, and it took several seconds for Arden to calm him down.

'I am pleased that my friend is being kept well,' she said once Sean was behaving with a measure of resentful decorum. 'But this is not a situation he can remain in, sir. We were supposed to leave Equus this morning.'

'That may still happen. But Malachi tells me that you came here because of a curiosity about Miah Anguis. At the mention of our brother's name, you cast all caution to the wind and came here at once.'

If Arden could have gone back to scold her self of a half-dozen hours ago, she would have done so. She had given entirely far too much away to Malachi Abaddon.

'I made a . . . rash decision. But I came concerning a mutual enemy of ours.'

Mr Cleave's eyes narrowed. 'Ah. The Queen.'

'Yes, I—'

'Take your coat. You have your meeting with our man of the hour. He might like to know more about our mutual enemy.'

She blinked, almost disbelieving him. 'He agreed to talk?'

'Don't linger, he has a habit of changing his mind.'

Arden quickly dressed for the weather and ran after Mr Cleave over the wet sandy duckboards of the dunes, struggling to catch up with his long strides.

The pathway was rude and the boards were little more than ad hoc pieces of metal sheeting torn from old factory ruins. Fortunately the sand was too coarse to become mud. Her skirts and coat gained a few curious looks from the trouser-wearing inhabitants of the tents and caravans. Apart from staring, they kept their own counsel.

One of the structures had been erected apart from the others, out of sight behind a mound of old machine parts and the rusted remains of a dinghy. Yellow flags snapped in the wind.

At the opening, a bleached plesiosaur skull balanced on a stick. Jaundiced ribbons tied to a guy rope fluttered in warning.

A quarantine tent, larger than the others. She heard a cough within, and another throat moaned.

Not much light inside. The venom of a *maris anguis* tended people towards light-sensitivity. Clearly the hunt had come at a cost. She counted at least ten people here, bound up in stages of rigor and palsy upon their stretcher beds. Another four sat upright, limbs and torsos bandaged by an attendant in full plague-worker garb.

The beak of herbs turned Arden's way as she stepped inside, then went back to its corvid nursing.

Mr Cleave was loath to enter, so only pointed Arden to a puddle of illumination in one corner.

Miah Anguis had found something more important than tending to his own wounds, and that was in cutting the charms from his face with a pair of iron shears. He stood with his back to her and gave Arden no greeting. He wore the plain flax-linen shirt of the deepwater folk, the edges embroidered with protective signs, curlicues in a dark bronze sea-silk thread. A small brass mirror nailed to a nearby tent pole was his only guide, and he reflected one uninterested look at Arden before he went back to his business of removing the squid-beaks and shell-charms at his face.

Once freed, each venerated object was cast into the small fire of a nearby brazier. He murmured words of prayer with each offering.

She met his pale eyes through the mirror.

'Drink the liquor,' Miah said offhandedly, mid-clip. He tilted his head towards a green glass jar on a plank that had clearly spent a good portion of its life being rolled around in seawater, before being scavenged and repurposed. 'Anyone who uses heavy blood nurses the mother of all headaches afterwards.'

She made a bitter face. 'I'd rather a *sanguis malorum* headache than a rockblood liquor one.'

'Still, drink. It's kelp spirit, not rockblood.'

Miah was not wrong. When Arden pulled up the broad glass stopper and gave the contents a cautious sniff, only the clean, slightly greenish scent of high-proof kelp spirit and juniper came back at her.

Not wanting to seem too fussy, she took two mouthfuls from the jar, and coughed each time. The liquor burned, but within seconds the lingering aches faded to a background hum, and the small clarity that the relief brought was welcome.

With the last charm thrown in the fire and the greater part of his beard shorn by the sharp edge of the scissors, Miah Anguis turned to her.

Bare-faced now except for shadows, Jonah's features came and went with every flicker of lantern-light. Perhaps more so than Malachi Abaddon, this man was similar in looks to Jonah, but broader of face than Jonah had been and his profile was slabbed like the side of a granite outcrop. He cast more shadows, his brows were heavier, lips fuller, a front tooth crooked like Jonah's, but of the left rather than the right. Everything in his appearance was only a suggestion of her dead lover. Miah Anguis' semi-familiar facade teased her but never showed Arden an image of Jonah whole.

She wondered why Malachi had called him an *outsider* before, when he was clearly one of these people. Easily forty or more years lay upon the man's brow, and he suffered under the Fiction-pale complexion that made a person look older before their time. Oceanic deprivations and hard work had hewn his thick body into a hunter's instrument. Apart from his tattoos, he was not so much a carbon copy of Jonah at all. Miah had none of Jonah's lean nobility, though all, if not more, of the brute strength.

'Excuse me,' he said, looking away from her as he dropped his wet leathers. She turned her face while he reached for a cloth to wrap about his hips. He gave a grunt of discomfort as he slumped upon a plank-chair made of driftwood. The gash in his leg had stopped bleeding, but the torn flesh gleamed wet in the half-light. 'Mr Banks has to patch me up before I can go out.'

The medic had been standing quiet in the shadows, with the patience of an eel. Then he slipped forward with a courtier's diplomacy and knelt at Miah Anguis' thigh, needle in hand.

Miah looked her up and down while the camp doctor worked. 'So. *Arden Beacon*, your ship guard said your name was. Woman out of Clay City, all the way from Lyonne. Wearing a coat given to you by Jonah Riven, who once lived on the Vigil promontory.'

'Mr Ironcup spoke truthfully.'

'And Jorgen Beacon's . . . *niece*, am I right?'

'Yes, he husbanded the flame at Vigil's lighthouse. I took over from him when he died last year.'

Miah shook his head, his expression distant. 'I didn't think Jorgen would last so long after Zach was killed. What brings a Lyonnian sanguis here, Beacon?'

Disquieted, she put the kelp-spirit bottle aside and arranged her skirts beneath her coat. So many useless questions knocking into each other. So many important ones, so many too late.

'Bellis Harrow. Once upon a time you chased her off his island and she never came back.'

The deepwater man's face tightened, and he gestured with the scissor blade to a nearby stool. 'You have your audience. Sit.'

She sat. Mr Banks' needle darted into the bruised flesh of Miah's thigh harder than it should. He grimaced, and in the half-light, exhausted and crudely shorn, he didn't quite seem so intimidating, and Arden questioned her ridiculous earlier reaction upon the beach. She even began to question the reason she had come here. He was certainly physically commanding, but Bellis had bettered many big men. Had this all been a misunderstanding?

Miah did not take his eyes off Arden. He tracked her in the way a carnivore will not ignore his wounded, captured prey, knowing it still dangerous.

'We have had many dealings with that woman over these past years,' Miah said guardedly. It did not escape Arden's notice how he too did not use the petrochemical Queen's married name. 'Most of them unpleasant. She came to us once, seeking shelter, and exile. We did not allow it.'

His words belied the truth of Bellis' first attempt to enchant these folk with *orientis*. Jonah had told Arden what had happened. Not allowed her to stay? They had attacked Bellis as if she were a witch, and only Jonah's impromptu deepwater marriage had saved her. Marriage or not, these people had driven Bellis off Equus, for good.

And this man had something to do with it.

'Mr Anguis, she's grown even more powerful than she must have been when she first came to Equus. But she never did come back for revenge. Why not? She speaks the name of *Miah Anguis* with genuine alarm. She's afraid of you, sir. They say . . . I have heard that every island has fallen to her army, but she has never brought her wickedness to these shores.'

'There has always been wickedness on these shores.'

'But hers is kept away because you have an influence over her. Is it true? Did she really go to Libro and kill them all? Couldn't they have stopped her in the way you and your people did? Even Jonah couldn't stop her, in the end.'

She had not meant to say the last, but it had come unbidden. A wrinkle of distress moved over his brow.

'It is true what happened to the people of Libro Island, and I'll tell you why she has not returned. We know too well what happens if you give evil shelter, permit it to set root in the guise of smallness, and innocence.

'We saw clearly from the beginning,' Miah continued. 'Under that pretty little face was a monster. We mourn for the people of Libro Island, but we made sure Bellis Harrow learned a lesson she would not forget, not until the end of her days. It was not me alone who cast her out.'

He returned to watching Mr Banks work upon his leg. A

wounded hunter coughed on the other side of the spacious tent. A voice nearby murmured to the nurse for water.

'I understand you acted quickly, but how? You must tell me!'

Miah frowned. 'This meeting of ours seems to have been arranged hastily and without thought. You ask me of Jonah Riven and Bellis Harrow in the same breath. Malachi says you conveniently invited yourself to our hunt. A Lyonnian woman is very curious about me when I have not made myself available to her. These things are suspect.'

A thrill of panic made Arden hasty. 'Mr Anguis, it's true once this opportunity presented itself, I grabbed it with both hands!" she insisted. 'Wouldn't you have done the same in my position, trying to find answers about someone you lo—'

Almost too late she held her tongue. She had said too much. He squinted at her. The word *love* dangled between them. His lip curled.

'Perhaps you're a Bellis Harrow, coming here in the guise of innocence but also incredibly dangerous,' he said slowly, shook his head. 'My good sense tells me we should do to you what we did her. Cast you out so you will never think of coming back.'

'I was never here for you!' Arden protested.

'Your actions say otherwise.'

Arden gathered the last scraps of her pride. 'I came out to the Islands because Jonah Riven asked for a deepwater funeral prayer. It's an old rite—'

'I know what the Deepwater Rite is,' Miah sneered, but half-heartedly. His weariness meant there was no real vigour in him. 'Go on.'

'We were initially bound for Libro, but *our* ship broke down and we ended up here. It was not at all on purpose. I never would have come otherwise.'

'Well, at least you are honest.' Miah nodded.

'You can tell?'

'Yesterday your ship-guard boy told us everything. All about your dalliance with Jonah Riven, this ill-fated excursion to

Equus. Barely two days you were together as lovers according to your boy, and here you are, risking life and limb to secure a funeral rite to a man wedded to somebody else.'

'I was on my way home, but your people have stolen my boat! That boat is a man's funeral boat, you can't just take it away!'

He blinked once, as if confused, then his eyes widened as he at last understood.

'*Funeral* boat? You call her a funeral boat?' His face split with a great grimacing smile. 'Oh. *Oh*. I see. A *funeral* boat. You intend to enact a common shorefolk funeral, set an ill-gotten boat on fire and have his memory sent on its merry way to the bottom of the ocean?'

Arden could not have bit her tongue any harder and not drawn blood. 'It's not as if I know anything about the *Deepwater Rite*, how could I? That seems much your area of expertise, sir.'

The atmosphere darkened. Even Mr Banks looked up from his last stitch. The medical man clipped the last threads and stood up, made his apologies and left, throwing down a curtain so they might have some privacy.

Arden awkwardly turned her head as Miah stood up, pulled the leg of his breeches back on.

'I cannot doubt you are strong, Beacon, to have survived him, and her. And to go through all this pitiful search for absolution when there is none to be had. Not here, when the machines have taken so much.'

'Then respect the strength that it has taken me to come out here in the first place, and let me take the boat and the boy home. Mr Anguis, there are people who depend on me for their lives, right now. You understand what it is to have people depend on you for the same thing.'

'I do understand and accept your gratitude. And this is why I say you may go unharmed, as much as my conscience says otherwise. But the boat and boy stay with us.'

'No, it's not right!' Arden leapt to her feet. 'Jonah Riven

passed *Saudade* on to David Modhi of Fiction before official witnesses. You cannot keep her!'

Miah grabbed the jar of kelp spirit off the bench where Arden had left it, and drank half its contents in one swallow before sucking air through his clenched teeth.

'You have chased a ghost. *Saudade* never belonged to Jonah. Thalie's son was never one of ours. He never completed the *terrible rite*. Given that he has high-bred sanguis ladies from Clay Capital chasing him across these islands, I can assume he even died intact with an exceedingly pretty cock.'

The suggested violence of the Rivens was spoken of so matter-of-factly, as if their lives were signposted in death and dismemberment.

'The *terrible rite*? Like Malachi's injury?' she shot back, not allowing him to intimidate her. 'You appeared intact yourself when I passed outside, so you haven't gone that far either.'

'As in removed altogether and fed to the ocean? Blessed and free from weakness? No, theirs is a greater call, their strength cannot be matched. I was cut differently, but still *cut*.'

A defiance in him. His thumb fell to the waistband of his breeches.

'I gave pain to the water. I shall show you if you wish.'

How strange, those curiosities towards the violent rituals of lesser folk. If she hadn't been so acutely aware of her captive position, or that she did not know this brutish man's intentions, for an intense lurching moment her mouth would have met his challenge and replied, *yes, go ahead then. Show me how you maimed yourself in sacrifice to the sea.*

But the moment had passed, and he'd only been teasing her. Miah had already tucked his shirt back into his breeches. After testing his balance he snatched a simple ichthyosaur coat from a nearby hook and walked out, leaving her in the tent.

She had no choice but to follow him out of the sick-tent into the dreary morning. The deepwater man still had a limp as he walked ahead, but his stride eased out before long and he arrived in the camp centre, a rough construction of lean-tos and canvas awnings. Rainwater dripped about huddles of the mostly young and infirm, people who were not strong enough to join in the hunt.

Miah stepped underneath several shelters, shook hands, murmured words alongside grateful faces, and Arden could not interrupt, for what kind of person would she be to intrude upon them now? He was respected here, and she was the interloper the way Bellis had been, once upon a time.

Miah's social duties done, he took a shortcut over the dunes. They crested at a point where the entire beach was a long black vista against the grey water.

Below them upon the black sand, the serpent's coiled body was both massive and pathetic in its death. Its eye was a milky agate and each scale around it had to be as big as a serving platter. Several yards down, a row of deepwater folk had together disembowelled the creature, sending coils of iridescent purple intestines puddling onto the black sand. Waves of dead serpent stench buffeted her even from far away, the smell of fermented salt and melting road-tar on a hot day.

The cryptid aromatics reminded Arden of the kraken hen Jonah had caught, and their first kiss. A whirling despair followed the feeling. Jonah and Arden had shared a brief moment where all had seemed possible, but those hopes had been nothing more than a mirage. The Lions had been watching. Their days had been numbered, even then.

Arden expected that Miah Anguis would keep going down the dune. To her surprise he stayed on the crest and looked down like a bleak stone monument at the prize he had taken from the ocean. A muscle moved in his cheek.

'Your ship-watch boy said it was Bellis that killed him?' Miah asked gruffly. 'Jonah.'

Arden nodded. 'Yes. At summer's end, when she caught us south of the Tempest. She was in *Sehnsucht*, a boat I'm sure you are familiar with.'

He hissed a curse word and squatted with a wince of pain,

before throwing out his wounded leg and sitting awkwardly, one knee drawn up.

Arden watched in silence as he fished about in his pockets for a pouch of tobacco, and lit one of the thin leaf-wrapped twists with a strike lighter, before sucking an agitated lungful of smoke.

She joined him on the damp sand, her knees tucked under her dress. If she was going to argue for *Saudade*'s return, perhaps a more personal approach would be best.

'Did you know Jonah well, sir? I know he was here to marry Bellis, but other than that . . .'

He rubbed his injured thigh. 'Know him? He was my cousin.'

'Cousin?' she started, then all the puzzles in her mind about Miah Anguis' provenance, the name they had called him, fell into place. He *was* Jonah's cousin. His family and blood. Miah had to be Jeremiah, the son of Zachariah Riven. She gasped at the surprise, as if the wind had stolen her breath away.

The flash of euphoria was followed by an equal worry.

'Mr Anguis, I thought everyone died that night, when Jonah . . .'

'I did die,' he gritted, and sucked in more smoke. It was strong and bitter, reminiscent of graveyard bogs and swamps that swallowed men whole. 'I did die. When the first of the creatures came into the compound, some of us fled into the ocean. It made no difference. The monsters followed. Circled us as we clung to a rock in Dead Man's Bay. I was the only one to survive the first night. Stayed there three. Three days burned from salt-scores. The water leeches flayed my back bloody and raw. I made promises to foul gods those days and nights, to keep me alive.'

He finished the tobacco twist and discarded it.

'The deepwater folk found me on the third morning, once word came to them what had happened. They could have left my rotting body there among the other corpses, but this land is not kind to us and they needed the numbers.'

Down on the beach the folk had wrapped rope cables around

the serpent's horns, and ten heads at each cable hauled the serpent's tail away for the flensers to access.

'I'm sorry,' she said helplessly.

'You don't need to apologize. The crime was Jonah's burden to carry.'

'Mr Anguis, he lived with it every day. He spent fifteen years in Harbinger Bay. He was a pariah in town. They might not have been shorefolk themselves, but they never forgave him.'

Miah stood up with a grunt. 'Well, he is free of it now, thanks to his wife.'

He didn't wait for Arden and took a track down through the clumps of coast-grass and back onto the beach. She hauled herself out of the sand and followed him.

The folk had set up a long driftwood table near the serpent's head. A roll of canvas and old, well-worn knives were set in a row upon the table. Another reminder chewed at her heart, for Jonah had owned a similar set. Worse still, from this angle she could peer beyond the dune ridges where their boats were anchored, and *Saudade* was among them, twice as large as any other.

'Sir, I still need to discuss *the boat*.'

'We've discussed it,' Miah said. He nodded to a pair of clan fellows, and Arden waited anxiously for them to collect their butcher's implements and pass, so she might be allowed privacy. Every minute here seemed time wasted.

'I cannot impress how staying in Burden Town is a death sentence,' she continued urgently once the other folk were out of earshot. 'They've already descended into cannibalism in that city, and soon they'll fall further. *Saudade* is our only way off. We will die if we stay!'

Miah yanked a flensing knife from the canvas roll with such vehemence that she needed to step back or get cut to ribbons.

'Listen, Beacon, you are young, and rich-looking, and obviously have no taste at all in lovers. There are men in Burden Town who would give you an unnecessary boat for a night in the sheets with a Lyonnian bloodworker. You do not need to take one of the few family relics I have left. Not when Jonah took everything that was mine, everything that I loved, my respect and even my name, whether he did it on purpose or not.'

Miah pointed the blade at the encampment, and then at her chest. 'Besides, Mr Cleave tells me your boy made an agreement to stay. Him and his friend, who Malachi will advise as soon as he returns.'

Arden gave an incredulous gasp at Sean's disloyalty. She pushed herself forward until the point of the rippled steel poked into her breastbone.

'Sean cannot make that bargain. He doesn't understand what he asks for.'

'Is he not Mr Modhi's *lover*? The boat's true owner, as you say? Then Mr Ironcup has some right to ownership, where you and your filthy licentious loyalty to Jonah Riven do not.'

'What if I take this question to Mr Cleave?' she retorted. 'Your young stormcaller is in that quarantine tent, bloodless, with no-one left to light the rockblood fires. What if I were to offer my services in return for a boat far too gaudy for a clan trying to keep hidden up here and away from a hundred thousand starving men?'

Her aim hit true, for Miah winced and pushed the blade, and had there been any pressure, it would have sliced open the dress-cloth at her sternum.

'We have been getting along so well, you and I. Don't make your removal unpleasant. I have butcher's work to do. Mr Cleave will see you back to the river.'

'But—'

'You speak of exchanging all the things but not the one thing obviously most precious to *him*,' Miah said sharply. 'That which you have not offered.'

A dark caution loomed over her. A weight, like a coming storm, the same as she had felt inside the Burden Town alley-church, and the priest's growling invitation. They'd been dancing around the boat's true worth, and the limits of what Arden would give.

'Most precious to him? Jonah had nothing except *Saudade*. She was his whole life.'

'Until the end.'

'You make no sense. Look at these people around you. You say you have no respect, but I see the love in these people's eyes. Jonah never had any of that.'

'Yes,' Miah countered sharply. 'Look at these people around us. They were there when I was dragged half-dead to the Equus shores after my family's massacre. They voted to keep me alive, even though I was shore-born and tainted by the shallows. Now how would they feel if I just upped and gave my father's boat to his killer's lover? I would lose this *love* you think comes so easily to me. Unless recompense was made.'

She swallowed a suddenly dry throat. Asked, even though she could see it in his face, the way his eyes racked over her, hungry. 'What recompense?'

He paused, deliberating on what he would say next. When he spoke, his voice was hoarse with a malicious ferment.

'Return to me what I lost. The three sunrises I saw on that rock while I watched my family die.'

'How can I return those days?'

'My people will see what I ask from you and know it payment. I will not lose face by giving my cousin a funeral-boat like a coward. You tell me he had no family, no respect. I will have taken something from him more than a boat, something that he cannot recover.'

Though white-hot inside, Arden gave Miah Anguis the same cool stare she'd used to close down arguments with Lord Abaddon, Mr Justinian, and scores of lesser men.

'I am not a thing to be bargained with.'

Before she could stop him, Miah seized up her arms and dragged Arden to press his torso forcefully against her own. She might have fought against the sea for all the effort her struggles achieved in his hands.

Up close his tattoos had left deep gouges upon his collarbone, and the ink upon his chest, the sea-serpent glyphs nestling in the dark hair, appeared as violent as wounds.

He jutted his face at hers. Not to kiss. His jaw slid abrasive upon her cheek, hot breath in her ear, murmured words in a mocking growl.

'It is not the boat. You are correct, I have enough boats and my father's is gaudy indeed. I will take something more precious to my family's killer, something that he cannot reclaim from the dead. If you ever have a memory of Jonah-fucking-Riven, it'll be my tongue on your clit and my cock in your quim you'll feel when you think of his name. Always. I'll defile any love you have left inside, and when I'm done I might even be generous and retrieve my fool cousin's body from Bellis fucking Harrow and burn it in front of you for good fucking measure.'

He pushed her away, mouth twisted as if it were even worse for him to have suggested such perfidies as payment.

'Anyhow. That's the price for your funeral boat,' he finished, with exaggerated politeness, as casual as if she'd offered a purse of Lyonne silver dollars and he'd declined with a request for gold instead.

Arden rubbed her arms, for they burned from where he'd held her so hard. Her speechlessness was more from the venom in his proposal than the content. In the wild surrounds of the swordgrass dunes her fevered imagination conjured him as misshapen in engorgement as the serpent upon the beach.

Her voice came back, trembling with indignant emotion. 'So, I suppose you find it amusing, to speak to me in the manner of a fiend . . . about a serious exchange.'

Miah had obviously been expecting her refusal. It had not been an offer made to ensure agreement, only to underscore impossibility. His behaviour had not changed since he was Jeremiah Riven of Vigil, taking tobacco off a young girl. He was not offended by her lack of enthusiasm. He waved Arden off, as if he'd meant to present her with an unreasonable choice that she could not accept.

'Then go with grace, Arden Beacon. I'll treat the boy well, and his friend likewise. But don't come back here again.'

10

The fumes from the refineries

The fumes from the refineries made a sickly blue hour when they returned on Lys' boat. They journeyed through wet, jaundiced fog, crawled at a snail's pace through the river's cloacal murk. Lys would have been navigating blind if not for the plaintive wails of the foghorns carrying across the river. The weather had turned upon them, and the chill sank down into Arden's bones. Her hands hurt, even when she tucked them inside her coat for warmth.

She had lost *Saudade*, and the hope of Jonah's funeral. She had tried and failed again. Arden hugged herself as if she'd become an empty vessel without purpose, everything internal having drained out, leaving behind an exhausted shell of skin. She could still smell Miah Anguis on her, the limestone water on his breath and the thick animal ferment of his fevered skin, so *like* and *unlike* Jonah it confused her memory of him. Had her Mr Riven smelled like that? Had he *felt* like that?

Along the river, Malachi blenched each time the small boat hit a current or wave. With the excitement of the hunt having worn off fully, his bruised ribs and swelling wrist pained him with an awful ache. She regarded him suspiciously. He would be the one to tell David about Sean, and the harbour Sean had negotiated on his behalf. What would David do? Follow him heedlessly? The deepwater folk lived a rough Arcadian existence, but with Burden Town's collapse coming, they could not hope to remain that long.

By the time they reached the House of Abaddon, far too late for a furtive entrance, Malachi's face had taken on a pale tinge of green.

The guard Harmal waited for them at the deck of the House of Abaddon. His expression grew stonier as Arden heaved herself up the ladder.

'Been away too long,' he grunted accusingly.

'Where's Miss Quarry?' she asked carefully. Chalice had not shown her face, when she should have been tapping her foot alongside Harmal.

'Lord Abaddon has escorted her into town,' he replied, and gave a grey, gimlet stare at Malachi. 'He was not happy to find you gone.'

'We brought a peace offering,' Arden said and pointed at the object by which their return would be smoothed over. Two sack loads of sea-serpent meat cut from a cryptid spine, almost as big as a man.

'What . . . what is that?' Harmal suddenly dropped his air of unapproachable stoniness. All of a sudden he looked like a child given a precious gift only dreamt of. One clear, rockblood plastic sack bulged, and he saw within the opaline bone, the dark blood, the promise of a feast. All his planned chastisements were forgotten.

'Give it to the chef. I'm certain he'll prefer this to the usual *long pork*.'

He sniffed, as if trying to show disapproval. Ratcheted the bloody package up on the lift platform nevertheless.

'Where are the others? Mr Le Shen, Mr Modhi?'

'The librarian is still in. The boy tells me he is out with boat business.'

Arden exchanged a pained glance with Malachi. By now David would have discovered both Sean and *Saudade* gone.

Arden took her leave of the men, hung up her skirts in the drying-closet and – too tired even to take off her damp gloves – collapsed upon the satin daybed as if she'd been felled by a divine and ironic arrow.

Jonah Riven murmured in her memory, and in her agitation she might have lingered upon his ghostly voice. The morphium of the night pressed too hard upon her to stay awake, and before she could even cobble together a pleasant thought, she . . .

The commotion woke her. A yelling in the foyer.

She thought about pulling herself back into her damp skirts, but the urgency of the moment combined with the added torment of having to stand up when her head whirled so had her settling on one of Malachi's faux-silk robes instead.

She stepped barefoot along the corridor to find David Modhi remonstrating angrily with Harmal.

'Where the hell would they have taken him, guy? Where could an entire boat go?'

Arden cleared her throat. 'Mr Modhi, it's all right. It is under control.'

David Modhi shoved past Harmal, gasping with panic. 'Mx Beacon, my God, they've taken Sean!'

She caught him by his shoulders before he could rampage any further.

'Calm down. Keep some wits about you, Mr Modhi. I know where Sean is.'

David stared at her as if he had been slapped. 'You do?'

This was not a conversation she wanted in front of Lord Abaddon's guard. The guard squinted at them, no doubt considering that they both be tossed into the street. Arden snatched David's elbow and led him through the dank oily corridor and back into the guest room, and the modicum of privacy it offered.

Once inside, she shut the louvre doors and pushed him onto a shabby ottoman the colour of a bruise.

'Sean is fine. *He is.*' Arden sucked her lips, and realized she could still taste serpent sauce and sweet fig tea from the meal

Mr Cleave had given her and Malachi before sending them on their way. Deeper still, the kelp spirit lingered on her breath. Now she'd been thrust into an unwanted position of responsibility. David would hear her voice first, her argument. Malachi might come later, but he was a stranger bearing the news of Sean's decision. Arden would have more influence on David's eventual decision. Suddenly the duty weighed on her and she silently admonished Malachi Abaddon for putting her in such a position.

David would not let her go. 'Mx Beacon . . . Sean. The boat . . .'

'Sean's with Malachi's people on the northern shore.'

He shook his head, not understanding. 'He's where? How did he get out there?'

She threw up her hands, helpless to explain it all without falling apart herself. 'If Sean had a choice, he would stay there, rather than in this poisonous house in this cannibal city. But David, they also took her. *Saudade.* They took Jonah's boat. And where the hell is Chalice? Shouldn't she be back by now?'

David tugged at his sweat-slick hair in agitation before making a non-committal gesture towards town. 'Still in Burden, with the Lord Abaddon.'

He turned a trapped-rat circle within the pink-pillowed confines of the room before returning to Arden.

'How did they take *Saudade*? She didn't have an engine. Sean hired guards!'

'We had eyes upon us in the harbour. She has a history of ownership. Now she's been acquired by former owners who think they have a claim on her. The same people who have Sean. The deepwater folk of the northern shores and . . .' Arden brought herself up short. Miah had feared the reach of Lyonne deeply enough to discard his birth name.

'And Miah Anguis.' Arden nodded.

'Miah Anguis! You found him?'

'And found him odious. He's the one claiming *Saudade*. Even he himself admits she's too much boat for them, but he won't give her back.'

'Couldn't you have offered something? Money? Kraken oil? Your blood, or mine?'

She felt her face twist. 'I offered all of them. Mr Anguis wanted something else. Something I couldn't give.'

'What? Mx Beacon, you *have* to give them what they want! Tell them we'll pay anything.'

'It's not so simple, David! Think, lad. Don't make me spell it out! What would a brute like that demand from me?'

Her cry seemed to correct David's mood somewhat. He paused, and in his face came the gradual awareness of just what sort of terrible payment she meant. He deflated from his position of high dudgeon. 'Cup's definitely not in harm's way, then?'

'Not yet.' She sighed, knowing that soon Malachi would wake up and tell David the offer. 'I am not so certain about *us*, however. Did Chalice even give an inkling of when she intended to return?'

It turned out that Chalice would stride haughtily into the foyer not long after their difficult conversation. Little in her bearing suggested that she'd had anything less than a most pleasant squiring about town, but she coolly let them know Lord Abaddon had developed an illness and would not be able to join them for supper.

'Indigestion,' she said matter-of-factly to Arden. 'Which is a shame, as I have an interest in going out again. Seeing the sights that I missed. Hearing what my sanguis friend was up to last *bloody* night when we lost both a boy and our *bloody* boat.'

She shot daggers of reproach at Arden. David folded his arms and took a great interest in his feet.

Arden sighed and fetched her travelling coat.

As they walked along the worn limestone boulevard by the cloacal river, Arden relayed to Chalice an abridged account of her journey with Malachi to the northern crest of Equus, and the itinerant folk who scratched an existence out of sea-monsters and kelp harvesting. Although Arden could not quite see

Chalice's face, there was no mistaking her level of upset, judging by her verbal objections.

'Oh Arden, darling, what compelling nonsense could anyone find in north Equus? Most of it is a mess of broken lich-machines and rockblood bandits.'

'I was safe enough from bandits. We went by the channel course with a very experienced river-pilot.'

'Oh devilment, right through the badlands!'

'Well, I needed to know!' She heaved a breath through her charcoal mask. 'All this time, in my journey from Bellis' army, from Vigil to here, I've been told of a man who is invulnerable to Bellis Harrow—'

'—and you wanted to see if you'd missed anything, am I right? See if there is something either your poor dead fisherman or you, our poor living woman, could have done against her?'

'It weighs on me. The curiosity made me a little reckless,' Arden admitted.

'More than *a little*, I would say.'

'It was a good thing I did go in the end. How else could I have known who had both Sean and *Saudade*?'

'Darling, let them take care of themselves. You could have been killed out there! Strangled by a pipe! Ravished by a bandit and left for dead! Leave the espionage to the experts, please.' She tapped her chest.

'We must get them both back. Is there anything in your Lion purse you could pull out to help, Chalice? Look, I saw—'

'Another Riven?'

Arden was startled into silence. How had Chalice guessed?

Chalice continued, 'It is rumoured that not everyone died that night when your fellow came into his monstrous talent. One got away, the Order thinks, rumoured to be on Equus shores.'

Arden wrapped herself in false disdain. 'I was going to say I saw them pull a sea-serpent out of the water. A *maris anguis*. I thought they were extinct at least. Goodness, Chalice, a *Riven*?

One of Jonah's people, still alive? Why have you not told me of this rumour before today?'

'And provide more reasons to go off half-cocked for some family reconnaissance? I'm not even entirely certain the information is reliable, myself.'

'And did this information come from Mr Absalom's locket too? Why, he must have kept a veritable encyclopaedia on a square of silk.'

'No need to be snooty. Right now the Order is rather upset with you having run off on them. An unaccounted-for survivor might have been influence we could have used to placate the old Lions when we get home. They rather take a dim view of gaps in their genealogical knowledge.'

Arden shook her head again. 'If there were people there who held deepwater names, they were distant relations to Jonah only. His family left these shores a century ago.'

'And what about this Miah Anguis who aggrieved Bellis so much? What kind of man was he?'

'I was not in a position to ask much of him,' Arden replied frostily. 'Their leader was a man named Amos Cleave.'

'Ah, like Jonah's stepfather, Ishmael?'

Arden nodded. 'Yes. He seemed quite the patriarch. There are a lot of Cleaves on that coast, I think.' She stopped and made Chalice stop in front of her. 'So what are we going to do now? Miah Anguis is as impenetrable as a stone wall, but Amos Cleave seems someone very open to suggestions.'

Chalice appeared to think briefly. 'Perhaps you don't need suggestions. Or the boat for that matter.'

'What are you on, Chalice? We need her!'

'I may have already come up with a solution. This changes everything, darling. I've heard a whisper of another Order contact in the city. He arrived this morning from Maris Island, flying the Queen's colours apparently. Someone who might know what has actually happened to your benighted fellow.'

Chalice Quarry, who always knew the most right and wrong things to say. Chalice Quarry, who had lied to her before. Arden found herself rooted to the spot, as if her feet had petrified into the stone.

'You mean . . . he'll know what actually happened to Jonah?'

'Well, are you coming?' Chalice pressed, when Arden didn't follow her. She was reliving the moment when Jonah was last alive, how hurt he was, how vulnerable . . .

'Is it the truth this time?'

'When we meet them, you'll know if they speak truth or not.'

Arden took a deep breath and steadied herself. 'I follow because I'm running out of options, Chalice. Not because a Lion has won me over with a fantasy.'

Chalice took Arden's gloved hand and brushed her thumb over the coin. 'The fantasy is that you have any options left.'

Burden Town pressed in about them, concrete, canvas and stone. Her Lion took Arden through a different path to the one she'd taken to see their scoundrel of a holy man. An older section of city, still bearing the remnants of that lost and forgotten civilization. The narrow streets took on the slanted camber of old stones worn by a million footsteps.

Chalice used no map this time, only steered them down a broad flight of stairs that should have been at the front of a grand hall or library, except no such things existed here. The street became an expansive underground space, a remnant of a sunken amphitheatre or courtyard that had been built over by successive generations, leaving only a low, deep gallery.

A sizable crowd of people milled in the subterranean dark. The crowd made the space damp, and hot, and the few petralactose light-fittings gave off a yellow cast, like a sickness. An acetone smell tainted the air, smell of too many people, not enough proper food. Bodies bunched in knots and fists, murmuring like a wasp-nest drone. Much to Arden's dismay, Chalice marched over to a sullen group guarding a staircase in some iron-gated mezzanine, her shoulders set squarely. One of the taller men she tapped on the shoulder.

'Excuse me,' she said. 'Is there no help for the Widow's Son?'

The man whom Chalice had interrupted mid-conversation turned about. An iron-grated brazier flame reflected in his goggles, his face obscured in his charcoal mask.

Arden's thumbs twitched. Was she going to have to drag Chalice away to safety? She should have brought David along, then she might have the chance of creating the same kind of fire as she had on the Equus beach.

Instead of challenging this odd woman who asked strange questions, the man slid his mask down to his chin and revealed a Lyonnian smirk.

'Why,' he said in reply. 'There is always help for the Widow's Son, if the Widow asks nicely enough.'

He slid his goggles up upon his silver head and smiled at Chalice, one tooth gold and winking.

It was Mr Absalom. Bellis Harrow's sergeant-at-arms.

11

You have made a journey indeed

'You have made a journey indeed,' Mr Absalom said, fixing his charcoal kerchief about his neck as if he were fixing a scarf. 'Truthfully, I worried that the Widow's Son might not make it.'

He had taken them up the rusted staircase to seat them at a small balcony table, a high place for men of status, or what little passed for status in this city.

'Did you come alone?' Arden asked Mr Absalom breathlessly, still not having yet recovered from seeing Bellis' right-hand man. When last they'd met, it was upon the ghostwood *Sehnsucht*, Mr Riven half-burnt from a fire he'd survived and Mr Absalom admitting that he was in actuality a Lion spy there to inform upon Bellis.

'I was unable to bring many people with me. Bellis' influence grows unchecked, since recent events. As has her capacity for seeking revenge on anyone who has slighted her.'

A cold, invisible hand brushed along Arden's arms. Of all the things she had told herself to make Jonah's passing easier, it was that he had died without suffering. Not long enough to be hurt, or tortured. Mr Absalom's words did not suggest a quick ending, or that Bellis had not humiliated him first.

Arden could bear their casual exchange no longer.

'Tell me what happened to Jonah, Mr Absalom. What did she do to him?'

'Arden,' Chalice snapped. 'Be patient. There are other issues of equal importance here.'

Mr Absalom leaned back from Arden's passionate plea, and circumscribed his gin glass with a gold-tipped finger. The quinine in the gin made the glass glow with the blue of arc lightning across an electrical coil. He wore rings of pig-iron, a yellow druzy on his thumb the size of a crooked sovereign.

'She did not kill him that day on the *Sehnsucht*.'

His evasiveness made her fretful. 'Tell me, sir, what happened to him. Tell me, and I'll go back to Lyonne. I will do whatever the Order asks.'

Out of the corner of her eye she could see Chalice suck in her cheeks. Arden was Chalice's prize to bring back to the Lyonne Order, not Absalom's.

'Your absolute compliance in exchange for information?'

'Yes.'

He took the glass and swallowed the contents abruptly. Gazed at the remains as if he were inspecting a document of deep mysteries.

'I can give you something better than information.'

'Better?'

'Give me this night to make the arrangements. Tomorrow I will bring Jonah Riven to Burden Town.'

The words were not making sense. 'His body?'

'The man.'

Her chest tightened. The air became thick, like treacle in hot sun. The cold press of her skin became hot. *Alive*.

'He is alive how, sir?'

Mr Absalom leaned in close. 'Mx Beacon, I know where Jonah Riven is being kept. On an island not far from Equus. The Queen could not bear him alive, but could not bear him dead either. He was sent into exile.'

'If he is alive then . . . oh, did Bellis hurt him?'

He shook his head. 'Not physically.'

The crowd on the floor below stirred and muttered. Some sharp words sounding above the din. A fight starting, and it became clear the focus was on a man about to be thrown to his death for meat and his companions not altogether happy about it. The time to move on had come.

Chalice tapped the glassware with a fork. 'I hope we can wrap this up now,' she said. 'Coming so far just to end up on the menu is not on my agenda. We have transport that must be arranged since Arden has misplaced Jonah's boat.'

'I have transport,' Mr Absalom said. 'And I *can* secure Riven's freedom. But you must keep this promise, Mx Beacon. You must return to Lyonne at once. Bringing Jonah Riven here ruins my standing, destroys my cover forever. I will never be able to return to these islands.'

'I promise, sir. Bring Jonah back to me and I will go wherever you ask.'

Mr Absalom stood up, reapplied the goggles to his face. They gave him the appearance of an insect with eyes of flame.

'Tomorrow night, meet us on the market harbour at the Cloaca's mouth. The man you seek will be there. And then you will come back with me to Clay.'

Mr Absalom pushed back his chair and prepared to rise.

Through a throat choked tight with an invisible hand Arden said, 'Wait.'

'Time runs short, Mx Beacon.' He tilted his head to the riot threatening to breach the stairwell. 'Speak quickly.'

'You have my promise. What is your guarantee that you intend to do as you say?'

'The guarantee is that you know me as a brother of Lyonne and those fellows down there do not. Even an incautious whisper in this place could be the absolute end of me. For my own protection I will act with honour and receive it in return, I hope.'

With that, he gave a nod and adjusted the brocade of his vest before sliding back into his behemoth-leather coat.

With no small measure of huffing Chalice let the Lion spy go, before turning back to Arden.

'What a show-off. Don't let him forget that you were *already* headed home. I'll not have him stealing my thunder just because he's enacted a rescue.'

Arden quickly kissed Chalice on the cheek, too overwhelmed and overjoyed to do much else. Even the shouts and ruckus from below could not put a dent on her whirling elation.

'Oh Chalice, is it not a miracle? He's alive! He's alive!' The coins in her hands pinched and snagged. Her blood belonged to another heartbeat. Jonah was alive, and alive, and alive.

He would come home with her. He would be safe in Clay, with Bellis far away. And the sea was not so far from the city, the Clay river mouth spilled onto oceanic estuaries where the shorefolk made their lives. He could be happy there. They could be happy together.

'I could find a salve for those,' Chalice said, peering down at Arden's gloves as she helped her up from the table. 'To keep the infection from spreading while we wait for Mr Absalom to return.'

Arden smiled, tremulous and almost fainting with joy. 'A salve would be nice. Yes.'

The creaking and crashing of the mezzanine's staircase failing under the load of hunger-crazed insurgents put a bookend to their conversation. A fight was spilling over into other fights, and now the eyes were turning upwards. The time for leaving had come.

Chalice took Arden's elbow as if she was an impossibly delicate thing, but her fingers held on tight, and hard.

'Let's go.'

As if the riot had summoned up the strange demons, nightfall brought rain upon Burden Town. Under the cold rockblood streetlamps, the aqueducts rose up brimful with yellow water, spilled their banks along with the discarded rubbish of a year. The devilfish of the river underwent a metamorphosis, and in the space of hours grew rudimental legs to drag their silvered bellies along the alleys and streets, looking for food.

All through the long night and into the sodden morning Lord Abaddon's helpmen patrolled the edge of the veranda. Every once in a while they would poke the risen water with sticks as a demonic imago chanced the oily wood.

Safe and dry, Arden could not sleep, and paced the sheltered walkway like a prisoner along the perimeter of their cell. By morning, she was exhausted. She could not escape the primacy of rockblood here, the suffocating feeling of it.

Arden's high view from the veranda included the wasteland boundary beyond the city and the true species of an automated island. Through the grey rain, a gargantuan wheeled dredger crawled along on wheels higher than a watch-house. Animated by old *sanguis mandatum-orientis* instructions, it shared a ghastly affinity with the lich-ships travelling from Equus to the Fiction refineries. Smoke wreathed the rusted funnel, a clawed bucket dangled upon an articulated arm. The petrichor of disturbed dirt wafted in the air.

The waiting had dulled Arden's initial excitement of discovering that Jonah was alive. Now other worries slipped past her defences. It did not help that when she thought of Jonah, Miah's face and body seemed to slide over his image, like a ghostly projection. It was as if the memory of the deepwater man sought to dominate Jonah even when they were separated by years and miles.

At the chiming of the clocks for the daylight hours, Chalice joined Arden upon the veranda. 'Darling,' she said. 'The rain has slowed. It's time. Mr Absalom will be at the market harbour.'

She blinked out of her imaginings, and gave Chalice a weary smile. 'Wait, let me talk to David Modhi first.'

Madame Lion gave an aggrieved mutter and fastened her rain bonnet under her chin. 'Don't take too long. Another deluge will close off our route to the port.'

Arden went to locate David, and found him with Malachi. They were both in the boudoir, dressing for wet weather. Lord Abaddon had made himself absent. It had only taken a sharp word from Chalice for him to withdraw, in high dudgeon, to the safety of his own quarters.

'Leaving already, Mr Modhi?'

The boy – a man now, she reminded herself – stopped buttoning up his oilcoat and took Arden into a hug. She hugged him back.

'I will miss you, Mx Beacon.' He glanced sideways at Malachi, who nodded, and moved away so they might have some privacy.

'So, you took up on their offer, I see.'

'Sean was a quick thinker to make the deal. He's really smart, Mx Beacon, he is. My mother always used to say that Hillsiders were foolish and clumsy, but that's not been the case at all.'

'Well, he is a credit to his people,' Arden said kindly, even though her heart pained her, seeing David look so happy in the face of such an uncertain future. 'But I would be remiss not to ask – can you reconsider coming with me? There's still a place in Clay. They'll treat a *sanguis ignis* well. It can be a constrained life, but for some it can be a long one.'

David shook his head with a gentle regret, gestured to Malachi, inviting him back into the conversation.

'David is strong enough to withstand an initiation,' Malachi said, knowing what exactly they'd spoken of. 'My people will accept him in time. Maybe they'll give him captaincy of *Saudade*.'

'Well now, don't cut all your parts off,' Arden said faintly, wanting to feel happiness for the lad but finding the emotion abut hard and painful against her own cautions. She would have to tell Jonah about *Saudade*'s loss. 'The tip of a finger will be fine.'

'This is not a parting, Mx Beacon,' David said. 'And tell Mr Riven I will see him again one day. I am certain of it.'

Malachi lingered, waiting for them to finish. At last he cleared his throat with a polite cough. 'This is no ordinary storm. We must get along.'

After her goodbyes, Arden put on her krakenskin and joined Chalice at the wide cedar overhang of Lord Abaddon's mansion.

The rain had slowed. Curtains of water still sheeted off the cornices, and the two menservants in the foyer battled with a four-legged monstrosity not willing to die from its double impalement upon boat-hooks. It was somewhat a cross between a lizard and a dog, with a translucent membrane between its front and back legs. The creature snarled and hissed every time one of the men poked it with a hook, dribbled venom from its inverted snout.

Arden wanted all of a sudden to tell them to stop and let the animal go. She couldn't bear to see a cruelty on the hour of her reunion with Jonah. It didn't fit right.

Chalice took Arden's hand, and patted the numb parts with attendant care. 'All good, darling? There's a bit of a walk ahead of us.'

Arden turned away from the pitiful scene. The creature let out a ferocious, cackling slather of rage as Chalice passed, but after an equal riot of venomous hissing, ignored Arden completely once she put on her krakenskin coat.

'I'm good. I only feel a little strange. I never expected to find Jonah so suddenly and so unharmed. I expected it would be different.' She clasped her damp gloves together and willed more feeling into her hands. 'Even in my most impossible dreams I expected some level of damage. And sacrifice.'

'Isn't that what that alley-priest said you would need?' Chalice asked, curt with sympathetic disapproval. 'I completely own and condemn his foolishness. He'd have you thinking you'd need to cut out your heart to win Jonah back. Bloody deepwater nonsense. My fault for even taking you to him.'

'I must admit, he was very convincing.'

Chalice stuck her hand out from the veranda, then withdrew it with a disappointed smacking of lips. 'If one were drunk with religious puffery in a place like this, one could make anything believable. Thank goodness some good sense has made a reappearance, Arden. By this night we'll be heading home, all will be right with the world.'

'Oh. I can barely imagine what I'll say to Mr Riven when I see him again.' Arden put her hand on her stomach. 'I have such butterflies.'

'Don't fuss too much. Tell him he needs to appreciate the hard work we've all put into this rescue of his.'

'I barely did anything.'

'Apart from nearly turning into serpent food with that little jaunt upriver,' Chalice tutted. 'Or, heavens, nearly getting mauled by some tattooed savage who has never seen a soap-washed Lyonnian in his life. Chin up.'

Chalice leaned over and properly fastened the hood to Arden's krakenskin, before retying her own bonnet mummy-tight.

'I'm only glad it's over,' Chalice continued. 'By the week's end I expect to see myself sunning myself on a Clay City balcony with a medallion on my chest, and that will be the fitting finale to my career with the Order. I'm quite done with all the gallivanting.'

Arden thought of some likewise good thing and dared not even chance either God or the devil with it yet.

Like any stormbride used to hard weather Chalice knew when the rain clearing was as good as it was ever going to get, and they ran out into the streets at her command. Arden grabbed her skirt hem and knotted the fabric high over her kidskin under-trousers. Ended up getting all her layers wet all the same.

Luck continued its unlikely companionship. Their run to the docks was unimpeded by soul or devil. The poisoned sky remained bilious overhead but did not break apart from a few fat drops of water. The docks were close. Arden's feet ran beyond her head, and Chalice grabbed her waist when her travelling shoes slipped about on the stone.

'Don't rush.'

'I need to see him.'

'He's not going anywhere.'

Then the rain began to fall again, and the spilling river rose once more. The previously chaotic markets at the wharfside lay empty and sodden, an ankle-deep sheet of floodwater moved between the trestle tables. Huddles of bodies stayed in the eaves of the buildings, watching.

'Hoy!' cried a voice. 'Hoy.'

Through the intermittent sheets of lightning they could see the figure of a man, upright and aristocratic, with a Djenne shawl across one shoulder and a monocle like a third eye about his neck. Mr Absalom, at one of the private docks. An iron ship listed at the main harbour, lurking in the water, its stack warmed up and belching bunker-oil fumes. The rest of the harbour had been rendered deserted by the weather and the devilfish, and an eerie abandonment echoed along the wet moorings.

'Hoy,' Chalice cried through the rain. 'We're here.'

'And not yet devoured!' Mr Absalom replied cheerily. 'Quick, our gangway is about to float off.'

Chalice had Arden's hand tight, tugging her towards Mr Absalom, towards the iron boat, and her way home, but something felt wrong, something . . .

'This is a bloodworked storm?' Arden asked as they approached. She recalled Mr Stone's pathetic attempt at holding back a thunderstorm. This storm had the clean edges of Lyonne training.

'Is the storm that obvious?' Mr Absalom looked about himself. 'I thought it rather natural myself.'

'I can smell it. I didn't think there was a decent stormcaller on Equus.'

Mr Absalom gave a great proud smile despite his drenching. 'Mx Greenwing is from Morningvale. This is her boat that I have requisitioned, along with her blood. Welcome aboard, Lightmistress Beacon, and on behalf of the Order, welcome home.'

A smartly dressed woman in a Lyonne Seamaster's uniform nodded from the deck. She had the look of a sanguinem, down to the gloves and the exhausted expression of letting too much blood go.

Arden dug her heels in. 'Wait. No. Where's Mr Riven?'

'Inside. Come. He cannot show his face on this island.' Mr Absalom now spoke with a touch of irritation. His impatience only compounded Arden's hesitation. Surely he could spend a few seconds alleviating her worries?

'If I don't see him – I'm concerned, Mr Absalom. I don't know who to trust.'

Mr Absalom nodded. 'I understand. I'll have him come out. Only for a moment, mind – he still suffered a great deal in the hands of his wife, and he does not like the open air.'

He signalled to another man on the deck. The rain fell harder, hurting her, the storm fighting with Arden's natural lightkeeper abilities, making her eyesight falter, her danger-sense overflow.

Someone said Arden's name. In the gloom, a figure stepped from the ship's low doorway. Her name said again in a Fiction accent softened by Lyonne vowels. He wore a coat of bronze krakenskin, darkly metallic in the rain, rimed in blue.

A coat torn below the shoulder, where a crossbow bolt had gone through.

The coat Jonah had been wearing when he'd had it torn off him upon *Sehnsucht* . . .

Dizzy, she said, 'Jonah?'

The figure spoke again. 'Arden. Come inside please.'

He beckoned her towards him.

Just a little way. Up the gangplank . . . that's all she had to do . . .

Then stopped as her foot touched the gangplank. A wave of doubt. She backed up onto the dock.

'Strange . . .' she found herself saying. 'I never heard of a stormcaller called Mx Greenwing in Morningvale.'

Mr Absalom stilled. 'She has strayed from the Order and works freelance.'

'Nobody strays far from the Order. Chalice, this doesn't feel right.'

Chalice did not even have time to protest her innocence, for everything happened all at once. A pair of hands threw themselves around Arden's shoulders, pinning her hard and lifting her feet so she kicked only air.

In a jumble of arms and limbs and breaths the so-called *Mr Riven* came at a run down the gangplank . . .

. . . it wasn't Mr Riven, but a stranger wearing Mr Riven's

coat. Arden lashed out with her foot, landing squarely on the inside of his thigh, folded him over with a *hoof* of pain.

The commotion drew out the locals, locals who had not left Lyonne on the best of terms and were touchy about foreigners making a drama of their docks. Mr Absalom whistled to his cronies. 'Quick, release the hawsers!'

Arden wedged her boot hard into a bollard. 'Put . . . me . . . down . . .'

Only by sheer luck did her thrashing connect the back of her head with a too-close nose. A crunch and shout of agony, and her captor flung her upon the cobbles with such rage it winded her.

Another ruffian darted behind Arden's back, to snatch her shoulders. He kept a firm grip on her arm.

Chalice ran to Arden, her traitorous face going double and triple in Arden's vision. She seized up Arden's hands at once, endured being slapped away, and pulled them up again.

'You're dying, Arden. Dying from the coins in your hands! Please get on the boat!'

'And you're despicable, Chalice Quarry!'

Face a ghostly circle surrounded by dark oilskin. Face pale with distress and grief and yes, even stubbornness.

'Arden,' Chalice implored, close to tears. 'Come with us now and survive this.'

She was imprisoned. She had lost. No Jonah. No *Saudade* funeral boat or Deepwater prayer. No sacrifice, only an empty few days on this cursed island where she had achieved nothing.

Was my fault I trusted a Lion again, Chalice. Was my fault for being that fool again.

Mr Absalom waved off the concerned bystanders, and stood next to the two men Arden had disabled. He raised an eyebrow in appreciation at the damage she had wrought, even though Arden would have rather spat at him than take his compliment.

He gestured for her captor to release Arden a little, then nudged the fallen Riven-impostor with his toe.

'Sorry, Enoch.' He spoke to the man in Jonah's coat. 'That

coat belongs to the lady. I have to give her some recompense for her feelings at this moment. Take it off.'

The man cursed, and once on his feet was glad to rid himself of the bronze leather.

Mr Absalom folded it over his arm and offered it to Arden with a gesture of apology.

Arden glared at him before snatching the coat. 'May the devils eat your liver, Mr Absalom.'

'Please don't think too badly of me,' Mr Absalom said. 'As it is always, I am under greater instruction.'

She darted a loathing glance at the weeping Chalice.

'So, since I am a prisoner, why doesn't one of you tell me the truth. What did happen to Jonah Riven after I left him on *Sehnsucht*?'

Mr Absalom shrugged, though not dismissively. Regret in those broad, noble features of his, one could almost believe he'd actually wished the best for them.

'Jonah still took breath when I left Maris two days ago, and that I can confirm. But he was not long for the world.'

Arden's lungs were squeezed with invisible fists. 'What does that mean? Is he alive or dead now?'

'I left him in chains upon the main island of Maris and Bellis was building a pyre for him. A flaming execution to the sea. Two days ago. He has been in her captivity for almost a full season, and she has taken her revenge all that time.'

Arden swallowed the bile in her throat, the anger that tasted like blood and metal. 'He was alive, and you left him there!'

'Believe me, Bellis would have put *me* on that pyre just as quickly. There was nothing I could have done. My duty was over.'

'If I'd been told earlier I could have saved him! I could have taken my boat straight to Maris and saved him!'

'Would have made it worse. All your *evalescendi* talent can do is make Bellis Harrow stronger in her own bloodwork . . . and her madness. You know this to be true, Arden Beacon. This journey of yours was only ever a grieving woman's folly.'

Arden shook her head. 'No. No, you can say all the words, but nobody saw Jonah die, there's still a chance—'

Chalice, fretting, stepped as close as she could. 'It's too late now, darling, think of your own life.'

Arden recoiled from her touch.

'Get away from me. Maybe I couldn't have rescued him myself. But *you* Lions could have! All this time, you could have!'

Chalice retreated, wrapped her arms about herself. Enoch grabbed Arden's arms from behind, and would not let her go.

'Come, Mx Beacon, there is no time for despair,' Mr Absalom said over the storm, his voice warm with an infinite, grotesque kindness. 'Even the Lyonne Order could never have helped him then, or now. Where would we find men immune to Bellis' powers here, or boats fast enough to outrun her *Sehnsucht*? This place is death. Come back to *life*, my child. When you are well and if revenge still haunts you, find a powerful enough patron to fight a Queen and her army. Hire mercenaries with the money you earn in Lyonne. Conduct your business of retaliation. Raze Maris into the ocean, if need be. By God, raze all the islands if you must. Right now there is only—'

Before Mr Absalom could finish his speech, a flash of silver barged into Arden, sending both her and her captor sprawling across the slimed basalt cobblestones.

'*Argh! Devilment, get it off!*'

Enoch writhed on the ground as the devilfish savaged him. Arden threw up her arms uselessly against the flailing fin-feet as they clawed their way over her prone body to get to Enoch. Somewhere, Chalice shrieked. A rifle fired, once, twice, stopped with another scream.

Flood-monsters. They would eat her. Any second, and those teeth would sink into an arm, a shoulder. Any second . . .

One of the monster-fish peeled a ribbon of skin off the screaming Enoch, then slithered over to Arden as she curled on the slimy stones with only a pair of krakenskin coats for protection.

Her heart stopped beating, or at least, what else could she

feel other than this high, singing paralysis, her blood crowding in her veins like so much cement? The monster-fish's jaw was so close to her face she could see the bloodless fronds of human meat between its crystal teeth.

The flat, dished head swayed from side to side, smelling, smelling. Enoch's skin slapped crimson upon the kraken bronze.

But not seeing. Just like the impaled fish in Lord Abaddon's foyer, the creature was oblivious to krakenskin. The fish-monsters could not see past the leather. She might have been a hole in the centre of the world as far as the creature was concerned.

A million miles away someone called her name.

The rain was back again, sleets upon sleets. The boat fretted against the dock. The sanguis captain screamed for them to get back on board. A wave of broken aqueduct holdings fanned out muddy water across the docks.

When you are well and if revenge still haunts you, find a powerful enough patron to fight a Queen and her army.

When she was well. She would never be well. They would keep her in a state of grieving forever if they could.

In the watery world more of the ghastly menagerie of the aqueduct crawled their way onto the wharf, hungry for meat. The petrochemical stink rose up, choking her. She pulled herself up from the slimy puddle, Mr Riven's coat wrapped about her like a caul of invisibility.

Chalice was crying out in the rain. '*Arden. Arden, oh my darling, come back!*'

Behind Arden lay darkness. She had imagined grief a pain. It was only an absence. As if her chest had been hollowed out. The *aequor profundum* in her blood bound her to no-one and nothing.

She turned away from the harbour and walked into the rain, out of the dock streets and towards the ancient boulevard that followed the flooded river, her dress tattered, her coat sodden with a man's blood.

Mr Absalom shouted behind her, 'There's nothing out there,

Arden Beacon! Nothing! You walk into the wastelands and you'll be bones come out the other side . . .'

It didn't matter where her orient was. Only an instinct that the long river would lead through the calamitous settlement and out of Burden Town. The thread of her blood sang to her, a hot scarlet thread intermingled with poison, pulling her towards Jonah Riven, ghost and demon. The ties that bound her wended their way down into the underworld and into the ocean, and it was where she must go, yes, she thought, yes, to the northern ocean at the edge of the world, and his funeral. His. Her own.

This place is death.

In the background a song that she would close off in her eyes and heart.

Oh Arden, Arden, come back . . .

Book Two: Maris

THREE DAYS BEFORE THE STORM

12

Three Days Earlier

In her limestone office in the highest tower of Maris, Queen Bellis Harrow-Riven held a glass to her lips but did not drink. A tea-flower bloomed in the amber water, opening from a hard leafy knot to a thistle-bloom of violet and blue.

On the back of her pale, powdery neck was a black chevron, the shape of a fish scale, or a tooth. A marriage tattoo, the mark she'd been given when she aligned herself to Jonah Riven. The marriage which had saved her life.

Ozymandias Absalom stood behind her, rocked back on his heels and waited for instruction. The monarch of the Sainted Isles stood both shabby and resplendent in a seed-pearl and lace wedding dress. The musty dress was ten seasons old and at least three sizes too large for her, an engineering miracle puffed up with steel hoops and plesiosaur bone that was forever in danger of catastrophic collapse.

Over the Queen's shoulder a bull's-eye glass window let in some light but was impossible to see out of. Each insert was crazed from both the milky afternoon light and the constant acidic etch of the sulphurous atmosphere.

Maris Island, the southernmost of the Sainted archipelago, was the tip of a still-active volcano and on the constant verge of eruption. Like the Queen who had made the small steaming rock her home, it bubbled and complained but never quite boiled over.

That time was coming to an end, Absalom thought. There had been too many seismic rumblings from his monarch to ignore what was about to happen.

Only three inserts were missing in the window, enough to give Absalom a slice of sky and pale, dusty courtyard. Down in the fortress yard the prodigal husband swung a hammer upon an iron wedge into a slab of yellow rock the size of an ox-wagon.

From the moment she had brought Jonah Riven here, Bellis had put the man to work. Over the course of a season the sea had slipped from his lean body, the forced labour binding him in a casement of flesh and muscle, anchoring him to the yellow ash of Maris.

'How many people are under my command now, Mr Absalom?'

'By my latest census, just shy of two thousand, nine hundred and eighty souls, Your Majesty.'

'Quite a lot, for this place.'

'It is.'

'Did you know when I first came to the islands, I could rouse barely a fifth of this army, and then only for a little while? I first went to Equus, such an industrious place. But my loving people on Equus soon lost their sense of direction. I could not hold them. They were lost to me. Then they turned on me.'

With a toss of her head she swallowed the boiling water, tea leaves and all.

'Was the brute Miah Anguis who gave me this scar.'

Bellis pulled down the high neckline of her dress, showed Absalom where the pink jag across her throat ended, the scar puckered from stitches that had gone in hurriedly. Though Bellis had never spoken much of her first failed excursion to the Sainted Isles, it was oft whispered as to who had cast her out. A man on the northern beaches called Miah Anguis, a figure well known among the Libro Islanders and the fishermen. He had cut Bellis' throat with a hunter's precision – not deep enough to kill her, but enough to teach her a lesson about who was the true power on Equus.

As for the clumsy stitches, new-married Jonah Riven would have threaded her wound himself, not knowing how he'd chanced his own fate by keeping her alive. Still halfway in love with her even then.

'Yes. During your first forays into magnificence, the deepwater folk abducted your royal person. Jonah came to the rescue, wedded you in the old ways so the folk could do no harm. Jonah took you home a Deepwater Bride. You owe him the life Miah Anguis was seconds off taking. Bellis, if I can suggest an opinion, I believe he doesn't deserve this torment that you impress—'

Bellis whirled on him. 'You call me *Your Majesty*! I'm the fucking *Queen*! Jonah was supposed to stay away. I'd almost made a proper legend out of him before he came back and scattered everything I'd built like a house of fucking cards!'

The room turned silent, save for the sound of water on windows. Bellis whirled back to the window and glared down into the courtyard.

'That Lyonnian *cunt*. What did she do with him, do you think?'

No question of who Bellis meant. The woman. Arden Beacon. Her part remained a puzzle to Absalom. Last summer the Order had used a young woman to rile up Riven's buried affections. She was attractive enough in an old-family Lyonnian way and Riven must have been a man desperately alone. Yet any pretty girl could have effected a seduction. The Order had instead sent along a *sanguis evalescendi* to grind Riven's gears, thrown chaos into the mix. Such an action was more than just them rattling the bars of Bellis' island cage. If the Order had brought two people together like that then they intended an *outcome*.

Though what that outcome was, Absalom was at a loss to figure out.

Under Bellis' acid stare, Absalom shrugged helplessly. 'I'm not sure I can speak of their suggested intimacies without causing offence . . .'

'Then just say it, fool. I see you talk to him in the yard. Does he talk about the slut who rutted and fornicated with my husband? Were they clothed, or unclothed, fucking like animals? How many times? Did he spend himself inside her? Does he think of her in the night and pleasure himself when he does?'

Absalom rocked back on his heels again.

'I would not presume to know what your husband thinks of her. My desires have never included the female kind.'

'Can you not *guess*, you pompous shit? I've had you among the work-crews for long enough. Or must I shackle you in the barracks so you have your ear next to Jonah's adulterous mouth?' She turned back to him, a small blood-bright flush appearing in her pale, waxy cheeks. 'Oh, that would be pleasing, wouldn't it? I see the way you look at my husband, the lust unbridled upon your high-born face.'

Bellis was working herself up for something outrageous. With a survivor's instincts Absalom could sense her escalation. His hand went automatically to his side, where once he had kept a gold pocket-watch in his vest, which he liked to rub for good luck. The watch had long gone, a barter for the small, sharp axe head that had taken its place. His insurance policy, if things with Bellis became too complicated.

Under the Lyonne Order's instruction, Ozymandias Absalom had been Bellis' sergeant-at-arms for the better part of four years. He doubted he would see a fifth.

'Those creatures down in the work yard,' Bellis went on. 'They are aware, are they not, of how my husband so easily discarded our marriage vows? And if *our* vows can be discarded, then *their* vows to *me* can be discarded!'

It is not vows that keep them tied, but your orientis *illusions,* Absalom considered saying, then wisely considered otherwise.

'That *woman*. She's behind this, I can feel her presence like an *itch* that won't go away, Absalom! She should be *dead* and I can *feel* her!'

He stood at attention as Bellis paced the room, voiced more discontent, about the weather, about the slovenliness of the guards, about the dreams that had risen and extinguished upon the day of her test moot, eighteen years ago, when the testers had spotted something – rockblood, they said – then discarded her back upon the shores of Vigil instead of taking her into the bosom of Clay Capital.

The sequins on her wedding dress fell off piecemeal, left fish-scale flecks on the grey stone. The two other servants in the stone office apart from Absalom cringed by the doorway.

And then she stopped abruptly in front of the bull's-eye window.

Down in the court, Riven had stood up from smashing a block of stone down into component dust, ignoring an overseer's yell. His back gleamed with sweat in the intermittent slices of afternoon sun, work-swelled musculature ridged and corrugated under his tattooed skin. It did not suit him, to appear so land-locked. On his arrival here he had for a few days even refused to eat – until Bellis made the guards force-feed him as one would a goose bound for the dinner table.

Her breath steamed against the glass. 'Does my husband seem tired?'

Absalom let out a relieved breath. He would not experience Bellis' anger today. That ire belonged to Riven.

'Yes, my Queen. The man appears weary.'

'I wish to spend time with him.'

Before Absalom could respond, Bellis whirled out of the room in a storm of tatty white lace, her scuttling servants trailing her the way woodlice might move after the shade given by a rock.

He had barely made to follow when a brief whistle interrupted him. One of the war-tapestries moved slightly.

Absalom paused, stepped back. The tapestries had been 'liberated' from Libro Island, when Bellis had first come upon them with her nascent army. They hung in her offices as testament to her power, though the drapes were old and decorated with old-time deeds. He looked a little closer. One frayed manticore fighting with a unicorn had a definite human shape behind it.

Absalom laughed without humour.

'Best get moving, Wren. Bellis will be wanting her assistant in wifely duties or else someone's face will be cut to match the other side.'

The little Libran moved out from her hiding place. Her oiled black hair and saffron dress were covered in cobwebs and moth-dust. Her broad, pretty face was marred only by a weal upon her right cheek, the same size and direction as one would have if given a backhanded slap from someone wearing the sharp steel wedding rings of a Deepwater Queen. The Libran girl had a cursed knack of appearing in the most advantageous and illicit places, catching her small flies of information, binding them up in her own secret webs. The Queen should have given her the name *Ariadne*, not *Persephone*, but Bellis never thought long about her re-namings.

'Oh, it will take some time for the turnkeys to drag him out of the yard,' Wren-not-Persephone said. 'Jonah never lets himself get *that* tired.'

'Oh, *Jonah* is it?'

'We have a relationship, him and me,' she said. 'I am with him during his debasement, I watch him when he sleeps and cries out for his lost family, and for *the woman*.' Wren stepped to one roughly hewn limestone shelf and pulled down a small, greasy jadeite chest. She tucked the box under her arm.

'How long were you hidden in the curtains, anyway?'

She shrugged. 'Most of the morning. Why?'

He sighed. 'Can I ask your opinion and have you be honest about it? One penitent to another.'

'As long as it won't cost me my head, I shall be honest.'

Absalom touched his axe-head pocket, and noticed how Wren followed the movement with her eyes. Though he had never told her, he was under no illusion that she was unaware of his concealed blade.

'Has Bellis been odd of late? Out of sorts?'

Wren tilted her head to the side. 'Bellis is always preoccupied,' she said. 'Her *orientine* blood whispers to her like a dissatisfied lover. She knows she could do more with her endowments, but she's trapped here. All she could conquer, she has conquered.

There are no more cities to burn except the one in Burden Town, which she cannot attempt again.'

'She's made a grudging peace with that prohibition, I think. No, I'm talking about her mood since her husband has been back. Do you think it's changed?'

Wren pressed her tongue against a chipped tooth. 'Maybe. She hasn't been visiting these offices so much. She stays in her rooms and sulks over books she cannot read. Why?'

'I'm hoping we need no more concern in our lives, that is all.'

Wren peered at Absalom. She knew Absalom never made small-talk. 'Is there a problem, Ozzy? This behaviour isn't like you either.'

She was right. Most of the time they existed in a semi-antagonistic relationship of odd mutual conveniences. Wren Halcyon Libro was a handmaid and a prisoner of war, whereas Absalom was here voluntarily, and a spy.

He decided to let out a little of his concern. '*Sanguis orientis* needs a mythology, a big idea to use as its influence. Bellis has been coasting on the sails of having a monstrous husband waiting in the wings and instilling a reign of terror since the day she was married. Now that he's shown up all mortal, her illusion cannot hold. Therefore her reign cannot hold. I fear she might do something drastic to re-establish her authority.'

'Like what?'

'I'm not sure yet. Our Queen has never been the easiest of subjects to pin down.'

They were interrupted by one of the servants dashing back into the room, his face sweaty from running and anxiety. He saw Wren with a panting relief. 'The Queen needs you, Persephone Libro.'

'I will be there, friend. Go and tell her I am preparing.' Wren moved to a stone shelf, and pulled down a small chest of acacia wood. She lifted the lid, and sniffed the opalescent grease inside it. Sea-serpent oil, a pungent mix of cryptid monster glands and soft paraffin.

Wren turned to Absalom once the servant had fled. 'So, shall we be of erotic assistance to our beloved Majesty and her husband in the meantime, then? If she has a secret upset, then let neither you nor I be the cause of it.'

How proper Wren made this despicable ritual seem, while at the same time the distaste dripped from each word. Mr Absalom joined her in their moral dejection.

'Let's.'

He slid his hand through her thin, saffron elbow.

As they descended the tower, their view alternated between distant ocean and sinking prison yard. A few corpses rotted upon the old steam-shovel gears. The real entertainment was the successive views of Jonah Riven being set upon by Bellis' guards, and him not going quietly. He gave a good fight, but in the end he was a lone man in chains, and there were four guards, and that was that.

They emerged from a short section of sea-cave and onto the slimed rock of the ocean's edge.

Bellis loved this part of Maris the most. Old volcanic activity had created blisters and pavements of dark granite about the long shore. The tide lay at its furthest point, an aching distance away. Sulphur fumes slunk across from white-crusted rents in the ground.

Behind them were the jagged mountain remains of the Maris caldera's last eruption of a century before, curved about like a natural amphitheatre. Bellis sucked in the poisonous fumes, deep, deep. Her yellow-white dress faded into that fog, as if she too were a spirit come out of the smouldering ground.

Then Jonah Riven, blinded with a rag and naked as he was on the day of his birth, arrived in shackles. Any other man might have been pitiful in such abjection, but he only radiated such danger from his bared, bloody teeth and sweat-trembling flanks that he might have been clothed in splendour. Her only concessions to mercy were the old, unlaced boots he wore, for this ground would cut a man's feet to shreds were he to walk on it without shoes.

Then Riven stopped struggling, and dipped his head, his other senses alerting him to dangers. What did he hear? The hiss of the waves out of his reach? The crunching of those few dozen footsteps meant to witness this indignity, as the stone flakes shattered under boot soles? The rock that was Riven's punishment faced away from the ocean. It was sharply ridged so that a bound man could not lean easily against its surface. This was the rock he was shackled to by hoops of rusted iron.

Bellis beheld her husband with a carrion-eater's countenance and had one of her guards take off his blindfold.

There had been a time when he had cursed her face. Today he only considered her without emotion, as if she too were a rock.

'Who do you love?'

He swallowed, trying to speak, not managing so well. A guard had been too rough, had throttled his already-damaged throat.

'Who? Who, Jonah, speak if you have any manhood left?'

'You,' rasped the voice from his bloodied mouth.

She pressed her bony palms to his sweat-slaked chest, before laying her ear upon his sternum. 'Your heart beats fast, husband.'

Bellis jutted her chin towards Wren. The Libro stepped forward with her box of cold ointment. Bellis flicked off the lid and took a violet handful. Used the unguent to touch him in a way that would be pleasing, were they lovers in a secret grotto and not players in a degrading theatre in front of several witnesses.

'When the Redeemer of Lyonne came to the Sainted Isles,' she murmured through her caresses, 'the Islanders were not grateful to receive His wisdom. Their ears were blocked, their hearts chained. Their god was the Deepwater King, and they would suffer no interloper. They tied the Redeemer to a rock like this one and let the ocean take Him.'

A cold wind blew in from the water. Wren turned anxiously to Absalom. Bellis had been content to bind and caress her husband like this, but she had never before invoked the symbolism of the Lyonnian god and His inglorious end, killed by Islanders a thousand years ago.

Interesting, Absalom thought. *It appears our Deepwater Wife is beginning to yearn for her childhood religion.*

He surveyed the gathering to this rite of thwarted, malignant love. With the rock at the focus, ten men stood in a semicircle of attention several paces away.

Nine of them were familiar faces, old-time shorefolk of Bellis' first successful incursion. The tenth was Leyland Tallwater, the patriarch of the little Hillsider family Bellis had recovered on *Sehnsucht* prior to Bellis' husband turning up.

Mr Tallwater had thoroughly ingratiated himself among the Marians. He wore a crimson sash of a senior officer upon his left arm. Where others glanced aside from Bellis' intimacies, Leyland sneered at the man on the rock. A remnant, inexplicable hatred moved across his gaunt Hillsider face. His wispy yellow hair lay flat in the squally breeze.

Bellis closed her eyes, not finished. 'Yet even after the tide swallowed Him, God let the Redeemer live,' she murmured. 'He was still alive when the water receded.'

When she opened her eyes again, they quickly became narrow. Something had changed in her husband's demeanour. Riven had developed a vacancy in his expression; there was no vigour to him, no returning of love.

Not that he'd shown much before, but he had fought her touch once and cursed her loudly, daring Bellis to kill him and send him back to the Deepwater King. Now nothing, not even acknowledgement. She pressed her face up to his, and there was such a difference in their heights, her head could not clear his chest.

'You wish that I leave you here until the ocean swallows you? I will give you no watery escape. I should have had you *burned*.'

She turned about so he could not see her face, glared at her ten servants, daring them to speak. 'What say you all? Shall we burn him? Speak to me, fools!'

Absalom, immediately to one side of the shackling rock, saw what the distracted guards did not. Riven's fist clenching inside a rusted hoop of metal that was not tight enough to enclose him securely, the knuckles popping white against his scarred, work-abraded skin.

As quick as he could, Absalom reached up, grabbed Riven's wrist and pressed it to the sharp rock. 'Wait!'

Then Riven's terrible gaze was upon him, if something had looked up from the abyss in cold rage and seen Absalom's face.

He almost let go. No *man* had looked at him just now. No *human*.

'*You strike her, and she will do what she promises*,' Absalom signed with his free hand. Harbinger convict-talk, that secret sign language of the penitentiary. Riven would understand it, having spent the better part of his life there. '*Calm down*.'

Riven glared at him still, but as a man this time, and a man who obeyed. Bellis had not moved from where she had taken to scolding her entourage.

Still shaken, Absalom said to the others, 'Time to bind up our prisoner, lads. He has done his duty for today.'

The guards shackled Riven up again, and Mr Absalom hid a sneer behind his hand, for these tough men were all a-flutter over the ignominy of the act, too empathetic, too scared. They would have been happier chopping heads from necks and burning men alive than watching this. Why could Bellis not have crucified Riven on the lava blisters and be done with it?

'Get him out of my sight,' Bellis said, her cheeks flushed with pink anger. 'Have him beaten. I want him screaming when he goes in his cell.'

Riven's attention only faded, as if his mind were unmoored and somewhere in the clouds.

Bellis picked up the ridiculous train of her wedding-dress uniform herself and stomped back towards the sea-cave. Wren ran behind, the watchers scattered, and once more Mr Absalom found himself the last man standing on the pavements.

Alone, except for one of the town women.

She was a short, delicate little madam clothed in ragfish leather. She came to Mr Absalom's side, folded her arms against her shallow bosom and spoke.

'Curious that the Queen should be upset. Her husband finally does the very thing she wanted of him, attained the stone countenance of the Clay Redeemer.'

It was not that the voice was male, for this was not a place of usual social graces and dress. The accent made Absalom pay attention. Pure Lyonne.

Mr Absalom pressed his lips together and took a moment to still that first flush of unbidden anger before turning to the *woman*.

'I'd have thought the Order would let me do my business here independently.'

'Well, the Order never lets anyone stray far from their sight. As you are aware.'

'Good afternoon too, Mr Lindsay.'

'And to you, Mr Absalom.'

The last Absalom had heard of his fellow Lion was of Mr Lindsay's appointment to Vigil, and the managing of the Harrow-Riven problem from the mainland. It was not altogether a welcome sight, seeing a high-ranking Order member here in Maris. One spy was bad enough, but two suggested that his superiors had lost their faith in Ozymandias Absalom.

'That is a lovely outfit, Mr Lindsay.'

'I try my best. One gets away with a lot more when one wears a dress.'

Mr Absalom squinted at him. 'Why is my door being darkened, Brother Lion? Let me guess. It's not about Riven because he is back with his wife and is no longer a concern. And Bellis Harrow is *my* assignment. The Pride would not be so bold as to replace me without warning. The only other obligation left is Mx Beacon. The *sanguis evalescendi* that Bellis found so curious. She really is alive, isn't she?'

Mr Lindsay inspected his cuticles, bore an expression of disagreeableness. 'Yes. Our colleague Miss Quarry was exemplary in her chaperone duty. There will be a medal at the end of this for her, if she keeps up the good work.'

'At the end of all this. Meaning that it is not ended, is it?

I saw it on *Sehnsucht*, the look in that woman's eyes. She was fond of the man. I doubt she would have so easily slid back to her Clay Portside gin-halls like a nice obedient girl once it was all over?'

'Hmm,' Mr Lindsay mused, and Mr Absalom deduced all he needed from the sulky silence. Bellis had not been wrong in her obsessions over Riven's lover at all. Lindsay would only come out here because a client was close by. A Lyonnian sanguinem could only make it to the Sainted Isles by either order or evasion, and Mr Lindsay would never order Arden too far out of his reach.

'So what happened? Has she slipped her leash the way Bellis did? This is twice you've let an asset out of your sight now, brother.'

Mr Lindsay sucked in a barely controlled breath. 'She is not out of my sight. We know where she is, and I have had new orders telegraphed to me from the Clay office.'

Mr Lindsay slid a finger into his bosom, brought out a medallion of the Order, the coin of instruction.

'She is travelling to Equus as we speak.'

'Equus? How will she survive there? I thought we burned that bridge with our agents long ago.'

'We left a bridge open. For extreme circumstances. By tomorrow they will have made contact.'

Though Absalom was careful to show no strong emotion towards Mr Lindsay, the twinge of annoyance was real. A bridge. Their one precious contact in Equus. The librarian Lord Abaddon would give her shelter. Good Order men had died in Equus seeking safety, but they had never been permitted to darken the house of the Lord. What was this woman to win such a lifeline?

'Take this instruction,' Mr Lindsay said as he held out the coin. 'Go to Equus tonight. Tomorrow, make contact with her and escort her off the island. Bring her back to Clay City.'

Absalom sucked his teeth. 'But what of my work here? I'm Bellis Harrow's only trusted insider.'

'Bellis has become too much of a liability. Right now she thinks only of ruling the Islands, but one day, she will think of lands beyond, and to the north. Can you imagine her in Lyonne? In Clay? No, I will deal with her in my own way, but for now the task before you go is to *remove* Mr Riven. He causes her grief, and a grieving Bellis is an erratic one who may be encouraged into action long before we are ready to manage her.'

'Remove? You mean kill him.'

'Remove is remove. I don't care how you do it.'

'Lindsay, the cost is too high. There are *hostages* involved.'

'Then work around the *bloody* cost and the *bloody* hostages.'

Mr Absalom took the medallion. The inscriptions on the gold surface were worn under his fingertips. Many instructions had been given under its command. Easily worse ones than these.

Remove him.

Absalom sighed in defeat. 'I will do what the Order requires.'

'Good. Come into town afterwards,' Mr Lindsay said. 'Find me in the Ivy House.'

'A brothel. How appropriate.'

'The Order shares the same saint-patron as the night people. Ours is a common profession.' Mr Lindsay smiled tightly. 'Good day.'

Absalom stood caressing the medal as Mr Lindsay moved off the pavements. Poor Jonah Riven. Such an ignominious end.

Burdened by duty, he put the coin in his coat pocket. No sooner had he straightened himself to return to the stone offices than another voice spoke.

'Oh, so that explains my suspicions about you, Ozzy.'

Mr Absalom startled, and whirled on Wren. 'You mendacious—'

She stepped out from behind the binding-rock and fluttered her saffron robes. 'How did I fool you twice?'

He reached for the axe head and pulled it from his waistcoat. '*Twice* is a harsh word if there are no witnesses around to hear it.'

She leapt aside, out of reach of his blade-arm before casting her eyes over the pavement. 'I didn't know Ozymandias Absalom had a woman from Lyonne. Such a tough little thing with a pretty face. Such strong features, and a husky voice. Did not think a woman whetted my friend's taste.'

He did not rise to the bait. Palmed the axe head, then with a sigh slid it back into its hidden place. 'Will I regret this overhearing of my business, Wren?'

Her expression became solemn as she gestured to where Mr Lindsay's path had taken him. Down into that roil of sordid vice that called itself a town. 'Few men have the privilege of one master, Mr Absalom. I understand this, I do. But I couldn't help overhear. Are you leaving us? With an instruction to kill Jonah before then?'

'I have been commanded utterly, Wren,' Mr Absalom said. 'I can make it quick for him, quicker than Bellis would.'

'But the *children*.'

For the most brief and unwelcome time a wrenching guilt filled him. The children. Easily one hundred Libro children, from babes to almost-adult, taken from the shores of the northern island as collateral against last-gasp Libran heroics. Later they became the blackmail Bellis had used against Riven on the night he had first come to Maris, bleeding and beaten. She'd gathered the children on the pier and said to him: *if you attempt to leave me, husband, by escape or by a knife to your throat, all these children will join you at the bottom of the ocean.*

He reached out and touched her cold cheek. 'Come with me when I go, Wren Libro. There is a place for you in Clay. The Order could use someone with your skill.'

'I cannot,' she replied with true regret.

'You were forced into enslavement. You owe nothing to either Bellis or any of the people who remain on Libro. They gave up their children willingly, ran away to save their own hides.'

'I made a promise to my mother, Ozzy. A promise to the court of Libro in front of everyone I have ever loved, to bring them all home.'

'There is no home for them left. Libro will soon be forgotten and slide beneath the waves of memory.'

The tide drifted in, each wave sending creeping foam fingers over the lava blisters.

'When?'

'Tonight. After she has her opium tea. Come with me. Back to Lyonne.'

Wren stood back. Her little bird-eyes fell on him, black and accusing, before she gave a shrug and fingered the weal on her cheek. Certainly, Wren could tell Bellis about this plan of Absalom's, but then she would be in harm's way too.

'Oh, all right then. I have grown tired of this place anyway. Where shall we meet?'

He let out a breath, glad that she had agreed to come. The Order would find a place for a girl so good at sneaking around. If she kept out of mischief for another twelve hours, she could at last be free.

'I won't see Bellis until midnight, Wren. Then I must lay my traps and be gone. There is an iron boat in the Maris docks crewed by Fiction men and a captain called Mx Greenwing.'

'Then I will be at the docks after midnight.'

'Don't be late, I cannot stay.'

Wren turned to go. Absalom hailed her once more. 'A word of advice.'

'Speak it, Ozzy.'

'These are dangerous days. Don't do anything foolish. This plan of mine does not allow for surprises.'

'Oh,' she said, 'I have always been able to look after myself.'

And with that she was gone in a flutter of ragged saffron yellow, over the blisters and towards the yawning mouth of the sea-cave.

13

Twilight fell hard

Twilight fell hard on Maris, leaving the factory cathedral ruins in darkness. The moon had not yet risen, and the evening star gleamed small and white in the orange sky. It would pass below the horizon come the midnight hour, and then Ozymandias Absalom would pour hot tea and poppy-milk into a cup of obsidian glass, climb the high steps into Bellis' tower and convince the Queen that Jonah Riven had to die.

Wren Halcyon Libro sat in her rooftop eyrie and contemplated the scenes of the day. Wren's thoughts rarely went to her home, and for that Wren was glad. She too had been royalty, before Bellis and her hundred ships and her thousand love-mad servants stormed their saltwater parliament. It was Mr Tawfik, the armada captain, who had placed her mother's neck against the barrel of a blunderbuss loaded with broken glass. He had given a sincere apology as he did so. Bellis was the one who had given the order.

Wren went upon her knees before Bellis, seeing instantly in the melee of that first attack to whom she must give her respects.

My Queen, let me serve you in the name of Libro.

Bellis, pale as white topaz, looking down at her, amused that this girl had identified her out of the crowd. Bellis had come to Libro a day before her army did, secretly working her *orientis*, turning the people into automatons under her control. Nobody had noticed the interloper among them, for the stranger's Fiction-pale complexion had hardly made her stand out in an island of equally mist-hued southern folk. Wren's deduction was cunning indeed.

Clever little Libran girl. Will you not beg for the life of your mother, yellow bird?

Her teachers had always an ill word to say about Wren. Undisciplined. A shirker, eavesdropper, tart of tongue. Talked back and ignored instructions.

But never ever, not once, did they call her a fool.

A hush fell upon the subjugated hall when Wren had replied, *it will never be my place to ask for anything other than to serve.*

Voluntary submission fascinated Bellis. She was so used to coercion that consent came as a pleasant surprise. Bellis took this clever girl under her bone-white arm. *I have need of clever girls.*

In her mind Wren saw her mother and sisters weeping while Bellis' soldiers rounded up a hundred children. Wren among them. In their eyes a terrible, wordless plea. A hundred lives in her care now. A hundred responsibilities. She remembered as if it were only hours ago, her last sight of the Libro docks from the deck of *Sehnsucht*, her charges huddled about her in a sea of tears.

And her mother, succumbed to *orientis* at last, walking into the sea.

Let me be clever tonight, Wren thought to herself.

After the seasoned workers returned to their cells upon the downing of tools, Wren slid down a rusting gutter pipe and padded through the shadows. She reached the watch-house at the last blush of sunlight. One of the foreign guards worked there tonight. A Lyonnian man.

From him she received a ring of keys in exchange for a hurried act of fellatio more marked by his terror at being caught out than by his gratification in the act.

In the end he didn't climax so much as grow soft with anxiety, for even the few *orientis*-resistant northerners were caught up in the Queen's requirement of loyalty and fidelity.

'Don't tell her,' he said as he passed over the keys.

'Honestly, Gregor,' Wren said, wiping the vinegar of him from her mouth. 'Do I look like I have the time to entertain such a complication as the Queen's wrath?'

His fingers fumbled on the trouser-button. 'I just feel like I . . . I can't, any more? This. My vigour is gone. I can't even lie with my wife when we are given that dispensation. Helena thinks my affections are elsewhere.'

Wren clucked sympathetically. 'Your affections *are* elsewhere. Everyone's are.' She glanced meaningfully at the Queen's tower.

'It worries me what she does to *him*. It's not natural.'

'No, it's not. And you know what they say, all unnatural things meet their comeuppance sooner or later. Nature abhors such abominations.'

She prepared to leave, then Gregor said, 'Wren?'

'Yes?'

'Just ask for the keys next time.'

She returned to pat his face. 'My dear Gregor Tallwater, that would mean I would owe a favour, that I am *beholden*. A debt is a terrible thing to carry.' She motioned at his crotch. 'In this way, our act is an exchange of services as clean and without obligation as possible.'

'Just bring the keys back. Don't run away or anything.'

'Where else can I go? Throw myself into the volcano?'

He made a face, and Wren melted into the stone shadow, leaving the Hillsider in his awkward place.

The shift had swapped over to the night watch, those men happy to read books and talk among themselves without much thought as to what went on behind the locked doors. Wren slipped into the last of the cells, a dry room that had once been occupied by an anchorite in the early century, some reclusive holy person. Unlike the communal cells stacked high with twenty wretches each, this one held a lone man.

A lamp burned in an alcove, a perpetual flame kept alive by petralactose aromas from the deep earth. There were still crumbling frescoes on the walls, saintly faces ringed by haloes. With her breath stilled, she took her place next to the low stone bed and stood over Bellis' husband.

Riven lay upon the thin straw mattress in a ghostweed doze, gold twilight on his skin only serving to deepen his tattoos into slashes of black. They'd close-cropped his hair and beard, left him no spare flesh to call up the leviathan.

Exhausted, his eyes moved under his lids, as he moved in a dream. How awkwardly put together his face was, deepwater folk and Northman, and something else she could not put her finger on. The long limbs did not quite fit on the short stone slab. The strength in him was undeniable even in sleep, hard-hewn, lain in by years. An uneaten tray of meat beside him. Wren snatched up a mutton-bird leg and gnawed it like a little beast, wiped the grease upon her thigh. Riven did not stir.

A curiosity took her.

'Let's see who ignites such dreams.'

She touched his face, said words in a passable Lyonne accent. He opened his eyes, dilated by both low light and arousal. His face soft, his eyes distant as if he were miles away. Though Wren had never had much of a yearn for anyone, male or female, she could tell that he was at his most beautiful then, a true creation of God.

Then those eyes turned to pinpricks of rage, he rolled off the stone platform in his rush to get away from her.

'Devil!' he cursed her, though it came out a croak. 'Do I not do enough that you people have to assault me in my sleep?'

'Was not me who quickened those loins,' she retorted. 'Bellis hasn't taken your hunger away from you yet.'

Riven turned away to stick his head in a bucket of water, let the water slosh over his scalp and back.

'Get to the point, Libro. I'm not in the mood for advice.'

'I came here to give more than advice,' she continued. 'You

think your bad luck revolves around Bellis and her violent court, but it is Mr Absalom who requires the most caution.'

With the remains of his shirt, he resignedly sopped the water from his head and shoulders. Wren had told him nothing new.

'We have an understanding. Ozymandias Absalom knows I am no danger to him.'

She moved closer.

'You are less than dangerous, Jonah. You are *extraneous*. You and I both know he is a spy. Absalom's Order brought you back under the wing of Bellis Harrow to control her, and instead she has become even more erratic. It's made them nervous, so you must be got rid of.'

'Get to the point, Libro.'

'Absalom has been instructed. Through the Queen he has to kill you. *Remove*, was the word, I think, but we all knew what the other spy meant.'

He shook his head wearily and discarded his shirt. 'That was always going to happen one way or another. I shall welcome it.'

Wren scoffed at him. 'Devilments, you give up so easily. The woman you committed adultery with, that Arden Beacon? She is alive.'

A great cold wind could have blown through the room at that very moment. He did not look at Wren as she spoke, but his senses surrounded her like a storm and they were huge and tumultuous. Shame, that she had no true desire for sex, because it would be magnificent to make love to this man upon this very moment, feel in his body the fracture of vulnerability and the chasm of despair. Almost enough to quicken her own stony little quim.

'Alive? Talk sense, Wren.'

'You feel her, can't you?' Wren continued. 'She is alive and has returned to the islands, maybe even looking for the man she loves. Equus, I think.'

Riven shook his head, a dark panic flaring in his face. 'No. No. Equus is the last place she should be.'

'Well, not for much longer. Absalom is about to go out and fetch her. He's leaving on a bloodworked boat before first light.'

He jerked to the end of his chain. 'What, fetch Arden for Bellis?'

'No. For his own people. To bring her home to Clay. Either way, Clay or Equus, your Lyonne girl is in a very precarious place indeed.' Wren sighed. 'As are we.'

Riven snatched up his chain, tugged the links, then paced the room back and forth, leaving wet footprints on the stone dust. In his self-absorbed state Wren didn't expect him to lunge at her. Before she could stop him, Riven had his hands around Wren's waist and reached under her skirt to tear the keys from her belt. With powerful deliberation he placed her upon his thin mattress, where she could not have easily made a dash for the door.

'Stay there,' he said, and thrust each key into the lock at his shackles. Each failed to turn.

Wren watched him struggle. Made a face and layered her saffron silks about her.

'We haven't finished our conversation.'

'Fuck your conversation.'

'I need a promise, Mr Jonah Riven, it's why I stand here, and have not hidden this key in a loaf of bread, or some other anonymous gift.'

His glare would have been fearsome. By then she had taken out another key from her slipper and had balanced it on her knee.

Riven was quick to learn. He did not lunge for the key this time, and waited for Wren to hold it out to him with her conditions.

'What promise?'

'The children,' she said despairingly. 'They must be saved.'

He rolled his head back, grimacing. She had seen him in pain so often, and this was an emotion not so very far away from it. 'No. You Librans got your children in harm's way by inviting Bellis onto your island, not me. Don't make them my business.'

Wren said, 'What else kept me here, when I could have run away a thousand times over?'

'Then do it. Give the Queen double her potion, the one that makes her sleep. Make her sleep forever.'

'And have nearly three thousand minds go mad from seeing Death? Three thousand madmen hysterical upon this island, tearing the flesh from their bodies, and each other's? I doubt I would do that even for you, Deepwater King.'

'I'm not the Deepwater—'

She held the shackle key out to him and he stopped speaking. Riven eyed it, and her, suspiciously.

'I am asking for help, Jonah. One Islander to another.'

'I'm not an Islander.'

'Those are Islander marks. The old blood is in your veins. Nobody else can steer a ship through these waters faster than any of Bellis' pets. Ten men a week try to flee these islands, and ten are caught, and tortured. I know the Queen takes a special delight in making you watch.'

'Wren . . .'

'Take it, fool. Do you want to see your lover again?'

'Damn it,' he muttered, took the other key and returned her set. 'I'm going to use this *very soon*. I can't wait for your bloody extended family.'

'Yes, because if the woman is on Equus, she is not safe.' Wren nodded. 'I know who is on that island. I know his name, and Bellis knows his name, for he once cut Bellis' throat from ear to ear and to your woman he will undoubtedly do the same.' She darted her head forward and mouthed. '*Anguis.*'

He paused, and swallowed. 'Then giving me this . . .' He thrust the key at her. 'This is not helping your people. I'm already burnt with guilt for killing my own family. I cannot live with killing yours.'

'Take the key, Jonah Riven. What have we done, every hour, every day since coming here? We have prepared ourselves for a Deepwater King to lead us off the island and home.'

A stray lance of moonlight caught his cheek and he winced. 'The title doesn't belong to me.'

'It is what it is. Please wait until I come back. I'm going to ready my people. Then we take the boat Ozymandias Absalom intended for this midnight, fit as many passengers as we can on board and go.'

Wren sidled out into the nighttime. Silence, save for the cough of the sea, the hiss of the fumaroles and their sulphurous stenches. Wren had never considered herself sensitive to the eddies of fate or the whisper of her old oceanic gods, but tonight felt them intently.

I have started something, she thought. *There is no stepping off this path.*

The corridor lay cool and empty. Even the group prisons had their moments of quiet, in the dark when men stopped cursing and instead began to sob. In her mind she mapped out the best place to get information into town, via the Libran night-soil merchant who trundled by a certain guard and could take messages.

She had not gone five paces when a body fell out of the shadows and collided with her, scrabbled for the keys she held in her hand.

The sweat of Gregor Tallwater filled her intake of breath, for how else could he have known where she was and what she held? This time she gave them up easily, for she knew enough of his scent to know his fear.

A glance shared between them, more intimate than any other. A terrible apology. Then Gregor cried out.

'Intruder! I have an intruder!'

She made to flee, and the leather of his glove tightened upon her wrist, hard. 'My friend, there was no other way,' Gregor croaked, the guilt ragged in his voice. 'It was either this or Leyland would have told Bellis . . . and she'd have killed me.'

'You told your damn father?' she hissed back at him. Leyland Tallwater, that despicable Hillsider who had risked his family and sacrificed his grandchildren, still commanding his son to jump and jig to his awful commands?

Gregor shrugged in broken surrender. 'He likes it here.'

Behind her, two other guards barged into Riven's room. The sounds of a body in rough assault, the collision of flesh and the breaking – maybe – of bone. A shout, and silence followed by choking. Then they withdrew.

One held up a key in bloodied fingers as he left the room.

'Tried to swallow it,' one said. 'Would have choked if he'd got it down.'

Wren turned to her betrayer, her heart hammering.

'How did your father find out, Gregor? Who told Leyland?'

He sighed. 'The Queen's sergeant-at-arms. Ozymandias Absalom.'

14

The guards forced Wren

The guards forced Wren to wait the rest of the night and most of the day in the cell they'd put her in. At first she had pleaded at the cell door to the Lyonnian guard charged to her first watch. 'I have things to tell Bellis,' she said. 'Important things!'

'Shut up,' the woman replied. 'The Queen will see you if she wants to, and not a moment before.'

Curses of all the sea. Without the right words from Wren to mollify her anger, Bellis' fury would overwhelm what little charity she had left in that stony heart. Absalom had fooled Wren, and she was never a fool. Given his head start, the Lyonnian spy would now be close to a day's worth of sailing away, easily within sight of the Equus Needles, if not the city of Burden Town itself.

Don't do anything foolish.

How could she have fallen so stupidly into his failsafe? Absalom might have believed Wren would run away with him, but he would not have discounted the possibility she would try to rescue Jonah Riven and the Libro children.

Our children. She closed her eyes. Heard the voice of her mother, crying even as the *orientis* took her soul away. *Take care of them, Wren. Be good for the Queen. Take care of our babies.*

I was barely more than a baby myself, Mother, when this promise was urged upon me.

Later that afternoon, she heard the clang of the warning bell.

'Who's escaped?' she asked the second guard who came to replace the first. This time Leyland Tallwater darkened her door. Gregor Tallwater's odious father, come to gloat. She could smell him, sour and envious through the bars of the cell. He had completely embraced his position among the servants of Bellis Harrow, wore Islander ink on his hands and cheek so new that the skin was still bruised from application.

'Who is it that's escaped, Leyland?' Wren repeated, firmer now.

'Not an escape,' he said. 'We're having a lament, a funeral for a King.'

'A lament?'

Leyland grinned meanly. 'The Queen has seen sense. She didn't need no King anyway. They are building the freak a pyre as we speak. He will burn up well. Those little Libran brats just the same. Then those mendicant refugees can love the Queen with their hearts unencumbered with fretting over their spawn.'

She pressed her face to the bars. Hissed the words. 'Mr Tallwater, consider that such an execution would be unwise given that Riven is worshipped among the armada. Bellis has trained them well to believe in such things as abyssal kings. Killing one in front of them may be enough to break any enchantment.'

He studied Wren, suspended between triumph and disgust. 'You have been too long in these walls, harlot. Even I'm more Islander than you. Tonight is the Night of the Serpent. Tonight a King may die and they will forgive it.'

Leyland closed his eyes, already in raptures just thinking of the event. The sour smell remained even when he left the cell window.

Once footsteps had faded, Wren retreated to the corner of

the stone room and wrapped her arms about her knees, suddenly trembling with an unholy chill. Leyland had not lied. This was the Deepwater season. This was the time when a death could be forgiven.

Despite her situation Wren slept, albeit fitfully, and in the late evening was roused up. This time Gregor, Leyland's son, had come to deliver the orders. A taunt from Bellis, sending the man who'd betrayed Wren.

'She will see you now,' Gregor said.

Did Bellis ever sleep? Was she ever not adorned in the garb of the bride, perpetually in those final hours before the dress was torn from her upon the wedding night and her abyssal groom appeared?

Behind her the Lyonne Redeemer died naked and chained upon His rocky wall, forever waiting for the tide to drown Him and the monster who would devour Him.

The bas-relief was a remnant of the old cloister built by missionaries upon Maris before the buildings had been repurposed into an industrial dormitory. Bellis had not removed the icon from her wall, perhaps delighting in the artist's ability to carve true suffering from the wood.

'My father had this very same icon in his church,' Bellis said. 'The Redeemer would look down upon me as I said my prayers each night.' Bellis picked up a stiletto of silver from the stone desk, pressed the tip to each finger-pad. 'I have prayed to him tonight, for the first time in many years.'

'And what did you pray of, my Queen?'

'You,' she said. 'My darling Persephone, I asked God if you really did what Mr Tallwater accuses you of.'

'And what is it the senior Tallwater says I did?'

'He says you visit my husband for *trysts*.'

'Leyland Tallwater is a false witness,' Wren said. 'He'd tryst with your husband himself if he could. You've seen yourself how he always volunteers to administer the beatings.'

Bellis went to her favoured window, the one that faced out

towards the barrack town and the armada of uneven boats, dark shapes on a glitter-sea. The risen moon danced on the horizon. Her stiletto dug into the windowsill, quicksilver in the moonlight.

'To accept false witnesses would mean accepting that people lie to me.'

'They—'

The stiletto whipped about so fast it would have impaled Wren at once were Bellis not so laden with dress-beads and lace.

Wren grabbed the small bony wrist and hung on grimly. Her chin wedged into Bellis' bony shoulder as the woman tried to bear her weight into her weapon, pierce her flesh, drive the spike into Wren's belly.

'Slut. *Whore*,' Bellis gasped. 'You fuck my husband? You wish to bear a Riven child!'

'I don't, my Queen! Stop!'

'How many times has he spilled inside you, my little Libran harlot? He rises easy enough at your hand. Yet it was not enough! Are you gravid yet? Is that little womb poisoned with snakes?'

By sheer force of effort Wren managed to kick herself free. A tea set came crashing down as Bellis collided with her desk. The sound of delicate porcelain shattered across the iron floor as loud as a scream. Wren paused for barely a second, terror flooding her bones, before wailing in feigned ecstasy, '*Oh my Queen, oh yes, yes!*'

Let the guards think the crashing was vigorous love play and not a fight. Bellis skipped to her feet, stiletto held out.

'No need for deceptions, my sweet, I'm not calling in reinforcements and ruining this moment between us.' She kicked aside the crown that had fallen from her head. 'I'm halfway of a mind to let you live, grow big, to watch you suffer.'

'Oh, *please* tell me what *sufferings* are in store for me,' Wren mocked back, her slippers testing the lay of the floor. The Queen would lunge again, and Wren must not fall, for if she did it would be the end of her.

Bellis' grin grew huge and yellow, her incisors as sharp as thorns. 'There was a mansion in the town where I lived, the house of the Justinians, our wealthy custodians. They kept a jar in one room, filled with a creature that never lived but might have done – a thing grotesque and misshapen, tentacles of human flesh. A twin birthed with a live child.'

'An interesting nostalgia,' Wren returned breathlessly, her smile equally grimaced.

'My husband's twin, birthed the moment he was birthed. It is what is inside you, *growing*. It is what will kill you, day by day. I should keep you in my offices, so I might watch.'

Wren showed the Queen her teeth. 'Indeed, that should bring pleasure enough.'

'Or I might cut it out and have my own creature in a bottle!'

And Bellis darted forward again. This time she did not come from the front but the side, and Wren barely caught the stiletto as it grazed past her neck. Held it tight, *tight*, and Bellis flecked spittle upon her face.

Wren took a breath for a final wail of dying, and to her surprise the killing blow never came. Bellis gasped, looked up, and above the pair of them loomed Riven, scarred and terrible, his bleak blue eyes hating the both of them utterly.

As fast as a snake he snatched Bellis' neck up in the crook of his arm and squeezed hard. Bellis' eyes rolled into the back of her head, and her body fell on top of Wren as if she were a spent lover.

15

Devilment

'By the abyssal gods, I thought I was gone for certain . . .' Wren said.

'Will she stay asleep with your potion?' he interrupted. 'We have a long way to go with her.'

Wren nodded. 'She won't wake for hours now. The tincture is strong.' She pulled the gold needle off the glass tube and let both fall back into a vase of rock-spirit. A flower of blood bloomed from the tip of the needle. If Riven had kept the chokehold on Bellis, the Queen would have stopped breathing completely. His act was a move to win a second's reprieve in a bar-room brawl, not to incapacitate a powerful *sanguis* who could be as damaging dead as she was alive.

Then Gregor Tallwater, impatient, spoke over the top of them. 'Must we bring her?' He gestured impatiently at Bellis. 'I don't care how little she is, dragging that weight will only be a burden.'

Wren tutted at Gregor Tallwater and his wife. Not seconds after Riven had shown up to rescue Wren from an impaling, the Hillsiders had arrived behind, dressed and packed for travel. Clearly these journeyfolk thought the archipelago underworld had chosen themselves a suitable guide, but from their expressions she could guess fair well they'd not agreed upon a detour into the Queen's offices.

'Bellis is too dangerous to leave here,' Wren explained. 'What if someone finds her like this and wakes her? The alarm would be raised across the islands.'

She shoved Bellis' body over to slide the coat underneath.

'We would be halfway to Fiction waters by then,' Gregor retorted. 'Nobody will look in a locked trunk. Hell, kill her even. That witch deserves it enough. What does it matter?'

'She has half the population under bloodwork enchantment and the other half ready to do what the first one does,' Riven said, standing up and scouting the room.

'Yes,' Wren said, slapping the dust from the floor off her hands. 'We have all been lucky that we are not under *orientis* command. Until tonight we've never challenged her to the point where she's needed to expend the energy on turning us. She saves it for her most malcontent folk.'

She winked at Riven. 'Except you, Jonah, but she enjoyed seeing you writhe under her thumb.'

'You're her servant,' Helena said warily. 'How can we be certain she's not used her ghastly powers on you during this scuffle and this escape will all fall apart?'

Wren went to the window and looked out of a missing glass into the dark rather than let the Hillsider woman see the expression on her face. She was transported back three years, the day Bellis and her army had come to Libro.

Wren might have been clever, but the others of the Libran Council were not so quick. It had taken a full day for *orientis* to take hold of them. A day where they went from fighting prisoners to mindless followers, placid as cows.

Including her mother, who in the end could not recognize her daughter's face.

Walk into the water, Bellis had said that evening, and Wren's mother had done so, walking obediently into the slate-coloured sea until the grey waves covered her head. Wren had said nothing, not even as Bellis watched her with cold amusement. Had said nothing about it for three years.

She turned back. 'Because *orientis* takes more than the span of a scuffle to take effect, and I have to keep my mind clear to assist the ten dozen people who will be travelling with us.'

'Ten *dozen*?' Helena Tallwater protested. 'Sir, my husband gave his help for *us*, not ten dozen passengers.'

Wincing, Gregor tried to bring peace. 'We owe him, Helena. He saved our children too, remember? Back when we were shipwrecked in Vigil last summer.'

'But the boat will be . . . why, there is hardly a boat in the harbour that can safely fit that many people!' She gave Riven a mulish squint. 'Leyland said a pyre has been readied, sir. That pyre will be waiting if we don't travel quick and light.'

Riven ignored them. They were beneath even the pretence of a reply. With all his strength he pushed a massive slab of carved wooden side table two feet to the right, revealing an equally formidable door.

A door locked and immovable.

It took both men's efforts to conclude that their escape path might have well been solid concrete for all it gave, though Riven was the last to accept this, driving his shoulder into the wood and iron that for any smaller body might have broken bones.

Wren put her hands on her hips and shook her head. She had seen how the outside of the hinges had rusted into orange lumps.

'Wait,' Wren said. She went to the stone cabinet and brought down the stone casket of serpent oil. 'It needs something to loosen the hinges a little.'

Jonah Riven had had enough experience with that particular ingredient that he visibly recoiled. 'What is that supposed to do?'

'Settle down, sailor, it gets more things unstuck than merely a man.'

'Well hurry up about it,' Gregor said. 'The guards will be back from their watch, and my father with them.'

Wren scooped out wads of the cold grease, nearly emptying the box, and squished it into the gap between the door and frame. The astringent smell wafted over, so intimate and so reminiscent of torture Wren could see from the corner of her eye Riven press his hand against the wall and clench his jaw in an effort not to vomit.

Despite the bad memory, serpent oil and metal in combination had the rusted parts frothing mightily. At the end of a minute, Wren could easily shift the door a crack, and once the men were involved, had it pushed open wide enough to slide a torso through.

Riven hoisted Bellis' limp form onto his shoulder. Gregor had brought a storm lamp and followed close by, with Helena and Wren at the rear.

Wren couldn't help lingering a few heartbeats. This place had been her home for years, and now she was leaving.

'Libro,' Riven said. 'Let's go.'

Gregor's lamp cast its paltry illumination. The eternal stairs had survived a lahar flowing down from a previous eruption a hundred years ago, so where the treads had corroded away, stone remained. They descended through the shadows to the muddy beach outside the old cathedral wall.

Wren took a breath, and even though it was the same sulphurous air she breathed up in the cloister-prison, it seemed fresher, cleaner. The rain had returned, needle-like splints of white in the full moon. Once the blush of freedom wore off, Wren wished she'd had the foresight to bring a coat, or better shoes. A gunky grey mud turned her slippers into stone clogs.

Down by the bay, the cluster of hastily erected buildings that was Maris' armada town was brightly lit for the night hours. Voices and song reached them on the wind.

Everyone seemed up unusually late. Gregor and Helena paused, whispered to each other, and then looked at Riven sulkily. Wren did not have to ask where this opprobrium was coming from. It was glaringly obvious that Riven would stand out as a stranger in town. Not only were his clothes prisoner's clothes, worn down to rags, but Bellis had fed him and worked him, so even physically he could not pass for a gaunt member of her army.

A pair of figures strolled by, not more than a dozen paces away.

Riven shuffled them all back into shadows of the stairwell. But the passers-by were shambled and drunk on rockblood spirit, and they wore crude masks of painted wood that showed them as being town revellers, not guards.

Wren gave a little gasp of understanding. 'Tonight is the Serpent night! It is a carnival for the King, and they all wear a costume.' She pointed towards the lava blisters on the eastern curve of Maris, the pyre that was meant to have burned Riven and turned him into Bellis' legend, the *orientine* image she would use to control her men.

To their surprise Riven pulled off his shirt and scooped up the white mud at their feet. He began to slap it over himself, coating his torso in a shield of grey-white. Wren quickly went to do the same thing. Within heartbeats she had daubed her arms, her clavicle, and her face.

'What are you doing?' Helena Tallwater demanded.

Wren tore off a length of yellow fabric from her dress. The silk was so worn from wear that her fingers easily pushed though for eyeholes.

'Your mask.'

Helena took her disguise with exasperation. Riven fastened his own around his head so that he became more maggot than man, white skin and featureless yellow face. A true monster.

And then he was the first to move, his hated package secure over his shoulder.

The town closed in, small mean streets that stank of sulphur and excrement. Once it hadn't been much of a place for a few dozen to live, before the Queen came with her three thousand besotted men, now it had the air of a little hell permanently on the moment of ignition.

Men bullied through the street with the malicious intent of

those set on making trouble later. A sea-dragon of canvas and burlap over a skeleton of barrel hoops followed them. Ten figures danced inside its frame, beat iron-sheet drums. Riven urged them to keep moving.

The gaslights glowed hot and bright in the house of ill repute. The Ivy House. Wren had had only two previous occasions to visit, both of them to refill the jadeite box of serpent oil the Queen required for her lovemaking.

Riven barged through the door and confronted the madam at the foyer's velvet table.

'I want to see the Clay woman.'

For all that Riven was a sight, the Matron of the Ivy House would not be cowed by any man.

'She is busy. With a client.'

Riven laughed, the first time Helena had seen a smile from him. Then he grabbed the Matron's arm, pushed her towards the stairs.

'The woman,' he said again.

'All right. Hold your horses.'

Riven followed, not waiting for the invitation. When the Matron stopped at the uppermost room, he pushed the door open forcefully, would have closed it on their faces if Gregor hadn't had his wits about him to quickly follow.

No woman in here, only a small handsome fellow of middle years sitting neatly upon a brocaded chair, drinking tea from a chipped china cup. He wore a waistcoat of green-gold threads, and trousers of black wool, and his face was fine-featured enough that he could have passed for either man or woman had the occasion required it.

'It's all right, Irene,' he called to the muffled pronouncements of *Mr Lindsay, I tried to stop him* of the Matron. 'I was expecting these visitors.' He turned to Wren. 'Hello, dear Wren Libro. It is nice to make your acquaintance at last. Mr Absalom speaks most highly of the Queen's handmaid.'

'I cannot say the same for you,' Wren replied with a frosty graciousness.

'And Mr Gregor Tallwater, with his lovely wife Helena, still looking fresh as when I last met you in a Vigil alley, willing to take lives and pay blood money to get out to the Sainted Isles. Is your father Leyland about perhaps? The family unit?'

The Tallwaters hunched in mute stubbornness.

'Don't talk to them,' Riven said. He snibbed the lock shut, then dumped Bellis upon the chaise longue. Mr Lindsay attempted to not show surprise, but the tarnished silver spoon that stirred his tea paused with a *chink* of metal against porcelain.

'She's yours,' Riven said.

Mr Lindsay resumed stirring with some agitation.

'Well. An odd gift. Would have rather she came to us under our reckoning and not this one.'

'The Order has chased her for nearly twenty years,' Riven gruffed. 'I'm done. Her leash is tightened. You deal with her now.'

'Now what might bring a man away from his matrimonial happiness, Jonah Riven? To me, and with such a gift?'

Riven's lips worked over his teeth. Then, 'Our marriage is annulled. I surrender my oaths to her. We have no more business, you and I.'

Wren noticed a furrow appear and withdraw upon the small man's smooth forehead. 'How interesting. I thought Deepwater marriages could not be annulled.'

A look of disgust, then Riven went to close the window where a hot volcanic wind gusted in along with the clatter-noise of carnival cymbals. Gregor and Helena huddled together by the door, clearly wanting to flee this second imprisonment. Wren propped herself up on the vantage position of the huge four-poster bed.

Riven leaned over Mr Lindsay and with a coarse expedience checked him for weapons. Mr Lindsay submitted graciously, and spread his arms.

'Is Absalom collecting Arden Beacon off Equus?' Riven asked mid-search.

Mr Lindsay's smile became thin. He tucked his shirt back into his strides. 'Arden Beacon is complicated by many more things beyond missing a hard fuck by a savage and wanting more of it. She needs to go home and heal, resume her place beyond her people. What *we* do with *our* property does not concern others.'

Wren could feel the room heating up. Riven's fists creaked. She jumped off the bed and in between them. 'Calm, gentlemen, we still have a way to go tonight.'

The small man scoffed. 'You should have killed your wife, sir,' Mr Lindsay said to Riven. 'Look at me here, alone. She will annihilate me when she wakes and take this town with her.'

'Then you both should come with us.'

Helena gave a squeak of protest, hushed by Gregor, who laid his hand on the door handle, silently pleading for them to finish the conversation and move.

'Go with you where? In what transport? The only spare boat that could steer out of these waters faster than the local Marians just left with my Order colleague this morning.'

Wren saw Gregor Tallwater exchange glances with Riven, then heave a sigh. They had committed to this, and planned it well.

'We have a boat.' Gregor held up a white staff carved in a milky, opaline ghostwood. From his expression Mr Lindsay knew at once what the Hillsider man held, a priming handle for a *white* ship. Only one in the harbour.

Riven took the handle, nodded at Gregor, before returning to Mr Lindsay, and only now did he allow the triumphant note to enter.

'We'll be taking our leave in a royal boat, you me, and ten dozen hostages. We are leaving in *Sehnsucht*.'

16

Jonah

'Jonah?'

Wren touched Riven's painted shoulder and he jerked under her touch, before turning to face her. He had not been sleeping while they waited for the others to arrive. For a moment, though, he had been absent from them, as if his soul had grown wings and flown away.

The air moved warm under Maris' largest pier, which was built over a low, blind-end lava tube even Wren needed to stoop in. The sand radiated heat through Wren's thin slippers. Same heat that would provide the warming currents through the Sainted Isles, draw the sea-monsters from their abyssal kingdoms to the hunting shallows. Gusts of sulphur and iron-scented air wafted from the black lava-tube cavity behind them. The stone cave was not particularly large or deep, but it provided cover from the cold night.

And their waiting.

Jonah, closest to the entrance, was outlined in moonlight. The steam from his breath surrounded him like a mist.

'Jonah? Are you all right? We cannot have the captain of our ship distracted.' Beyond their hiding place, the hard, full moon in the west cast white peaks on the waters. They had chosen the worst of all times to go. They had no dark cover.

Riven only asked, 'Have your people arrived?'

'We are here,' said a voice in the gloom.

'All of you, Mr Abel?' Wren asked.

'As many as we could. Maybe all.'

The man who had spoken came into view from the other end of the cave. He wasn't much more than Wren in age, less than eighteen. One of the older children. He beheld Jonah in silence. Wren knew what he was thinking – *is this him? The Deepwater King who will lead us from captivity?*

Had they enough time Wren would have counted the arrivals off, made certain they were not missing a guard or a child. She was still her mother's daughter, and in the matriarchal line of Libro the responsibility for escape became her burden. Why, even in the days of the Redeemer it had been a woman who ordered the Clay Messiah tied to a rock and left for the high tide.

They should have done the same when Bellis came, Wren thought. Not welcomed her with arms wide open.

Hiding a crowd – fully two-thirds of them under-age – in a stoopy tunnel was no easy feat. They would not stay hidden for long, not with the carousing town puffed up with liquor and stir-crazed men looking for fights.

From their vantage point *Sehnsucht* berthed no more than a hundred paces away. She wallowed pale and fat with only five fellows watching her. Behind Wren, the breaths of all the refugees echoed loudly in the culvert.

Riven stayed so quiet beside her. He had the quality of an ossuary about him, a collection of bones, lifeless, beyond waiting.

'What's wrong?' Wren asked him quietly. 'Speak to me, Jonah.'

'There's too much light.'

'I thought the same thing.'

'We can't make it to the ship. Not without being spotted. Everyone is awake.'

The night had brought the carnival to full boil. Phosphor rockets sizzled into the sky, exploded their hot, crimson innards. A child cried and was hushed.

'Deepwater King,' said a child's voice, and they were hushed too. Jonah Riven's expression was one of fear and pain. Bellis would soon stir and wake, and then every eye in the town would turn towards her. Their only hope was to be a thousand miles away, so when she woke, she woke alone and powerless.

Or at the bottom of the sea.

'What can we do?' Abel asked. 'We can't go back into town.'

Riven stood up outside of the tunnel mouth. 'I can distract them.'

Wren caught his arm 'How?'

'I stay here, you go.'

'Jonah?'

He passed *Sehnsucht*'s priming handle to Wren, pressed it into her palm. In his face . . . An ending there. She'd seen the same in suicidal men. She tried to push the handle back.

'Jonah, no. Think about your woman on Equus.'

He tucked his hands behind his waist, and his face softened in sympathy. 'I am thinking of her, Wren. I wanted to be the sort of man worthy of her love. I wanted to *earn* it. But the Deepwater King requires his sacrifices.'

She swallowed, sensing in the solemn way he spoke that he had already made his mind up what he was going to do.

He looked over at his rescuees, sought out every face. 'Wren Libro knows the route out of here as well as any sailor,' he said loud enough for them all to hear. 'Those of you with navigational skill, set the course to Libro beneath the storm wall of the Tempest.' He gave Mr Lindsay a cool, baleful stare. 'And have Mr Lindsay deposited somewhere distant with his package. Somewhere he can be recovered. Or not. It makes no difference to me.'

Riven turned to Wren. 'You have my permission to drop both of them over the side if they cause trouble.'

Overcome with gratitude for him, she stood on tiptoes so she might bring his jaw down to her, kissed him on his hard cheek. 'My love always, my brother.'

He seemed so confused and young with the affection she had shown him, her cold little heart skipped a beat.

'Stay safe, Jonah. God lives below you and above you.'

He nodded, and accepted from Gregor Tallwater a knife that gleamed thin and sharp. Bellis' stiletto.

Then he was gone into the night, half-loping like a beast who could not be held in captivity.

Wren did not smell the blood in the air so much as sense it. Sanguis blood, the thick, cloying secrets that it held. Even Bellis, on the edge of unconsciousness, murmured at the recognition. A summoning smell. Wren remembered an old ritual from her father's death. The blood on the waters. A Deepwater Rite.

A sound in the darkness. A cry in the distance. A man's scream. Something was coming, whatever it was Riven had called. Coming in multitudes and as one.

The rockets in the town fired off twice more, and then a silence followed, an awful undertow of anticipation. Four of *Sehnsucht*'s keepers left the ship and ran towards the town.

'Now,' a voice cried, and they were all in a dash down the pier towards *Sehnsucht*. The remaining guard made an attempt to stop them, and Mr Abel, weighted down with his cargo of Bellis in a sack, barrelled through him as if he were a twist of fog.

They needed no instruction to board the white boat, and the children crowded across the deck, mouths open at a town burning, the flames reflecting off the battlement walls of the Marian caldera. Silhouettes of shapes dark and massive writhed in the inferno. *The old King of the deep, the canyons of the sea.*

Before Wren could climb into the wheelhouse, she needed to look around. Jonah could not have gone far in that restless dark. She could not leave him so easily.

Mr Abel whistled shrilly from the gangplank to get her attention. 'Look sharp, the men are coming back.'

She exhaled, and let Jonah go. 'Untie us, Abel, we're leaving.'

Mr Tawfik had always kept *Sehnsucht* in the same fine condition in which Bellis had first acquired it. It took Wren next to no time to pump the petralactose into the engine and ignite the pistons. *Sehnsucht*'s side wheels bit into the black water, and the screw-propellers stirred up a froth.

Goodbye, Jonah Riven, she thought to herself. *I hope you find your way back . . . from wherever this night will take you.*

She opened the fuel pumps on the ghost ship, felt the engine thunder beneath her feet. *Sehnsucht*'s bow rose and bobbed. Freedom, and her return home with the children as she had promised. She'd heard tell that some survivors had hidden deep in the Libran forests. Wren hoped they would recognize her after all this time.

Book Three: Anguis

AFTER THE STORM

17

Arden, come back

Arden, come back.

Chalice's cry still echoed in her head as she stumbled away from the Burden Town docks, away from Mr Absalom and his iron ship, away from transport back to Lyonne and forward to . . .

To something. To nothing. She had chased a dead man to this island. More ghost than ever now. All those wasted weeks and he had been alive. Now he was something else. Neither alive nor dead, and she had not the resources to help in any way. Mr Absalom and the Order would not have helped her even if she'd asked. They'd have taken her back to Clay, reinserted her into the machinery of a sanguis bloodworker, and kept eyes upon her always. By the time she could have slipped away she would be old bones and Jonah would long be dust.

Time slowed and stopped, and Arden Beacon followed the river channel out of the river mouth and into the pipelands where men could not go. The rusted flood walls of the aqueduct, overbrimming with rain, gave way to the natural banks of the original watercourse. It became as if she were walking through eternities and seeing the collapse of civilization in the span of minutes. She existed as a creature outside of time. The stars circled overhead, wheeled and shone bright, then died upon each footstep.

And still she fled along the river's way, out of Burden Town, away from the Lyonne Order, from her failure.

The cement and basalt of the old pagan city's foundations stuttered out to reveal the bedrock beneath her feet. Night fell, rockblood clouds obscured the moon, too dark to see. She shuffled in a stoop through the driving rain, listened for the sound of the aqueduct so she might not fall into the murk and drown.

Water sopped at her calves and ankles.

All night she walked by the glow of the dimly phosphorescent water, guided by the methane fires along the muddy banks and the moonlight high and distant. A murky morning came over the horizon, and she walked all day driven by her poisoned blood and duty and regret and all the weight of her longings turned bitter beneath her skin. At that second day a traveller walked with her a little while, and when he turned to her he had Jonah's face and he said, *do you know me?*

'You're Jonah Riven,' she said to him, but it was too late and he had put on another face, some gnarled visage with watery eyes and cheeks ruddy with rock-spirit poisoning.

You don't know me. You never did. I was only a dream you had, once.

Her traveller did not stay long, for his path meandered away from her and into the muddy plain.

Self-doubts crept in with the midday demons, and the land became black as a *memento mori* with marcasite outcrops and the brassy remnants of pipes, like the gold findings from a torn necklace. If she became weary she did not feel her body's lament, so when her feet could no longer hold her she crouched in a huddle in the scoop of a broken steam-shovel's bucket, pulled Jonah's krakenskin coat up to her neck.

The smell of blood tainted the leather and Jonah Riven came to her in that dream, burnt and burning upon Bellis' funeral pyre, his face crumbled into ashes. *Sanguis ignis*, he said with a voice like a tolling bell, *you will not burn when I touch you.*

But she did burn and she woke with a startle of anguish, found herself back in the bucket again, her cheek rough against a corroded metal tooth. The images took longer to fade. Such grotesque intimacies while she slept through the night.

It took a great effort to climb out of her small shelter on the third day, for it seemed her legs had locked up overnight like rusted machine parts. A sea breeze had taken away most of the choking fumes, but what remained was not better. The blackened land showed no comfort or horizon. A bloodworked dredger laboured in the distance, hauled up bucketfuls of dirt only to dump its load behind its trundling wheels. Every rock and uplift of soil was chewed down to mud as far as she could see. The rain came in diagonal sheets, hard icy needles. If she were to leave the bucket, she'd be wet at once.

I could stay here. I could stay here a day. I could stay forever.

Such a strange, unbidden thought, and had Arden been in the mood for superstition she'd have thought an angel whispered in her ear.

If not an angel, then one of the old sprites of Equus, toying with a lost mortal. The old copper devil of Malachi's childhood.

Through that lure of oblivion, Arden fought back with the last of her resilience. *I do not wish to die here*.

She got up with effort, for her knee hurt, and her ankle had at some stage rolled within her boot. She was so cold her hands could only ball up and ache. Her coins were small portions of numbness in the pain.

It took no more than a few paces for Arden to realize how her dress uniform weighed her down. She released the strings and let the skirt fall before once again committing herself to the terrible journey in only her coat, blouse and kidskin leggings. Jonah's coat she rolled and placed over her shoulders.

The rain stopped, and with it came a fresh wind, clearing the last skeins of noxious fog. For the rest of the day she trudged through fields of oily mud and twisted, useless pipework. The entrails of Equus. In all the blackened ground not one shred of green showed. The only trees were the pipes installed by malfunctioning automata, twists and roils of metal that went nowhere. The forests of the endless mechanical night.

Later she came across another steam-shovel, long ago broken and still compelled by *mandatum* to keep working. Like the dredger it dragged its broken bucket through the oily slop.

Mandatum, she intoned with each step. *Mandatum* and *orientis*, the powerful blood soaking itself into this soil, this rock, this island. Her own minuscule sanguis shadows were nothing against the immense power that had wrought the automata from the copper and steel, had commanded and compelled.

Such dread obsessions that outlasted even the death of that one individual who had commanded them.

The agony of her body dulled, and her mind became clear. She had reached in her mind a spiritual journey's end, had found the answers she'd searched for. She needed nobody to help cure her moral injuries, no priest, no intermediary. The words of those sacred waters would be her own. She would give the proper graces. Give sacrifice, like they used to, in the days of the Deepwater King.

Arden walked on through that third day until the pain in her limbs came back, and this time they overrode her discipline. Each borne weight jarred her joins as bone upon bone. Her feet dragged, caused her to fall, at first once a mile or so, and then she could barely make twenty paces without stumbling. Her throat became so parched she chanced a puddle-rut left behind by an ambling shovel. However it made her gag, so she decided that it would be best not to drink at all.

By the afternoon a blue smoke rolled across the pipe-fields, the first real evidence of life she had seen since leaving Burden. A bunker-thief town of rockblood bandits, a rude dwelling where iron barrels turned red-hot over fire pits and dribbled aromatics from rusted spigots.

Arden stumbled into the middle of the thieves' encampment for no other reason than it would take more effort to go around them. Hungry children's faces daubed in rock-seep turned up to watch her go past. A sight she must have been, in her double-bronze and glowing blue rings, wrecked and bruised by her journey.

Someone stood in her path, pushed a steel cup into her hand. 'God, love, drink it.'

A day without water made even this small offering cramp up her stomach, and Arden knelt and retched. When she finished, she noticed with a dull despondency that she had lost one of her gloves.

The woman who had handed her the water cup tried to take her gloveless hand to help Arden to her feet, turning her palm up to see the coins buried in her inflamed flesh. 'Sanguis,' the woman breathed on seeing the coins.

Arden shook her hand free, stood up by herself.

'I'm all right. I must not be helped.'

The woman's face corrugated with wrinkles and sorrow. Her hair was equal parts white and stained black from rockblood. 'Where do you go, little sister, so far from home?'

The grey sky melted around them. The muddy ground slurped and shivered as if it were a living thing. 'To the sea,' Arden said. 'To the sea.'

Heard as if from a distance someone else say, *don't try to stop her, she is heading towards her dying, let her go.*

But the pipelands are that way . . .

If they take her, they take her, said the woman, and they allowed Arden to pass by unmolested.

Onwards. The pipelands rose up in their tangled copper thickets in clumps and tangles, replacing the vegetation that once grew in Equus. During one resting moment Arden watched a length of copper tube order itself upon a threaded joint, then flip, end over end, to join with another.

She got up to move only when the living pipes came too close for comfort. She could sense the saint's work in them like a sickly sweetness, the *mandatum* of their hard bodily commands, the *orientis* of their meaning and spirit. Those powers together had wrenched and sullied the order of the world, made the ships, the derricks, the dredgers.

Eventually the ground she walked upon became sludgy and acidic. The exposed metal of pipes and cogs wore patinas of verdigris. Familiar shapes caught Arden's attention. The great steel-lined pools of the canal locks, leaking water and rusting in the afternoon sun. The lich-ship harbour off to her left-hand side. Under her feet the sticky dirt became sand, black as diamond hearts in the low dusk light. The sharp, bladed sedge of the shore returned to form a carpet, the hard nubbins of beach succulents erupted from the heavy grains. It was the first greenery she had seen in days.

Arden gasped a salty breath. She knew this place. Here was the rickety pier where she had come with Malachi, here was the ridge they'd climbed before looking over the hunting coast. Through instinct alone she'd followed the watercourse here, through fate and faith. Jonah's people, his family, the only ones who remembered his name. This was the encampment of the deepwater folk.

And they had *Saudade*, Jonah's boat.

'Oh,' she panted. 'Wait for me, I'm nearly here, wait . . .'

Faint from hunger and hope she pulled herself up upon the high dune where the folk had camped and stood up on legs as weak as a new-born colt's. The wind whipped oily strands of hair across her face, bit deep and hard.

And disappointment crushed her.

Nothing but an empty clearing. If there had been tents set up alongside that scorched circle of ground, they had long gone. Some broken boards and iron-scrap littered the edges of the clearing, not worth someone's effort to move. The sand had already begun to obscure even these remnant remains. Given another day, the sand would drown the encampment completely.

The old lookout platform, just visible above a crescent of grassed dune, was empty.

'No . . .' Arden said to the empty ground. 'You can't have gone. The serpent . . .'

She understood how the serpent must have been small despite all the people it had taken to bring to shore, and the deepwater folk had made short work of butchering it. She waded through the remains of driftwood and rubble to the beach proper, and found vertebrae of the serpent in full cryptid decay, a fine crystal of opal bone that disintegrated at Arden's touch.

The small platform where Mr Cleave had given instruction creaked and hummed.

This is the place where it ends. You can go no further.

She climbed onto the watch-platform and lay with her cheek upon the driftwood planks until the night came, and in the dark the petralactose smell began to give way to stale freshness. The moon in the sky, waning.

Let the Deepwater King take me into His cathedral, let Him take me down to the bottom of His cold, dark kingdom . . . and let Him return what He has taken.

She could not even sleep, only lie as if she had been discarded upon the platform the way one would discard bait for a monster.

Bait, she thought dully. Rolled the word about in her head, fed it to the emptiness in her heart. The *sanguis evalescendi* in her blood gnawed at her bones. Under the cacophony of *mandatum* and *orientis* lurked a deeper, older sensation, a shadow of the deepwater people's bloodwork when they would pull beasts from the water and the leviathan from his lair.

She'd felt it the same way she'd felt Mr Stone's brief potentials with the rockblood in the barrels.

Her mind threw a memory at her, enclosed in the confessional of the Burden Town priest. *I have a talent that can increase that shadow of yours.*

With slow, careful movements worsened by her injuries, she descended down the rusted pipe-ladder. Her necessity only increased as she approached the shore. How exactly had Jonah died? Could she call him back, in flesh or in spirit, the way he'd once called for his stepfather to return?

She waded into the sloshing, foaming water, found it colder than the air itself.

Once it reached her waist she grabbed a hank of her hair, cut it off at the root, threw it into the ocean, then with her bodice knife stabbed and stabbed her hands, opening her coins.

Find him, maris anguis, monstrum mare, Deepwater King. Bring him back . . .

Let him come back to life. If he'd been put into the sea, then let the sea return him. If he'd been shackled, then let him slide out of the metal.

Return him.

It was not Arden calling the storm, for the oceans required no blood from her, and she hauled off her sodden krakenskin coat and would have walked into the wave if someone had not come behind her and swept her out of the water, half-dragging her back across the wet sand towards the watch-platform.

She did not want to be carried so, and kicked free. Her intruder dropped her beyond the reach of the water, long enough for her to feel something hump and roil in the sand beneath her palms. The person pulled her up again, and she cried out for Jonah, for his name was the only word that came to her lips.

A phosphor flare ignited, crimson-bright. Pipework had erupted from the sand, alive, alive.

'Climb!' the rough voice barked in her ear. 'Climb!'

Arden was thrown against the ladder the way someone might haul up a bag of rocks.

'Get up there—'

Her hands gripped the bars and fell. 'I can't, it's too much . . .'

'Climb damn you, woman, else we will both end up dead!'

The platform might have been an unconquerable mountain. She'd climbed it earlier, but she could not climb it again. The days and nights crossing the pipelands of Equus had broken her body. A Fictish curse exploded from behind her, and Arden watched in exhausted remove as the person turned to pull up his sleeves.

Arden recognized the Riven eyes there, achingly familiar. 'Jonah.'

'Shut up.'

Miah Anguis cut himself and sucked the blood from his arm, before spitting it into the darkness. The sand writhed up in broken metal, the arbours and gears of a devil machine. He yelled Fictish words, then once more threw Arden onto the ladder.

Mandatum, she thought dully. Only a *sanguis mandatum* could instruct soulless metal like this.

Weeping with pain and terror, half-supported by the hard thighs and back below her, she climbed. He paused to shower another mouthful of blood at the pipes once more, then came up after.

Her voice, when it returned, came at a tremble. Her lungs felt as if they were burning each time she sucked in a breath. 'I did not need saving, sir.'

Miah seized her shoulders and pushed her against one of the poles, his face in hers, trying to scry the madness in her, his own bloodied mouth a twist of horror. 'Monster-calling will kill you, Beacon! How can you even try to use the blasted poison when you have not the skill for it?'

'Jonah is still alive,' she screamed back at him. 'Days ago he was still alive! There's still time to bring him back!'

'A blessing that he is gone, woman! There is no funeral promise to keep! If he did not die under your watch, he's not your business, you're free of him.'

'Don't *woman* me,' Arden yelled, and dived for the ladder, only to have him grab her about her waist and hold tight. Wrapped her up in the prison of his arms until her struggles turned to puppet-jerks against his thick immovable torso, then to nothing. His blood-scented breath hissed hot on her neck, his heavy pelvis pressed tight against her own. The *evalescendi* hammered through her body the same way it had done when

Jonah had brought her back from near-death. The blood from his cut forearm coursed down her belly and one leg of her kidskin stockings.

Slowly, the flares faded against the sand. The dark returned and the awful feeling drained away. She no longer yearned for the ocean, and the absence exhausted her. She slumped in Miah's arms. He did not let go, and somehow she was glad that he did not, otherwise she would have been lost.

'I don't like restraining a fellow human,' Miah Anguis hissed in her ear. 'But I'll not have a sacrifice to the devil-cogs just to send a love message to my family's murderer.'

'Then why not use *mandatum* to ward them off?' Arden croaked in between her torn breaths. Talking hurt, but she wanted him to know what she had seen.

He dropped her then, suddenly. Offended terror in that shadowed face. 'I wasn't using *mandatum*,' he said, the denial too abrupt for Arden not to have been correct.

'I'm sanguis, and I know a bloodworking command when I see one.'

'Sit down. You are having fever-visions.'

'I am . . .' she started, then stopped, for there was nothing else she would rather do than collapse and sleep forever. She crumbled like a marionette with its strings cut into a cross-legged heap.

Miah gave an annoyed curse under his breath that was so much like Jonah she had to squeeze her eyes tight lest she cry into the bargain. He slipped off his dry coat and laid it across her back. She pressed her hands into her eyes until the after-image of the flare turned green, then looked at her unwanted rescuer. 'I thought everyone had gone.'

Miah made a dismissive gesture towards the sand. 'Someone always stays behind when the encampment moves. Two hundred people are not easily hidden, and someone might follow.'

'What would follow so many out here?'

'Whatever lives in the pipelands. The old copper devil.'

She pulled the coat around her. It smelled of the deepwater

man, both animal and hot and metallic, like iron in a smelter. 'I thought the big machines couldn't get past the mangroves,' she said with a sulky curiosity.

'It doesn't stop them trying. At least nothing's out there tonight. That's a complication we don't need.'

The flare burned down to char and cinder, leaving the sands black once more. A gear meshed out of time with a cog, and sparks flew beneath them. The automata screeched like little animals. Miah tested the fuel contents of the rusted red-glass lantern. Managed to get it alight so they were not lost to the immense night.

The platform turned a deep, louring scarlet.

Cast as red as a devil in the light, Miah took a leather bladder from a satchel about his torso and unstopped the seal, held it out to her.

'It's just sweet water,' he said at Arden's hesitation. 'I won't give you liquor yet.'

The water was slightly warm and brackish with an undertow of rockblood sulphur, but she accepted it without complaint. When she had choked down as much as she could bear, he stuffed the bladder back into the travelling satchel.

'Who brought you here?' he asked – casually and yet with such urgency she knew this was no small question.

'I walked. When I found out about Jonah, I walked.'

Her reply was met by a scowl and squint of disbelief.

'From Burden Town? Impossible. The trail goes go through the pipelands. The lich-metal there will turn a body to mincemeat before they go three hundred paces.'

'Well, I saw them.'

'But you were not attacked.'

'No.'

He hovered on the edge of speaking, thought to say something, then changed his mind. 'Hmm. Maybe you have a slight sympathy towards, some kind of . . . hmm.'

Now Miah didn't look at her as if she were an annoyance. Something mercenary had appeared in his expression now;

perhaps a recognition that she could be useful. He rummaged around in the satchel. Gave her an unleavened bread, a hard cheese, a saltwater melon pickled in vinegar. Took a knife and cut small slices, not enough for her to become ill from eating after so many days without.

Arden was grateful enough at this unexpected bounty to weep messily as she ate the bread in small bites.

'Who told you my cousin was alive?'

'Lions.'

'Then you should be with them, and not here.'

She shot him an aggrieved look, full of anger and despair.

He merely shrugged and passed over a small bladder of liquid again. This time it was kelp spirit, and even though she had not called anything with her bloodwork, the liquor helped quell the pains sparking through her body.

'Eat more, if you can keep it down.'

Even as she ate, even though her raw, bloodied appearance would have made her quite the horror to look at, she felt his eyes upon her. Those quick, critical glances. 'This was an unusual path for a woman to take.'

'I just had to get away from them.' She shook her head. The food had revived her a little, made her thoughts clearer, made her understand how truly lost she had been when she had begun her walk.

'Them?'

'Lions. The Lyonne Order. They wanted me to return to Lyonne.'

'Ah. I suppose they had *transport* available as well,' he said roguishly.

'I was not ready to go.' Her next words came out in a whimper. 'I can't go home without him.'

'Like I said, if my cousin survived Bellis, he needs no funeral.' He cut a melon slice off the fruit and wedged it into his mouth. Spoke with a cheek full. 'Which made your excursion into the water beyond foolhardy, not to mention your trip out here.'

She glared daggers at Miah Anguis. Her increasing clarity

brought back her sense of self-respect. If she had ever recognized Jonah Riven in his cousin, the quiet strength of him, that feeling had fallen away. Miah was coarse and self-assured in a way Jonah never was.

Then he stood up with a grunt and squinted out into the black ocean. 'We might not find out for a while yet if the calling has drawn monsters to shore. If luck holds, they'll not come at all.' He nodded inland then. 'Fortunately the pipelands are quieter tonight. When the light comes we can move,' he said. 'It will be a day's journey to catch up with the village. I can find someone to sail you back to Burden Town by the sea-road. Maybe the Lions have waited for your return.'

'And what about my boat?'

'*My* boat. We've had this conversation.'

Yes. The conversation, and the wretched agreement he'd proposed. A feeling was growing in her, a decision igniting in her belly that Miah Anguis' presence had only accelerated like fuel on a fire. An understanding of one of the last things Mr Absalom had said to her.

Where would we find men immune to Bellis' powers here, he'd said, *or boats fast enough to outrun her* Sehnsucht?

Yes, where? In all her walking, Arden realized she had not been directionless. She had orientation, a goal. She had unconsciously sought out the one person who could help rescue her lover. The certainty grew in her, a single, incendiary purpose.

'Keep *Saudade*. Help me get to Maris Island. Just put me in front of Bellis Harrow.'

'Huh. Would have been easier to suicide in a Burden Town canal than come all the way out here and ask me to facilitate your undoubtedly quick death at her hand.'

'I wouldn't die. Not if you came with me. Not if I face her, and you're around, with whatever talent you have of keeping her at bay.'

Miah dumped his satchel in front of her crossed legs.

'All right, so you have gone mad. Rest now. I'm not going to carry you back to Burden Town come morning.'

'You are a coward, Miah Anguis!'

He wagged his finger at her. 'Now, now, insults only get a person tipped off this platform. It's not about my cowardice, it's about me not giving a shit about my family's fucking murderer.'

'Then if Bellis is so intimidating to you, at least let me know for certain what she did to Jonah. Discard me on Maris and scuttle off back here to hide with your tail between your legs. I don't give a shit about that either.'

Miah's face twisted. 'Forget going to that godforsaken place! If my cousin is alive, he will not have survived her intact.'

'I don't ever want to return to Burden Town. You have to help me.'

'Have to help?' He laughed. 'You *demand* so many things. Look at you. *Ordering*. This island has chewed you up and spat you out, and here you are presuming to give me orders.'

'Bargain, not orders!'

'Bargain? With what?'

More sparks from below, illuminating the shoreline, and the opaline remains of the serpent. It was true. She had nothing, not even the scant remains of attractiveness, for everything about her was damp and wind-scored and abraded.

Miah reached for his satchel, prepared to rise, already tired of her. 'If all I'm going to get is arguing all night, you stay here. I'll come back at daybreak. It will be safe to move then.'

Arden watched him going, saw the chance close. She stood up, his coat falling from her, stood in his way as if there was ever a chance she could stop him leaving.

'Take me to Maris, Jeremiah Riven.'

'Don't call me that name.'

She took his rough hands in her own. He was immobile as if she were touching a statue, yet inside trembled from an indignant tension. This was the price she always knew she must pay. Her skin turned to stone. Her body had petrified into a lump of granite. *Give the Deepwater King what he wants*.

The priest had told her, in the Burden Town alley. Had spoken with the voice of the deepwater god.

She pressed herself against Miah, ragged and pitiful.

'You offered me *Saudade* if I gave three nights to you in return. I will give you her and three nights. Tonight, two more. Just take me to Maris when it is done, do what you do to keep Bellis Harrow toothless and help me rescue a man.'

She fumbled open the sodden ribbons at her salt-stained chemise and bared herself to him.

Only then did he understand what she meant, and scowled at the clumsy offering.

'You said no to me, before.'

Spoke those words, but his breath came loud and his voice grinding, his eyes falling to the welts and weals across her neck and torso, the marks of her desperate journey, and how many more irredeemable things she might do before this was over.

'I did not know what I wanted. There is a difference between a ghost and a man.'

'The deal was made once only, and was refused. I won't make it again.'

She'd never been much good at seduction. Either too chilly with men or ploughing forward like a demolition ship that was only going to make a mess of things. Still, Arden reached up and around the broad resisting neck. Her muscles cramped and aching, her remaining clothes still stinking of raw petralactose and sweat, and yet determined to win this brute's will.

He avoided her mouth as if she were repellent to him, tore her hands from around his neck and held her away, his eyes wide with resentment, at the favour she asked, at all the things she represented, at the tremble that went through his body at her touch. 'It is too dangerous.'

'For me, or you?'

A second passed where she feared she had tried for too much with too little, before he released her wrist.

She met his eyes as she pulled open the leather belt buckle at his waist. This was the moment she would strip herself raw of all the civilized flesh and wear the skin of a wild thing . . . but something she needed to keep to herself. *I will not ever love this man.*

She stroked between his legs as she spoke, as if she were invoking her own gods. 'Three nights, Miah Anguis. Three times where you take from Jonah what he loved and then you take me safe to Maris so I can get Jonah back.'

He swelled in her hand. Let him retract his promise and she would take away hers and she would walk into the pipelands, the ocean, shed her blood into the sand, come back as a ghost the way the deepwater people feared. She didn't care, she was beyond dying. In the glow of sand-sparks Miah's eyes glittered with a long-buried reckoning.

'Three nights,' he repeated, hoarse. Desire or surrender, hard to tell. 'And he will know of it, when we meet again.'

Even in the dark she closed her eyes and slid down her kidskins. Turned about, upon her knees as a penitent might before a cold image of his god. The iron snagged rough both on her palms. The wind hissed through the metal bars, cold upon her walk-chafed thighs. The waves sloshed. Thankfully, Miah was measured in his act.

In a distant landscape his hips jolted against her as he searched clumsily for her opening within the dry folds of her quim. Only for the quick, urgent memory of another man did this one's entry not hurt so, yet still Arden gritted her teeth and exhaled the way she'd needed to do the first time she purposefully used a bloodletting knife to pierce her skin.

Then the sting of his entry, he was inside her, a hot violation of her body, and the promise was sealed.

She smelled a stink of sex and salt and her own unwashed skin. She pushed back against his weight, bore his hands gripping her pelvis, the restrained violence in each jerky thrust. She arched her back so he might finish quickly and this thing would end. His hands bunched at the back of her neck. Barked out the name of his god in Old Fictish – shouted of the hate, and revenge, and the hungry sea.

Miah was careless in what he took, for this was not pleasure, but retribution. Was barely half a minute of graceless rutting that followed, the skin stripping from where her knees abraded against the iron platform before he became rigid, dug his fingers into the meat of her hip, said the name of God once more.

Then his climax, spilled ejaculate hot down her thigh and upon the iron of the platform, a debt partially paid in *aequor* and blood. Shuddered behind her, reached around in belated acknowledgement of her sacrifice, to press her close to his sweating torso and enclose her breast in his hand.

'Even the gods hate you,' he groaned. He wasn't speaking to her but to Jonah. To his cousin he hated so utterly it swallowed him up. 'You should have died.'

When he collapsed from effort, Arden pulled away from Miah and stood up. Looked down at the man as he rolled skywards, a red figure in the lamplight, wrecked by orgasm and anguish. Felt her heart harden and turn into stone.

18

She did not sleep

She did not sleep. The platform was too hard, the waves too loud. The man was an awful complication thrown into a life that should have had a singular path . . . and up until last night had been dying here on this island.

At one stage he rolled over, and in unthinking sleep threw a casual arm across Arden's chest as if to pull her into an embrace. Arden slid away, and he did not stir.

She counted the days in their deal and Miah's help to get to Maris, which meant there were still many mornings before Jonah's return. She was under no illusion that intimacies were hard to stop, once started. But if Miah could keep his word even at the moment she stood before Bellis . . .

Then she might have one more chance to save him.

At first light Miah recovered both her coat and Jonah's from the sand and waited with his back to her as she climbed into another layer of wet clothes, before leading her, limping and bloody from her terrible journey, to his small pony and cart. A disturbed ring of dirt about the shaggy animal along with some bright copper shaving was evidence of protective bloodwork. In this unclaimed territory between wilderness and the lich-machines, there were bound to be casualties.

She observed Miah surreptitiously as he hitched the pony back into its harness. How much *mandatum* power did he have? She rubbed one of her naked, inflamed coins uneasily. Half her palm was numb now, except for a little bite of sensation at their centre. Of all the talents that would make the Lions chase their exotic sanguinem to the ends of the earth, how did they not know of Miah's existence?

Or perhaps they did. Arden recalled Chalice's sly question, about a missing Riven. If they'd not known of him, then they'd certainly suspected his presence.

Along the road back to the shorefolk Miah asked no further intimacy of her. Arden began to entertain a hope that perhaps the next two nights might pass without a repeat of the night upon the serpent-hunter's platform. It was not as if he'd seemed particularly enthusiastic about the deal, and she was quite a wretched mess. It couldn't be in any way more than a chore, a saving of face. She sat in a huddle upon a sail-canvas roll at the back of the cart, too stiff and chafed to walk, the salt on her skin having turned into a crust, her face so wind-burnt it hurt even to move her mouth for the food and water Miah passed along.

Billows of smoke from far-off bunker-thief fires made lazy revolutions across their blackened path.

'This place,' she said, when the silence leaned too much like a weight about her. 'It's as if the land is injured, somehow.'

Miah only nodded. 'It is injured. Hurt beyond imagining and no way we can change it,' he said.

'Not even . . .?' she gestured at his arm, the blood beneath his skin. 'Could nothing be done?'

'I am no saint.'

They stopped once in a clearing, and she steeled herself that he might request her again, for his hand brushed her thigh, and he looked at her thoughtfully from under his heavy brow.

Instead he shared the last of his food. After the pony was given time to graze, they continued along a track that still bore the worn cobblestone ruts of an ancient civilization, most of which had sunk beneath the waves. Before the coming of the missionaries, Equus Island had been populated by the old ancestors of the deepwater folk. Anything that was not metal belonged to them. Then the waters had risen in an ancient cataclysm, leaving only the islands behind.

In the late afternoon they passed into estuarine country, inlets and streams fraying the coastal edge, and stopped for a while at a broken granite causeway that appeared to head out to the silvering sea. Miah pulled the pony up short, and they waited there for a little while in the blustery day as the tide retreated, leaving behind the braided remains of an old road indented with puddles. In some pools a knot of tardy, transparent eels skipped in panic, having been caught unawares by the fast departure of the sea. Miah gave the pony its own head as they crossed, occasionally leaving the cart to pluck the eels out of their shallow prisons, dump them in a small barrel of water he'd kept in the back of the cart. When Arden peered into the barrel, they were small, almost transparent versions of the sea-dragon the folk had brought to shore. They roiled in their own slime, indignant at capture.

'Are they food?'

A shadow of a grin on that stony face. 'Dragon-fry. We release them past the poison waters of Equus. They'd die here otherwise, or grow small, and stunted.' He gestured out towards the horizon. 'The waters here used to team with leviathan, back in the days before this place was corrupted. Sea-dragon schools so dense there could not be a boat piloted from one island to the other. Only the old blood kept the monsters at bay. There was pride in such work, then.'

As the light behind them was sinking into reds and golds, a smell of salt water heralded the return of the tide. Miah urged the pony forward and to the other side of the estuary. The land might have been desolate if not for slabs of basalt plates showing through the wild grass, a slight smell of onions and liquorice rising from grass that had been previously crushed from the forward camp of the deepwater folk. The trees here were hardly tall, but after the mud of the badlands, their scrubby presence was like a veritable forest.

They stopped for the night at a ruin so degraded by wind and storm it was impossible to see what it had been before. More stone underfoot, and a great rusted iron dish full of holes and ashes. Maybe it had once been a temple or pilgrimage way, for the lone building was far too small for a house.

Still, the locals appeared to still use it frequently, having added some journeyman comforts. A rockblood lantern in one corner. A raised bed-platform of old wicker, so one was not forced to sleep on the cold stones. The ceiling had been replaced with a haphazard construction of steel ribs and crackling oiled flax-canvas.

Miah disappeared for a while. Arden waited with the pony, staying close to its shaggy hide as a loom of anxiety made her fret about Miah's return. The journey had tipped something inside her. After days of isolation she now feared it utterly. Miah was her only tool against Bellis, her only instrument of saving Jonah.

The thwacks of an axe echoed in the distance. When he returned, sweat shining in the fading light and dragging a sack of wood, she found herself panting in relief.

He noticed her straight away. 'What's wrong?'

'Just worried when it took so long, is all.'

He gruffed a laugh. 'Huh, there's nothing out there. Only the machines and the devilfish.'

He threw logs into the iron fire pit with kindling, set them alight, and she realized then she was crying, for fat tears rolled down her face and dripped off her chin.

'This is not a punishment,' he said irately. 'I am not your executioner.'

She waved him off. 'It is nothing. The journey has tired me.'

'You can stop this whenever you want, Beacon. As soon as we reach the encampment I'll have Gareb take you back to Burden Town. Forget the agreement.'

She remembered the man Malachi had introduced her to on

the Deepwater Night, and shook her head, but found herself squeezing out more angry tears because she could not get even those chaotic emotions under control. 'I need a bathroom, and a damn wash.'

'Latrine bucket is around the back. Water too, but it's cold.'

'I don't care if it's cold. I stink like I've died in this coat,' she said impatiently. 'I've had enough of wallowing in my discomfort.'

Miah shrugged, as if it didn't matter one way or the other. He was not meant to be with her for his pleasure. Whether the agreement was settled with her smelling of roses, or several days of dirt and sweat, it made no difference.

Unable to bear her wretchedness any longer she left him to unpack the rest of the provisions, and slipped into the near-dark. The fresh air had blown the rockblood scent away, and the sky sported a few translucent clouds across the northern horizon. The waning moon skirted close to the water line, washing out the stars.

Arden found the stone wash basin directly under an iron pump handle. Some remaining ceramic mosaics crunched underfoot. The water came out nearly freezing, but she didn't mind, for it was a clean pain, sharp and real. She slipped out of the coat and the remains of her kidskins, and with a dented pewter dish sluiced down the salt from her skin even as it turned to gooseflesh, did her best to clean her wounds without soap.

When she looked up she found Miah sitting on a slab of driftwood, watching her.

A brief annoyance crossed her mind, to cover her nakedness to preserve the brief scraps of her honour, for there was something in his unreadable expression that worried her, as if he was going to ask something impossible.

Then her small pride was gone. She had resigned herself to this agreement and he would see everything before these days were out. She ignored him as best she could and scrubbed herself marginally clean. Oh, she thought, for hot water. And soap.

He watched Arden emotionlessly as she rinsed the blemishes

from her skin. One leg stuck out, he was favouring the hunting injury, for their activity had likely snagged his stitches. A bottle of spirit in his hand reflected the rising moonlight.

As she finished washing, a scream echoed beyond the harbour, making her jump. 'What was that?'

'A machine, trying to get through,' Miah said. 'They never stop trying to cross the estuary. They won't stop until the entire island is mud and we are driven into the ocean.'

'Have you tried to stop them from coming too close?' She gestured at the wound on his arm, which had scabbed up as dark as one of his tattoos.

He gave a mocking grunt. 'Me against the saint's wickedness?' He shook his head. 'All the blood in my body will not keep them from this shore.'

The wash basin was big enough to sit inside if she tucked her limbs in at a huddle, and truth be told it was better that he did not look at her further with such dour blankness. The cold water made her abraded skin numb, took the assorted pains away. She wrapped her arms about her legs to conserve warmth as she let the wind dry her. The distant screams were sometimes metal, but sometimes very human.

He rubbed the thigh which held the stitches. 'We will be back by the afternoon. The day after that we will be headed to Maris.'

'Thank you.' Then, 'It wasn't Jonah's fault. The rite he did, which went wrong and brought the monsters to your home. It was Bellis. She suggested it to him.'

'He should have been stronger, said no.'

'He was a fourteen-year-old boy, and grieving. Bellis is your enemy. Not him.'

His brow creased. 'Do you very much long to see my cousin again?' The liquor had softened his words, but not the intent. He didn't bother to hide a critical curiosity.

'I do, yes.'

'And then what?'

'Take him home with me to Lyonne.'

'Marry him, even though he is already married?'

She felt herself blush as she hadn't thought that far ahead, then understood why Miah spoke with such a scoff. 'We aren't like deepwater folk. Under Lyonnian law he is allowed to divorce Bellis.'

'He is lucky.' This said aside, almost at a mumble, as if he could not bear to compliment Jonah, even so abstractly.

'Were you ever married, Miah?' she asked, and prepared herself for any number of answers, including an annoyed spouse waiting back at the encampment followed by an onerous night of adultery.

He shook his head. 'I have wanted to marry, several times. But I was never permitted a bride either by choice or arrangement.'

'Why ever not?'

'A Deepwater marriage has to be agreed upon, by all of us.'

'No eloping into the mangroves?' she said too light-heartedly, then regretted her words, for he was too solemn, and silent as he shook his head. Arden wondered why trouble gnawed at her even in this moment of gratitude. Still, her relief that their agreement remained firm disarmed her, and when he came to her with his hand offered, she took it without hesitation.

'You'd best come inside. It's safer.'

She rose from the basin and her breath steamed in the cold air. As insubstantial as a wraith she followed him into the plain stone room. He seemed somewhat kinder now than he had been on the platform, offering her a clean linen shirt to dry herself off with, and held out the bottle of kelp spirit.

'Drink. This doesn't have to be any more difficult than it already is.'

She took the bottle, drank, and coughed from the fumes. Drank again, enough to make her head spin even before she had finished swallowing.

He gestured her to the bed, removed his clothes. She didn't want to look at him though a moment arose, brief and awkward, when he wanted to have her that way. Face to face, like lovers.

Even with the liquor dulling her mind, she knew she could

not bear such closeness. A body was one thing, but her mind, her emotions – those had to remain unyielding. They had both revealed small vulnerabilities, put cracks in their armour.

Arden turned about and effected a position, saved herself from witnessing the sudden wrenching passion in his face, the hard, upthrust excitement of him, the scars and markings on his body so like Jonah's, yet so different. In the half-light he was inhuman, losing the outline of a man and replacing it with a shape that was at once bulky and sinuous.

His eagerness extended into his act, and he did not last long in his labours before finishing; afterwards he embraced her until he grew soft, and sated. Arden lay as still as a small creature caught in the jaws of a much larger one, each heartbeat a pained squeeze of survival and emotional turmoil. Not long afterwards Miah fell out of her completely, rolled over and settled into a doze.

She lay upon the pallet. The toxin in the serpent oil unguent had had a peppery heat that burned within her even though they were apart, stopped her from escaping fully into that comfortable numbness the kelp spirit offered.

Another cup of spirit, she thought, and she might be drunk enough not to care.

19

Drink

'Drink.' He stirred against her, having woken wanting. By then it was not completely dark, and dawn was on its way.

'Ugh, no more drink.' She winced from her pounding head and wondered how long she had slept. Her legs creaked like old machinery as she moved under the rough blanket.

'Drink,' Miah said again, offering the bottle of spirit in urgent generosity, as if he thought it a kindness. Even though she was still halfway intoxicated from the first round she took a small sip from the bottle, rinsing the fuzz off her teeth and the blood-taste from her mouth.

If it was meant to take the edge off the act it did not work, for she could not put herself outside herself when he seized her up in his thick, scarred arms and murmured words of hoarse instruction, could not drift away into a netherworld where everything was fog, and nothing mattered, because he was too present, too absolute, too insistent she not slip away.

Worst of all there followed a moment when the hot, fevered closeness of his scarred, naked body, the oceanic rhythm as he moved within her, dragged her off the precipice she'd been clinging to and plunged Arden into a dark, shuddering orgasm.

Her body's treachery horrified her. The confused guilt which followed that awful sparking delight made her gasp. Miah took it the wrong way and held her close, murmuring words as if they were prayers. The months she'd spent hoisted inside a cage of sadness were not meant to be erased so simply and with the presence of another man.

'Get on with it,' she gritted, close to tears again and doing her best to hold them back, because if he saw her crying he would stop, and she would have come this far for nothing.

'Get on with it?' he said in return. He turned her over and made Arden look at him. 'There was joy in that, don't deny it.'

'I'm not denying it.'

'Then give me these days. You will have Jonah for the rest of your life.'

Pliant with despair she allowed him to examine her body in a way she'd not have allowed him the night before, let his lips work across her collar, to her sternum, to each nipple one by one so she might startle from the shock of his mouth there so unexpectedly. She did not push his head away when he thrust his stubbled face between her legs and into that place both root and crown, or when he tongued the key of her so she sobbed from the obliteration of her principles.

The jags of sensation wounded her so that when she cried out in climax again it was less in bliss and more in hopelessness.

Afterwards he embraced her like a lover and kissed her with a damp mouth still tasting of her surrender to him. An almost bitter triumph was in his face.

'He was never there, was he?' Miah said, smirking. 'Never did that.'

'It is not a competition,' she said, and pulled on her blouse. It was thankfully dry, as were her kidskin leggings.

He grinned and propped himself up on his elbow. 'Still. It will certainly be a memory I will hold close in long nights hence.'

Had she not needed to maintain politeness, she might have given him a tart response. By now it was daylight. There was no more food apart from some figs Miah had liberated from the wild coastal trees the evening before, and the water tasted even more strongly of limestone. It left a dry taste in her mouth.

They left the way station and returned to their journey along the coast. Just before noon they came upon a muddy, dour harbour encampment, a combination of shorefolk tents and ruins, fogged with the bunker-smoke and rimed with rockblood.

The deepwater folk who on the Deepwater Night had seemed so alive and invigorated were reduced to shades among the mechanical wreckage, grey and bowed by work. The rough leathers and linens of clothing made them shapeless.

On their arrival, Miah became agitated. His foot drummed on the baseboards of the cart.

Two dozen tanker-ships in various states of breaking and decay rested forlornly on the nearby beach and in the sloshy breakers. Sparks showered from the end of one ship's rusted hull as a beleaguered work-crew set about cutting the vessel apart for its bloodworked iron.

The ruins of a pier jutted out into the grey water. At its end, *Saudade* bobbed dark and huge against the smaller fishing boats.

Arden took a sharp, almost painful breath at *Saudade*'s appearance. Whatever doubts were over her disappeared with the sight of that proud ship. This was the vessel that would take her to Jonah.

Miah's passage into the encampment did not let Arden look at *Saudade* long, for he took the cart down a street of shanty huts, and towards the mouth of a temporary foundry falling into some despaired ruins. Hardened iron-melt lumped on the edge of salt-dusted crucibles. Creatures moved in the high eaves – not birds. Something else. Their guano had a cryptid smell.

She glanced at him, sensing a sombre change in his mood. He dismissed some fellow folk greetings with a terse mumble in Fictish. His foot juddered on the wood of the cart, and he spoke with an odd impatience when he finally came to the cart's grey-coated owner. The owner pointed at Arden, spoke in a tone that was undoubtedly disapproving, and fell into a sulk when Miah tipped up his head and high-handedly replied in his old language, along with a word in old Lyonnian that sounded like *restitutio*.

With that business done he led her over some duckboards in the wet sand to a small and bare room that was hardly an improvement on the temple, with one wall merely a sailcloth awning against the weather.

Its interior contained a rug, a bed pallet, a side table with slumped, re-fired glassware and a jug of water. He lit a small petralactose light above the bed.

Arden looked about her, and hugged herself to quell the sudden race of her heart.

'This is your apartment?'

'Yes,' and then he let out a little disbelieving, wry laugh.

'What?' she asked.

'I've never brought a woman here before.'

'I find that hard to believe.'

'I mean, not *here*. I am not allowed a bride, but since we are enacting a deal of restitution, it is permitted to have a temporary bed mate.'

Miah nodded, and she could smell him in the room, the yearning of him, but under it the sharp metal smell of his secret sanguinity, *mandatum*.

He took her hand and pulled her to him. His mouth went under her ear and he breathed loudly. She avoided his mouth when he pushed for a kiss.

'You never told me why you are not permitted a wife in the first place . . .'

Miah didn't answer her, only yanked at the laces of her dirty undershirt, pushed her stockings down off her hips. Had her rejection of a kiss angered him? Their coupling afterwards was sullen and quiet compared to the previous night in the way station, and he did not bother to undress. Even in the midst of his sweaty, huffing exertions and her own murmurs Arden could hear the stray voices of people in the other rooms, a constant distraction. He finished quickly and lay upon her with his crushing weight. A knot in his shirt was sticking into her sternum. She took note of all her discomforts and found one was more pressing than the others.

She tapped his heaving shoulder as his breath steadied.

'Can we get something to eat? I'm starving. We haven't eaten anything since last night.'

For the briefest of seconds it appeared as if he would take offence at Arden's priorities, but then he nodded. 'All right. I need to do some business. I'll be gone until the evening time. These last days have been a trial, I will not deny it.'

'So,' she said as he tucked himself back into his leathers. 'Since my clothes are torn to rags . . .'

He hesitated, then nodded. 'I'll have one of the women bring some more, and food.'

'Thank you.'

He hesitated at the edge of the door-canvas, and Arden halfway expected that he return to the bed pallet, but he nodded once more and was gone.

Not wanting to spend another minute in this room, Arden put on her coat and stepped outside onto the duckboards. The air had the iron smell of chemical cutting torches, and down on the littered beach lay an entire tanker-ship broken in half. She had seen many boats in various stages of dismemberment on the Clay Portside docks, but had never seen a boat built like this one, a countless jumble of springs and gears about a long central arbour. Why, it really was more like a clockwork toy than a machine.

'Hello?'

The woman's voice startled her, and she turned about. The visitor had arrived with a steaming bucket in one hand, a dress of grey wool and some undergarments of flax-linen in the other. She carried herself tall and stern, silver hair knotted with a braid of leather. Serpent-scale chevrons on both cheeks.

'You are Arden . . . Beacon?'

'That's right.'

'Come with me,' said the woman. She had such an air of

authority about her, Arden did not argue or ask questions. Each time her braid moved, Arden caught sight of the tattoo on the back of the woman's neck. A chevron, a marriage mark.

She followed the deepwater woman to a basalt-stone communal bathing area that had not a single privacy wall save for a few desultory bed linens drying on a line.

Without a word the woman laid the dry clothing across a nearby guy rope. Showed Arden a shallow green copper tub next to a cirque of flat stones. A sliver of foamy lard-soap greyed the top of the steaming water. She pulled some linens from another rope and hung them up to give Arden some seclusion.

'There's meat after this,' the woman said with an indelicate gesture. 'If you're still in the mood for meat.'

After the woman left Arden put her coat aside, stood in the tub and scrubbed herself as best she could, as the brush and soap kept knocking from her hands if she did not concentrate on holding them. Along with every other little torment, her heart hurt from general self-pity and anxiety for the next day, when she would sail to Maris, and a man who might not be alive. Would he understand what she had done to save him? Would Jonah think unkindly about these nights?

Hard to linger too long on worries when the soapy hot water and the shallow copper bath brought so much relief. She stayed until the water cooled, then dried herself off with a brushed-linen towel. When she was dry and goose-fleshed, she found to her delight that the woman had hung boots of fleece-skin along with the dress. She had even been supplied some fingerless gloves of a sea-serpent leather, a nod towards them knowing she was *sanguis* and what her hands required.

Arden struggled to dress herself gracefully. Her fingers did not want to follow her mind's instruction, and the gloves required repositioning with her teeth. The woman returned to Arden after she finally slipped into the fleece-skin boots.

'My husband Amos tells me Miah Anguis made an agreement of *restitutio* with yourself,' the woman said. 'My husband was only just informed.'

So this agreement had a name, and if Miah was telling people about it, then it was formal, and sanctioned.

'If your husband is Mr Amos Cleave, you may tell him that is correct.'

'What happens when the deal is done?' Mrs Cleave asked. Arden could sense a guardedness to her question. No ordinary curiosity had prompted the woman to ask such a thing. She recalled the cart-owner's annoyance at seeing Arden, the way Miah had said *restitutio* as if it were an explanation for her unwanted presence.

'Tomorrow I intend to leave this place. I have somewhere I need to be, and he will take me. That is our agreement.'

'Rescuing a man whom you once loved, apparently. A man of our acquaintance, Bellis Harrow's husband.'

Arden bristled at the name. 'Yes.'

Mrs Cleave closed her eyes and nodded solemnly. 'If you go to him, you will not come back here?'

'If I survive his rescue, I will not.' Arden shook her head. 'I'm passing through, Mrs Cleave. This has been a necessary diversion, and very soon I will be gone.'

Mrs Cleave nodded then, as if Arden had satisfied a worry.

'Well then, go ahead and have some food by the central fire. If a woman is intending to carry out a rescue, then she needs her strength.'

'Say we go to Maris tomorrow, and find out my cousin didn't survive her. What then?'

Miah's late-night question took her by surprise. He had not said anything on his return that evening, only sought out affection with an almost sulky neediness. She had responded kindly to him, buoyant with joy at the upcoming journey to Maris, and feeling the first bright sparks of hope she'd had in a long while.

Why, she decided, this agreement had not been altogether awful, for the day had allowed her rest she sorely needed. On his return she found Miah experienced enough to not be clumsy in his urgent lovemaking, or ending up accidentally hurting her with his muscular bulk. Curiously, her good feelings made her think warmly of Miah Anguis. After all, he was going to risk himself by taking her and facing Bellis again. Perhaps she would think of him in times hence, and his memory would be a warm and pleasant one.

But even as they finished up the last few moments of the agreement in the dark-time hours, there seemed to be a strange sort of tension in him, as if he were holding something back.

Then as they'd lain alongside one another, exhausted and rimed in sweat, he'd blurted out the possibility of Jonah's death.

'You may have to consider what happens afterwards,' he concluded with such gravitas it sounded as if he had been practising the speech. 'Remember, Bellis' people are deserting now. She'll not be in the best of temperaments.'

'I won't believe Jonah's dead until I see it myself. I won't consider it,' Arden said. She climbed out of his bed-pallet and slid the dress back over her shoulders. 'I've come so far and I miss him so much.'

'Don't put all your figs in one basket, Beacon.' Miah discarded the now empty kelp-spirit bottle, then looked at the scab on his arm where he'd cut himself two nights before. 'I know what it's like to be cornered into a situation you can't get out of. This talent. *Mandatum*. It has no use to me except as little tricks upon the copper.'

'But *mandatum* gives immunity against Bellis, turns her power on herself. The talents are so similar, she could not use her sanguinity against you.'

'Even saving the lives of every soul here could not win their full trust. I have been lonely, set apart from the others. Despite bringing me home to Equus, making me one of their own, I have never been truly accepted by my people.'

'Ah. The no-marriage thing.' Arden knew at once where the conversation was going. The night and their upcoming separation had made him maudlin. They were words for a lover, not her. 'Miah, no sooner than I am gone, one of your young admirers will step in my place, bed-permitted or not.'

'In secret, and with no acknowledgement after.' He reached for her hem and rubbed the cloth in between his fingers. 'Was fine when I was young, but my days are growing shorter, and I have yet to accomplish all I wished to. I am prohibited to marry a deepwater woman, but I can choose someone else. A foreigner. If she would accept me.'

He did not look at her, kept rubbing the woollen hem. The mood was tilting into something worrisome. It would be so easy to give in to him. Let Jonah's ghost go. A life without Lions. A life hidden, and maybe all her own.

A sanguis in Clay never lived such a free existence, but a *sanguis mandatum* had lived here for decades untroubled. The evidence was real that she could too.

'All right, we'll see what tomorrow brings. If the outcome is bad I will consider it, but only if worst comes to worst.'

'Consider it,' he said, with a thoughtful smile. 'It could work. I could get the permissions.'

He then spoke for a little while on a plan he and his companions had come up with to enter Maris Island. They would disguise themselves as stateless Fiction pirates who had stolen a boat and its lone passenger – Arden – before asking to see Queen Bellis in the hopes of a reward. When she was within speaking distance, Miah could reveal himself. Command Bellis, the way she commanded others.

And in the shelter of Miah's strange bloodwork Arden could rescue Jonah.

It seemed a good plan, and Arden told him so, and she let him make love to her again, even though it was just about morning and by rights the agreement had ended at midnight.

The machines screamed in the badlands and Arden imagined that she was holding Jonah as Miah claimed her in his raptures. Bit her tongue so she would not say Jonah's name when she reached her peak, but it was him in her mind all the same. This would be the last time another man would take Jonah's place.

She had spoken to Miah of an alternative life only to placate him. She was being kind in her evasions, not cruel. Any other relationship would be an impossibility. The coins in her hands tied her to Lyonne, and Arden was returning with Jonah Riven by her side.

Miah offered her another bottle from a tea chest at the foot of his pallet, but instead of being a spirit, it was a sweet cordial that tasted of fennel, of wild liquorice.

Dawn light filtered through the canvas awning. She lay next to Miah and drew the blanket up to her neck to escape the chill of the mist creeping under the canvas wall. His arm went about her as he slept. Impatience made it hard for her to do the same. Something moved in her, the kick of sanguis recognition, the same feeling that had come when she'd first sailed into the Burden Town docks.

She tried to banish her doubts from her mind. The agreement was finished. Within hours she would be sailing to Maris.

20

Arden woke

Arden woke – groggy as if she'd been hit – to find the bed pallet empty, and Miah Anguis gone.

Groaning from the aches about her body, Arden pushed off the rough blanket. The sky through the gaps in the canvas wall was brighter than she would have expected, since she'd only slipped into a doze. How had she slept for so long? Why hadn't Miah stirred her awake when he moved? A lighthouse keeper was meant to sleep light. A person outside walking by should have put her wide awake.

Then Arden hiccoughed, and the taste of fennel filled her mouth.

Along with the taste of something bitter, and medicinal. Like the sleep draughts the doctor would give her as a child.

She snatched up the cordial bottle where Miah had left it. He'd had none himself. It was untouched since she'd happily partaken of half the contents.

'No . . .'

In her rush for the tent wall she fell over the pallet, and yanked aside a fold of waxed sailcloth. Instead of a morning falling over the harbour, it was a solid grey day.

Saudade was no longer there.

'Devilment, Miah!' She struggled into her donated shoes and ran out onto the pavements that surrounded the encampment. If *Saudade* was not there, then Miah had gone, and for no small time either. There was no sun in the sky to show through the rainclouds.

A woman strolled past with a child on her hip, and Arden caught her attention.

'Sister, what time is it?'

The woman gave Arden a little panicked startle before replying, 'Mr Cleave has the clock, but I would say it's noon-time at least.'

'Noon!' Arden cried, and left the puzzled mother to run down into the encampment's centre.

At the central campfire, thin strips of serpent meat festooned the smoking-pits. A scent both nauseating and enticing filled the narrow walkways between the semi-permanent shelters of flax-canvas and salvaged iron. Her stomach pinched from hunger but her anxiety made her too sick to consider eating. She marched as best she could along to the docks where the men stood in knots, eating their midday lunches and smoking tobacco. She sought out any face who could know what they were doing. To add to the injury, it began to rain, and she reached the end of the decaying harbour a bedraggled mess.

'Excuse me,' she said to the back of a grimy ichthyosaur coat. 'Where's the black mangrove boat that was here last night?'

The face that turned about belonged to Mr Cleave. He looked her up and down with no small surprise.

'How the devils are you still here?' he said without greeting. 'My wife said you'd be gone by morning.'

'Maybe ask Miah Anguis that. He's broken a vow of *restitutio*, taken the boat but not me.'

Then it came over her, the full extent of what Miah had done. What he'd planned.

Miah had gone to Maris without her.

She tried to suck in a breath but it wouldn't come. 'Oh devils. Oh God.'

A low, careful look came over Mr Cleave as he witnessed Arden's terrible epiphany. Resentment mired in concern. Mr Cleave then tilted his bristly chin towards a shack of iron. 'This rain has made a mess of you, Clay woman. Get yourself out of the weather and let us discuss this.'

A lean-to shelter propped against the remnant hull of a ship. Inside had just enough room for a desk, with two salt-mottled ship's chairs tucked underneath. He pulled out one – stuffing bleeding from an un-stitched side – and gestured that she should sit.

The affectations of a harbour side office amid the ruin and decay made her want to either laugh or weep. Even the formal way Mr Cleave took the other side of the desk and put the papers into a drawer seemed comical, for they lived such a rough existence she'd have expected them to continue business about the fireplace.

'So, he could be fishing,' Mr Cleave said evasively once he had settled into his chair. 'With some others.'

'*Saudade*'s a lot of boat to go fishing in, especially when there's already a half-butchered sea-dragon in your possession.'

Mr Cleave would not criticize one of his own in front of a stranger but an aggrieved tic had formed in his eye. 'The contract was a private arrangement between the pair of you,' Mr Cleave said. 'I would have preferred for him not to have brought a Lyonnian here, but that will be for Mr Anguis and I to discuss.'

Arden's fingers gnawed at the arms of the chair. Rainwater fell off the corrugations of the iron roof in stripes, like prison bars. 'I was supposed to go to Maris Island this morning.'

'Maris Island?' He was taken aback. 'So that was the rescue my wife was talking about. You were to leave today.'

'Yes!'

'Perhaps,' he said thoughtfully, 'I could arrange some of my men as an escort, if leaving is still required.'

Arden almost jumped at the chance, until reality intruded. 'I *needed* Miah with me. He's the only one who can control Bellis, command her to let Jonah go. That was our deal!'

A harsh reality washed over her. Miah had never forgiven Jonah. Her payment of three days had not put out the fire of his revenge, only focused it.

Oh Jonah, if Bellis was bad . . . what if I just delivered something worse?

'If it is of any help,' Mr Cleave said, 'under contract of *restitutio* it is honourable for both parties to adhere to the terms of the agreement. He won't do anything that will make him lose face among us. Sometimes a reputation is all a man can truly own.'

'Does he have that reputation? He's always saying how he doesn't fit in here, how you won't permit him to marry into the deepwater folk.'

Again Mr Cleave kept his face emotionless, but the tic in his eye almost had him winking. Under his calm appearance, he was as aggrieved as she was.

'Well, we cannot do anything about it now. Go and eat in the meantime and don't waste your day worrying. There's a perfectly good reason for his absence. I will inquire when he gets back.'

Arden was being urged to leave, but when she stepped out of Mr Cleave's damp office she did not go far. She slipped behind a rusted hull-section of a broken boat and watched in the drizzle as Mr Cleave departed his office in a near-jog. He quickly seized up a passer-by and remonstrated with him. Much pointing towards the dock, and Miah's room.

The worry turned into a stone upon her forehead. The hollow feeling in the pit of her stomach turned into a chasm. Miah had not just broken a vow to her. He had escalated it to include his adopted people as well.

Saudade did not return all that day, and in the evening there were already grumbles about the town that the several fishermen who had gone with Miah were late in returning. It did not help that they were still not far past Deepwater Night, when the monsters spawned close in the shallows.

Arden spotted David and Sean near one of the sorting tables, as an older woman in a ragfish coat showed them how to unspool the bright wire mechanisms dug out from a gutted ghost ship. Arden kept her distance. Until this complication with Miah worked itself out, she would be a liability to them, and their chances of being properly accepted into their new family. Mr Cleave's upset was clearly no small thing. She felt eyes upon her, as she paced the ship-breaking beach, the old encampments.

Night fell, and she was driven back to Miah's room. The cordial's effect lingered. So deeply did Arden sleep she did not hear a man's return in the dawn of the following morning, a man stinking of blood and the sea, his arms crusted with scab. Monster-calling marks, a long journey. Became only half aware, caught up in a faceless, wordless dream, of the weight of him as he knelt upon the bed pallet, him pulling himself erect from his damp breeches with one hand and yanking up her skirt with the other.

'Quickly,' the voice came, hoarse and urgent.

She was still sleep-drunk when he slid himself hot between her legs, the cold buckle of his loose belt scraping the skin at her thighs.

Dazed with drunkenness, words fell: 'Jonah, wait!'

She had not meant to invoke his name. But the kelp spirit had dragged her mind into a fog of the past and he had come upon her so quickly that she had not the wit to deny what her whole body and spirit yearned for.

Miah's lustful exertion dashed up against the name of his hated cousin. He froze as if struck by a paralysis of reality. A Fictish curse fell out of his mouth.

Her eyes flashed open and instead of her ghost lover, the deepwater man was on top of her, and inside her. 'What in God's name? Where did you go? Get off me!'

'Why do you love him *still*?'

Arden kicked him off the bed pallet and yanked the dress down.

'Devilment, Miah! What sort of savagery was that? The

agreement ended yesterday, and you damn fled, breaking your vow! Mr Cleave is furious! I'm furious!'

With a hiss of irritation, Miah pushed himself back into his blood-stained leathers. 'I saw you stir in desire.' He yanked the belt buckle tight, and final. 'You've not been honest with me.'

Arden sat up. 'Honest? You took *Saudade*! When we said three nights, it was three damn nights in a row, not extra days whenever you feel like it!'

His jaw worked almost imperceptibly save for the popping of muscle at his cheek. He turned around for the carafe of kelp spirit, found it nearly empty, threw it aside. He smelled of blood, of *mandatum* – that constant metallic undertow, but this time it was as thick and cloying as anything she might receive of the saint's remains in Burden Town. Stronger, even.

'Did you hope *he'd* come back instead? Is that why you woke so eager?'

For several seconds she was speechless. Miah was *jealous*?

'Are you . . .' she started to say, then stilled her tongue; for with his back to her Arden saw what she had missed. Swinging from his belt-loop at the back of his hip was a cylinder of brass and black mangrove wood, close enough for her to touch.

Saudade's priming handle.

Urgency dashed through her. Could she grab the handle? Could she strike him over the head with it and outrun him? Get on *Saudade* and out of the harbour before he could come after? And then what?

'Where did you go, Miah?'

His scowl deepened. He stood up, yanked his coat back on. The handle swung at his side. There was an unreadable expression in his heavy brow.

'Get dressed. You need to see something.'

'See what?'

'I said *dress*.'

Arden reassembled the shreds of her dignity with her shore-folk linens and followed Miah out into the grey day. Several folk greeted him with nods. He strode on ahead, not checking to see if she followed.

On reaching the breaking yard at the beach, Arden noticed at once an odd structure there, a cage constructed from pipework and oil-rope. Something roped together quickly by the materials at hand.

Inside it, a man in a velvet coat sat lordly on an overturned barrel. He recognized her at once.

She recognized him too. After the surprise of their reunion wore off he gave a huge cat-grin.

'Well then,' Mr Lindsay said. 'I never thought we would meet here. I always thought it would be Clay City at least.'

He glanced at Miah, less than confidently. His jaunty grin faded, and his eyes creased with caution. 'And you've made friends since I last gave you a ticket home, I see.'

Miah folded his arms. 'I take it this man is familiar to you, Beacon.'

'He is a member of the Lyonne Order,' Arden said warily. 'Where did you find him? Maris, obviously.'

'There is no Maris. Not any more. We recovered this man from a rock in between here and the island. He had quite a story to tell. A Queen captured. A town overrun by bloodworked creatures called out of the ocean. Who could do that, I wonder. Who?'

Arden held her breath. Danger loomed. Her grommets prickled through the numbness. *Jonah*.

'Miah, do not trust this man.'

Without warning, Miah grabbed Arden by her arms and pushed her against the bars of the cage.

'You lied to me.'

'When?'

'About everything. About your willingness to a marriage. Two nights ago. Made it seem you were all for it.'

'Miah, all we spoke of was a fancy, what we'd do if Jonah was not alive.'

'Is this a fancy?' He kissed her roughly, his tongue in her

mouth tasting of charsmoke and kelp spirit. She gasped at the imposition of it, struck him – a little weakly – across his face. She bit his lower lip, tasted blood. *Mandatum* there, as thinly bitter as anything left behind by the dead saint.

He grunted, pushed Arden away, using his weight against hers and mashing the steel into her back. He wiped the blood from his mouth with grim humour.

'Mr Lindsay and I had an interesting talk. You can make a sanguinity stronger? Amplify what is already in a person's blood? *Evalescendi*, my friend here says.'

'Of course, I told Mr Cleave what I was,' she started, then stopped, for she had not told him, not really. He probably still thought it *sanguis ignis*, or something common. And she had been cautious with Miah, not altogether trusting him.

'Not everything came to our bargaining table, Beacon. You never told me what you could do for me, how you made your way across the badlands without getting sliced to ribbons. Our deal is not broken if one party lied about everything from the start!'

'Miah, I cannot bargain with something I don't fully control.'

'Since neither Bellis nor my cousin are on Maris, and you were slippery about your assets, so *our deal* is *forfeit*.'

'If it is forfeit, then let me go.'

'No. I've decided to forge a new agreement. Mr Lindsay here tells me how truly useful a *sanguis evalescendi* is. I've also decided you will marry me and make me leader of these people. Their Deepwater King.'

'What are you talking about? You cannot marry me without my permission.'

'This is the Sainted Islands. A marriage is not your decision. It's the decision of the clan and the people in it, and you've won me some leverage in that argument.'

'If these clansfolk forbade the great Miah Anguis a bride before today,' Arden hissed in her most blisteringly supercilious tone, 'a new argument will not sway them.'

'Says a *sanguis evalescendi*, who can make powerful what is weak?' He jerked his chin towards the tussock-dunes, and gave a clenching, victorious smile, his teeth stained red from his bitten lip.

'The old copper devil still makes these people afraid in the night. You'll marry me in blood and body and when it's done I'll use your blood's power to clear out the mechanica from this island once and for all.'

21

Don't

'Don't talk to me.'

'Please, Mx Beacon,' Mr Lindsay called gently. 'Mx Beacon, I hope you're not thinking of doing something foolish like trying to escape.'

She turned her head so she would not have to look at the Lion, and pressed her coins until they hurt, and distracted her from the chill. The dreary afternoon rain had eased off, and were it not for the scrap of iron sheet over her enclosure, she would have been soaked to the bone. Miah had not taken any chances of her fleeing before the *wedding*. He'd made good on his promise. Locked her inside the iron-pipe cage next to Mr Lindsay and pocketed the key to an iron padlock as big as her fist.

'*Keep you out of trouble*,' were his exact words. '*Until I can bring everyone the good news*.'

Mr Lindsay continued in a wheedle, 'He believes he's made a very prudent decision. See, an unmarried man cannot make a case for leadership among these people, and it appears certain factions of this antediluvian community do not wish him to assume the mantle of leader. You quite fell into his lap, a Lyonnian woman not bound by deepwater strictures, and useful to boot! One cannot blame him for taking advantage of the situation.'

Some women chatted behind the half-broken ship on their way back from the sorting tables. Snatches of voice. A child's shriek. Sometimes they cast glances her way. Arden stewed in an enraged sulk. The only bright spot in all the miserable day was Jonah's confirmed survival, but it was all spoken of so remotely it could not be but a dent in her current predicament.

'Also I apologize for telling the senior Riven about your potential. I thought you may have already told him, being so intimate and all.'

'Sod off, Mr Lindsay.' She frowned and then turned on him. 'All right then, if you want to talk. What happened to Jonah, what did Miah mean by a Queen captured and a town overrun?'

Mr Lindsay affected an expression of sympathy. 'He took his own freedom. The Librans made off with Bellis and me. Your fellow called a hundred monsters to shore as a diversion. Just like he did the day he killed his family. Where he went from there, I don't know. He did not come with us.'

Beyond the shipyard, a group of men passed by, longboat oars slung over their shoulders like spear-fighters. One of them was Miah. He did not look in the direction of Arden's cage.

Mr Lindsay noticed the frosty snub immediately. 'You've waded into a pickle, dear. He desires leadership and respect from his deepwater kin far more than he desires human companionship. He's like a shark with the scent of blood now.'

Arden scratched her gloves agitatedly. Mr Lindsay found her actions interesting.

'Do they itch, those coins I had installed last year? They are not so far off being rejected from your body. Your time grows short and you know this.'

She knew it, but she would not let him see.

The rain fell all that morning, miserable and cold. The shelter gave anything but, and she shivered through the day, hungry and aching, pain upon her skin and in her heart.

* * *

Late past noon a pair of sea-wives came to escort her from prison to a longhouse of twisted branches and iron plates. She rushed to the fire in the iron grate, warmed her numb hands in the heat, and her toes, and her face. Sitting in a cold tub for several minutes was one thing, but a half-day wet and frozen in little but a thin knitted dress was something quite torturously else. On a nearby carpet, a large king otter the size of a sled-dog raised his grey muzzle and the wet nose moved as it sniffed the unwashed newcomer, before curling itself back to sleep.

'Any closer to the fire and you'd be hugging the flames,' the older woman said. 'Stand back and let me put more briquettes on.'

Arden reluctantly sat back on a low bench, though she did not want to leave the heat, and the woman poured more coals from a black-dusted linen bag into the fire pit, before patting the otter's great wedge of a head.

'I am Mrs Seaworthy,' said the woman. 'I am a widow.' She pointed to her younger companion, dark-haired and generous-fleshed, a beautiful face that seemed quite at odds with these simple folk. 'This is Mrs Stone, who was only a year ago married to the young man you may have met upon the beach where we hunted the serpent. Our stormcaller, Mr Stone.'

'Hoy,' Mrs Stone said in her flat Islander accent, smiling with a little too much friendliness. 'Together we sew your wedding dress! As Deepwater Bride you'll become one of us.'

The dress turned out to be an unadorned and simple shift. As Mrs Seaworthy laid it out across the salvaged wood, Arden noted the fragility of the fabric, its frayed seams, how it might barely last a night. Still, it shimmered under their hands, a cunning weave that imitated tiny scales, a bone-ivory dress of snakeskin tending to gold in the firelight.

Once she had taken Arden's measurements, Mrs Seaworthy brought food, a salty soda bread, cheese and pickled melon, a prickly-pear fruit for desert, an eel-berry wine.

Mrs Seaworthy asked, gently, 'Has it been explained, what will happen tonight?'

Arden tore her bread into small pieces. She was hungry, but her nervous stomach would not hold enough food. 'I haven't thought about it.'

What she had thought about, was escape. And every permutation in her mind kept ending up with her being chased into the pipelands and Miah Anguis in a jealous rage draining every pint of blood out of her.

In between the man who had fished her out of the ocean and the one who now wanted to bind her in marital captivity, a disturbing transformation had taken place.

Mrs Seaworthy spoke as she sewed. 'There is an old legend among our people, of the first Deepwater Bride. A beautiful girl, a King's daughter, would walk the beaches of Equus. Then one day the Deepwater King saw her and fell in love. He pursued her, made her his bride, took her into his watery kingdom.'

Arden chewed nervously on the bread. '. . . And?'

'After the initial ceremony, the groom pursues the bride while she is barefoot,' Mrs Seaworthy said matter-of-factly. 'The serpent-call will be made and either it or the Deepwater King plucks the maiden off the beach and takes her to his cave—'

'Tent, really,' Mrs Stone interjected to Mrs Seaworthy's tut of impatience. 'She is ravished, and then it is done. Oh, it is not so bad at all,' Mrs Stone finished with a giggle. 'Mostly we run down the shore a little, trip up and roll around together.'

'Peg, we are not talking about your common conveniences and your clumsiness,' Mrs Seaworthy chided. 'Go on back to minding the children dear, I need to speak to our guest on her own.'

Mrs Stone frowned. 'But Amos said we were not supposed to leave her alone in case she—'

'Go,' Mrs Seaworthy said, harder.

Sulky and making faces, the younger woman left the long-house with the huge otter at her heels. Arden sat up straight, sensing the import of the moment. Mrs Seaworthy spun a black-iron wedding ring on her finger, leaving behind a red oxide stain upon her skin.

'So my dressmakers are guards too. Am I expected to make an escape if I'm left unattended?' Arden asked flatly.

'Where would you go if you did?'

Arden didn't reply, and Mrs Seaworthy stood up, walked to the other side of the longhouse and opened a door.

'Henrietta,' Mrs Seaworthy called softly. 'We're ready.'

A tall woman entered the lodge, bearing a flax woven satchel. A woman in an embroidered dress of grey wool, with chevrons on her cheeks. It was the same woman who had helped her bathe on the first morning, Mrs Cleave. She projected such an authority Arden halfway wondered if she should stand up at the woman's arrival.

'Should have thought it too easy,' Henrietta Cleave scolded. 'I actually believed Miah would keep the agreement and let you leave us before he spun ideas about getting married. How on earth did you fumble such a simple *restitutio* deal, and with *him*?'

'I didn't fumble the deal, Mrs Cleave. The agreement was broken from the beginning. He's the one who should be driven into the pipelands.'

'Yes he is. But I come to bring a repair of sorts.'

Mrs Henrietta Cleave sat down before Arden, placed the satchel by her side, and nodded at her. 'You are Arden Beacon. Your uncle was Jorgen Beacon, of Vigil, and formerly Clay.'

'Yes.'

'I knew him,' she said. 'He was a good man. Respected among the deepwater folk, and a good friend of Zachariah Riven, who was a distant cousin of mine.'

Of course, Arden thought. It was where Henrietta's sharp, sea-bitten features came from.

'So I will talk to you with respect,' Henrietta Cleave continued. She placed her hand on the satchel meaningfully. 'Has it occurred to you, Clay woman, to wonder why Miah is unmarried at his age? Why the women have steered clear of his name for twenty years even though they are not averse to brief trysts in the mangrove forest?'

Arden shook her head and rubbed the coins in her hands. They did not pain her. The heel of her hands remained numb, as if the fire had not warmed them up at all. Her anxieties crowded about her, a suffocating weight.

'He said because you have never properly accepted him.'

'It's not acceptance,' Mrs Cleave went on. 'We don't *want* him married to anyone. Nobody wants him as Deepwater King, or have him replacing my husband, Amos. The monster in him cannot rule this town. Yes, the title was held by Jonah Riven for a night and a day to save his demon Queen, but at least he left when all was done.'

Next to Mrs Cleave, Mrs Seaworthy nodded and made the circle of the serpent upon her chest. 'Thalie's son left, and took that devil Queen away from us. She could terrorize the rest of the islands, but she had no place here.'

'Because of Miah.'

'Unfortunately, yes. They are a pair, repelling each other. Thank the deep sea gods they shared a hatred from when they were children in Vigil.'

'Thank those gods,' Mrs Seaworthy repeated and made the serpent sign again.

'But that still leaves you,' Henrietta Cleave said. 'I have been Deepwater Bride for thirty-five years. Amos is my second husband. I have kept this community alive through all the encroachments of mechanica and sanguis devil queens, I am not about to make way for a helpless Lyonnian interloper who has *no* control over that man's worst obsessions.'

'I don't intend to stay, Mrs Cleave, married or not.'

'You won't. Miah Anguis will not keep you around much longer afterwards.'

'What are you talking about?'

Mrs Cleave stared at Arden intently, willing her to take with the utmost gravity what she had to say. 'Only the Bride can challenge the King's leadership. There's little you can offer him once the marriage rite is completed except the risk of losing his position.'

'What – are you saying he'll kill me?'

Henrietta did not blink. 'As a man given the abyssal crown he will have utter say over your life and death.'

'He will not kill me.'

'Really? He will suffer being second in command?'

'He still needs my blood to use his power.'

'The blood. Not the woman.'

Arden must have appeared resentful enough that Mrs Cleave did not linger on the awful outcomes.

'But there is still a way to survive the ceremony and secure – if not escape, then at least time.'

'How?'

'*You must run*,' Mrs Cleave said.

'That's what I want to do,' Arden started, then stopped, for Mrs Cleave had opened the satchel and in it were her forbidden sturdy signaller's boots, cleaned and rescued from the long walk.

'You're giving me my boots back?'

'And your coat. Enough for you to survive that first night unconsummated. He may claim you as wife, but without the first night's ceremony he cannot claim the position of leader. We are too *thorough* for that.'

Just as Henrietta said, a krakenskin coat lay folded neatly below the boots. Hers, not Jonah's, which Arden quite accepted she would never see again.

'As soon as you are on the bridal beach, get dressed. You have a head start, and you must run far. Grab a stick and beat him if you must, throw your blood-fire at him! Do not let your husband catch you. If he does not catch you on the wedding night, the leadership challenge will be forfeit. He cannot marry you, he cannot be King.'

Someone outside was talking, and Mrs Cleave stiffened and dared not speak further. In the silence Arden's mind was a whirlwind. Boots, that meant she could run. A beach, far from here, meant an escape.

Mrs Cleave was cunning enough to see the gears turning behind Arden's eyes. 'It's not a complete escape, dear. The wedding will take place here, first. Then the second act, on a small island north of here. One night out of his reach . . . that is all. Afterwards with the ritual incomplete, another agreement can be made. But my husband will remain administrator of these people, and you may yet have your freedom.'

Arden exhaled. 'If you think it will work.'

Mrs Cleave nodded at the boots again. 'They'll be hidden on the longboat that is meant to take you out. Don't let Miah see. He will take grave offence that we intend to trick him out of his ambitions.'

She stopped talking as the big otter slid back into the room and let out a bark.

The door opened a few seconds later. Miah stood bulky and tall in the shadows, watching them in judgemental silence.

'Were you not supposed to prepare a dress, Mrs Seaworthy, and not indulge in idle gossip?' His eyes went to Mrs Cleave, and anger darkened them. 'Or you, Mrs Cleave?'

'Mr Anguis,' Mrs Seaworthy said hurriedly, leaping to her feet so quickly she knocked over the bench. 'Your bride is in seclusion. She must not be spoken to.'

Mrs Cleave rose only slowly. 'I am giving the next Bride advice on her duties to come, Jeremiah. It is no simple task, leading these people.'

'Leave us for a moment.'

'Mr . . .'

'Get out of here, Henrietta.'

Mrs Cleave give Arden a pointed glance. Mrs Seaworthy had already fled.

Miah came up to the table, took up the hem of the discarded dress. Rubbed it between his fingers before glaring at Arden sulkily.

'Will you stay here without trouble, or will the cage be better?'

Were it not so ghastly cold she would have rather had the cage. There was no ambiguity there. This warm lodge meant to seduce her with homeliness. She was trapped between Miah Anguis and Mrs Cleave's warnings.

Too late, she realized the forbidden boots were on the same table as the dress. Mrs Seaworthy had hurried so much that she'd forgotten to hide them.

Arden lunged to him so he might turn about and not investigate the package upon her table, or the knife, or the instruments of her escape. 'I'm supposed to be in *seclusion* here,' she said, snatching the dress up and folding it upon one of the other tables, drawing him away. 'You impress upon me all the rituals of your people and then cast them aside to suit your whims!'

Miah snatched her arm and pulled her close to him. The change was in his face, a caul of strange obsession covered his eyes.

'I called the serpent to the shore,' he hissed. 'Me, not Mr Cleave, or any of the men. The Deepwater King moves in *me* and in *my* blood. I make the rules, and when you are Deepwater Bride the damn rest of them will follow me.'

'It must not be much of a following if they can't elect you naturally.'

'What were you all conspiring about?'

Arden's heart raced so hard it would have been impossible for Miah not to have heard.

'How to be the Deepwater Bride,' she said sullenly, even though underneath she was jumpy with excitement. 'Since I have been roped into that position without my consent.'

'Well, you certainly know the mechanics of that position.'

Her mind boiled over with quick thoughts. Though they were her chosen avenue of escape, she would not rest her entire chance on Mrs Cleave and the women. They all thought her merely a tool, and perhaps that was mostly true.

Miah Anguis will not keep you around much longer afterwards.

But Miah couldn't be completely mercenary. Even a shark in bloodied waters might have some recognition of its own kind. She took the dive, same as she had on the platform.

'I know the mechanics of your heart, Miah. When first you spoke of this to me, it was not through sheer ambition, out of wanting to be King. It was a *man* who wanted not to feel so lonely. You didn't need to have treated me so abrupt and cruel.'

He scowled. 'You will never feel towards me the same as you feel towards Jonah. Not while he is alive. Only a fool would continue to hold hope.'

I will run from you. I will run and you will not see me again.

'These last few days have made me a realist. We can still work something out, you and I.'

She moved close to him. A dark, unbidden passion leapt into his eyes, a confusion of thoughts he'd not allowed himself before. He snatched her up and pressed his mouth to hers, great gasping, hungry kisses she was powerless to fight, so did not.

Then he discarded her, his breath wheezing like a steam train. His hands worked at his belt buckle, and she laid her own numb palms upon his raw knuckles.

'You must leave,' she said. 'We cannot make love. It is forbidden until after the wedding.'

A moment when she thought he'd laugh at her, and mock her small protest. Then he nodded.

'Until after the wedding,' he gruffed, and left her standing alone in the longhouse, shivering as if she'd run from one side of Equus to the other.

22

Thunderclouds massed upon the horizon

Thunderclouds massed upon the horizon, great mountains illuminated internally by violet lightning. The sunlight faded long before the day's end, casting a monochromatic gloom over the rusting hulks of the ghost ships and the thin, hungry coast.

In the fading light the women came for Arden and sat her upon a stool. Mrs Cleave thumbed the skin behind each ear taut, murmured Fictish prayers. The application of the wedding tattoo took a long hour. As a thin line of kraken ink fell down into the bodice of her dress she tumbled over the instructions Mrs Cleave had impressed upon her.

Delay the moment Miah consummated the wedding. Hide for the night. He would be fighting mad, but Mrs Cleave would, with her grateful husband, supply a boat for her when she returned from the ceremony. Because he was not King and leader, Miah could not stop Arden from leaving.

She would go to Maris after this, Arden decided. Even if it was abandoned it would be a start. Someone must have remained to tell her where Jonah had gone.

Mrs Cleave took Arden's chin in her hands and raised Arden's face so it might meet her own. 'Remember,' she said firmly in Lyonnian, 'what you have to do tonight. The boots are in the front of the bridal boat, along with the krakenskin.'

The day was late by the time the boats were ready to sail, the sulky sun behind clouds and a song on the wind, the callers of the King. Upon the dock, the young folk gathered to see Arden off in her decorated longboat. David and Sean were among them. Their gloomy expressions didn't stand out so much among the others. Today was an anxious, waiting day, not a celebratory one.

David took a step towards Arden's bridal party, only to have Sean catch his arm, hold him back.

Arden took her seat in the bow of a decorated longboat. Miah paced the dock with predatory restlessness, uttered sharp words to anyone that displeased him. She was just as restless, but for other reasons entirely. Her feet could not keep still, as if an invisible music were playing the cacophony of freedom.

Arden's boat left the harbour first. At an appropriate distance, the captain, a small, sea-bitten woman, switched over to the petralactose motor. A kick of power made the bow rise, and Arden hung on grimly as the boat hauled through the water.

Past Equus, the shallow seas turned grey, and the waters became oddly flat and clear, as if a wave-break had caused it to stagnate into a still, lapping pond. The bride-boat passed over mineralized forms resting just below the water. Arden guessed she might be looking at floating pumice stones or Sargasso shoals, only for Mrs Cleave to lean forward and say, 'Skeletons. Because of the rockblood and the mechanica, these waters are toxic, and barren of life. It's why they are so clear.'

She turned to Mrs Cleave, feeling hopeful. 'Which means it will be hard to call monsters?'

The woman nodded. 'Exactly. He cannot summon reinforcements where we are going.' She gave a sigh and then asked over the clatter of the engine, 'Is it true? Miah says you have a sanguinity that can increase his *mandatum* talent, that with your help he could clear the mechanica from the island.'

Arden shook her head. 'All the *mandatum* in the world won't make Equus like it once was,' she said. 'They were lain in with *orientis*, too, and that's hard blood.'

Mrs Cleave closed her eyes and nodded. She seemed a woman well used to casting aside impossible dreams. 'Then make your flight swift and we will meet again in the morning.'

By eventide a small, mountainous island rose up from the dead waters like the tip of a great sunken castle. Arden's confidence faltered as she marked its dimensions. It was a small, solitary outcrop close to five miles wide, craggy and desolate. If she didn't find somewhere to hide within its intimidating vertical aspect, she would have to quickly learn the feminine wiles of manipulating a king.

Devilment, she thought to herself miserably, if I knew how to make a man do my bidding, I'd be Mrs Richard Castile.

'Mx Beacon,' said a voice in her ear.

She startled. Mrs Cleave had not spoken this time, only one of the bridesmaids. The former Deepwater Queen had retired to the back of the longboat to unspool the anchor.

The bridesmaid nodded at a package at Arden's feet. 'Put on the boots. We're going to beach this boat. Get ready to run.'

The singers sang the song of the Deepwater Bride, daughter of a wealthy King, who had chanced a shoreline where she was forbidden to go. Arden fumbled with her laces, feeling the boots at once too loose and too tight.

Not so far behind them, the bridegroom's boat cut its motors and unfurled the black sail.

She had halfway imagined a long, unbroken shore, like the beach at the Clay mouth. Instead, they'd arrived at a dirty, wave-broken scramble like a twin to the ruined coast they'd left, a dump littered with boat parts and broken machinery. Gnarled skeletal remains of tree roots tangled in grey spools at the tideline.

In the setting sun the shadows cast out long and black against the flame-tinged sand. The engine clattered louder, the bow raised, skipped and jumped.

'Hold on!' shouted the woman at the tiller. 'Duck down!'

A dreadful jolt and scrape. Arden's shoulder rammed into the bow. The bridesmaids let out a collective yelp of protest at the rough landing. The woman at Arden's back gave her a push.

Arden snatched up the krakenskin coat and stumbled out of the boat, before splashing through the skim of water. Half-buried debris caught and snagged her feet.

Almost to the second of the groomsboat reaching the shoreline, the sun set behind the island's great rock. Arden heard the bullroarers behind her, the calling of *maris anguis*.

Run.

23

In the pelting gloom

In the pelting gloom, her feet fell over a length of iron, and she quickly traced out a ragged edge with her foot. Only a bruise, no skin broken. Her dress caught and frayed.

She pulled off a glove, slipped the wax from a coin, bit into her new healing skin. Foxfire jumped in her palm, a tiny orb of *ignis spiritus* that glowed no brighter than a gleam of moonlight on still water. Not enough of a light for anyone to see but her own Beacon-sharp eyes.

She stood up and looked around wildly. 'Gods and devils damn it,' she said under her breath. The beach had ended as suddenly as if a mountain had fallen there. A sheer slab of extruded granite, stretching into the sky.

In the distance some male voices sounded in song, echoing off the rockwall.

She had to get off this beach. As for shelter, only a narrow copse of black mangroves against the battlement wall of the island mountain provided the slightest cover. She might as well have been put in a box.

I'll double back, she thought. *It's nearly dark. If I can make my way past the landing . . .*

She came across a small trench in the sand that might have

been a creek mouth once, and Arden turned inland to where the dead mangrove trees twisted in their eternal dying. Some animal had left behind a narrow path through the trees. She moved through, willing her breath not so rasp so loudly past her lips.

Through the gaps in the foliage came snatches of lantern-light. The wedding party had set up their tents at their landing spot in preparation for a vigil.

By the morning they would have a King.

Or not.

Make it not, Arden thought fiercely. *Make it not.*

And then . . . she was past them . . . and the track was wider . . . she was around the corner of the rocky spit and headed out of their sight. A vaulting excitement made Arden drunk on her own narrow escape. She held out her hand before her and burst out onto the far beach.

Snatches of half-moon silver winked through the clouds, casting her shadow long and dark across the clean white sand.

Arden was no more than a dozen paces into the beach when a thickly muscled figure flanked her, lunged at her and pulled her tight into tattooed arms scabbed by monster-calling.

'No!'

She fought the arms that held her, hard, shrugged and contorted and suddenly Miah was standing in front of her where he'd been lying in wait, and where she would have stumbled if—

'Cousin,' Miah growled. 'Let her go.'

What? Who's holding me?

A rockblood fire ignited in a shallow trench. The waves roared behind him. Arden let her body grow still, and knowing. The arms around her were unfamiliar. Too heavy, too coarsened by work.

The heart which beat at her back lubbed with a rock-hammer's strike.

Miah stood wearing the grey-blue leather of his moiety's giant serpent over his bare chest. He had not bothered to chase her.

Had lain in wait instead, ensconced himself within a circle of sharpened pipes concealed in the sand. The fire made their shadows jump and writhe like snakes.

Or maybe they did move. *Mandatum* instructions.

'I don't wish to fight you, Jeremiah,' rumbled the voice at her back.

That voice. She felt the strength leave her. She sagged into the arms that held her. She knew this voice.

'Why not? Would be nothing for a murderer to bring those dark things to the shore like you did the first time.'

'I have paid my debt for that.'

'Really? What happened to the last woman taken from us? Turned into a scourge worse than your monsters ever were. How fitting, that everything under your influence becomes an abomination. Oh, you'll destroy this one too.'

The muscles tensed behind her. The rain began to fall again, sleeting lashes of pain. Her heartbeat pounded a name.

Jonah Riven.

Jonah Riven.

Jonah Riven.

Arden wanted to turn around. Look at Jonah's face. Be certain it was him and not a ghost.

When Jonah did not reply Miah said, 'Look down, cousin, she is injured.'

I'm not injured, she wanted to say but the distraction was enough and without warning Miah charged at the pair of them, his fists swinging.

In the time it took to heave a breath she was tossed aside. Someone shouted her name, the rain thundered upon them in a deluge. The fires were up. A pipe writhed near her face. The ground shook.

She clambered upright, her hair falling about her face so she could not see.

'Get away,' Jonah's disembodied voice shouted in the rain. 'Get out of here, Arden!'

'No, I can't lose you again!'

Out of the darkness, as if he were a creature rent in two, Miah loomed out and seized her ankle. Lightning illuminated his face, a rictus of rage and hunger.

'Stay . . . here!'

He seized her and threw her onto the sand, before following with the weight of his body. For a terrible second she thought he might try to ravish her among the stakes and pipes, but instead he grabbed her hand, bearing down hard upon her coins so her fingers splayed in agony. His mouth enclosed her fingers, teeth bumping over her knuckles.

Was not his tongue that she felt, but a hard circlet of metal.

Arden yanked her hand free, but it was too late, the copper ring was already upon her, tightening.

Gasping, she kicked Miah away and stumbled into the storm, called up her weak, stuttering foxfire into her palm once again. Her sense of direction lost itself to the sideways sleeting rain, the howl of wind buffeting against the forest and the trees.

'Too late!' he screamed, laughing with maniacal hysteria. 'You wear my fucking ring. Beacon! You belong to the fucking Deepwater King!'

A conflagration of air built behind her, same sense of massive weight and displacement as the storm that had brought the giant serpent a week before. Sanguis feeling, blood-called . . .

Then a screaming, a man on the beach, howling in rage . . . and agony . . . and she turned about, afraid of who it might be. The lightning flashes rimed what seemed . . . almost seemed . . .

A figure lumbered out from the rain, illuminated in fire, bleeding from a cut at his side, and Arden staggered from the relief and exhaustion of seeing him again.

'Jonah . . .'

He was bigger than she remembered, seemed older even though a full season separated them. His tattoos hard and black, like scars on his pale skin. An unfathomable weariness in his eyes. His face had harshened, his head shorn down to the root. In grief Arden had dreamt of seeing him again, of rushing into his arms.

But all that had happened between them made him remote as the storm.

She embraced him in the rain and pressed kisses to his mouth and he was alive and real and confused at her return so utterly that she had to let him go.

The elation of reunion was tempered by an almost unbearable sadness, and Jonah frowned at her wedding dress and the band on her finger.

'You *married* him?'

At the shoreline, an incapacitated Miah was yelling, screaming Jonah's name.

24

I had to

'I had to, Jonah, there was no other way.'

The terror of losing him made her cling to Jonah's wrecked and hard-scarred body as if he were a precipice she might fall from, and to her death. He had to peel her grasping hands off, wrap them up in his own.

'We haven't time,' he shouted over the storm. 'You have to move.'

This stranger-lover slung his bare arm about her torso. He was so cold, she feared him not real at all, a ghost, a revenant come back to life to help her for this one awful moment before fading back into the nothingness of death.

'Hurry, the fin-folk won't keep him occupied for long.'

Jonah grabbed her hand. More little insults to her pride followed, for she could barely walk in a straight line. Arden tripped over an exposed root, and he fell on top of her. She felt the bellows of his breath and knew then that he was drained too. However he had come back to her, he had not come back altogether healthy or whole.

They held on to each other in the darkness, panting for air as quietly as possible.

'How are *you* here,' she gasped once it was clear they were in nobody's earshot. 'How did you know *I* was here?'

'Jeremiah knew I was here,' Jonah said between breaths.

Arden knew the depths of Miah's envy of Jonah, but the extent still made her gasp. 'That devil. He did this on purpose.'

In the half-light his grip tightened. His breath was a hot tide on her forehead, the curious alcohol smell of starvation. Her fretful mind fell back to Mr Lindsay in the pipework cage. His talk of Jonah summoning the monsters of his childhood. It had to have left a mark on Jonah's soul.

He pulled her upright, abruptly. 'Can you walk?'

Nodded wordlessly, indicated she was fine.

'Good. There's shelter up ahead.'

They continued to climb through the sloppy mangrove forest, on a laddered path slippery with leaves. Even with her dark-sight freed from the veil of the saint's powers, Arden struggled to see. The forest was so close, so tangled. The arms held her secure as stone and they came upon the great granite wall that stretched up into the clouds. Warmth surrounded them, for the granite radiated a fecund heat.

A tiny miner's elevator-cage, barely wide enough for one person. At two people abreast, they could only stand in an embrace. Jonah held her close, and in the wet she heard the chatter of a chain running through a gear mechanism, the airy whoosh of descending counterweights, and their little iron platform began to rise.

As she embraced him, she felt his muscles trembling with fatigue, and something else, a high, singing tension. Was it her causing this anxiousness or something else?

Their ascent slowed. The cage moved through a thin layer of cloud. The rain eased off into a fine mist. Lingering smell of sulphur in the air, a heat from the rock like a night-road after a hot summer day. Jonah tied off the ratchet chain so they could not be followed.

With her terrors far below her, Arden realized how fiercely she was shivering. They had come upon a courtyard of stone. All around her were the same undulating designs as in the city of Burden Town carved into the flagstones, balustrades and fire pits.

But unlike the worn, corroded stone of the Equus city, these carvings were preserved unmolested as if the compound had been frozen in time. Eternal blood-lamps flickered within stone lantern houses, gave the stones a slinking yellow glow in the fog.

Some kind of church or monastery gone to ruin, she decided, or a priory for a religious order, with a main building flanked by smaller ones.

Jonah tested a door, then leaned into it until the wooden lock gave way. Once in he tapped around in the gloom until he found the flint that could light the fire pit.

As the flames jumped, the carvings upon the walls shuddered and flexed. Men and sea-monsters, at sport and at war.

'What is this place?' she asked, teeth chattering. 'A church? A temple?'

'Holy ground.' He stopped at the doorway boundary. 'I can't stay. I have to deal with my cousin.' He paused, and in the firelight his face became older, and she saw Miah in him, and at once was both repelled and ashamed for feeling it.

The King's cedar-carved face, wreathed in kelp leaves, gazed down at her from above the doorway lintel, sly and knowing.

Jonah saw her reaction, and saw it perhaps the wrong way. 'I have to deal with my cousin. You'll be safe here.'

'Jonah—'

He slid out of her grasp and into the night. She attempted to run after him, and her courage failed her at once. Because they were high out of the rain, a wicked fog had swept in with the storm, made the world as blank as a cataract.

She retreated into the chapel, shivering too much to consider another attempt at following him. Closed the door to the chill. Pressed her cheek against the carved wood. Took a breath, let it become a sob. Leaned upon the door and wept.

For the relief. For the loss.

* * *

She stumbled in the sand and the Deepwater King was on her at once, Miah's face looming above hers—

Arden jerked awake. The moment had been brief but she was certain she'd felt him here in this room, his hands on her skin.

But she was alone, and the terror drained out of her, leaving her wrung out. The damp wedding dress steamed on her body. Arden had come to sleep, or had been placed, close to a stone fire pit, the krakenskin coat bunched beneath her head to make a pillow.

She remembered the copper wedding band on her finger, and attempted to remove it again but to no avail. It had tightened beneath her knuckle. She could spin it, but the only way it was coming off was if her finger went with it. She was well and truly stuck with the evidence of her marriage.

A whispering in the high eaves caught her attention. Monstrosities up there in the dappled gloom, little flying devils, leathery and pale as death-doves. She moved closer to the fire, knowing that it was blood they liked best.

'Jonah?' she murmured.

'He won't come back here. It's holy ground, and he has not yet been forgiven his sins.'

The voice startled her and she turned about, disoriented in the uneven light. The accent had been Lyonnian, and could not have belonged to Miah or one of his men.

'Who are you? Show yourself.'

A wrinkle appeared in the darkness. Then a face moved from the shadows as if he were surfacing from a black lake.

That face. Her voice caught like a chain snagged on a gear. The word came out in a croak.

'*Father?*'

25

No

No, no. Too young, by years, only the embracing dark had made him seem that way, the pepper in his beard. Not Lucian Beacon, with his stout sternness, but paler in his complexion, as if he'd never seen the sun. This man was younger and taller, with a Clay Portside common-blood cast to his features, and his black curling hair cut so short it was like a tight knitted cap upon his high forehead. He wore the simple robes of a minister, with a ceremonial brace of skeletonised albatross heads on each shoulder. His eye sockets were smeared with charcoal and nacre, making them seem as if twin abysses pierced his skull.

But a Beacon all the same.

'I know your face. Have we met?' the man asked hesitantly, his eyes reflecting the firelight as if his skin was merely an envelope for flame.

'I'm Arden Beacon. Of Lyonne.'

'Arden.' His brow furrowed. 'My cousin had that name. They used to say we looked alike, that we could be twins, even.'

Even in her despair she wanted to wail with relief, like the drowning man who finds a rope thrown to them. 'I am your cousin! It is me! Your father and my father were full brothers.

You're Stefan Beacon, son of Jorgen, who worked the Vigil lighthouse. You are family!'

'Family? You are Lucian's daughter?'

She nodded, giddy with relief. 'We met in Clay Portside, just as you arrived to study for the priesthood. You lived in Vigil, the town at Fiction's end, you served as pastor for the land between Vigil and Garfish Point. They said you died, cousin, after Bellis Harrow disappeared. They said Jonah Riven was to blame . . . and he was not! Not at all!'

Stefan dipped his head, closed his eyes as if he were recalling an old, forgotten song. 'Yes. I am from Vigil. And I did die, in a way. I am Pastor John Stefan now. Or I was. Then I came here. How is it that you know Jonah Riven?'

'I took over your father's lighthouse in the summertime. He still lived in the compound on the promontory. We . . . and then Bellis . . .' she stammered, hardly able to breathe from the surprise of seeing her cousin again, here, when she thought him dead at Bellis' hands. The pair had sailed away from Vigil together over four years ago. Arden had feared he'd become yet another one of Bellis Harrow's disposable *orientine*-controlled servants. It would be difficult to survive such a condition.

'I understand, if it involved Bellis. Now wait, I must finish my prayers.' Her cousin fell back into the shadows. A door rattled in the dark, and she was once again alone.

'Stefan . . .' She followed him into the gloom, and the doors he must have gone through, and entered the cathedral.

For all its carvings and cavernous space, the fire-pit room had merely been an antechamber. This was the true gallery that opened up, a void both dark and expansive. Her breath echoed in her throat, then disappeared into the immensity.

As if at the end of a deep well, its bulk sunken into the rock, a massive cedar-wood icon overwhelmed the far apse-wall.

Instead of the Clay Church Redeemer spread helplessly and chained on His Libro rock, this icon was completely different. A sea-serpent tangle at war with a kraken, and a nude male figure entwined within them. The statue had cold abyssal eyes of jet, skin painted with the same oyster-shell nacre as on Pastor John Stefan's eyes.

Arden couldn't help but avert her eyes a little.

'I have asked the King,' he said on her approach, 'what you are doing on my island sanctuary in a deepwater wedding dress, and He tells me that it is a question my cousin best answer herself.'

'Stefan,' she said with a click of impatience, disturbed by his presence and that big violent icon where the Redeemer of God should have been, 'there's a man on the beach who is trying to either kidnap or kill me or both! And where is Jonah? It's not safe for him out there.'

'Jonah can keep himself safe, if that is your concern.' He gestured about himself. 'And nobody is coming here, the chapel grounds are forbidden to the Equus folk. I assume that is what they are, for you wear a sea-silk wedding dress.' Stefan nodded up at the icon. 'Now. Walk with me. It is not wise to gossip in front of the King.'

Nautical morning, when there was light enough to see by, not enough for the sky to court a sunrise. Stefan brought her to the pergola of a smaller temple, its overhanging roof writhed in carved kraken-symbols. Seaweed faces peered over the lintels.

The rain fell soft here, and a row of wooden time-clocks in a contemplative courtyard garden nearby bowed under the weight of water. They chimed against three hollow bellies of granite in succession.

'Are you not missing morning prayers? Or do you not have them?'

'The King can wait. Breakfast first, then we shall speak.'

Despite Arden's anxious buzz, Stefan made her sit patiently as he rolled up the sleeves of his linen shirt and fetched two bowls of a slow-cooked fish stew left simmering from a previous night's meal, cut pomegranates, tuber bread, goat's cheese, a weak foamy mead to drink.

She'd thought herself too broken to eat, but as soon as the

food was in front of her, Arden wolfed down her meal without pausing to speak. Yet even as she ate her first substantial meal in days, she stole careful glances at her cousin. What were they supposed to talk about? Stefan was a stranger to her, and as to his allegiances, he seemed far too given over to his kraken-wrestling god for comfort. A priest with a big Deepwater King idol in his main chapel, and who suffered impromptu weddings on the beach, couldn't be entirely on her side.

In the end he initiated the conversation. 'The dress becomes you, but is not quite suitable for the weather, even with a krakenskin coat.'

'I wasn't given much of a choice,' she grumbled past a mouthful of stew. She paused to look around her. 'Who is this church for? Is it to the Deepwater King or the Clay Redeemer?'

'This little rock has been sacred to nearly every civilization that has crossed its path, and they all leave a mark on it one way or another.'

He pointed upwards. A map was carved on the pergola's undersides. The Sainted archipelago. The three main islands were surrounded by a scatter of islets like a constellation of stars.

Gilded in gold leaf was Stefan's crooked little island. It lay off the coast of Equus, the last crumb of land before the immense and endless void that was the Darkling Sea, and the abyssal lands beneath the waves.

Arden ate until she could not manage another bite. Stefan smiled, and his expression was so much like her father Lucian's, it made her twinge with homesickness.

'It is good to see family again,' he said.

'If you are family, Stefan, why did you not visit us more? I would have liked to have known my full cousin more than some stranger who slipped in and out of my life.'

'There was work to do.'

'God kept you so busy, John Stefan?'

'At first I thought it was God's work, but then I came to realize it was something greater. I was to look after a very special girl trammelled in *sanguis orientis*. I was to keep her here safe while she overcame the becoming of her talents.'

Arden mentally counted the years since Bellis had fled Vigil. Four years. 'Jonah told me once you brought Bellis to this place for *sanctuary* and *reflection*.'

'Yes.'

'And to hide her from the Order.'

'Yes too.'

'Why? She should have been delivered to the Lions! Jonah was practically an outcast. The entire town thought he'd murdered the both of you.'

Stefan gave a regretful nod over his stew. 'Back then we still believed we could prove the Eugenics Society and the Lyonne Order wrong about *orientis*. We thought, all we need is time. The time and seclusion worked for the Saint of the Isles when they were coming into their power, why could it not work for Bellis?'

Too exhausted to be polite, Arden let out a sharp laugh. 'I'm certain she reflected on her power well enough.'

Stefan lined up the beads on his worry-bracelet, counted them and his head jerked forward. 'To no avail. *Orientis* became too much for her. It is like a waking dream. She could not sleep. Days. Weeks. The call of her blood . . . I prayed day and night. Once an entire fortnight passed and in that time neither of us laid down our heads, not even once. But ultimately a man must sleep, otherwise he dies, and when fatigue overcame me, Bellis fled my church and took *Sehnsucht* with her. She never returned.'

'Have you been alone since?'

He shook his head. 'I was not always alone. The Librans came each month to pay fealty and ask for blessings. Every moon-day, bringing their songs and tithings. I didn't think too much about Bellis after she left. I believed her bones at the bottom of the ocean and her poor tongue stilled. It is no easy burden to bear, *orientis*. It asks so much of you.

'Then there came a month when the Librans didn't show. Two months I counted without a single boat at the eastern pier.

Fortunately I had my goats, my wild honey, otherwise I'd have starved.'

'Because she had found Libro.'

'Yes. After a year of no word from them, a coracle washes ashore. The sailor wore a scar across his teeth and a stone in his mouth. Tells me Bellis came out to their island with a dreaming army. Killed their leader. Stole their children. She had stopped fighting her true nature. All this was my fault, the man said, because I'd helped Bellis come here, because like Jonah I thought I was doing the right thing.'

'Oh Stefan. You foolish boys. It was the Society's business to manage Bellis from the beginning!'

'And how would they have managed my dear friend? We all saw what happened to the Rivens when even the whisper of *mandatum* made its way to northern ears.'

She swallowed the guilty, knowing lump in her throat. The ring on her finger felt as heavy as an iron shackle. Miah had called his *mandatum* a secret.

'The Lions never confirmed *mandatum* among the Rivens. They only suspected.'

'You think, cousin? I too thought that Jonah killed his people because Bellis had told him to. Then I realized differently.'

At her cousin's words a chill went through Arden's belly.

They knew.

The Lions knew, from the beginning, when she had read Harbourmistress Modhi's letters on board *Saudade*, the ones Bellis had painstakingly copied.

'They used Bellis to give the *orientine* instruction,' Stefan continued. 'There were a lot of merchants from Lyonne that year. Strangers. Men with deep pockets and golden coins. I think the Lions knew by then. *Orientis* is all about the dream and the direction, but only *mandatum* moves the metal. It was the *mandatum* the Society and Order worried about most. Harbourmistress Modhi was in communication with the Lyonne Order. She was not sent to keep eyes and ears upon my Lightkeeper father alone. Oh not at all. The Order suspected a *mandatum* carrier on Vigil's promontory shore. Effected the death of everyone living in that compound. We couldn't have the same happen to Bellis.'

'Two wrongs don't make a right, Stefan. Bringing Bellis out here cost so many lives!'

'How many people in Vigil are related to the Harrow family? What would the Society do to get rid of those bloodlines? They wouldn't have removed Bellis alone. They'd have done exactly what they did to the Rivens, they'd have razed the entire town and every living soul off the map. A thousand innocents.'

Arden heaved her breath and choked on a piece of soft cheese. A thousand. How about two thousand? How about the entire island of Maris, driven into the sea? When she was done with her sputtering she gasped air like a landed fish.

'What's wrong?' Stefan asked.

Her crisis over, Arden tried to explain. 'The Lions couldn't get all of the Rivens, could they?' She pointed to her neck. 'Jeremiah Riven calls himself Miah Anguis now, he's *sanguis mandatum* and my damn Deepwater husband.'

26

Jonah did not return

Jonah did not return that day. Arden gave up on waiting. She fell into a salty, chafed doze upon a narrow wooden bed in one of the retreats.

She woke at noon. She was rested enough to go into the washhouse for her first proper bath in weeks, soaked in a tub of cedar wood until her fingers wrinkled and a layer of skin was scrubbed away.

Stefan had found Arden spare clothes to wear – a linen top, drawstring trousers, the creases sharp as they must have been decades ago when first stored away by the remnant clergy. While she had slept he had set the sea-silk dress to hang along with her boots in an airing closet over a dry, hot volcanic vent that had the smell of burnt stone about it. She fetched her boots, and the leather warmed her toes.

The largest structure apart from the temple was a chapter-house that housed a library's worth of books. Of those remaining from a century of pilfering, there were volumes too frayed and worn to touch. Her coins hurt even as her hands lost feeling. Stefan came with a salve of lanolin and honey.

'Rub the salve into your hands,' he said. 'Don't put the gloves on. Give them air. Let's see if it can ease the pain.'

She took the salve and rubbed it in as best she could. Her palms had gone mottled as if a blue lace had woven beneath them. The numbness had already crept past her wrists. He watched as she turned her palms over and back, inspecting the damage.

'The coins will need to come out before the end of the month. Maybe sooner.'

'Are there instruments here that could do it?'

Stefan shook his head. 'Needs a phlebotomist, perhaps the one who put them in. Sometimes they can be found in Fiction. This leads to the question, how can we get you to one in time?' He dropped his gaze and lifted her hands. 'Would your husband take you somewhere?'

'No!' Arden jumped to her feet. 'No! I'm not going back to him. God and devils, Stefan, I've completely proven myself untrustworthy. He'll only want revenge now.'

A shadow crossed Stefan's face. He'd had experience enough of people losing their way under his care.

'One would not be particularly in the best of minds, if one's wife ran off with one's cousin. May I assume your relationship with Jonah Riven went beyond good neighbours?'

'I do not have to justify my feelings for Jonah to anyone but myself,' she retorted. 'But when is he coming back? I must speak with him.'

Stefan made the sign of the serpent upon his chest. 'I cannot say. Jonah came here on a boat which barely survived the journey. Since then he has never stayed in the church premises. He won't sleep on holy ground. The deepwater people have a strange relationship with guilt and sanctity and following strict moral laws.'

Arden rolled her eyes. 'It has not escaped my notice.'

'Then wait. If his love is strong, then he will come back.'

Stefan fetched some Libro-knitted socks for her boots, so she might walk beyond the priory grounds. Even though in the sullen afternoon light it looked very much different, Arden's direction-sense quickly found the trail that she had taken from the cliff face the night before.

The compound was built on a high basalt plateau. If not for the pine and cedar trees, there would have been views in all directions, as if they were on the mast of a great ship.

In broad daylight the lift-cage seemed especially fragile. She would not have so willingly climbed into the rusted bucket had she not been so desperately distracted by Jonah Riven climbing in with her.

The coming twilight had brought a mist, but not enough to obscure the waters. Far below, a familiar boat anchored off-shore, kraken-oil sparkles visible from its spout. A pair of shoreboats moved from the boat to the pier.

Miah had brought back reinforcements, and *Saudade*. Arden winced from the anxious wrench in her belly.

'So,' Stefan said when he came to join her at the cliff-side. 'Your husband is tenacious. Definitely a Riven. Shall I winch you down?'

'No.' She turned to Stefan. 'Miah's doing it on purpose. He's trying to taunt Jonah out.'

'I would expect he's more doing all this for his Deepwater Wife.'

'I'm not his Deepwater anything. We never consummated the marriage.'

'The tattoo on the back of your neck says otherwise.'

Arden pushed past him. 'You're so infuriating, cousin. I'm not giving up on Jonah.'

She left him on the cliff edge. It was still light enough to go to the other side of the islet. She would not stop looking for Jonah's hiding place until it was absolutely too dark to see.

Beyond the compound to the island's north, there were old basalt quarry-ruins slumped alongside newer abandonments. A small community had at one time flourished, then faded. The inhabitants had been wealthy, whoever they were, for the ruins of a house still nestled in the basin. The square, stern style reminded her of Vernon's decaying Manse in Vigil. She wondered if Jonah might take shelter there, but most of its side had caved away, and the empty rooms faced the sea.

She went to the opposite cliff-side, and looked out across the cold waters beyond the archipelago. Rubbed her lanolin-sticky hands together. If she went back to Miah, he might still kill her. Consummated wedding night or not, the tattoo on her neck made him Deepwater King, and gave him that right. Then again maybe the promises of sex and the words of love might give Arden power over him in a way Henrietta Cleave and the others could not imagine. He would need a more permanent source of *evalescendi* if he intended to work *mandatum* on more than just a strip of swampy coast. He wouldn't kill her straight away.

Stefan barely took notice of her arrival when Arden returned in the gloaming, violet hour. He'd taken to the contemplative garden, balancing flat stones upon a rock so they made a tower, ten stones high.

'Have you exhausted your curiosity about our island?' he asked, not looking at her.

'Some of it,' she said, feeling grumpy at his air of unconcern. 'Who owned the mansion house on the north side?'

Stefan shook his head. 'Rich Lyonnian farmers, from the days before the Equus automata set in. Most of the communities took flight after the saint's machines caused Equus to become functionally uninhabitable. Only a few stayed.'

'It reminded me of the Justinian estate, a little bit.'

Stefan gave a smile that was nostalgia and benevolence combined. He balanced another flat pebble. 'It does, doesn't it? The old Baron owned a lot of properties around the islands. He even convinced the deepwater people to work for him.'

'Rather than starve in poison waters.'

'They never had much of a choice.'

She sat on the broad flat stone next to his rock tower. The wind blew cold, rustled the tall trees.

'I don't think I have much of a choice either, Stefan. What do I do? Do I stay with Miah Anguis, or do I try and find Jonah, and a way off this rock?'

'Well,' Stefan said as he stood up. 'I think one always needs to make important decisions after supper, and a sleep.'

27

The two siblings

'. . . the two siblings and the eldest grandchild were each given a boat by Jacobin Riven,' Stefan explained over their evening meal. 'To Zachariah the ghost ship *Sehnsucht*, to Thalie the black mangrove *Saudade*, and Miah got the golden *Sonder*.'

'Miah said Zachariah owned *Saudade*.'

'His memory is not correct. Yes, Zach used *Saudade* more, but the boat was not his. Thalie would not go out to sea. She distrusted it, which made it hard for her as a shorefolk woman.'

Two sunsets had now passed since the wedding. Arden had hoped that Jonah might be drawn out by the smell of food, but he made no appearance. Only *Saudade* still waited in the half-moon light of the ocean, her smokestacks glowing with blue sparkles.

Miah would be in there, stewing on her absence. Whatever malign influence had motivated him to turn from the uninterested man of their first meeting to this infatuated devil, perhaps having her gone for a few days might make him reconsider what he really wanted.

Stefan remained gently genial around Arden's preoccupied absence, treating her with a patient kindness. Over supper he told her about his time in Vigil, about the Rivens as he remembered them, the kraken hunts, the leviathans, the boats they owned.

'What happened to *Sonder*? I never saw another large ship among Miah's people,' Arden said. 'And if *Sonder* was Miah's, how did he lose it?'

'Some say *Sonder* burned the day the Rivens died. Others say that the Lyonne Order took it, or fishermen stole it. My father – your uncle Jorgen – kept the other two boats in a remaining seaworthy condition. Had he known Jonah would return for those boats, he'd have torched them into ashes as soon as he could. He had no love for Thalie's son.'

'They were lovers, your father and Jonah's uncle?'

Stefan coughed mead-foam. 'I . . . I never really thought about it.'

She squeezed her hands into fists and released them. 'I'm certain of it. It burns hot in our family, that all-or-nothing kind of love.'

'I have never fallen in love,' Stefan admitted. 'I am aware of it intellectually, of course. And I have seen its casualties. God has been kind to keep such a torment from me.'

'He has been kind to keep such a terrible fire from you. Only I fear that portion has been given doubly to others.'

They finished eating in an almost funereal silence. Stefan took his leave to go to bed. He still had the early morning prayers to attend to.

Arden stayed awhile at the supper table. When the light extinguished in Stefan's room she lit the foxfire in her numb palm and headed towards the main chapel.

Like the northern counterpart, this Clay Church outpost required no prayers between midnight and dawn. Stefan slept those hours and Arden was left alone with the great pale statue within the vaulting apse. The Deepwater King regarded her approach with His black-pearl eyes, and His confronting figure seemed to hold back both the giant serpent and the monstrous kraken until she had said what she had come to say.

'Good evening,' she said. 'It seems we have reached an impasse.

I'm renouncing my marriage to Miah Anguis. I hope you don't mind.'

The flickering of fire gave motion to His face. The shadow under His lips moved, as if He had opened his mouth to speak. The stuffy incense still burning in the censer from the evening rite cast a certain dizzy, soporific effect. She could feel Jonah here, close, close.

Then she saw the footprint.

A votive had spilled perhaps not more than a few moments before. A reflection shone across the waxed wood. Oil puddles, one the shape of a man's bare foot, gold in the lamplight.

A thrill went through Arden as if she'd wrapped her hand about a sparking electrified coil. A man thinking about death on a lonely rock would not skulk about the priory.

'Oh Jonah, you'll not escape not so easily,' she breathed. 'Bellis isn't going to win this one, *orientis* or not.'

The silver footsteps moved out past the eastern side of the compound, where the salt-stone moss poked through the flagstones and swallowed the ruins.

She poked one glowing stain with her toe. Not water. It had an unearthly luminescence, the way phosphor might glow in a glass bell. A glow leading her down a path she had not before seen in broad daylight. Crumbs of light, leading her away from her reality and into a fairy-tale underworld.

The land began to cant down and into terraces, each one punctuated by a stone cell. Mausoleums by the look of them, part of the extensive cemetery grounds. Human skulls were carved above each lintel. An anatomical heart upon the doors. At the lowest internment, the drops of silver faded.

One door hung open. She blinked in the darkness as best she could, saw the disturbed dirt, the clear impression of a human foot.

Arden had imagined taking him by stealthy surprise as he'd done to her. Instead the dark and the gravesite mist made her courage fail. 'Jonah,' she said as loudly as her trembling voice would go. 'Jonah, I want to talk to you.'

The door creaked on broken hinges.

'I know you needed to do things to survive. I know I did too, to get back to you. Please don't be angry at me.'

No word from the mausoleum entrance. Was he waiting in there? Listening?

'If you won't come out, I'll come in.'

The glow in her palm wavered as she pushed the door open. Cast little light. The smell of salt water up strong. The slosh of the ocean sounded in a chthonic depth just out of her hearing. Her fragile illumination caught cobwebs moving in the corners, the edge of a funerary vase bristling with sticks. A miasma filled the air, made the space bow and flux.

'Devilment—' she managed to say at the instant her foot bore weight upon a marble tile and felt it crumble. 'Devil—'

And then the floor gave way as if it were made of dust and she fell . . .

28

Instinctively she fought

Instinctively she fought the hands upon her body, flailed her fists until the same two hands caught her and bore her down upon warm sand—

but so dark

—until she could fight no more.

'Quiet!' hissed the man's voice, ragged and unfamiliar. 'Quiet.'

Arden did not so much relax as give up entirely. She could still feel the throb at her wrists where his hands had needed to grip hard. When she finally recovered enough to lift her head, her vision sparkled with a thousand points of blue and silver.

The cave was warm as blood, darkness scattered with the same luminescence that had led her here. A hundred bodies writhed in the back reaches of the great stone gallery, most of them turning nose-less, lip-less faces towards her. Their cold glassy eyes reflected the blue light from a million points of worm-light.

'My—'

The hand was on her mouth, muffling her. 'Shh, they'll not hurt us if we are quiet.'

She stilled, nodded, and then Jonah released her. More merfolk than she could count lolled on the opposite side of the grotto.

A slimed horde of pale bodies, wide-set yellow-silver eyes, mouths filled with crystal teeth.

The fin-folk, merrows, *homo marini*. Up close, one would be hard-pressed to explain the erotic legends of fair maidens upon rocks with seashell combs. They were like people starved down to bone before being daubed in silver silk and ragfish slime. Their eyes were large discs of silver on either side of their heads. Long crystal teeth erupted from their jaws. Their cheeks sunk, fleshless.

One of their cadre stood up. Membranes as thin as a slime's meniscus spanned the sharp spikes upon his back. They glistened as he turned to glare cold yellow eyes at Arden. *He*, she decided, had a man's body with no genitalia, only a vent between his legs.

Jonah stood protectively between them. Arden pressed close behind, terrified to lose him again. He gave a soft, low warning hiss. For several heartbeats the two creatures of the sea glared at each other with naked antipathy before the merrow decided the human man not worth his time.

Without asking, Jonah reached down to pull Arden to her feet. He wore the same leather breeches from when he had first rescued her, ripped at the knees, otherwise he might have been one of the naked merfolk for all the clothes he wore. But he was not at full strength despite the oddly forced musculature of him. His skin had sunk into the crevices, puckered at the scars.

'Should have made a better hiding place,' he said wryly. 'Made certain I had no worm-glow on me.'

She had not noticed it much on the night, but noticed it now. An odd rasp roughened his voice, causing him some difficulty speaking.

'I'd have followed you off a cliff if it were the only way.'

He searched her eyes, her face as if she were a puzzle. Nodded. 'Yes, you would have.'

He took her hands and turned them up so she could see the damage her fall had brought. She had to restrain herself from grasping at him. But she felt so jangly and nervous now, excited at his return but well aware he was very much damaged by all he had done.

In the luminous blue half-light her hands were covered in bloody scratches from dropping through the mausoleum floor. Above her the web of tree roots and dark vines had caught her body, arrested a drop that might have otherwise killed her.

'It's not bad,' she whispered. 'My hands don't hurt. I'm not feeling pain.'

As soon as she spoke, his face told her everything she had wanted to hide. Jonah had been a neighbour to Jorgen Beacon for years. He knew what numb hands in a coin-implanted sanguinem meant.

'It was the payment the Deepwater King required,' she said to his unspoken question. 'Jonah, I sacrificed so much to get back to you.'

He released a breath, and nodded. 'I know the King's ransoms. Still, if only . . .'

'Was mine to choose, Jonah.'

There was a breath, a half-second when she thought he might kiss her, but it passed and she did not chase the moment. To have done so would have broken whatever spell had brought her here.

When he spoke, it was a sailor's curtness. 'Can you get an *ignis* lamp going? The light will make our houseguests behave.'

'I think so.'

This grotto, or sea-cave, or whatever its purpose before Jonah had chosen to hide here, had provided sanctuary to others before. The cave angled up from the sea, which ebbed and retreated several feet below. High storm tides had brought sand into the upper reaches, along with other lost treasures.

Arden stumbled over the dry remains of a beached longboat to a scattered pile of random articles above the tideline. Broken crockery, silverware, an ornate chair missing a leg, a marble vase with silk flowers.

Among the discards were at least three brass storm-lanterns

meant for a sanguis flame. She thumbed the sharpest needle and quelled the stab of worry that followed when she could not properly feel its bite.

The lantern gave out a feeble but steady glow from where Arden could take stock of the other salvages. Ship's bells and compass roses, water-damaged barometers. A magpie hoard of shiny shipwreck things. A chest of drawers, a side table for a mansion's hallway. Some scattered buttons, broken jewellery. Not collected by humans with an eye for usefulness.

Jonah invited Arden to sit upon one slab of marble she suspected had come from another cemetery collapse, then proceeded to gently bind up her hands with rag strips torn from a silk bed sheet.

'I used to have a bedside table like that back in Clay,' she said, her voice coming out high and dizzily frantic from finding Jonah again. 'When I was a girl. Oh, and a locket like that one, when I was in the Clay Academy, my first year. I lost it in a canal not more than a month later.'

'Take the locket if you want. The owners have long gone.' Jonah gave a snort of dry acknowledgement before tearing out another strip from the sheet. 'Other hand now.'

She examined his shoulders in silence, watched the muscles play under the lamplight with each movement of his arms. They'd travelled so long and so overwhelming a distance from the close, warm surrounds of *Saudade*'s hold. The evidence of welts and beatings appeared upon his back like ghastly tattoos over his old ones. He seemed almost flayed, as if he'd shed a skin during his time away from her and not yet grown a new one.

'You cannot stay here,' Jonah said once he had finished binding her wounds. 'Not here and not with me.'

She snatched her hands back. 'Jonah, what needed to be done to escape Maris was—'

'Was a crime. I am a murderer. It's what I am, and what I do. The Lions should have kept me in that damn Harbinger Bay prison.'

Jonah pulled away from her. He rubbed his face wearily, sat back on the high-tide beach and slung his hands over his knees. 'I'm not Lyonnian, Arden. What morals your people have are not our morals. This—' He motioned to the sea-cave, the surge of water below, the fin-folk on the opposite side. 'This is all I have left after what I've done to those people on Maris. They were under Bellis' control. They didn't deserve what I did.'

'They would never have been free of Bellis otherwise. She had hostages, didn't she? You freed them too. And you have me now, Jonah.'

'And you gave yourself to my damned cousin!'

Arden gasped at Jonah's outburst. An arrow went through her heart. Jealousy was not something to be entertained, she should not allow it, she should put him in his place and scold him.

'I gave myself to Miah Anguis, the same way you made Bellis Harrow your damn wife!' Arden returned hotly. 'To save a friend. To save *you*.'

The man swallowed, and utter despondency blanketed him. Not even the martyred saints upon the church walls of Clay's grand cathedral could have matched the agony in his face.

'You gave too much.'

'It's not for you to decide what I should or should not give.' When he did not respond she went to kneel in front of him. 'Jonah Riven, you listen to me. There's still time for us. Come back with me.'

'I can't go to the chapel.'

'Not the chapel. To Lyonne, and Clay. I want to bring you home.'

He gave a half-hearted laugh of ridicule, and in the *ignis* lamps, his blue eyes were bloodshot and fierce with scorn. 'Someone like *me* in Clay City? Displayed like a sideshow?'

'It wouldn't be like that.'

'It *would* be like that.' He shook his head. 'I'll not be made an object of pity.'

It was his hunger talking, and the exhaustion, and the remorse for what he'd done. She took his hands in her own numb ones, skin on his knuckles still broken from the scuffle he'd had with Miah. Older injuries beneath. She turned them palm up, pressed her face into the hollow they made.

He murmured, resistant enough to not relax fully, but did not pull away. He stroked her cheeks with the calluses from the work he'd been forced into, the weight of old stone in his hands, guilt and fear and yes, hope too. Because he had loved her and lost her, and feared that place again.

'Would only be pity,' she said, 'if I'd known you'd not survived.' She glanced at him, trying to scry his emotions from his inscrutable face. 'Miah wanted things from me, but there are places in my heart I let no man go.' She pressed his hands between her own. 'Unless I allow it.'

'I have not told you exactly what happened on Maris,' he said hesitantly, his breath loud as if he'd been winded. 'Maybe you would think differently of me if you knew. Not just the people I killed. How I was greedy, and clung to life, and did everything Bellis asked. Even the dishonourable and shameful things.'

'She tried to tear you apart, Jonah. But you conquered her.'

Arden raised her face to him, murmuring this wild man into her surrounds and her trust. Her lips had barely brushed over his wind-scored own when a tile fell from the root-bound ceiling and crashed upon rock.

Jonah jumped upright. 'Someone's up there.'

Across the grotto crevasse the merfolk hissed in agitation. A thin grey daylight cast through the looping vines of the mausoleum, and a voice called down most plaintively.

'Arden?'

Arden took up an *ignis* lamp and held it before her face. 'I'm here, Stefan! I'm all right.' She stole a glance at Jonah. 'We both are.'

Stefan's face appeared in the gap she had made by falling through the mausoleum floor. His face shone in the glow of a magnesium lantern.

'That's good, but I don't know how much time you have. There's someone coming up the wall.'

'What's that mean?'

'It means you've lost sanctuary. They've decided their immortal souls are less important than the boon they'll get by invading—'

He slid away.

'Stefan?'

A scuffle, another falling tile and silence. The fin-folk began to hiss like a thousand adders trapped in a stone. Jonah moved Arden behind him, before dashing the lantern out of Arden's hands, plunging them into darkness.

Seconds later, a head appeared, outlined in a harsh chemical glare.

'Hoy, is anyone in there?'

Another voice, muffled. 'I swore he was talking to someone down there.'

'It stinks of fin-folk. Get Anguis. The woman might be hiding.'

Jonah's hand found Arden's. They didn't need to ask each other what had happened.

Miah had come back for her.

Miah glowered in his plesiosaur coat, still wearing marks on his face from the wedding night three days earlier. Mr Cleave did the talking.

Arden could barely hear them from behind the carved blinds of the anchorite's passage that linked the church with the solitary retreats. Their figures were obscured by the morning fog. Jonah had not wanted Arden to go, but she couldn't abandon Stefan to Miah's wickedness. If the deepwater folk had sullied the holy ground of the Deepwater King's chapel, they would have no hesitation in hurting its keeper. Stefan had sheltered Arden, and that made him vulnerable to Miah's resentment.

And his anger.

Clearly upset by the turn of this morning, Mr Amos Cleave tried his best to maintain a semblance of politeness as he explained to the priest why they'd made such a trespass on such sacred grounds. He might have had the mantle of leader torn from him, but the old habits did not so easily break.

Miah Anguis shouted interruptions in coarse Fictish for every few words Mr Cleave managed to speak. In the middle of a belated apology the new leader lunged forward, struck Stefan down with a fist. Arden would have cried out if she had not jammed a knuckle in between her teeth. She pressed her cheek to the latticed grille meant to hide an anchorite from the pilgrim come to ask spiritual forgiveness, felt distress leap in her chest.

Mr Cleave and the other Equus Islander did cry out, in horror for such a sinful violation. They hauled themselves onto Miah and held him back.

'He's still a holy!' Mr Cleave shouted. 'God will know if you hurt him, Anguis.'

'You don't tell me what to do any more, Amos Cleave! Get your hands off me.'

Miah shook the older man off as if he weighed next to nothing, then dragged Stefan up by his collar. 'You're just as slippery as you were when you were a boy, Stefan Beacon. Where is my devils-damned *wife*?'

'I won't fight you, brother,' Stefan murmured, dazed, and blood in his mouth.

'You're not my brother.' Miah punched him to the ground again, and Stefan did not move.

Panicking, Arden searched about her wildly for Jonah. Where was he? He could not have fled, not with his friend being tortured like this . . .

When Miah kicked Stefan in the stomach, her cousin wailed with such agony Arden could not bear to witness any more. 'Stop!' she cried, and fell out of her hiding place. 'Leave him alone!'

She stood on the pergola stairs, defiant. Miah forgot about Stefan completely. Anger and desire wrecked his face. Had she thought a few days apart might have broken whatever spinning absurdity made him imagine he was in love with her, it had only sharpened it.

Something had, at least. She felt the itch of *evalescendi* beneath her skin.

Miah looked like he'd not slept for days. His eyes were sunken and bruised, his lips chafed, his knuckles raw in the way only striking a fist repeatedly on a wooden wall would bring.

'Miah, this is not you. Something's making you not think straight.'

She pressed her numb hands together. *Evalescendi*, she thought wildly. *Have I caused this in him the way I made Mr Stone light a fire from the rockblood? But shouldn't it be physical objects he trammels, an unstable mind belongs to* orientis . . .

Beside him, Stefan slowly tipped onto his hands and knees, his attention warily on the deepwater men and their new leader.

'Remember when we first met?' she said, trying to keep her voice as steady as possible. 'Remember our agreement? You were not thinking of leadership then, Miah. You were even arranging to send me back to Burden Town. Nobody would rearrange their life and burn down their own people after three days without the cause being unnatural. Please think about it!'

'Jonah had you two days, and you gave up everything for him,' Miah said mulishly.

'It's not the same. *Evalescendi* is poisoning you. We cannot be together.'

He grimaced, as overcome with agony as if she'd plunged a spike of hot metal into his temple.

'No! Since I've been with you, all I can sense are the machines in the badlands, the *mandatum* grown strong like a fever! I must be rid of them, for Equus' sake!'

'I'm sorry, I should have thought more about my shadow talent, I never knew it could be so strong.'

'But you only cared about Jonah Riven. Didn't care about how you could hurt others with your sinful blood.'

She closed her eyes in despair at the word *sinful*.

Next to him Mr Cleave pleaded, 'Brother, this is holy ground. Take the woman and leave the priest be.'

Miah was trembling, his fists clenched, but he did not take a step towards her. Arden panted, light-headed with terror. He could easily grab her and take her away but . . .

. . . he can't act without my consent.

Stefan gasped a few more pained breaths, then, wretched and proud in his albatross coat, picked himself off the ground with an effort that almost destroyed him. 'What if she does not wish to go?' Stefan said between gasps. 'She sought sanctuary with the King, and you must honour the true church.'

'The true church? Look at this place,' Miah raged. 'These false carvings, these embarrassing rituals, all while our island starves and suffers. You have never been in the water with *maris anguis*, never fought it on sea and on land. The true church is at the bottom of the damn ocean in the drowned cathedral of the fucking Deepwater King.'

'And to get there completely you must die,' Stefan replied.

The words enraged Miah again. He shrugged Mr Cleave off and struck Stefan down once more. Blood spattered across the wood as Stefan's nose made contact with the planks.

'Stefan!' Arden cried.

With deliberate slowness Miah walked to the pergola steps to the courtyard and towards Arden. The wood creaked under his boots. 'Come with me and I won't kill him.'

'No. Kill him and I'll burn you.'

'Like flame on the beach? Barely a spark without a stormcaller around. There's nothing sanguis here and you're all used up, aren't you? Feverish from blood poisoning and untrained in *evalescendi*.'

'Then you know I have not long to live.'

'We can fix that. A woman doesn't need hands to—

It happened so quickly Arden was not certain of the order in which it came, only that there was a shout as one of the men was knocked down by a rock flung from an unknown source, then another from a startling angle. A body fell out of the pergola rafters to tackle him. For all his surprise, Miah caught the blows, came out swinging against the half-naked wraith. He flung his attacker sideways so powerfully they both fell against the pergola rails.

The weight of two men made the rails give a loud and audible crack like a musket's report.

Jonah moved quicker than the older man, dodged the blows to his face, and caught a couple to his bare midriff before yanking up Miah's arm in compliance. Wedged his hip into Miah's own. Arden heard Miah's shoulder joint creak before the deepwater man, red-faced, gave an animal howl of pain and bobbed on agony-weak knees.

'No closer,' Jonah Riven barked at Miah's escort. 'There will be no more serpent hunting if he loses an arm.'

'You little shit, Jonah,' Miah foamed through enraged spittle. 'There's no upper hand here!'

'Except over *you*, cousin.'

'Must have felt good, *cousin*, when I took your lover into my bed,' Miah hissed through his pain. 'A throb in your pretty, uncut cock?'

He screamed once more as Jonah yanked his arm back harder. 'I said no closer!'

Jonah had seen the danger before Arden did, and even then too late. One of the deepfolk creeping up with a hefty switch of mangrove wood. Before Jonah could move, fouled up in Miah's arms, the switch cracked across Jonah's head, breaking the wood.

Not enough to stun him. But enough for Miah to slip out and shove Jonah prone upon the ground.

Arden let out her own shout of fury. 'Enough! Enough! I will not be made a pawn or a trophy or a reason for anyone's own bedevilled problems!'

'Get back here!'

Before anyone could prevent her escape she had turned from them and fled through the fogwood forest, twigs and cobwebs festooning her hair, ivy tangling through her legs. She could not pull herself up, anger and anguish and guilt an inexorable flood rushing through her veins. The *evalescendi* there, burning harsher than *ignis* ever had . . .

Then there it was, the end of the island, the Darkling Sea bleak and infinite beyond this last outcrop on the end of the world. The cliff face roared and threw up its own gush of wind, sea-spray like a thousand tears, soaking her utterly.

Arden pulled up at the last second, and teetered on the edge. Behind her Miah had stopped too, his face pale and grimacing.

'The fall will kill you from this height, Beacon.'

'Maybe I would prefer to die this way!'

'And leave me bereft, and grieving?'

'Do I care for your grief?'

'Your cousin Stefan might care. Mine own might care too, a great deal, were I to take my grief out upon him. Why, I might even blame Jonah for your death, and a shame that would be.'

He had come closer. The wildness in his face was tempered with the panic he might lose her. The sea beckoned.

'Imagine the fall, your limbs cracked and broken, your body tossed upon those rocks,' Miah crooned. 'Imagine it.'

She imagined it, and imagined what else could happen with her leaving.

Then she swallowed, and stepped back. Gravity smothered her as utterly as a *sanguis pondus* making her weigh ten tons, and she fell, only to have Miah catch her in his rough arms. With a grunt of effort he hauled her over his shoulder, and walked with his burden back to the chapel.

What if you had jumped.

What if.

She jumped. She had enough sense to point her toes and tuck in her chin, and were it not for the froth on the waves, she'd have broken both legs upon entry, sacrificed herself to a watery grave. The world tuned white, and she torpedoed through the slosh and into a blue-black purgatory of water, the Deepwater King's realm.

Her descent slowed just in time; the rocky bottom of the cliff face bruised her bare soles.

I will stay here forever, she thought. I will not rise. The world will cease to spin. Time will stop.

She would stay and be at peace. The sky was gone from her, the water's surface was the sky, her life would be measured in seconds, but that would be a full life, and her own. Her symmetries thudded through her water-chilled veins. She was alone. Evalescendi *meant nothing here.*

In the raptures of her breath-deprived brain she saw all about herself, the kingdom rising in pearl battlements and salt-stone, kelp forests towering, great behemoths of the ocean flitting though their fronds. The drowned city beneath the waves, before the Sainted Islands were flooded.

A kraken bull swam past, shimmering copper, flashing blue, scarred and terrible. A ray swam overhead, so large that its shadow fell like night across the cathedral of the King.

The doors of His great chapel opened wide and He emerged, clothed in the skin of maris anguis, *spiked harpoon in one hand, blade in the other, His face in shadow.*

What have you sacrificed?

Everything.

She said.

What will you give me?

Everything.

The Deepwater King came close and cold, and His great strong arm encircled her dying body and His cold blue lips pressed to her own . . .

29

Water

Water.

She was choking, drowning. Spluttered and woke to liquid going down the wrong way. No King, only Stefan nursemaiding her.

She squinted into the gloom as her darksight made out his face. One eye swollen shut from the beating, and blood drying to a dark crust in his beard. A yellow brazier illuminated half his face, and threw the rest into shadow.

'Oh, careful,' he said in a dockworker's Lyonnian. 'Take small sips. Swallow it, don't breathe it.'

Stefan sat back on his haunches. He looked about himself. A distant grumble resonated through the stones of the dark room. Thunder, somewhere overhead. 'Storm's up. Well. We've won a few hours' grace at least. Deepwater folk have their superstitions about storms.'

'Where are we? It's so dusty in here.' Arden blinked in the gloom and turned aside. A skull grinned back at her. 'Oh, devilment! Oh, goodness gracious!'

She was lying next to a wall of skulls resting on a framework of leg bones. A pale mortar held the larger bones into the wall. Smaller bones had been rearranged into the clay in the order they'd been in when alive.

One skeletal hand still held a sanguis grommet like the brad in a bootlace hole. She reached out to touch it, and imagined she could still sense the wisps of power even in the calcified remains.

'Easy, our friends won't hurt us. They'll only bear witness.'

Still dizzy from sleep, Arden turned away from the ossuary remains and took stock of her situation. She had been lying on a stone platform with her coat for a pillow. Her body ached so. 'Stefan, how long has it been?'

'Long enough. Been a little insensible for a while, and gladly so. We're locked in one of the chapel crypts, courtesy of our guests.' He held his hand up and closed his eyes. 'The wind has changed in the caverns below. By the tide breeze, it has to be night.'

Arden sat up with effort and patted her head for injuries. 'I don't think I hit anything when I fell into the merfolk grotto earlier. At least I hope not.'

'That, and the cave gas.' He leaned close and spoke in the dockworker's patois again. 'Your husband is quite single-minded about you taking up the mantle of Deepwater Wife. Unnaturally so.'

'Yes,' she replied miserably. 'He started halfway decent and it all went frightfully upside-down. The fault may not entirely be his, however.' She rubbed her coins, then sniffed. 'What's that smell?'

Stefan gestured over his shoulder. The source of the bitter smell was a small brass apothecary's kettle nestled in the coals. A similar cup nestled in his hands, and he offered it to Arden again.

'They locked us up with a cup of tea?'

'I have it sequestered about. They've not suspected what my brew actually is.'

She sniffed again. She knew that smell. Fennel and liquorice masking a bitterness beneath. 'Tell me it's not a morphium, Stefan? Why is there morphium tea in this room?'

'You can sleep through this,' he said. 'You do not have to

stay awake this night.' He made the motion of drinking. 'One sip of morphium tea can put you asleep for an hour. A cup of it . . . well, a cup could end your problems sooner. We Lyonnians do not have the same prohibitions against taking our lives as the deepwater folk have.'

Arden stared at Stefan. 'Suicide? Are you mad as well?' She shook her head and pushed his cup away. 'We're not that desperate.'

'We could be.'

She gave him a withering glance.

'A little then, to tide us through this night?'

'No, I need my senses. If Miah's locked us in here, then we need to find a way out of this room.'

'There is none except the trapdoor.'

She was wide-awake alert now, and found the means to get to her feet. At once she knew that Stefan was right. Each wall appeared solid behind the carefully stacked bones. The crude entry stairs ended at a lone trapdoor. Had there been another way out Stefan would have not been so coy about it now.

'The clarity of our situation will only hurt you,' Stefan said. 'Cousin, I thought there was a chance of survival with him, but I saw it in Jeremiah's eyes. It was the same look as Bellis had before she fled me.'

Arden sought out his face in the gloom. '*Mandatum* is a bloodwork of physical objects. It's the mind that moves to *orientis*. He should not be affected by his mind.'

Stefan sighed, and put the cup back among the coals. 'Who knows what *evalescendi* does to other *sanguinem*. The talent a shadow mystery much as the other two, and had there been any more examples in nature, why, the Church would have put a prohibition on it as it did with *mandatum* and *orientis*.'

'Oh Stefan. We have to do something.'

Stefan remained bleak. 'If it's true what you say, and Miah has *mandatum*, then the man is not giving up. *Ever.* You know as well as I do. *Orientis* might direct and suggest a dream for as long as the user wields it, but *mandatum* articulates the hard orders and it lasts forever, just like the eternal machines in Equus.'

Somewhere in the night, a man's defiant, agonized shout lost to the storm. Arden stilled, and an odd, remote anger filled the places that were once empty with despair.

Stefan took the copper kettle off the coals. 'Jonah has become acquainted with withstanding torture since leaving Bellis Harrow. That knowledge will prove its usefulness tonight.'

She regarded Stefan in distressed silence as he retrieved his cup and poured himself some of his bitter tea. Watched as he sipped it with trembling hands.

'Stefan,' she said. 'Why would you have a numbing tea hidden in a crypt of all places?' She frowned. 'Tell me you're not sick?'

He paused, and placed the cup on the hearth. A sheen of sweat lay on his brow. She had thought before that maybe he ran Beacon-hot, and now she was not so certain.

'Was not through pure charity that the Clay Church allowed me to change my service to them, leave the mainland and come here.'

'I don't understand.'

His smile was sad. 'I am an *addict*, cousin. I'm enslaved to this drink. I suppose the first priest to show me how the tea worked thought he was doing me a favour, to ease my own homesickness. The King requires extremes.' He picked up the brass cup again, pressed it to his lips and closed his eyes. 'If I don't drink this, I die. If I drink too much I die. That's why I know the tea works.'

Despite her promise to herself, Arden still struggled not to give in and accept a cup of that sweet oblivion. She knew what Stefan was saying. There was no escaping what was coming for her. She'd dreamt of choice, but now had none left.

Unless.

She stood up, a quiver of resolution in her heart. Went to Stefan, and hugged him, despite the awkwardness of their embrace.

'I am glad to have met you, if only for a little while.'

'What are you intending to do, cousin?'

Arden met his gaze, then touched his cheek. His skin was clammy and hot.

'I will go to the extremes the King requires.'

Nobody came when she first yanked on the silver bell-rope with her numb hands. In the distance a bell gave an obstinate, unmusical clatter.

'Hoy,' she shouted. 'I need to talk to Mr Anguis. Open this door!'

Nobody responded, and soon she grew tired of being ignored. It was just like Miah, she thought. Making certain she knew who responded to whom in this new arrangement of theirs.

She returned to the pallet and hugged her knees, rocked back and forth impatiently.

Stefan had at last an inkling of what she intended. He put down his cup and went to sit beside her, his brows knitted in concern.

'You don't need to surrender to him, Arden. If you didn't want to before, you shouldn't now.'

'I appreciate the concern, cousin.'

'Desire might not stay his hand if he's even slightly aware what is going on.'

'But I have to try. It's not just about me. It's about Jonah. And you.'

'Are you certain it's not your sanguis endowment making you feel so much to blame? We become analogous to our blood, there's no escaping that fate.'

'Was Bellis influenced by her blood?'

'Very much so. *Orientis* personified becomes ambition.'

'And *mandatum* becomes obsession?' She lifted her chin. 'Oh God and devils, why did it take me this long to work it out? If only I'd stopped and thought rationally about how I might affect Miah!'

'It couldn't be helped,' Stefan said kindly. 'Us Beacons always blazed too hot and burned out too quick, *ignis* or not.'

Arden squeezed her numb hands. Imagined *evalescendi*

tilting her mercilessly towards symmetries greater than hers, making her blunder into trouble.

'I want to be more than my blood, Stefan.'

Eventually curiosity got the better of her captor, and one of the deepwater folk lifted the crypt door. The wind and rain washed in, a cold breath of salt and iron.

'He'll see you now,' gruffed the deepwater man.

Arden tipped up her head, haughtily, and threw a quick, covert glance at her cousin. 'It will be all right,' she said, and let the deepwater man close the trapdoor behind her.

The walk across the storm-drenched courtyard soaked her to her skin. In the centre, a post, and upon it a body slumped.

Jonah opened his eyes as she passed him. An incomprehensible emotion through his pain. He knew where she was going. An imperceptible shake of his head.

Too late, she thought. *Well, we'll see where this takes us.*

The rest of Miah's entourage had the hunched, beaten-down appearance of men under stubborn sufferance. She could tell by their bearing how in awe they were of Miah Anguis, how absolutely they'd defiled their own religion to follow their new leader. It was for this reason, Arden deduced, they had kept out of the consecrated grounds and had instead taken residence in the more secular storeroom.

She could not spot Mr Cleave among the men allowed out of the weather, but Miah took his comfort as his due, sat glowering at the end of a long table, the bones of a roasted mutton-bird on a plate before him. It was warm in here, and he'd divested himself of his coat and shirt. The crude tattoos on his broad, muscular body seemed hewn in, like violent injuries, scarred over but still showing.

He did not acknowledge Arden's entry, only pondered upon a thick, smouldering twist of ghostweed he held in one hand. Made her stand for several minutes in the draught while he fought his own *mandatum* poisoning.

'I am running out of goodwill, Beacon. Your coming here might have wasted your time,' he at last said sulkily.

'You hardly invited much goodwill to start with. Stefan was innocent in all this.'

He reached out to a candlestick with its stub of flame, and lit the end of his cigar. Puffed on it. 'He kept you from me.'

'He did not have the full story.'

Miah sucked in a lungful of ghostweed. 'Come to offer a trade, hmm?'

'I know there is yearning in you, Miah. Beyond being King of your people. But you must let Jonah and Stefan go unharmed.'

He gave her a look full of resentment. 'I have sampled the goods you offer. I found them inadequate. You give me nothing more than any other shore-woman will do.'

The pronouncement was uttered harshly, and afterwards he seemed both exulted and terribly pleased with himself, for fighting his blood's authority. 'Besides, I'm getting pleasure enough seeing my cousin punished. Come the morning, he will have been given a thorough education in justice. You may keep the remains. Isn't that what your heart wanted when you first darkened my door, Beacon? His burial? A deepwater funeral to commend him to the sea?'

A feeling was aroused in her. A rebellious, driven spirit. Miah could lie to himself and to her. But the truth could not be ignored. The *mandatum* preoccupation burned deep in him, in his eyes, the way his breath came hard as if he were struggling against an insurmountable weight. She knew its terrible source. She knew.

'Tell your man to leave,' she said.

Took another draw on the ghostweed cigar, stared fearsomely through the smoke. Flicked a glance at his companion. 'Leave.'

Miah's attendant was uncertain and hesitated. Miah waved him off. 'She wants to offer a trade. She'll not do anything foolish.'

The darkness licked the walls along with the flame. Miah pushed the chair back from the table.

'Come here, then,' he said.

Resentment at his casual command made her pause before

she walked to him. His eyes upon her. The snake-carvings behind him moving, almost.

'What do you want again? I didn't quite catch it.'

'Jonah's life. And Stefan's.'

Miah gave a forced, cruel laugh. 'We've been here and the answer is no.'

'If you were to just drag me back, I could make myself a ghost, and never acknowledge one word or touch. I know you now, Miah. You would never be content with half-measures. Only my complete submission would satisfy you. Give me Jonah's life with no more harm, and I will return to Equus.'

'That's a lot to offer. I'll need to see evidence of your full measures first.'

She took a breath of courage and slid out of her coat, kicked off her boots, pulled off the wet priest's leggings and discarded them. A thought crossed her mind how it might have gone better if she'd taken more notice of the burlesque dancers of Clay, who didn't make disrobing seem so clumsy.

The buttons of the shirt were too much for her hands, so in the end she yanked the shirt over her head. It dripped water over the floor. She sensed upon her eyes other than Miah Anguis', men made cold and wet from the weather, taken from warm beds and the embrace of saltwives to linger on this wet island. Their attention was not on the courtyard.

The ghostweed glowed red with Miah's vicious inhale. A rage behind his eyes that she was unmooring him so. He would not advance on her, give her no place to claim the excuse of non-consent. He put the cigar aside and drank from the cup of mead by his side. Maybe she was just humiliating herself, bruised and bedraggled, and he would realize just how little she did have to offer him. A wild deepwater wench would respect him as leader and King. He would not be reduced to chasing wilful Lyonnians who didn't appreciate his status, or his body.

Instead he shifted upon the bench. 'Kiss me, then. Make me believe you can love me without condition.'

A terrible determination. Arden straddled the leather-clad

thighs and kissed the hard lips though all her conscience screamed in opposition. He opened his mouth and the return kiss was full of indignant desire. His mouth tasted of char-smoke and grease-fat undercut with mania. His yearning was visible even through his leathers, and he gripped her forearms halfway between pulling her close and throwing her off.

Even then a small, still note of regret for this path. Each kiss only strengthened the bonds of his *mandatum* obsessions. Her mouth only stoked the fire in him. He raised her closer, mouth hungry on one breast, sent darts of sensation into her, and because her life and Jonah's life and Stefan's life depended on it, she surrendered to her own body's reaction. Murmured encouragement. Miah exhaled a grunt of awed delight and pulled himself from his leathers, trembling and eager.

'You see sense at last, wife.'

She would not allow him entry, only moved against him slowly, the resolution in her heart wrapped up in thorns and bitterness. Wished herself monstrous, venom in her flesh, a cartilage rasp of her skin and teeth in her vulva.

Because if she were angry, she would not feel so torn and undecided, as if she could surrender herself to him and lose herself completely.

But she was none of these things and he was close to overcoming the prohibitions of blessing, close to throwing her to the floor of the storeroom and taking his way among the wheat kernels and fig-sacks. If something was to break in him, it had to break soon. He clutched her close and ground his mutilations against her, believed her wetness was her desire for him. His face flushed hot as his excitement took hold. Tried to enter her and found himself stymied as she pulled away.

'Don't make me—' he grunted. A flush of arousal mottled his chest and shoulders.

On the edge of an awful epiphany Arden slid off his knees to kneel before him, kiss wider the damp thighs as heavy as oak-masts, he said *no* at first, for he had to know he was being watched. His men would despise him for his weakness. But his secret desire was greater than what was forbidden, he let her slide her tongue upon his scar, her mouth along his hot, wounded length, then to catch the vinegar traces of his seed as he came almost as soon as she had begun. His hands tangled in her hair as he trembled in jerky spasms, strangled pronouncements of joy from his throat.

She knew Miah well enough to recall the physical paralysis that followed his orgasm, and slid upon his lap as he shivered with aftershocks to whisper in his ear. 'I realized it back in the longhouse, but it took until now for it to make sense. The issue of a man is much the same as blood, really, in the scheme of things. Same blood as Mr Stone's when I called the fire to the shore. And *mandatum* is instruction that can be given both ways. You will leave the island, and return to your people and not come back.'

He had the presence of mind to hiss, 'Why would my men obey such a thing?'

'Because Mr Lindsay, the Lion, is there with his words and his coins and his issuing of instructions,' she said, with the copper taste of him still on her tongue. 'And because you will be blind.'

'What—'

She covered his eyes with her numb hands and then from the depths of her belly – though it hurt, oh how it hurt – willed fire.

And Miah screamed.

30

The storm

The storm drowned him out, and the men came running as soon as she'd yanked her wet coat back on and mutinously drunk the rest of the beer in his stein.

She did not try to run, Arden Beacon, who had not inflicted so much more than the remnant flame her whole family expressed, but that little spark of foxfire was all she needed to boil the fluid in his eyes.

With a strangled cry Miah rushed for her. The table's edge caught him and tumbled him to his knees. He spat incomprehensible words in Old Fictish. A snake on the end of a noose would be no less enraged. He tipped over chairs and trestles, lunged at her imagined noise.

One crewman had forethought enough to shove Arden aside at the moment he ran in, thinking that perhaps she had caused some grievous injury with a blade and might still be armed.

'Whore!' Miah screamed, one hand clawing the blank space before him. 'Lyonnian whore! Get her!'

His brother clansman lurched after Arden somewhat half-heartedly, for even in their wild deepwater ways such intimately violent scenes were usually caused by a man's offence to the woman, and the tough saltwives would punish him accordingly.

They didn't have long. The doors to the storehouse crashed open with the wind, and Jonah stood illuminated by dawn fire, bloodied but not broken, the chains still hanging from his wrists.

'Enough,' he thundered even as he gasped with exhaustion. 'You have brought shame upon the house of the King.'

The men stilled, cowed both by Jonah's presence, and the blade in his hand. Miah pulled back, baring chest and throat, laughing maniacally despite his vulnerability.

'What becomes of me, cousin?' he mocked the darkness. 'Here I am, prey ripe for the killing. Finish the sin.'

'I won't kill a fallen man,' Jonah growled.

'Oh no. Not one fallen man. Only *many*. Be careful with that woman,' he said, his voice gone hoarse and hysterical. 'One day she will tire of you the same way, and you will join me in Purgatory. Blinded or castrated, who the fuck knows?'

'Anguis,' one of the deepwater men implored. 'What do we do?'

Miah's lips moved without making a sound. He was fighting himself, the *mandatum* necessity, the obsession, and Arden's words whispered to him in his moment of weakness. Then with a breath of surrender said mockingly, 'We will return home to Equus. There is a Lion, waiting for us.'

They paused, then two went to pick him off the floor. He fought them at first, the humiliation of assistance far too great for him, then deigned to take a shoulder. His head tipped up, sniffed the air, and he turned to Arden.

'This is not over, Beacon. Don't think it for one second!'

Mr Cleave was the last to arrive, with two others. He evaluated the situation, Arden's defiance, Miah's sightless, stumbling anger, and Jonah still holding the monster-hunter's flensing blade. Knew at once that a drama had occurred and his political fortunes had reversed.

'Well,' Mr Cleave said. 'This is an interesting reunion.'

'Control your man,' Jonah gruffed. 'He has done enough damage.' He tightened his fist on the blade handle.

'Would that we had met again under better conditions, Jonah

Riven,' Mr Cleave replied, holding up his bare, unarmed hands. 'I never had much of a chance to say it when you last came to our shores, but I knew you as a boy, and your stepfather Ishmael could call himself a relation of mine. We have good blood between us.'

Jonah nodded, put down the steel. 'I remember. You were the one who stayed Jeremiah's hand the first time.'

Mr Cleave nodded Miah's way. 'We will take him back, give him treatment. But please understand that the black boat *Saudade* must be the payment that squares us and all that you've done tonight. You're taking a man's sight, and his wife.'

A wince of pain in Jonah's eyes, and then he nodded. 'Go then. She is yours.'

In the dawning light they took Miah down to the pier. Arden watched with bitter relief as they boarded *Saudade* in preparation for leaving. The big ship bumped up against the pontoons fretfully. Miah cursed the entire way.

But for all the relief she felt at having disposed of Miah Anguis, Arden could not shake the cloud of misgivings that settled permanently about her. She had facilitated this exchange. Forced Jonah to pay the price of his boat, his one possession and connection with his family. All this for her.

She waited, chilled by the dawn fog as the black boat cast off. When Saudade had been completely swallowed by fog, she turned away, and walked back to the crypt.

Found Stefan on the floor, his body cold and grey, the cup spilled at his hand.

She cried out for Jonah, and he came to kneel beside him, covered his body with an altar cloth.

'Oh Stefan,' Arden murmured, speaking even as she wanted not to disturb the moment between Jonah and his friend. 'If only he'd believed me! I was going to set us free.'

Jonah looked up. 'His addiction enslaved him. He would not have lived out the year.' Something in his face seemed incomprehensibly distant. A thousand seasons separated the man she had embraced on board *Saudade* and the one who now tended the body of her cousin. The man was gone, and the boat gone. A cousin Arden had hardly known had been Jonah's lifelong friend, and he was gone too.

Strange, how she felt no real weight but her knees buckled.

He stood up and went to Arden's side.

'Arden, do you need to lie down?'

'No,' she said. 'I'm all right. It's just . . .' She gave a grim laugh. 'The Deepwater King has exacted his coin.'

Jonah nodded. 'They are his ransoms.'

Across the courtyard, the doors to the Deepwater chapel hung open slightly. Arden could not stay still, did not feel ready enough to talk to any living thing. So she went to them, pushed the doors aside and entered.

The votive candles of the antechamber had all been put out. The eternal flames of the worship hall had been spilled across the floor and smothered. The kraken and serpent still sported, but the King was gone, sawn off the wood.

31

Jonah Riven

Jonah Riven, pragmatic as ever, recovered his krakenskin coat from the storeroom, which apart from the arrow-bolt had suffered little damage for all its journey back to him. He rubbed his small shoulder scar thoughtfully, then shrugged back into the bronze leather.

'We can't let Stefan stay in the yard.' Arden rubbed her numb hands with worry. 'We can't. We need to put him to rest.'

Jonah glanced at her hands. He was thinking, she knew, of her days' remaining number. He must have seen the same act in Jorgen Beacon, back in Vigil, the illness in him. The death.

'Is it customary for Lyonnians to prepare the body?'

She started to nod then blurted, 'I can't bear to look at him! My father, my uncles. I see them in Stefan's face!'

'Then don't look. I'll say when he's ready. We will cast him into the sea with the Deepwater Rite.'

'The Rite . . .?' She had almost forgotten what had started her on this journey.

'He is a priest of the old religion. It is how he will be returned to the King.'

* * *

Jonah had known Stefan best. They had been neighbours before Jonah's captivity in Harbinger Bay. When Jonah had returned as a man to Vigil, Stefan Beacon – *Pastor John Stefan* by then – became his friend. Jonah's only real friend, apart from Bellis Harrow. Three people united by hard sanguinities they could not control.

Arden wondered what Stefan's sanguinity had been. He could not have been driven to help Jonah and Bellis through empathy alone.

Now she would never know.

In the gauzy afternoon light Jonah took Stefan's body and prepared him for the funeral boat, murmuring the old songs. Arden stayed at the pagoda, gripped a column for both strength and protection. With his back turned he became a stranger wearing the ink of Miah Anguis. The chevron tattoos sank and rose into the indentations of his spine. His most recent trials welted pink and raised across his back. This death-song made her fearful, of what lay ahead, and of him. They had yet to speak fully of their reunion.

She had lashed herself to the fate of a man she did not truly know. There had been more days and words between her and Miah Anguis in their time together.

By evening, Jonah took long hollows of driftwood from the grey beach and fashioned a longboat as gnarled as a kraken's tentacles. Arden found a spiced tea in a tin among the last of the stores. Real tea, not the bitter morphium of Stefan's addiction. She hassled Jonah to drink it, even though the rite commanded he should spend the day refusing food.

'Take a rest and drink,' she said, giving her note of instruction. 'You may not eat, but you can drink.'

They sat on the edge of the bluff, overlooking the Darkling Sea. A storm wall in the distance sparkled with lightning. The sun slipped low behind them. The brewed tea steamed in Arden's hands.

'Such a far distance you have come to witness this,' Jonah said suddenly. For the entire day he'd been immune to small-talk.

'Did you know I was in Equus?' Arden asked.

He nodded. 'My last day on Maris Island, Wren Libro – the

girl in the saffron dress – she told me. But Mr Absalom was on his way. He meant to take you home. I was happy then, to know you safe.'

She examined the contents of her cup. The tea murked. A star-anise pod floated on the top. 'Are you unhappy the way things have turned out?'

'Of course not. I know survival, Arden.'

She nodded. 'Either my god or your god or the devils of the ocean have brought us together again. I want to be certain my path is the right one. Tell me – have I done the right thing? A man is dead, another blinded . . . how do I make up for that?'

'Ultimately, it's your decision how you pay those debts,' he said with a gruff casualness while tossing back the last of the tea.

'Yes.' Yes, it was her decision. She would not let *evalescendi* make it for her. It was her decision and she wanted Jonah to stay with her.

She leaned forward and kissed his rough lips and he responded with a generous fondness. She let the teacup fall and clung to him then, his raw, solid body as if he were the wood of the cathedral.

'Stay with me.'

He held her tight, but as an adult might comfort a child. There was none of Miah's yearning hunger in him. For a terrible instant she realized how he could have loved Bellis utterly but never consummated their marriage.

'There's something I must do first. Do something for me, Arden.'

'Anything.'

'The Librans will come back here soon. Tell them what happened here. Tell them my name, and have them bring you home.'

'Home.'

'Lyonne. Clay. You have done what you came for.' He kissed the top of her head tenderly. 'This journey of mine always ended with you. And it must end.'

If you asked me to follow, Jonah . . .

He did not ask. He hugged her close, but she could feel him fading from her, the way a ship will do in a midwinter fog.

* * *

Then the night came, the time for the fires to be lit in the sand, to call for the god of his people.

Jonah wore a linen shirt over his tattoos, bound his wrists and palms with strips of sea-silk and oyster shells as if they were armoured gauntlets from a strange war. Walked the boundary between land and water while at all times murmuring a song to his cruel god who would soon claim him.

The only clothing Arden owned that was not scrap was the bridal dress, and an odd rebellion made her slide back into the translucent silk and wear it for the funeral.

A funeral for both Jonah Riven and Stefan Beacon, maybe.

The ache returned, and if she hadn't exhausted her tears in the afternoon solitude, she'd have cried yet again.

Jonah gave her a brief, odd look when he saw her in the wedding gown, but said nothing. He returned to his prayers. Arden spun the wedding ring on her finger.

The wind whipped up, the waves rolled in and retreated. For a long time he walked the edge, a bullroarer of opaline serpent ivory circling above his head, one of the relics from the temple. It was filled with kraken oil and burned with a blue flame. Looked out to sea. Arden, higher up on the beach, experienced the same mounting tension as she had on the night the *maris anguis* had been brought to shore. Lightning on the clouds, behind the thunderheads.

She crouched down, watching. The yearn of her blood's shadow moved thick and coarse in her veins. The merfolk of the grotto had taken to the ocean, and they were dark silhouettes against the phosphorescent breakers, crowding in.

Arden thought about shouting a warning to Jonah, before accepting that he had called them, for the Rite of the Deepwater required an army, the court of the King.

Jonah suddenly swung the fiery roarer into Stefan's funeral barge.

Set him alight, pushed him burning out to sea.

And followed.

32

He went into the ocean

He went into the ocean.

The merrows avoided the burning funeral boat. They swallowed Jonah up instead. Bony webbed hands reaching out, tugging him under. Not even the splash of a fight. He didn't even struggle.

Minutes passed. Longer than a man could survive, even one so attached to the sea.

Arden said his name. Softer now. The wind took her voice away. Stefan's boat had burned hot, and as the fuel exhausted, it split into two pieces, one half sinking with a smoky sigh of extinguished flame. The other floated as a large fading ember for a long while, caught by a rip in the tide. The half-moon waned overhead.

The waves rolled in, stirring up the plankton in the water, making the breakers glow with disturbed shoals of light. Blood in the air. Something was out there in the dark ocean, bigger than the serpent *maris anguis*, bigger than the bull kraken of *Saudade*'s near-capsizing in the storm wall a season ago. The merfolk wailed their terrible song. Arden clutched the silk at her sternum and the very air beleaguered her.

Merrow song loud in the breakers, loud entreaty in throats

meant for deep water. Merrow backs heaped with the labour of the unforgiving air, the weight of the atmosphere. Merrows crawling out of the ocean, their crystalline teeth long and sharp, as delicate as fish-bones.

Arden stood up as they came in a clumsy phalanx towards her.

The entourage fell away to reveal a man staggering among them, as ungainly as if he had just been born.

'Oh Jonah, you're alive!'

Her exclamation came before she could think it. Before she knew how alive he was.

The merrows retreated and Jonah made his way further up the beach. The man came back to her. Wet, he stumbled up to Arden, and she flung her arms about his chilly neck.

'How did you survive? You were under for so long.'

His breath in her ear was too fast and agitated for comfort. She pulled away.

'Jonah, what's wrong?'

He pointed at his mouth. Opened and shut his jaw.

It came upon her what was wrong. She took his wet head in between her hands. 'Can you talk? Jonah, your voice . . .?'

I know his ransoms.

Jonah shook his head. He dragged from his deepest memories the most common hand-sign in a trader city.

Exchange.

Snatched Arden's hands and pressed them briefly to his eye sockets, and grimaced again.

'No,' she said vehemently. 'Maybe I didn't see you properly. You did not drown.'

He moved back on his haunches. His expression was not exactly impatient, but would broach no more fussing. Arden stood up.

'Let's go back to the chapel grounds,' she said. Her voice came out tremulous, and unsure. 'Somewhere warm.'

She led him in silence back up the trail, sensed him behind her but could not bear to look. How many strange stories had she read of lovers led from underworlds, only to disappear at the last minute by an ill-timed glance?

Arden could hear his footstep, yet her feeling was of an *absence*. A departure. As if with every step he were walking the other way.

At the top of the hill she made her decision, and led him to her sleeping room. The lamps cast golden glows across the darkwood floors.

Once there she turned to face Jonah. He was pale in the lamplight, otherworldly almost, with his skin translucent from chill and the merrow slime still upon him. His expression had changed again. Now it was serene, perhaps slightly curious. Almost . . . almost as if someone else was behind his eyes.

Alarmed and seeking comfort she raised herself on tiptoes, pressed her lips to his cold ones, and Jonah Riven returned the kiss with the hesitant welcome of a foreigner who knows nothing of such customs.

It was as if she had kissed a stranger.

'Your eyes . . .?'

They appeared to have taken on a bioluminescent hue in the dark. She thought to herself that she might be imagining it, for there was still a half-slice of moon left. Plenty of places to catch the light.

Jonah pulled back the blankets at the pallet, and motioned that she should get in, sandy-footed and damp. He did not follow. Instead he sat on the floor cross-legged, became circumspect and distant in the golden light, a frown creasing his brow.

'Is it even you?' Arden asked him with a frown. 'Or are you something else in disguise?'

One of her hands poked out from the blanket, and he took it gently, though her skin had lost all feeling. She opened her mouth to speak, could find no protest.

'I'm not going anywhere without you, Jonah,' she said firmly, trying to replace her confusion with certainty. 'Not until you get better.'

He pressed his mouth upon her hand and she returned with a kiss to his water-dark head.

33

At first light

At first light she dressed in the sturdiest clothes she could find in the priory's stores, and headed to a small creek near the ruins. Took a deep breath and waved her hands in the muddy water of the riverbank.

Within a minute three leeches were on one hand, four upon the other.

Arden swallowed her disgust and tried to look away for the minutes they stuck to her swollen palms, but after they fell off, she had to admit she felt much better. The swelling at her coins had subsided to a mottle of blue.

She finished her ministrations to find Jonah watching her quizzically from nearby.

'They're medicinal,' she said. 'I hope. I've seen surgeons use leeches in Clay City. I suppose they can't do much worse.'

Jonah didn't give the sense of understanding her, or even responding. Since that morning he had been silent and withdrawn. Distant. More than distant. As if a man had gone into the water but something altogether different had come out.

It must be an oxygen injury, Arden thought anxiously to herself. He was underwater too long. That's why he can't speak and is so strange. The bridge-builders of Lyonne, the caisson workers who laboured in the pressurized pylon-bases, often suffered similar diseases.

Then he gave a small tilt of his head, so that she might follow. She did so, and ended up at the observation tower at the priory's western end.

'Is there something on the water?'

Jonah made no response, only gazed at her with a calm quietude that only made her worry for him more.

Still uncertain, Arden climbed the rickety wooden stairs and fended off several decades' worth of cobwebs before arriving at the viewing platform. A copper spyglass spun on a fixed gimbal, the lenses long since milky with salt-scoring. The ground crunched underfoot, dried acorns having spilled from a small animal's cache.

She didn't need a glass. At once she saw what had made Jonah so worried. A big paddle-wheeled boat anchored in the sheltering bay. Arden grabbed the splintered wood of the balustrade and dug her fingernails in, hard.

Saudade? Was Miah back already?

Jonah joined her on the platform.

'I'm not sure what boat she is,' Arden said as calmly as she could. 'It looks like *Saudade*, but the colour is wrong. It's more bronze than black.'

Jonah knelt and picked up some pine cones, before laying three across the tower's balcony. Three. As if even in the depths of his change he was urging her to remember words he'd told her a long time ago. Three pine cones. Three boats.

It's Sonder, my grandfather's missing boat.

The landing craft was a small propeller-dinghy obviously secured from another vessel. A name was written on the side that was certainly not *Sonder*.

Two men and a woman arrayed themselves haphazardly about the dinghy's slightly overloaded ballast well. Arden stood upon the dock and suffered a prickly anxiousness as the shore-craft approached. Her heart settled in her mouth. Not the first time her fortunes had turned on such a meeting. Anything could happen. She was firmly placing her chances with the Fates by standing here to greet them, instead of hiding.

Once the dinghy beached itself, the men helped the woman out.

The woman, frowsy in a cabbage-tree hat and a raggedy petroleum-fabric coat, stared aghast at Jonah, then at Arden. Seeing Arden so glossily Lyonnian despite all her trials, in company with a Fiction man who looked more like a bleached whalebone scrimshawed by a bored sailor, seemed completely beyond the woman's understanding. She presented them with a most disapproving frown, as if she suspected them of having carnal relations and fornications in quite an ungodly manner.

'I thought you were searching for your husband, Mrs Castile,' the woman sniped. 'Not looking for a replacement.'

It was then that the recollection came thundering back, and Arden let out a cry of surprise.

'Mrs Cordwain,' Arden exclaimed. 'What happened to the Equus pilgrimage?'

One of the men, a stout, short fellow in a waistcoat over a barrel chest, took off his hat. 'Yes, what did happen? Things never work out as one expects.'

It was not a man that spoke. Arden felt her lower lip quiver as she met the round – and now bearded – face of Chalice Quarry.

'Would someone religious like Mrs Cordwain approve of a lady wearing a man's garb?' Arden said, her chest still a little fluttery from the shock of their reunion, and her eyes swollen from brief but fierce angry-crying. 'Even a Lion spy.'

'I managed to convince our Clay City sister that it is safer for her, and me, and all of us, if the golden ratio of gender remains weighted to the male. Besides, I needed a crew for that boat. It's a floating junker and I'm not much of a sailor.'

Chalice picked the last of the gluey whiskers off her face with a wince, then sat down at the galley table. She reached out across the faded golden wood and cupped Arden's hands in her own. 'I worried so much, darling. Walking off into the night like that.'

'Our paths needed to diverge for a while.'

'Then I'm glad our paths have come back together.'

Arden rubbed the steam of her breath from the glass of the smeared porthole. A pair of legs passed by, ostensibly Mr Le Shen's, for the librarian had also found what he was looking for and had joined Chalice for the return journey.

'Yes, and I'm glad they did.'

'Well, fortunately you had all the luck of an uncomplicated search for your fellow. God was certainly looking out for His favourites! My darling, even the Court of Gullibles would not believe all the fuss and bother I had to go through! I was quite in a state all week. Look at my skin! Dry as a mummy's bandage.'

Arden smiled, and not uncharitably. She would allow Chalice her sufferings. Theirs was no competition after all.

Chalice returned with another plate of saurian stew, and a side of soda bread torn from the loaf.

'I kept some aside. Your monster-caller has the appetite of a horse.'

'He's still, um . . . regaining his strength.'

'Hmm-hmm. Still as unfriendly as ever though, I couldn't get him to acknowledge me.'

Arden remembered the night before, the *absence* of him. 'He is recovering,' she said. 'From an accident. He may be preoccupied.'

Chalice made a sceptical face and returned to her meal.

Over her second helping, Chalice told Arden her side of the story. Mr Absalom had not been able to stay in Burden Town. Aside from his stormcaller, all his crewmates had been lost to the deluge. He had no resources, no friends apart from those who'd known him under the auspices of Bellis Harrow. Of course he would leave post-haste.

But Chalice had refused to go with him. Since she'd done wrong by both Arden and David, her only recourse was to stay in the Abaddon Library and re-ingratiate herself with Mrs Cordwain's group. See how to make things right. There had been something of a schism among the pilgrims, and Mrs Cordwain had found herself out on her ear with – as the tides of fortune would have it – the entire treasury of silver Djennes collected from the Hillsider congregation.

Together Chalice Quarry and a much-chastened Mrs Cordwain had journeyed to Libro with Mr Le Shen, and met with the locals there, very much in recovery from their terrible time as guests of Maris.

'I met our young lady from Bellis' army. The girl in the saffron dress. Wren Halcyon Libro, who Bellis called Persephone? She told me how Mr Riven had helped them escape.'

'He did escape. But what made you come here and find me?'

'Well, my good friend Ozymandias Absalom did mention a *Church of the Deepwater King*. Mr Le Shen is a helpful anthropologist. He suggested that a Fiction man under such a moral debt might pay it at the church of his forefathers, and I seem to recall Mr Riven's mention of Bellis having been spirited away here, way back when we were chasing the *Fine Breeze*.'

'That is clever of him, and cunning of you.'

'Indeed. Our librarian will make a good Lion,' Chalice said. 'I'll get some recruiter's medal out of this whole debacle at least.'

'And the boat. How did you come across *Sonder*? Everyone said she was lost.'

'There's the thing. The Librans had it, and they just *gave* it to us. As soon as I mentioned I needed to find your monster-calling fellow, they practically showered us with food and supplies they could barely spare themselves. Oh, he's a hero among them, he certainly is.'

Arden pressed her cheek against the porthole glass. Jonah sat up on *Sonder*'s prow, seemingly buried in his own preoccupations.

'Darling,' Chalice said, and the timbre of her voice changed. 'You spent several days among the deepwater folk.'

'I did.'

'Did you . . . look, I know it sounds foolish, but I must ask again. Did you really not see another Riven out there? A relative of Jonah's perhaps?'

'Oh, are we still going on about *that*?'

'Darling, have we not reached some measure of trust? Have I not proved myself enough? I knew you were keeping secrets from me, when you started asking all those questions back in Burden Town. Did I challenge you on them? No, I did not challenge you, even when the secret Riven causes such a stir among the Society and the Order. I left you alone with that secret out of love and respect for you.'

'All right, there was another,' Arden admitted, too weary to keep secrets.

Chalice slapped the table. 'I knew it! But, darling, did you say *was*?'

Arden shrugged. Anything could have become of Miah once he'd left Stefan's island. She did not know, and had convinced herself she did not care.

'It doesn't matter to us any more, Chalice. He and Mr Lindsay have made their acquaintance now, the Lions have their man. We can at last take our curtain calls and leave the stage.'

The sun settled on her left, the port side, a huge golden disc about to kiss the water. She supposed by dead reckoning, Garfish Point lay to the west, then the firth that separated the two countries of Fiction and Lyonne. Even the seawater had begun to change, from the grey-blue of the Darkling Sea to the cheery trade wind blue-green of the Lyonne Ocean.

Sonder tipped and yawed at the boundary, but she was well made despite her age and her run-down appearance, and they were soon into calmer waters.

Arden touched the scabs at the back of her neck, where the tattoo healed. Maybe she would find a place in Clay to have it removed. That, and the *mandatum*-set ring on her finger.

At once she sensed Jonah's approach. Tipped her collar back up.

'Oh hello,' she said nervously over the hiss of sea-spray. 'I wasn't avoiding you. I just wanted to be outside when we crossed over. On the wharves the shoremen sing songs about this boundary. It's quite legendary among Lyonnians.'

She hummed a few bars of a sea-shanty, then felt her cheeks flame. He stood a respectful distance away and his jaw seemed carved from stone.

'Is it such a bad thing, leaving Fiction and the Islands?' Arden asked.

Jonah said nothing, and his face remained expressionless save for a small, secret curiosity.

'We will be a hundred miles off shore when we pass Harbinger Bay. Then I will take you home. Clay could be your home too. You needn't worry.'

If only he could find his voice. If only he would be her lover again.

'After my coins are removed, we could live in the port,' she said. 'The neck between the east and western oceans. The water will not be far away.'

He took up position alongside Arden, looking out to sea. In the middle distance a pod of ichthyosaur breached the waters, chasing the schooling fish who flashed fire in the setting sun.

A Time For Endings

A time for endings.

Bellis Harrow upon her lonely islet, in a cave like a deepwater maiden. Bellis Harrow who had once been general and Queen, but was now exiled in the fashion of both. Left to die on a rock. Her blood muttering in her veins. Her resolve only strengthened by solitude.

A month here, her food stores running low. Water brackish, and intermittent. Time to consider how one might end it.

But she should not have doubted her darkling gods so.

One morning, a black ship arrived in the half-moon of the islet's only shelter. A boat she knew from her childhood, and her marriage, built both for the sea and the snarling Sargasso shoals of monsters.

She watched from her stone outcropping as a small boat made its way to the rocky shore. Counted five men, a killing number although only two headed towards her shelter, and left the others on the beach.

She did not expect the first arrival. Her old enemy. He wore welder's goggles over his eyes, had some discomfort in the broad daylight, and shaded his face until he reached the crude overhang of her lithic abode.

Even after years she still suffered the same lurch of discomfort around him. Her muttering sanguinities sensed wrongness, and there was something very wrong about Miah Anguis-Riven.

'Jeremiah Riven,' Bellis said bitterly. 'Have you come to ravish me upon the rocks? Was always a threat of yours, if I recall.'

'No,' he said. Jeremiah Riven pushed the goggles onto his forehead and examined her stone apartments. His eyes had something ill about them. The pupils reflected, like a night-dwelling thing.

Bellis kept watch on her visitor, wondered if he might be considering a crude assault upon her, some tiresome act of revenge for a childhood slight.

But he hardly appeared to acknowledge her presence, and if he did, it was with a tart impatience. 'I have never had an interest in you. Don't try any tricks on me. Are you alone on this rock?'

She hissed at him. 'Don't worry, *Miah*. My army is gone from me. I cannot orient anyone alone, and I am vulnerable. To the weather. To the sea. To unwanted guests. Am I to be a prisoner then?' She sniffed. 'No, too dangerous I would think. Best I be your conquest, your kill. But wait. What is that I sense? An . . . obsession? Ah, who'd have believed it? Jeremiah Riven has become weak and fallen in love.'

He crossed the room in three strides, snatched Bellis up by her thin neck. 'Shut up, *defiler*. You will speak nothing of me.'

'Then why are you here, brute? If you've lost your mind with some clumsy romance, I'm afraid I'll not make a good replacement.'

'Devil—'

'Lady, gentleman. Please. No fussing.' One of the other occupants of the shoreboat had finally made his way to the overhang. A slight, fey little creature, shorter even than herself, with a pretty face more suited to a girl than a man.

Miah released her and stomped off to the crudely mortared balcony, fists creaking inside his leather gloves. The little man smiled upon seeing Bellis.

'It's good to meet you properly, Mrs Harrow-Riven.'

'Well then,' she said, rubbing her throat. 'Why do I think I've seen you before, Lyonnian?'

'I am Mr Lindsay,' he said, still puffing from having to navigate rocks Miah had merely walked over. 'We have been in each other's orbit a long time.'

Bellis only sniffed uninterestedly. 'A Lion, then. I have always been followed by Lions. Perhaps you were always lurking in some shadowy room, thinking I wouldn't notice.'

'Did you notice?'

Her nostrils flared. 'Would I have run, if I had not noticed?'

He looked back at Miah, pacing the rocky balcony impatiently. 'I was hoping the pair of you would come together as colleagues rather than enemies . . . given the symmetries you trammel. Given how much stronger the sum of you would be rather than your parts.'

Much as she tried to keep the dismissive mask upon her face, Bellis' eyes narrowed. 'What is your friend talking about, Miah?'

'You wanted to go to Lyonne, to Clay once,' Mr Lindsay continued.

She laughed. 'Once. When I thought I was *sanguis petrae* and had a golden talent that anybody cared about. But I was kept from those places.' She darted a daggered glance at Mr Lindsay. 'Because I had a shadow in my blood.'

'Because we were cowards,' Mr Lindsay said. 'Because we didn't know what to do with you.'

'And you know what to do with me now?'

Mr Lindsay laughed. 'Not in the slightest.'

'I'm going there,' Miah interjected brusquely. 'I have business in Clay Capital, to take back what was stolen from me. He,' Miah nodded at the small man, 'he suggested you should come.'

Bellis raised one eyebrow. 'Are you implying, Mr Lindsay, that we form an alliance?'

Mr Lindsay grinned. '*Sanguis orientis, sanguis mandatum.* The two talents of direction and instruction. The hammer and furnace, the anvil and chain, same as our dear saint who was exiled to Equus and made their eternal mark. They do not have to exist in the same person to have an effect.'

Jeremiah Riven, known as Miah Anguis, only glowered.

'I can't say I'll behave much,' Bellis said.

'On the contrary, perhaps it is chaos that I require,' Mr Lindsay said. 'To Clay we will go, *orientis* and *mandatum* in union. You may at last walk the streets denied you, and my friend Mr Anguis will recover his wife and his pride, and let all that have wronged us discover just what grave mistakes they have made.'

Acknowledgements

The usual suspects have not changed but special mention where it is due: Sarah Endacott, Andrew Macrae, Cat Sparks and Helen Stubbs, the old school LJ friends Catherine Buck and Janna G. Noelle for their support through the long eternities, the Writer Beers gang, the Cave Clan Night Crew, my friends and my family.

And on the professional end thanks to my agent Sam Morgan, Vicky Leech from HarperVoyager UK, Michael White and Lara Wallace from HarperCollins Australia, and those unsung others who worked behind the scenes and are responsible in no small part for this book's existence.